HOUSE REPORT

HOUSE REPORT

Deborah Nicholson

This first world edition published in Great Britain 2004 by
SEVERN HOUSE PUBLISHERS LTD of
9–15 High Street, Sutton, Surrey SM1 1DF.
This first world edition published in the USA 2004 by
SEVERN HOUSE PUBLISHERS INC of
595 Madison Avenue, New York, N.Y. 10022.

British Library Cataloguing in Publication Data

Nicholson, Deborah
    House report
    1.   Women theatrical managers - Alberta - Calgary - Fiction
    2.   Murder - Investigation - Alberta - Calgary - Fiction
    3.   Detective and mystery stories
    I.   Title
    813.6 [F]

    ISBN 0-7278-6068-2

Typeset by Palimpsest Book Production Ltd.,
Polmont, Stirlingshire, Scotland.
Printed and bound in Great Britain by
MPG Books Ltd., Bodmin, Cornwall.

For my mom and dad, who taught me how to dream;
for my teachers, who gave me the skills to reach that dream;
and for Sandy Stockton, who helped me catch the dream . . .
. . . and counted every comma in it.

September 9, 2003   *Much Ado About Nothing*

House Manager: Katherine Carpenter

House In: 8:00

House Out: 10:54

Intermission: 9:05–9:25

House Count: 859

Liquor Sales: $1897.33

Lobby Sales: $598.95 (T-shirts not selling)

Ice Cream: $250.00 (Frozen yoghurt is very popular)

Ticket Report: No problems

Special Events: N/A

Maintenance Report
Please have housekeeping pay special attention to the men's washroom in the main lobby.

Manager's Comments
At 9:45 a bartender reported that a door in the men's washroom was locked. Maintenance was called and we investigated. Upon opening the door, we discovered a patron in the stall, unconscious. We began CPR, security was called, and paramedics were dispatched. The patron was pronounced dead on arrival at the hospital and police were dispatched to investigate. The theatre was locked and patrons were questioned before being allowed to leave. More details to follow in my incident report.

I pulled the report off the printer, which sat on the edge of my desk, and scanned it as I lit a cigarette. I looked up and saw Cam turn the coffee pot off. It was nice to have him here. We hadn't seen each other for a couple of weeks and, as much as I hated to admit it, I had missed him. He even looked good in his uniform of loose-fitting blue overalls. A strand of brown hair had fallen across his forehead and I felt the urge to reach out and brush it away.

'Will you pour me another cup before you throw it out?' I asked, leaning back in my swivel chair and stretching.

'How many cups is that tonight?' he asked as he crossed the office and handed me a coffee.

'Too many. What time is it?' I felt too exhausted to turn my head and look at the clock.

'It's three thirty a.m.,' Cam said, sliding into the chair across from me.

'I've got to get out of here,' I said, leaning over to pick up my backpack and dropping the package of cigarettes into it.

'Those are mine,' Cam pointed out.

'I thought you quit,' Graham piped up as he came into the office looking like it was three thirty in the afternoon, not the morning. He was such a typical non-smoker.

'I did.' I handed Cam back his cigarettes. 'Graham, there's the house report. Will you distribute it for me, please? And I'll need you back here by four tomorrow afternoon for a staff meeting.'

'Cool,' he said. Graham was my chief usher, but was only eighteen and sounded it. 'Do you want me to call the staff and let them know?'

'No, I'll help. You call A to Z, I'll call the rest.'

'Funny,' he said. 'Just remember, you don't pay me enough to laugh at your bad jokes. I'll see you tomorrow. Get some sleep, OK?'

'OK. See you tomorrow.'

Graham grabbed his keys and backpack and headed down the hall to the administration offices. I cleared the last of the coffee cups off my desk and stood up.

'You OK, Katie?' Cam asked, coming around to my side of the desk.

'Yeah, I'm fine.'

'Want to come to my place tonight?' he asked.

'No. But I'd really like you to come to mine.'

Cam smiled as he reached over and took my hand.

'Are you sure you're OK?' he asked, pulling me to him and wrapping his arms around me.

Suddenly I found myself holding him tightly. I think it was when he started rubbing my back that I lost it. I hate crying at the best of times, and now I couldn't turn it off. Cam wasn't helping – rubbing my back, muttering little reassurances. I had almost regained my composure when he reached up to my cheek and brushed away a tear. Well, that was so sweet that I started all over again. I realized I wasn't going to be able to control my tears tonight, but it was OK, this time I had a good reason. Six hours ago I spent fifteen minutes giving CPR to a dead guy.

Thursday

My name is Kate Carpenter. I am thirty-three years old and still single, as my mother is quick to point out. I have blonde hair, blue eyes, and a reasonable figure, which has been known to fluctuate by ten pounds or so. It's a good thing that my weight is fairly stable, since I hate exercise and love to eat. I have a trace of grey in my hair and wrinkles around my eyes, especially when I smile. I never thought it would bother me until I noticed them in the mirror one day – my mother's wrinkles on my face.

My apartment is a tiny loft on the top floor of a downtown high-rise. The landlord charges too much rent and gets away with it because having a loft is 'in'. It is located close to work and is quirky enough to appeal to my tastes. The balcony opens towards the west, which means I have a panoramic view of the mountains and can watch glorious sunsets. The bedroom is upstairs and it is my retreat. I had turned it into a great hideaway. My big indulgence was the bed, which is in one corner. It has a wonderful down mattress that cost me a fortune but was worth every penny; set in a beautiful brass and porcelain frame. I have four bookcases against another wall, crammed with books and music from my illustrious youth. I saved everything from my university days and, believe me, when you have a major in music, you end up with quite a collection. I have my stereo and CDs upstairs too, and a big cushy chair that's perfect to curl up in with a good book. There are some plants trailing off the ledge; a floor to ceiling window, and a huge and very well organized closet.

The day after I moved in, I realized that my clothes would never fit in the existing space. I went to one of those huge home improvement stores and bought every type of closet-organizer kit they sold. It cost me a small fortune, but it was worth it just to have my clothes organized. I would certainly never be accused of being neat or tidy in any other aspect of my life, but my closet was the exception. I have sections for dresses, skirts, pants and blouses and organizers for hats, shoes, scarves and jewellery. There are a few shelves that I have never been sure what they are for, but I am managing to fill them anyway. That's the best part, buying new clothes to fill it up. A spiral staircase leads down to the living room, where there is just enough room for a couch, piano, TV and my videotapes. Movies are another of my weaknesses – I can't seem to resist picking up my favourites.

The kitchen has all the amenities you could hope for, including a dishwasher and a tiny breakfast nook on one end. Then there is the bathroom. It has been renovated and features a trendy glass-brick shower, an oversized tub in which you can actually sink up to your neck, and soft lighting that would make Attila the Hun look good. It is probably the biggest room in the apartment.

I stood in the bathroom, staring at myself in the mirror. My eyes were starting to swell and were red-rimmed from my crying jag. Even the soft lights weren't helping tonight. At least I had washed off the mascara that had run down to my chin. I always hoped to look like Demi Moore when I cried, but all I ever pulled off was an Alice Cooper impersonation.

I ran the facecloth under cold water, held it up to my eyes for a minute, and then finally gave up. The puffiness was not going to go away. I picked my clothes up off the floor and threw them in the hamper, which was much easier than hanging them up. I pulled on an oversized T-shirt and turned off the bathroom light. I suddenly realized how tired I was as I climbed the stairs.

'Feel better now, Katie?' Cam asked. He was already tucked into bed waiting for me.

'Remember what happened last time you asked me that?' I warned him, then relented. 'But yes, I guess I'm a little better now.'

'Good,' he said, holding up the quilt so I could climb in beside him.

I reached over and switched the light off. Cam pulled me close to him and I certainly didn't object. I wrapped my arms around his waist and buried my face in his shoulder. I could feel the pulse beating in his neck and, somehow, felt comforted.

'Are you OK, Cam?'

'Yeah. I worked in a hospital before I came here, remember. I've seen dead bodies. That part of it didn't really bother me. The fact that he died in the theatre was kind of weird.'

'I've never seen a dead body,' I admitted.

'So I guess we both had some new experiences today.'

'I'm glad you came home with me,' I said, grateful that the darkness hid the tear rolling down my cheek.

'All you ever have to do is ask, Katie.'

'Let's not have this big relationship discussion tonight.'

I felt him kiss my forehead and whisper, 'I'm sorry.'

'Are you as tired as I am?' I asked.

'More.'

'I don't think that's possible.' I snuggled deeper under the covers, not letting go of Cam. 'I have to get some sleep. There's a ton of stuff waiting for me at the office.'

'I know. I'll be filling out incident reports for at least three days,' he said.

'Goodnight Cam,' I said, closing my eyes.

'Night, Katie.'

It was dark and quiet. I felt my arms and legs grow heavy. Then Cam started running his fingers through my hair. I really hated it when he did that; it was the one thing I couldn't resist. I hesitated for a moment, hoping Cam would stop. But he didn't let up. Sleep could wait. I turned my head and kissed him. I could see a sly smile on his face through the darkness.

'Are you always so sure of yourself?' I asked.

'Only when I'm here with you.'

'We've got to talk and straighten out our relationship,' I said as he kissed me again. 'Or maybe it can wait until tomorrow . . . We'll talk tomorrow.'

I felt my heart start to beat faster. Wasn't this one of the reasons I'd broken up with him in the first place?

Friday

I woke up around noon and felt like I could still use another twelve hours sleep. I smelled coffee and heard Cam in the kitchen, so instead of closing my eyes and going back to sleep, I threw the covers back and got up. Cam always got that hurt look in his eyes when he made breakfast and I didn't want any. Besides, it was one of the few times that I actually ate a decent meal. I pulled my T-shirt on and headed downstairs. He stood at the bottom of the stairs, waiting for me with a cup of coffee in his hand. He gave me the cup and a quick kiss.

'Morning,' I mumbled. Mornings are not my best time of day.

'You look tired,' he said.

'I am. How about you?'

'I'm fine. I had a cold shower, went for a jog and don't feel too bad.'

He was right. As usual Cam looked wonderful. He always had that healthy glow, the kind that I had to work really hard to achieve.

'I hate you in the morning,' I told him.

'I know.' He led me to the table. 'Come on, I made a fruit salad and some fresh scones.'

'It smells great,' I said as we sat at the table and he topped up my coffee. I grabbed a scone and spread it thickly with jam.

This is my wicker room. I had always seen these great pictures of kitchens filled with wicker furniture and plants hanging everywhere. There is only a tiny window in my kitchen, so the one plant I have isn't doing very well. My wicker chairs had pinched when you sat in them until I finally bought some cushions. But for my one attempt at interior design, it wasn't bad.

'You working tonight?' I asked, stuffing a second scone greedily into my mouth.

'Yeah, I'm on in an hour, actually.'

'Can I catch a ride?'

'Katie, you don't have to be there until four this afternoon. Go back to bed for another couple of hours.'

I also hated it when Cam was patronizing, but I wasn't up for an argument right now. 'I've got a staff meeting at four and a ton of paperwork to do. If I don't go in early, I'll have to stay late.' I explained to him. 'Besides, I haven't had a ride in the Fish for ages.'

'You need to take better care of yourself. And it's a Hemi Barracuda, not a fish. Show some respect for a classic,' he said testily.

'So you've said,' I snapped. 'Sorry, that was bitchy and I promised I wouldn't do that anymore.' I sipped my coffee, sat back in the chair and took a deep breath before continuing. 'Cam, I'm stressed and I'm tired. Last night was really rough and I'm still kind of freaked out by all this. Please let me get through this weekend and then next week you can redo my life. OK?'

'Katie, you know I only act like this because I care about you.' He realized that arguing wasn't going to get him anywhere this morning. 'But I'll try to behave.'

'I don't suppose you could try to call me Kate?'

'We've talked about that, too. You'll always be Katie to me.'

'You maintenance guys are so thickheaded!'

'Building engineers,' he corrected.

'You're too good a cook to be an engineer.' I spread some jam on the last bite of the last scone and popped it into my mouth. 'I'll have a quick shower and be ready in fifteen minutes.'

'OK, I'll do the dishes,' Cam said as he stood up and started to clear the table.

I stood up and wrapped my arms around his neck, pulling him close to me. 'One of these days I may realize that you're not so bad to have around.'

'It's these little rewards that I keep hanging in for,' he laughed.

'I'm going to take a shower now.'

'There she goes, folks, she said something nice, and now she's out of here.'

I swatted his head and left him to deal with the dishes.

We drove to the Plex in silence. I love riding with Cam. He has this great car, a gleaming white 1971 Hemi Barracuda that he spends hours oiling and polishing. It makes him crazy that I just referred to it as the Fish. No matter what it was supposed to be called, it kept me off the C-Train, which I hated, and kept me from having to walk. It was only about fifteen blocks to work, but that was too much like exercise and besides, Cam had his own parking spot right across the street from the Plex.

He opened the car door for me, a real treat in this day and age, and we walked slowly down the block towards the stage door. He put his arm around my shoulder.

'I've missed you,' he said.

'It's only been a couple of weeks,' I said. 'But I've missed you too.'

He stopped when we got to the stage door. 'So is this goodbye again?'

'I don't know, Cam. You and I seem to be very complicated.'

'I think you make us complicated.' He smiled at me.

'Probably,' I admitted. 'I guess you've noticed that I'm really bad at relationships.'

'I don't have an exceptional record either,' he said.

'Cam, come by tonight after the show goes in and we'll coordinate days off. We can spend some time talking and try and decide where we should go from here.'

'I can think of many other things I'd rather do than talk,' he said, grabbing me in his arms.

'We'll probably do that too.' I smiled, remembering the one good part of last night. 'We always seem to get along better when we aren't talking.'

'I have to go, but I promise I'll see you later.' He squeezed my shoulder and kissed my cheek.

I watched him walk into the building. Sometimes, I really don't know what's wrong with me. He cooks, cleans, isn't afraid to show affection in public and wants to be with me. What else was I looking for in a man? Cam turned and waved before he went inside. I smiled back and then headed for Grounds Zero.

Grounds Zero is one of those great places that you can smell before you can actually see. They roast their own coffee beans and there is always a smoky, aromatic haze hanging over the restaurant.

'Hi Gus,' I said, slipping on to my favourite stool at the end of the counter.

'Hi Kate. I heard you had some excitement at the theatre last night,' Gus said, coming over and leaning on the counter.

Gus made a point of remembering everyone's name and always seemed to know what was going on before anyone else did. He was somewhere around sixty years old, a retired oilman who hadn't enjoyed retirement a lot. Gus always liked to drink coffee and eat, so Grounds Zero was a natural extension of those habits.

'Yeah, more excitement than I need,' I said.

'Any idea what happened?' he asked as he put the lid on my usual – a steaming cup of cappuccino, no foam, extra chocolate sprinkles.

'No, not a clue.'

'You watch yourself, Kate. These things aren't always what they seem to be.' Gus's warning sounded ominous, but I wasn't worried. We made it through the worst last night, what else could happen?

'See you tomorrow, Gus,' I said taking the cappuccino and heading up to my office. I had the feeling that this was just the beginning of a long day of answering questions.

The Plex was an amazing white elephant of a building. It had been somebody's dream to have an arts centre in Calgary. They thought it would be a brilliant idea to house the city's main theatre groups and musical organizations in one complex. So a committee had been formed, money raised, ground broken, and here we are.

The committee had christened the building the Calgary Arts and Theatre House, hoping to encompass all forms of arts and entertainment in the city. There were detractors, who thought spending millions on the project was a waste, and they started referring to it as the Cat House. That was when the committee

11

had a vote and renamed it the Calgary Arts Complex, thinking very carefully about any acronyms that could be formed from those letters. Those of us that toiled there just referred to it as the Plex, which didn't thrill the board of directors either. They thought it was much more high class to refer to it by its full name. We were in theatre, they reminded us, we had to maintain a certain stature.

There is a 2500-seat concert hall for the symphony and the opera; a 1000-seat theatre, which the Foothills Stage Network shares with the Ballet; and a 500-seat theatre, which is run by the Heritage Theatre Company. There is also a tiny space used by the city's improvisation and theatre sports groups; another tiny space that is rented to community groups, and a movie theatre dedicated to foreign and art films. Upstairs we have a recording studio; rehearsal halls; private studios for lessons, practice or auditions; a theatre, music and dance library; and in the middle of the block is the administration tower. This seems to be where the whole plan fell apart.

The theatres are all separate entities but the admin tower isn't. The office staff of the Plex, the resident companies and all their boards are housed here, and the infighting is something to see. The best part of my job is that I rarely have to go up to the tower. All of the 'downstairs' staff are convinced that it isn't safe up there, and I agree.

I work for Foothills Stage Network and my title is front of house manager. Sounds great but just means I have to work nights and weekends. FSN is the resident company in the 1000-seat Centenary Theatre. That means that we run the place, no matter who's on stage. We mainly share our space with the Ballet. FSN runs all the production staff and stage crews. The theatre is filled with really expensive, state-of-the-art equipment, and our guys are in charge. I am responsible for all the front of house staff – merchandisers, ushers, bartenders and ticket takers.

I have ten part-time ushers and about twenty volunteers for each show. We use volunteers from wherever we can get them – our company and any of the others. I was not above stealing volunteers from the other companies in order to get enough staff for my theatre.

I walked down to the end of the block and let myself in through the side door of the theatre. I was supposed to use the stage door and sign in, but I don't respond well to authority or the rules and regulations that they try to impose on me.

The lobby was dimly lit and I noticed the police tape was still up when I walked through. My office is in a corner off the first balcony, at the end of a short hallway and beside the washrooms. Not a glamorous location, and the elaborate decor ends at my office door. Theatres don't waste money on areas that the public will never see. I have given up requesting that the walls be painted; even sleeping with Cam hadn't helped me there. I began to buy posters and now have the walls almost totally covered with everything from *Star Trek* to Monet. I have a huge south-facing window, which looks out over the parking lot, but allows plenty of sunshine. I brought in several plants that hadn't fared so well in my kitchen and saved their lives. I've been here over two years now, and I think it feels like home.

Getting this job was the result of my thirtieth-birthday crisis and my growing dislike of the secretarial work I had been doing for several years. One day, while I was volunteering with the Symphony, I saw this job posted. I thought it over for about thirty seconds, decided the corporate world could do without me, and miraculously got the job. I do have some experience in community theatre, some supervisory experience, and lots of stage experience in school, but secretly I always thought there hadn't been any other applicants.

I now take a university course every other semester, have most days to myself, and go to the theatre every night. It has turned out to be a good way of life.

Theatre people have great parties and I don't miss many. That's a bonus that isn't in my contract – an expanded social life. If there isn't a party happening, we have several restaurants and bars in the building, and you can usually find someone to go out with after work. Then there's Cam.

Cam is a building engineer. There are six of them altogether, covering all the trades. Due to the incredible underfunding of the arts, they not only perform their own, specialized duties, but do everything else from unblocking toilets to freeing children trapped in the escalators. They work twelve-hour shifts, four on and four off, so I see lots of them.

One night, Cam and I were both at the security desk, signing out at the same time. I had never seen him in street clothes before, and I don't think I had ever seen anyone else who could fill out a pair of jeans the way Cam did.

He asked me out for a coffee and I asked him why he wasn't going home to his wife. That's when I found out that he was getting a divorce. We ended up seeing each other for a year until I decided I couldn't continue the relationship until his divorce was finalized. That took him another six months, but somehow we never really got back together. But then, we had never really broken up either. Two weeks ago I told him I needed some time alone, to sort things out. I had been doing so well until last night.

I fumbled with my keys and finally got my office door open. This building is locked up like a bank vault and you can't get through a single door without a key. The lights were on in my office and Otis Naggy, a security guard, was sitting on one of the benches, flipping through a program. He has a name that sounds like it came from a book, and he looks like he belongs on the *Andy Griffith Show*, fishing with Opie.

I always hate running into Otis. He is incredibly young, incredibly naive, and thinks he is my best friend. I've caught him sleeping in my office several times when he was supposed to be on duty and had never reported him. Otis thinks I like him because I never turned him in. Truth is, I just didn't want to deal with the paperwork.

'Otis, I told you that you couldn't use my office to nap in anymore.'

'Funny, Kate. Lazlo asked me to wait here until you came in. He needs to talk to you about last night.'

'Otis, let me have my coffee, then I'll call Laz the Spaz,' I said as I took the lid off my cappuccino and flopped down in my chair. None of us have much respect for authority in this building.

'Sorry. I radioed him as soon as I heard you at the door. His orders.'

14

'That does it. No more free cookies for you.'

'Kate, the Spaz is really excited about this. This is the closest thing to a real police investigation he's come across in five years and you know how he is about things like this.'

'Yeah, yeah. Well you don't have to babysit me. I promise to stay right here until Lazlo arrives,' I told him as I thought about where I could hide for the afternoon.

'Do I still get free cookies?' he asked as he left the office.

'It depends on whether Lazlo ruins my day or my whole week.'

As soon as Otis left, I started the coffee-maker, pulled several files out and spread them over my desk. Hopefully, if I looked busy, Lazlo wouldn't waste too much of my time.

Lazlo Hilleo is head of Building Services, which includes security. He had been a cop for about three years but he likes everyone to think he had been on the force for much longer. No one knows why he left the police department after such a short time. There's a pool worth over five hundred dollars to the person who found out why.

Lazlo loves rules and regulations, which drives all of us crazy because he *makes* the rules. He is obsessed with numbers, logbooks, and signing things in and out. All these picky rules just create more paperwork for the rest of us. Lazlo is one of the few people who has access to the entire building. This is a big responsibility, because the lower levels of this building are like a maze, and if you accidentally leave an area you have access to, you could be trapped for life. There is a story circulating that a construction worker was lost over five years ago in the basement and he's still wandering around, trying to find his way out.

My guess is that Lazlo's attitude problem is caused by the fact that he is short. I once dated a short man who liked to be in charge, just like Lazlo. Plus, he is a born and bred chauvinist. Unfortunately, none of that helped me get along with him. I tend to react poorly to Lazlo and the authority that he represents.

I quickly hid my trash can under my desk before he showed up. Mine had gone missing a couple of weeks ago and I swiped this one from the Heritage Theatre. Lazlo has ID numbers

15

painted on everything, and if he saw a garbage can from another theatre in my office, he would confiscate it and write me up. I was sure he would figure out that Cam had used his keys to let me into the Heritage to steal it – also against the rules.

I had just poured myself a coffee when I heard someone coming down the hall. There are double doors at the far end of the corridor, so I always have a bit of warning when someone is approaching. I sat down behind my desk, opened a file, and tried to look busy.

'Excuse me, Kate.' He tapped at my door, waiting for an invitation.

I looked up. 'Hi, Lazlo. Otis said you wanted to speak with me.'

'If you can spare a minute or two . . .?'

I'd be lucky to get him out of here in a minute or two, I thought, but instead I smiled at him. 'Help yourself to some coffee.'

'No thanks.' He sat down across the desk from me. 'So how are you doing after last night? Did you get any sleep?'

Lazlo is in his mid-forties and wears a cheap toupee and an expensive suit that must have been tailor-made to fit his short, heavy-set build. He tries so hard to act nice, but usually ends up being patronizing. Everyone refers to him as Laz the Spaz behind his back, and a few of us have said it to his face. I often wonder if it bothers him. I always feel a bit guilty for thinking badly of him, but he can never carry off the nice-guy routine for more than a few minutes at a time.

'I'm OK,' I said, shuffling the papers on my desk.

He pulled a little notepad out of his pocket, like detectives in the movies use, and flipped it open.

'May we speak confidentially?' He spoke softly.

'Do you want me to close the door?' I asked.

'No, but I would prefer that this not be spread around the building. There are enough rumours flying already.'

'All right,' I agreed. 'What's this about?' I had a sinking feeling I wasn't going to like what he had to say.

'The police were here all morning. They sent an evidence and forensics team over and combed the place. I used to work with the detective in charge, so I encouraged them to speed

16

through the job. They've finished now and released the theatre back to us.'

'Released the theatre?'

'Yes. Which is why you were supposed to check in at the security desk before coming on site. If the police hadn't finished, you could have been charged with tampering with a crime scene. There are reasons for these rules, Kate, and you sneaking in the back is not setting a very good example for the staff.'

'OK, I promise I'll check in from now on.' I was lying, but at least it stopped the lecture.

'Now, since the police are finished, you are free to run the performance this evening.'

'Was there ever any doubt? I really think this is getting a little carried away.'

'Kate, there was a murder in your lobby last night.'

'I mean, I know this was a shock to everyone but . . . what did you just say?'

'I said there was a murder in your lobby.'

I finally set down my pen. 'A murder?' I asked in disbelief.

'Yes, there is no doubt it was a murder.'

'Lazlo, what are you talking about?'

'The victim had a nail driven into the back of his skull. I heard some talk from the paramedics when I went to the hospital last night and the police confirmed it this morning when they found a nail gun buried in the trash can. A nail gun with a Complex ID number on it.'

'Oh my God.' I almost dropped my calculator. I got up and took my half-empty cappuccino cup over to the coffee pot and filled it, holding out the pot to offer Lazlo some. 'So somebody here murdered him?'

'That sounds like an obvious conclusion. However, we both know that ID numbers and logging in and out does not stop certain items from wandering from place to place,' Lazlo said as he picked up a cup and held it out for me to fill.

I ignored his last comment and filled his cup.

'We are instigating a key and equipment inventory now,' he continued as he sat back down. 'If any keys are missing, the police can look into that. If not, then we check out everyone in engineering.'

17

'You'll have my full cooperation,' I promised.

'Good, then perhaps you'll go to the security desk and sign in. As you are supposed to do every time you enter the building.'

'Do they know who he was?' I said, still not believing that this could happen in my theatre.

'Excuse me?' he asked.

'The man. Do they know his name?'

Lazlo studied his notepad for a minute. 'I imagine it'll be in the evening papers, so I guess there's no harm in telling you. His name was Peter Reynolds. Apparently he was a stockbroker.'

'What?' I sat down on the window ledge, almost knocking a plant over.

'I said his name was Peter Reynolds . . .'

'I don't believe it.'

'Don't believe what?' he asked. 'Do you know something?'

'I knew him.'

'You knew him? The victim? Why didn't you say so last night?'

'I didn't recognize him. I'd only met him once before. He didn't have a beard the last time I saw him.'

Lazlo put his notepad away, looking quite excited by this news. 'I'm going to call Detective Lincoln. He's the homicide detective in charge of this investigation. He'll want to talk to you. In the meantime I would appreciate it if you would go down, sign in, and then stick close to your office, OK?'

I hated the fact that Lazlo seemed to know what he was doing, and I hated having to agree to do what he wanted me to do, but I nodded anyway.

'Good,' he said, standing and putting his notebook away. 'I'll call you as soon as I speak with the police.'

'Thanks, Lazlo.'

I waited until he was gone, then went to the security desk to sign in. I realized I should obey the rules, but he didn't have to know I was doing it.

It was three o'clock. I had finally waded through the previous night's sales figures. I spend hours every day reporting what we had sold in our lobby market and bars the night before, counting T-shirts, pins and mugs and checking how many beers had been drunk. The office staff thrive on these minute details and the money we make from selling it all. I also filled out an incident report, which would also hit almost every office upstairs. They like to know about the money we make and they love to know when something has gone wrong. Everyone except the public relations department, which, I'm sure, would be working overtime trying to make light of this whole event.

I was expecting my staff in for a meeting at four, the Spaz had called and told me that the police were coming at four thirty, and Graham was due in any minute. What I really wanted to do was go home, preferably with Cam. I wondered what he was doing and how he was going to react to the news that I knew last night's victim. And that it had been a murder.

I got the time sheets out ready for everyone's arrival, and poured myself another coffee. I really wanted a cigarette, but couldn't find one in my desk.

'Hey, Boss,' Graham said as he poked his head around my door. I had long since given up trying to keep my door closed and having people knock.

I looked up and smiled at him. Graham is very young – only eighteen, or almost nineteen as he likes to point out. He wants to be an actor more than anything else in the world. He had worked for me as an usher until he finished high school. Graham thinks that just being *near* the theatre is an education for him. He doesn't care if he's seating people, hanging up coats or serving drinks – he just wants to be here. He is tall, blonde, and quite well built for someone his age. I suspect he works out more than he admits. He looks vaguely like a young Kenneth Branagh and he is convinced that's who he is going to be when he grows up. He's pretty good, too. I've seen him in some children's theatre and have been dragged to a couple of his high-school productions. He sings, he dances, he acts, and he dreams of seeing his name up in lights. When he graduated and my former assistant quit, I decided to take him on full-time. Graham may be a smart-ass, but he works hard for me.

He looked like he'd got more sleep than I had last night, or maybe it was his youth. Had I ever been able to bounce back that quickly?

'Hi Graham,' I said.

'So what's new?' he asked me.

'Grab a coffee. It's been an eventful morning.'

'I'll stick to the healthy stuff.' He pulled a juice container out of his bag and sat down. 'Don't tell me you found more stiffs.'

'No, no more bodies. And don't be disrespectful.'

'Sorry.' He opened his juice and tossed the lid into the garbage can. 'Two points!'

'They have declared our stiff from last night to be a murder victim.'

'What?' said Graham, almost spitting his juice all over my desk.

'And I found out that I knew him,' I continued.

'You are full of surprises, aren't you?'

'Yeah, well the day ain't over yet. The staff meeting is going to be short and sweet because the police will be here at four thirty to question me.'

'Do we get to watch them grill you?' His eyes lit up.

'Graham . . .'

'OK, I'm serious.'

'Thank you. After the meeting, I need you all to go through the place with a fine toothcomb, make sure that all the police tape is gone and everything is OK for tonight. I don't want any patrons to find something lying around. Then you can take a quick break, but be back by five thirty. I'm going to need all you guys around here tonight. I have a feeling there may be some reporters around, and maybe a few kooks as well. Hopefully this will all die down quickly.'

'Bad choice of cliche. How busy are we supposed to be tonight?' he asked.

'Totally sold out.'

'Wow, I didn't realize so many people in Calgary want to see *Much Ado About Nothing*. A little publicity goes a long way.'

'That's rule number twenty-five in the publicity manual. When all else fails, kill somebody.'

Graham laughed. 'So after last year's dismal ticket sales, they thought they would open this year with a bang?'

'I wouldn't put it past them. Look, I've got to make some

notes for the meeting. Do you mind setting up the coffee in the Diamond Lounge for me?'

'Sure thing.'

'You can run down to Grounds Zero and buy some muffins,' I added. 'And put them out, too.'

'Right, see you down there,' Graham said as he hurried out of my office. I'm sure he was anxious to spread the news of the murder.

Three thirty. I had half an hour to get ready. I brushed my hair, put it in a ponytail and then freshened my make-up. I keep several outfits in my office so I can always change here. Saves a lot on cleaning bills. I put on my black jacket and pants with my yellow silk tank top. It was my favourite. I felt the need to look the consummate professional in front of the police. I headed down to the lounge and helped Graham finish setting up.

By five past four, everyone was there, in uniform, with coffee in hand. I had ten permanent staff, ranging in age from fifteen to sixty. Charlotte and Martha were my two sixty-year-olds, who had been looking for something to do with their days when our paths crossed. I snapped them up as soon as I found out they were interested, and we now work all the weekday matinees together. They do some weekend shifts too, when they are sick of having their husbands around and need a break from the home front. The rest of my staff range from high-school students to professionals to housewives – all people looking for something to do a couple of nights a week. Some want a little extra pocket money; others just want to be around other people. All of them have been with me for two years. I have virtually the same staff I started with, and am quite pleased with all of them. They work hard for the seven dollars an hour I can offer them and I, in turn, try to make their time here as much fun as I can.

So there they sat in their black pants, white shirts, black cardigans and bow ties, name tags in place, looking to me expectantly, wondering what I was going to tell them about last night. I took a deep breath and prepared to tell the story for the fifth time in twenty-four hours.

'Hi guys, thanks for coming in on such short notice. I'm

21

sure you all know that something happened here last night. I'm going to stop the rumours and tell you exactly what *did* happen, and then brief you on what to expect tonight. I have a meeting at four thirty with the police, so any questions will have to wait.'

No one spoke. I don't think I have ever held a staff meeting where I really had everyone's undivided attention, until now.

'We had an uneventful evening, got the house in on time, had a busy intermission, and got the house back in. One of the bartenders told me that there was a stall door stuck in the main lobby washroom. I called the engineer on duty. Cam came up and we went in to check it out. We discovered that there was a patron in the stall and he wasn't answering us. Cam got the door open and we discovered a gentleman who wasn't breathing and didn't have a pulse. We thought he had suffered a heart attack.'

'At least the play didn't bore him to death,' Charlotte joked. Charlotte looks just like somebody's elderly grandmother, but she has the fastest mind I had ever seen for a quick comeback. I don't think Charlotte has ever been stuck for words.

'Anyway, Graham called the paramedics and we did CPR until they arrived. They took over and transported him to the Foothills Hospital. We heard later that he had been pronounced dead at the hospital. The police arrived, the doors were locked and all the patrons were questioned on the way out. Two hours later, the only thing we discovered was that no one seemed to know the gentleman. We finally got out of here around three in the morning.'

'Wow,' Leonard butted in. 'We spend hours practicing how to evacuate a thousand people but never once did I think we would have to worry about how to keep them *in* the theatre.'

'Except during that one bad play last year,' Martha piped up.

'You read the *Herald*'s review,' Charlotte said. 'The theatre critic said we're going to have to start worrying about locking them in if the productions don't get better.'

'So I guess this was a good practice run for us then,' Leonard said.

Leonard is a philosophy major at the University of Calgary – need I say more? His mind works on a whole different plane from the rest of ours. He has all these great philosophy jokes that my best friend's husband always has to explain to me later. I would have to remember to introduce the two of them some-time.

'If we could just get back on track here,' I interjected. Somehow my staff meetings always seem to go like this. 'When I came in this afternoon, I found out that he didn't die of natural causes. The police were here all morning, doing whatever it is they do. Apparently the murder weapon was found. So that's where we stand right now.' I paused to let this sink in a little.

'So what is going to happen tonight?' Martha asked.

'Tonight, and for the next several nights, I really need all of you guys here if you can possibly make it. We're expecting some weirdos, the media, and who knows what else. I would like to try to keep them all away from the patrons and try to pretend like everything is normal around here. It is also very important to remember that some of the media we are trying to keep out are also our sponsors. So we've got to be firm but polite. And remember, no matter how dazzled you are by the spotlights, none of us is authorized to make a statement. And none of this "no comment" stuff.'

'But that's what they always say on TV,' Graham said.

'Well, back to real life,' I said, shooting him a dirty look for sidetracking me again. 'What you *are* authorized to say to the media, and I mean this, is that a Foothills Stage Network representative will be making a statement very soon.' I looked down at my watch. 'Is everybody OK with this so far?'

'Can we all go check out the bathroom?' Charlotte asked.

'You can check out everything. Graham is going to take over and let you know what needs to be done. I've got to get back to my office and meet with the police. I don't want to see any of you up there before six o'clock. A little privacy would be nice for a change.'

Everyone groaned.

'I promise I'll fill you in on all the gruesome details later.' And with that I headed back up to my office to tell my story for the sixth time that day.

* * *

Detective Lincoln arrived fifteen minutes late, which did not set me in good humour. I was running on a tight schedule and suffering from lack of sleep as well. I watched from my window as the police car parked in the loading dock and Lincoln got out. He looked much younger than I had expected. I had an image of someone in his mid- to late-forties, slightly over-weight, slightly balding, suffering from years of too many cig-arettes and too much coffee. He should have been wearing a rumpled raincoat, like Columbo, and should be divorced due to the pressure his wife had suffered from being married to a cop. This detective was young, slim, with thick black hair cov-ering his head and no sign of bald spots. He walked with a bounce in his step and certainly didn't look like he suffered from overwork or long hours of sitting at a desk. He also dressed much better than I ever expected to see a cop dress. I guess years of watching police shows on TV has ruined my perception.

I poured myself another coffee, lit a cigarette and waited for him to turn up in my office. I didn't have to wait long.

I heard the door at the end of the corridor open and turned to see Lazlo following the detective down the hall towards my office, trying to keep up with the policeman. I noticed Laz was breathing quite heavily by the time they arrived at my door.

'Kate,' he started, trying to hide his discomfort, 'this is detec-tive Ken Lincoln. He's with Calgary Police Services, Homicide Division. Ken, this is Kate Carpenter.'

Ken held out his hand and I stood up and shook it.

'Pleasure to meet you,' he said. He had a good, firm hand-shake.

'Nice to meet you too, Detective,' I said. 'Can I offer you a coffee?'

'Never touch the stuff,' he smiled. He looked even younger with that boyish grin on his face. Then he turned to Laz. 'Thanks for the escort, Lazlo. I'll call you if I need anything else.'

Lazlo's face fell, but he recovered quickly. I think he really wanted to be involved in this. He said his goodbyes and headed back down the hall. The detective waited until Laz was out of earshot before he began.

24

'Have a seat,' I offered.

'Thanks.' He sat down and reached into his pocket for a pen and notepad. I guess real-life cops actually did use them.

'Now, I'm told that you knew our victim.'

I took a deep breath and went through the whole story again. I was actually getting quite good at it by now. Detective Lincoln let me talk with few interruptions. He had even fewer questions when I was through. It appeared I would get him out of here and be back on schedule tonight. I was beginning to like him more and more. He finally closed his notebook and put it back in his pocket.

'Well, that should do for now,' he said. 'I'll give you a call if we need anything else.'

'Great. I appreciate you making this so quick.'

'Well, if I could impose for a minute longer?'

'Sure,' I said.

'Would you mind if I just used your phone for a quick call?'

Relieved that he didn't want to hear my story again, I quickly stood up.

'It's all yours,' I said. 'I'll just wait in the hall and give you some privacy.'

'Thanks, I'll be quick.'

I kicked the doorstop away and let the door close behind me. I perched on the window ledge in the corridor outside my office and eavesdropped.

'Hi, Rebecca? Hi honey, it's me. I'm fine. I'm just calling to let you know I'm probably going to be a little late tonight. Yeah, it's work. But it's good news. I've got my own case. Yes, finally my first! I'm really excited too. Look, I've got to go now, but I'll tell you all about it when I get home. OK. Love you. Bye.'

It's funny how people just assumed that a closed door meant no one else could hear your conversation – even the police.

The door opened and Ken came out. I grabbed it quickly to stop it from shutting when I saw my keys sitting on the desk. I wasn't about to get locked out again and have to call security to let me back in.

'Thanks,' he said, grinning again. 'I'll be in touch.'

I just smiled at him as he walked down the hall. Seconds

later I saw ten ushers heading towards my office, anxious to find out what had transpired.

I felt exhausted when I got home, but was too keyed up to sleep. I changed into a T-shirt and sweats, went to put the kettle on to boil and restlessly wandered around the living room. I reached up to straighten one of my prints, picked the dead leaves off a plant, and finally went over to the piano and wiped the dust off the picture of my brother. The whistle on the kettle went off and I jumped, almost knocking the picture off the piano. I went into the kitchen and made some tea, grabbed a scone and carried them out on to the balcony.

It was a beautiful, cool fall night, with a gentle breeze blowing. As I was looking at the stars I started thinking about my brother. He was almost four years younger than me, and lived thousands of miles away in Toronto, but we remained close. It had been almost six months since I last saw him, and I realized it must have been almost a month since I had talked to him. He was an airline pilot and frequently had overnight stops in Calgary. We always had dinner together and caught up with each other's lives. I thought my life was boring compared to his, and he thought his life was boring compared to mine. I like to hear about his latest trips and he likes to hear about my latest productions. I really missed him. This death business was making me very sentimental, which was something I tried to avoid. I finished my tea and decided it was time to go to bed. As I was coming in from the balcony, the doorbell rang. I set my cup down in the kitchen and got to the door just as the bell rang a second time. I opened the door to see Cam standing there, looking slightly embarrassed.

'I'm sorry I didn't get up to see you tonight,' he apologized.

'Don't worry. Lazlo told me he had you counting everything that wasn't nailed down. I didn't think I'd see you.' Seeing the look on his face, I realized my unintended pun. 'Sorry, wrong choice of words.'

'Do you mind that I'm here without an invitation?'

'No, actually, I'm really glad to see you. Come on in.'

'Thanks.'

'Want some tea?' I asked.

26

Cam looked tired. His face was pale and he had the beginnings of dark circles under his eyes. 'Have you got a beer?'

'Have you got a cigarette?'

'Katie, I thought you were quitting.'

'Don't you dare lecture me. You smoke.'

'Barely. But I also work out.'

'So you'll have healthy cancer cells?' I opened the fridge and pulled out a beer. 'Here, now give me a cigarette.'

He pulled the pack out of his pocket. I took one and he lit it for me.

'Thanks,' I said.

'Feel better?'

'No, now I feel guilty for smoking. Are you here for the night?' I asked as I poured myself another cup of tea, feigning indifference.

'Would you like me to be?' he asked.

'Do you want to stay?' I countered.

'I could. I don't want to infringe on your space, though.'

'I only want you to stay if you want to.'

'Katie, you said you needed some time away from me. I just stopped by to see if you were OK. So it's up to you.'

'Well I don't want you to feel like we're dating again. I think it's still too soon for that. So if that's OK with you . . .?'

'Only if you don't mind. I can stay for a beer and then go home.'

'Oh, for God's sake,' I said, turning away from him.

He grabbed my arm and pulled me back, slopping my tea on his shirt. 'OK,' he said, giving in, 'I would like to stay the night. And take off this shirt.'

'Good, because I would like you to stay . . . and take off your shirt. I need to talk and I really don't want to be alone.'

'You don't have to be alone. I don't just come here when I'm horny, you know.'

'I know, but I feel guilty calling you and asking for help. Two weeks ago I told you I didn't want to see you for a while.'

'Katie, two weeks ago you didn't have some dead man in your theatre. Besides, no matter what happens between us, I am always going to be your friend.'

'Stop this sensitive-guy stuff and let's go upstairs. I feel like listening to some music,' I said, heading up the stairs.

'You are such a cynic,' he said.

'Turn the lights off on your way up,' I called from upstairs.

'I'm just going to change.'

That was the one concession I had allowed him. He could keep one toothbrush, one razor, and one sweatsuit at my place. Anything else was more of a commitment than I'm willing to make. Anything less would be unfair to him.

'What do you feel like listening to?' I yelled over the loft.

'How about the Eagles?'

I popped Elton John in and climbed into bed. He came upstairs with just his sweatpants on. Sometimes Cam can be the stereotypical blue-collar male and it usually really turns me on. The accountant I had dated only succeeded in looking half dressed when he had his shirt off, but Cam looked like he was ready to go out and slay dragons.

'Interesting choice of music.'

'I knew you didn't really want to listen to the Eagles,' I said.

'This is really nice,' he said, noticing the candles I had lit. 'You definitely know how to create a mood.'

'Cam . . .'

'Yeah?' He was laying his clothes neatly over the chair. I saw a damp spot on his shirt where he had already sponged off the stain.

'I knew the man who died. I didn't recognize him last night, because he had a beard. But I knew him.'

'Oh, Katie.' He climbed into bed and hugged me. 'I'm so sorry.'

'I didn't know him well. It's just so weird to think that I even knew him at all.'

'Did you talk to the police?'

'Yes, they met me at my office this afternoon and questioned me.'

I reached over for the ashtray to put my cigarette out. Cam piled some pillows behind him and sat up.

'You going to tell me about it?'

I grabbed my tea and lit another cigarette. I propped myself against the wall.

'Well, you know I used to volunteer with the Symphony?' He nodded and I continued. 'There was this other woman there. It was her first time volunteering and we started on the same day, so we kind of stuck to each other. We went out for coffee a couple of times. Anyway, she works as an usher now. Gladys Reynolds. Do you know her?'

'Everyone knows her,' Cam said as he drank his beer.

'What?'

'She has a bit of a reputation for hitting on all the guys,' he explained.

'Did she hit on you?'

'Katie, a gentleman never tells,' Cam laughed.

'She did! When? Before you started seeing me, or after?' I asked, stabbing the cigarette into the ashtray.

'Before,' he confessed.

'While you were still married?'

'She said she knew I was married, but all she wanted was to have sex with me. No strings attached.'

'So? Did you?' I demanded, staring Cam straight in the eyes.

'Did I what?' he asked.

'Cam, you know exactly what I mean.'

'No, I didn't. When I was married, I was faithful,' Cam admitted.

'Did she leave you alone after that?'

'Katie, can we get back to your story?'

'OK, OK. Well, she hasn't changed much. Turns out, back then she was married. But she and her husband hated each other and were only staying together because of their dogs. The kids were already grown-up and in university, but they couldn't agree on who would get the dogs. Meanwhile, they basically lived separate lives. In the years they had that living arrangement, she never dated anyone.'

'Are we talking about the same woman?' Cam asked.

'Yes. Well she reached some sort of turning point. A couple of weeks after I met her, she told me she had met this very young usher and she really wanted to sleep with him. She felt it was time to break free, and apparently she was really turned on by the idea of sleeping with someone who was younger than her youngest child.'

29

'And you were friends with this woman?'

'We weren't close friends. I think I liked to go out with her just to hear what she had been up to.'

'Is there more?' he asked.

'Lots,' I said. If this wasn't such a gruesome situation, it would be funny.

'Let me get another beer first. Do you want anything?' Cam asked, getting up off the bed.

'More tea?' I asked, handing him my mug.

'Certainly,' he called as he went downstairs and turned the kettle on. I stood up and leaned over the half wall.

'So she ended up sleeping with this very young man,' I said, trying to get back on topic.

'How old was she at the time?' Cam stood in the kitchen, looking up at me, while he waited for the water to boil.

'Fifty-five,' I said.

'That's sick,' he said. 'It reminds me of that movie with Jacqueline Bisset and Candice Bergen, where Jackie sleeps with Candice's son.'

'Yes it was sick,' I agreed. 'But then so were the bartender, the ticket taker, coat-check attendant and the security guard; all of whom were under twenty-five years old. I'm kind of surprised that she hit on an old guy like you.'

'Oh, you're funny, Katie.'

'So the rumour has it she slept with every man under twenty-five and then a few women.'

Cam came back upstairs with the drinks. 'Women?' he asked.

'She met a gay performance artist and decided that gay was beautiful. So she went through a few of the women who work in the building before switching back to men.'

'I thought I'd heard it all.'

'Cam, this gets better yet.'

He lit a cigarette and offered me another one.

'After she had dated several of these boys, we were here one night, having coffee. The phone rang at about midnight and it was her husband calling. I still don't know how he got this number. He told Gladys that there was an emergency at home and she'd better get back right away. She left in a panic and I told her to call me if she needed anything.'

'Well . . .'

'Well, at about three a.m. there was a pounding on my door and it was Gladys. She said her husband knew everything. He had names and dates and places of everyone she had slept with. And she accused me of telling him.'

'Did you?' Cam asked hesitantly.

'Of course not. I would never interfere in anyone's life like that. So Gladys took off, went to the house of every man she had been with and accused them of telling her husband.'

'At three in the morning?'

'Uh huh.'

'That's every man's nightmare come true. Ever seen *Fatal Attraction*?'

'Yeah, well that was Gladys. We had coffee the next day. She said she never found out who told her husband. He went straight to his lawyer and was drawing up divorce papers and wanted to have her removed from the house. It was starting to get really messy. I don't think she ever believed that it wasn't me who told him.'

'Why?'

I paused and thought about Gladys for a minute while I took a sip of tea. 'She never said another word to me. I ran into her a couple of times after that and she just waved and kept on going.'

'I am so glad I never got involved with her,' he said with relief in his voice.

'Well, at this point, I wish I could say the same thing. It was her ex-husband who was murdered.'

'Oh shit. And you had met him?'

'Once. I had offered Gladys a ride to work and when I picked her up, he was at home.'

'Wow. Did you tell all this to the police?' he asked, amazed.

'Without all the embellishments. But I told them the story.'

'What did they have to say?'

'Just thank you and that they might need to question me further, so to keep them notified if I was planning on going anywhere.'

'This is just like the movies,' he laughed. 'Are you a suspect?'

31

'Cam, I am not having fun being involved in this. I would have preferred having him die at the opera and then I could just gossip about it like everyone else.'

'So how did the show go tonight?'

'Not as bad as I imagined. There was some press around and a few gawkers. The patrons were certainly there early, though. I think everyone wanted to get a good look around. Maybe I should have left the police tape up. We're sold out for the next week.'

'The headlines are sure helping.'

'I haven't had a chance to see the papers,' I said.

'Front page of the *Herald*: "FOOTHILLS STAGE NETWORK PRESENTS MUCH ADO ABOUT SOMETHING".'

'I'm sure they'll come up with every theatre pun ever invented.'

'The *Sun* was great too: "FOOTHILLS STAGE NETWORK'S SHAKESPEARE IS SLAYING THEM IN THE AISLES".'

'Oh, that's bad. How about you? Did you account for every screw and nail in the building?' I asked.

'I only made it halfway through the key count. Tomorrow the guys start with the equipment inventory and security is going to handle checking all the employees' keys. I imagine we'll be pretty busy for a week at least.'

'I don't envy you,' I said.

'Well, I'm off for the next four days, so I am not even going to think about it until Wednesday,' he said.

'I would say you are very lucky the way your days off happened to fall.'

'I'll consider myself lucky if I actually get through these days off. I have a funny feeling that Lazlo may be calling me in for some overtime.'

'So don't answer the phone,' I said.

'I don't intend to.' We sat in silence for a few minutes and listened to the music. 'The Eagles sound better than ever,' he laughed.

'Sorry, I didn't feel like the Eagles.'

'Why did you ask me then?'

'You might have said Elton John, and I was trying to be nice.'

'So what now?' he asked.

'About the music or the murder?'

'The murder.'

'I go to work, try to act normal, and hope this thing is figured out quickly so all the excitement dies down.'

'And on Monday?'

'What's Monday?' I asked.

'Your day off. Will you go to Banff with me?' Cam asked, rolling over and holding me close.

'It's too crowded,' I said.

'We'll go to the hot springs. Have dinner. Go for a walk. You used to love going to Banff.'

'I still do.'

'So, you want to go?'

'Yes,' I said as I relaxed and leaned back against him.

'Why don't you take tomorrow off and we'll stay overnight?' he asked.

'I can't. I just can't leave someone else in charge with all this going on.'

'I know. I figured you'd say that. But you can't blame a guy for trying.'

'I'll tell you what I will do.'

'What?'

'I'll go to a movie with you tomorrow afternoon. I might even neck with you if we can sit in the back row.'

'Not at the Plex,' he said.

'No. We'll go somewhere else, even if we have to pay.'

'Deal. How about blowing out those candles so we can get some sleep?'

'How about a game of backgammon first?'

'Katie, it's late and I want to go jogging in the morning.'

'Cam, it's already morning. Skip jogging for one day?' I whined and tried batting my eyelashes.

'How about playing backgammon now and you jog with me tomorrow afternoon?'

'I'll blow out the candles,' I said.

'Night, Katie.'

'Night, Cam,' I murmured as I pulled the quilt up around us and snuggled close to him.

'Why do I never win with you?' I whispered.

Cam didn't answer, but I felt him brush my hair from my neck and kiss me just in the hollow below my ear.

'I know a way where we both could win,' he finally replied.

'I thought you were tired.' It was only a half-hearted protest.

'Too tired to argue, not too tired to make up.' He had moved down to my shoulder.

'We haven't had a fight.'

'We will.'

'So this is like making up in advance?' I asked.

'Don't you think that's a good idea?'

'I think it's a wonderful idea.'

Saturday

Cam and I slept until noon and then went out for brunch at Victoria's on the new and improved Seventeenth Avenue. The city is redoing all the old run-down areas into trendy new shopping and eating districts, and Seventeenth Avenue was the latest. I used to live in this area, not all that long ago, but I barely recognize it now. Now it's just another area of town that I can't afford to shop in.

We saw a great movie at the Globe Theatre, which was my favourite movie theatre. Instead of taking a classic old theatre and closing it down, it has been renovated, keeping the style and romance, but updating the technology. We chose to see the movie playing in the upstairs theatre and sat in the back row of the balcony, holding hands like two kids. We also managed to go all day without any sort of argument. My mood was considerably brighter by the time he dropped me off at the Plex.

I waved goodbye as Cam drove his pride and joy down the street. I was pretty sure he would take advantage of this wonderful sunny fall day and cruise for a while, showing off his wheels, rather than going home. I walked to Grounds Zero and jumped up on my usual stool at the end of the counter. Gus started making my cappuccino before I had a chance to order. I pulled a cigarette out of my pocket, leaned over the counter to grab a book of matches from his stash, and waited for him to slide my coffee across the counter to me.

'Kate, I'm disappointed in you,' Gus said, sprinkling chocolate on top of the cappuccino.

'What do you mean?' I asked, having no idea what he was talking about.

'You knew this Peter Reynolds and I had to find out from someone else.'

'How the hell did you find that out? There are only three other people who know. You're amazing, Gus.' I took the lid off my coffee and took a sip. 'Have you got a video camera hooked up in my office or something?'

'No, I just know the right questions to ask the right people. And how to listen to the answers,' he said as he wiped down the counter.

'More like you're a snake in the grass,' I said. I pulled some money out of my wallet and slid it across the counter to him. 'Have you given the police the name of your source, or is this your own private investigation?'

'Kate, my sources would dry up if I told the police about them. Then what kind of fun would this job be, if I couldn't find out what was going on? You think I like making cappuccino and sandwiches all day long?'

'So are you going to tell me who's talking?' I asked.

'No way, Kate. Just think of me like a doctor or a lawyer. Anything you say to me is totally confidential.'

'I'll think of you like the nosy old cappuccino slinger that you are,' I joked.

'Oh, that hurts. I don't consider myself anywhere near old yet,' Gus said as he took my money to the cash register. He handed me some coins back and I tossed them into my pocket. Laundry money.

'Thanks Gus, I'll remember to call you before the police next time I find something out.'

'All joking aside, Kate, I think this is an inside job.'

'You mean somebody who works at the Plex is responsible for the murder? You've got to be kidding!'

'Think about it. Who could get into the maintenance department and get a nail gun? How many locked doors are there between your theatre and equipment storage? You think a member of the public could get in there? Nope, someone with a set of keys did this.'

'Gus, I think you're crazy, but I'll tell you what. I'll keep my ears open, you keep your ears open, and we'll compare notes tomorrow. Maybe we can catch the murderer before the police do.' I threw my bag over my shoulder and stood up.

'Just watch your back, Kate. If this person has keys, you're not safe either.'

'Oh, Gus, stop your worrying. I'm not in any danger; I just found the guy.' I put the lid on my coffee and headed for the door. 'I'll see you later.'

Like the reformed girl that I was, I walked the half block to the stage door and stopped at the security desk to sign in. The little glass cubicle that made up the security office was filled with guards. It looked like they had called in reinforcements since the night of the murder. Lazlo was in the back corner, giving orders, checking through logbooks, and driving everyone crazy. Nick Grey, one of the three security supervisors, sat at the desk, looking decidedly frazzled as I approached.

Nick had been at the Plex since it opened, though it wasn't his first choice of careers. He had been applying to the police department for a long time, but had to earn a living in the meantime. So he worked at the Plex, taking orders from the Spaz and supervising an ever-changing cast of rent-a-dicks.

'How's it going?' I asked him as I signed the book.

'It's been a long weekend,' he said, lowering his voice so the Spaz wouldn't hear him. 'Next time you find a stiff, could you report it on somebody else's shift?'

'I'll do my best,' I promised, then headed off toward my office. Nick buzzed me through the first door, which was easier than trying to find the right key, and I headed off down Tin Pan Alley.

All the backstage corridors are named alleys. Someone had thought it would be easier to find their way around if these anonymous concrete corridors were given names. This is just another of the big plans that hadn't worked out, since you can't tell one alley from the next. You can always tell when a new play is in rehearsal because the technical staff run long lines of coloured gaffer tape down the corridors that lead from the stage door to the theatre and rehearsal halls. If this isn't done, we can spend hours looking for actors who have taken a wrong turn somewhere and ended up stuck behind a locked door.

I passed by the prop shop and scenery workshop, but there was not much to see because the doors were closed and the windows taped over with newspaper. This is always done when a new set is being created. Can't take any chances that somebody might see it before its stage debut.

The door to the Centenary Theatre is at the end of Tin Pan Alley. I fished my keys out and let myself through it. I stood in a darkened hall, the green room and dressing rooms to my left, and access to the stage to my right. When my eyes grew accustomed to the darkness, I turned to my left, past the dressing rooms, and let myself through two more locked doors, leading into the main lobby.

The lobby was dark, the theatre quiet, and I was looking forward to two hours of peace before anyone started to arrive. I made my way across the lobby, up a flight of stairs and let myself into my office. I threw my keys on my desk, put the coffee on, opened the safe and called the switchboard for my messages.

'Good morning, the Calgary Arts Complex,' a voice greeted me.

Grace, the weekend receptionist, has the revolting reputation of being the most cheerful employee at the Plex. She is also the nosiest person in the building.

'Hi, Grace, it's Kate. Any messages for me?' I asked, prying the lid off my cappuccino and taking a sip.

'Hi, Kate. How's it going down there?' She ignored my request. 'You guys recovering from all the excitement?'

'Well, ticket sales are up and gossip is running wild, but other than that it's business as usual.'

'Well, your messages are brief today. Two volunteers won't be in tonight. Do you want their names?' she asked. I could hear papers rustling in the background as she tried to find my messages. Grace is also renowned for being the most disorganized person in the building.

'No, just put them in the volunteer coordinator's message box. She can deal with them for a change.'

'OK. Do you think it's this murder thing? I was wondering how the staff would react.'

'Anything else?' I cut in, trying to avoid that subject.

'A Detective Lincoln called and wants you to call him as soon as you get in. Do you need the number?'

'No, I've got it,' I said, wondering where I had tossed his business card.

'Leonard is going to be late, but then that's nothing new, right? And somebody named Gladys called. She said you would know who she was.'

'Gladys?' I asked, trying to contain my surprise.

'That's what she said.'

'Did she leave a number?'

'Yeah. Let's see . . .' Grace reeled off a number. 'She said she'd be at that number all day and you could call at any time. Is she related to this murder somehow?'

'Thanks, Grace. Talk to you later.' I hung up the phone before she could ask anything else.

I called Detective Lincoln right away. No point putting him off. He certainly wasn't going away. He sounded pretty excited when I spoke to him, explaining he had a few more questions to ask, and we arranged to meet in an hour. Meanwhile, I was trying to get through my endless round of paperwork before he arrived. You can't let the T-shirt or beer sales go unreported for even one day without the admin staff going crazy. I picked up the phone several times to call Gladys, but I couldn't make myself dial. I didn't know what I would say to her.

I balanced all the sales from the previous night and slipped the reports into my out basket. I counted out floats and put them into the cash boxes for that night's show. The ushers had to have something to make change with. I kind of miss the old days when ushers actually helped people to their seats. Not like now when they just hustle T-shirts and ice cream in the lobbies. I had just finished counting out the last float when I heard a knock at my door.

I looked up. 'Detective Lincoln, please, come in.'

'I'm glad you could see me on such short notice,' he said, settling in the chair across from my desk.

'No problem. I just have to lock up this money. The coffee is on. Please help yourself.'

I locked the cash boxes in the bottom drawer of my desk, then put the rest of the deposits into the safe and secured it. I was glad the weekend was almost over and I could get rid of most of this money soon. I had almost ten thousand dollars in the safe – something I made sure that no one but myself knew. That much money was too tempting.

The detective had pulled a bottle of mineral water out of his pocket. 'I brought my own today.'

When I, too, was sitting, he took a sip and began. 'Ms Carpenter . . .'

'Please, call me Kate.'

'Thanks. You're aware that the Complex has been conducting an extensive inventory?'

'Yes, Lazlo told me what's been happening.'

'Well, we have determined that the weapon came from the building maintenance department.'

'Lazlo's ID numbers on the hammer?' I asked.

'Actually, someone had tried to rub the numbers off. The lab found paint traces and was able to reconstruct the ID. We have an amazing police lab here,' he said. 'Have you ever seen the things they can do?'

'Sorry,' I said. 'This is my first brush with the law.'

'Well, I'll show you around sometime if you like. Anyway,' he said, steering himself back to the subject at hand, 'the nail gun is from the maintenance department.'

'So someone who works here did it?' I asked, thinking back to what Gus had said.

'It's a possibility. There are no keys missing and no sign of forced entry, so we would assume that someone who is in possession of a set of keys either committed the murder or gave the weapon to the murderer.'

'So that would have to be someone in the maintenance or security departments.'

'Why do you say that?' he asked, pulling out his notepad.

'No one else in this building has keys that access all those areas. I'm sure you've already found out that key assignments are quite specific here.'

'Kate, do you know a Norman Caminski?' he asked.

'Yes I do,' I replied cautiously. I can't control the smile that appears on my face every time I hear that name. 'But we call him Cam.'

'May I ask how you know him?' He looked slightly embarrassed.

'We are dating, Detective. It's not much of a secret around here, and I doubt that it is news to you,' I answered defensively.

'Well, I try not to believe everything I hear.' He grinned again. I was beginning to think he was using that grin on purpose, to disarm me.

'Why do you ask?' I asked, sipping my coffee.

'Mr Caminski would have access to the missing hammer.'

'You can't think that Cam had anything to do with this?' I couldn't hide the surprise in my voice.

'I can't rule anything out. You knew Mr Reynolds and his wife?'

'I told you before that I had met Peter Reynolds once. Gladys and I met while working here. We've gone out for coffee and attended a few concerts together. But really, nothing outside of work.'

'Now, you also stated previously that Mrs Reynolds has dated a lot of men who work in this building.'

'Yes, she did.'

'Did she ever date Mr Caminski?' he asked.

'No.'

'Did she sleep with him?' He wouldn't make eye contact with me.

'No!'

'But she approached him?'

'Yes. Cam told me that she made a pass at him.'

'Was that while you were dating him?' He was still scribbling in his pad, trying not to look up at me.

'I don't think so, Detective. Cam just told me about this last night. I would like to know if you are implying that Cam and I had something to do with this?'

'I believe I said I couldn't rule anything out at this point.' He finally stopped writing and looked up.

'Cam and I found the body. We tried to revive him.'

'I'm aware of that, but I am also aware that, as a building engineer, Mr Caminski has access to all areas of this building.'

'Cam would never do anything like this. He isn't capable of it.'

'Has he ever taken you to restricted areas of the building?' Again that boyish grin. I felt my defenses going up.

'He's shown me around, but anyone can get permission for building tours.'

'And did you get permission for a tour? Or did you and Mr Caminski just decide to go on a tour on your own?'

'Detective, this is not the Pentagon; it's the Calgary Arts Complex. Half the people around here don't sign in or out or follow most of the other procedures they are supposed to.'

'I'm aware of that, too,' he replied.

It was infuriating that I was allowing him to make me angry. He was my age, I knew he was inexperienced, but I was letting him get to me anyway.

'That's what is making this so difficult,' he continued. 'It's hard to determine exactly who was in this theatre on Thursday evening.'

'Let's get the time sheets,' I suggested. 'No one ever forgets to sign those. No time sheet, no pay cheque.'

'I'll ask for those. Tell me, Kate – your garbage can ... Don't those ID numbers belong to the Heritage Theatre?'

I started to rethink my opinion of Ken Lincoln. Even though this was his first murder case, he was good. 'Yes, it's a bit of a practical joke around here. This stapler is from the Concert Hall. The Heritage has my scissors and an empty cash box; and I'm sure there are a few other things at the Concert Hall, too. The other house managers and I thought all these ID numbers were really stupid, so we go on raids once in a while. Lazlo hasn't noticed anything yet, which proves our point, I guess.' I suddenly thought it all sounded very juvenile.

'How did you get into the Heritage Theatre to get these items?'

I took a deep breath as I tried to decide what to say next. Truth or lie? 'Cam let me in,' I admitted.

He started to stand up. 'Well, I think that's about all for now.'

'Detective, I'm telling you the truth. I had nothing to do with this and I know Cam didn't either. No matter what it looks like. I will do anything I can to help you find the murderer.'

'I understand, Ms Carpenter – I mean, Kate. Look, I'm not accusing anybody of anything right now. I just need to understand what goes on in this building and try and figure out who might, or might not, have done this. I'm not trying to pin this on someone. I hope you believe that. Besides, this is all so new to me. I've never been to a live play. I'm just trying to learn something.'

'Thank you, Detective.'

'Thanks for your time,' he said, tossing his empty bottle into the recycling bin.

'Is there anything I can do to help?'

'You can keep answering my questions and stay out of everything else.'

'Detective, you sat here and practically accused Cam and me of being involved in this. How can you expect me to just sit here and wait for you to throw him in jail?'

'Kate, everyone in this building is under suspicion, not just Cam. I will find out who did it and I don't need your help. You get any ideas, you call me. Otherwise, leave it to the police. OK?'

'OK.' I was getting pretty good at lying to authority figures.

'Good. I'll call you if I have any further questions,' he said. 'Thanks again for your time.'

After he was gone, I refilled my empty coffee cup and sat on the window ledge to drink it. I had to think about what to do next. I wasn't worried about myself; I had an iron-clad alibi. I had been in full public view all night, seen by at least thirty staff members and close to a thousand patrons. But I was terrified for Cam. The fact that he had access to that nail gun before it went missing wouldn't look good. I had to do something to help him. I felt a hand on my shoulder and jumped, spilling coffee all over the floor.

'Graham, don't you ever sneak up on me like that again!'

'I said hello three times,' he defended himself, kneeling to mop the floor. 'Where were you?'

'Worrying. Sorry.' I got down on my knees and helped him clean the spill.

'Worrying about what?' He had finished with the floor and started wiping off his shirt.

'Have you got a clean shirt here?' I asked.

'Yes, now quit avoiding my questions.'

'I was worrying about the police. Detective Lincoln was just here and we didn't exactly have an uplifting conversation.' I flopped down in the chair behind my desk, watching Graham trying to clean his shirt.

'What's up?' he asked.

'I probably shouldn't tell you,' I said. 'Have you got a smoke?'

'Of course not.' He gave up with his shirt and sat down across from me.

'I'm just going to go buy a pack and I don't want to hear anything about how I'm supposed to be quitting.'

'Fine. What if I tell you that it's bad for your lungs?'

I ignored him. 'The cash is ready for tonight and last night's sales reports are done. Would you mind starting the liquor inventory? I'll be back in about fifteen minutes.'

That's one of the joys of running the theatre. Before and after every show we count every drop of alcohol in the place. The admin staff say it's the only way they can balance the bar sales, but I think they worry that we all steal drinks. But most of the bar staff drink better stuff than we sell in the theatre – except maybe Burns Enevold, our local drunk.

'Take your time,' Graham said. 'I'll get everything else ready. But I just have to say that you also increase risk of heart and gum disease.'

'There's also an increased risk that I might fire smart-ass employees.'

'All right, I'll stop. See you in a few.'

I picked up the garbage can and stapler on my way out. I thought it would be best if I dropped them off at the Heritage on my way to the store. I went back into the main lobby, took the service corridor behind the main bar, and then headed down the fire-escape stairs and into the public corridor. By the time I got to the store I had a basic idea of what I could do about all this. By the time I got back to my office, I was sure of it. I sat back down on the window ledge and watched Graham filling out the time sheets.

'Anybody else here yet?' I asked.

'No, just us.'

'Graham, how do you feel about Cam?'

'He's a nice guy but not really my type. Puts up with a lot of shit from you.' He laughed. 'Why do you ask?'

'Because I think I need your help with something.'

'What?' Graham looked intrigued.

'It's not really work-related,' I started. 'And I shouldn't be telling you about this. I probably shouldn't even be thinking about telling you what I'm thinking about.'

Graham shoved the time sheets to the side of the desk and leaned forward. 'Now you've got me really interested,' he said. 'What do you want to do?'

'I want to find out who murdered Peter Reynolds.'

'Who doesn't?' He looked disappointed by my revelation.

'Graham, I'm serious. Detective Lincoln told me that they have traced the murder weapon back to this building, and probably located the last person who had his hands on it.'

'Cam?' he asked.

I nodded.

'Holy shit!' He sat back. 'Are you serious?'

'I'm serious.'

'Could he have done it?'

'No,' I said. 'Absolutely not.'

'OK. So we're going to make sure that the police leave no stone unturned?'

'You got it,' I said. 'The detective wanted to know about the men that Gladys Reynolds has been involved with. I want us to work on that list. I'll give the names to the police, but we'll investigate it, too. I want to find out where they all were at the time and how they feel about Gladys. When we're through the list, we'll see what we're left with.'

'OK, but maybe we should get Charlotte and Martha to help. It'll go much faster,' he suggested.

'Graham, no one else can know what we're doing. I'm counting on people telling us more than they would tell the police, but only if we can make it look like we're not really asking.'

'So what are we going to do?' he asked.

'Well, we know that the people in this building love to gossip, so I think we should start by listening to the gossip. Maybe ask a question or two – over drinks?'

'An acting gig?' he said.

'You got it. Everyone you talk to has to believe you are one of them. Can you handle it?'

'When do we start?' Graham asked, jumping to his feet.

'As soon as the show goes in. I'll start on my list and then after intermission we'll meet here and go over it.'

'OK. I'll go start the liquor inventory.'

'I've just got a quick phone call to make and then I'll be right down to help.'

Graham left and I dialled Cam's number. His machine picked up after four rings. 'Hi Cam, it's Kate. Please call me as soon as you get in. If you can't get hold of me, please come over tonight. I have to see you and I've got some really important news.'

I hung up, feeling disappointed that I hadn't got to speak to him. Then I picked up the phone again and decided to call Gladys.

Graham and I got the liquor count done and I did up an order for next week. These sold-out houses were really draining our supply. It seemed like the public wasn't only thirsty for blood, but for beer too. My staff had started to straggle in, so I had Graham sign them in while I changed.

I pulled a cute little navy and white polka-dotted dress with a lace collar off the rack and changed in the bathroom right outside my office. When I came out of the bathroom, Graham had everyone organized and counting programs. I poured myself a coffee, sat at my desk and pulled on my blue and white spectator pumps. Eat your heart out, Nicole Kidman, I thought. You're not the only one in the world who knows how to accessorize.

I made small talk with some of the volunteers while I put earrings on, and then it was time to send the ushers to their doors. I did a quick tour of the theatre, made sure everyone was in place and happy, and called security to open the main doors. All the lights and the main doors are controlled by the mighty computer at the security office. No theatre could be open to the public unless they knew about it. Another of Lazlo's ideas, I'm sure. I always seem to forget to call and have them opened on busy nights, and the ushers have to remind me. I usually apologize profusely to the line of patrons standing outside, covering up by saying there had been a computer glitch.

I made sure all the ushers were guarding their assigned doors before I entered the theatre. The lights were on and there were actors everywhere in various forms of dress and undress, doing their warm-up exercises. This is why we guard the doors and make sure no ticket holders enter the auditorium at this point in the evening. Seeing this would take away all the magic the public expects from the theatre. I sat in the back, trying not to stare as actors screamed, coughed, sang and did yoga, waiting for the stage manager to clear them out and let me open up. At seven twenty-five he got the last actor off the stage, dimmed the house lights and turned it over to me.

I did a quick check, making sure nothing was out of place, approving of the atmosphere, and then made my way back out into the lobby. I let myself into the technical booth where the lobby public address system is located, and began my official duties.

'Ladies and gentlemen, the Foothills Stage Network welcomes you to the Centenary Theatre and our production of *Much Ado About Nothing*. We would like to remind all patrons that the use of cameras or recording devices is strictly forbidden. We invite you to partake of our London Bar service to pre-order your drinks for the intermission before this evening's presentation begins. Ladies and gentlemen, the house is now open.' I could hear the ushers pushing the doors, hopefully as one, for a very dramatic start to the evening. We try to choreograph it so that all were opened as I say the word 'house', and it sounded like tonight it had actually happened.

I came out of the booth and told Graham that he was in charge and then went up to my office to start work on my list. I lost track of time until I heard Graham announce that the show was about to begin, and a few minutes later he came loping down the hall. The speaker in my office came to life as Beatrice and Benedick began their battle of wills onstage. I turned it down immediately. I already knew most of the lines by heart and decided I had listened to this play once too often.

'Coat check was under by five dollars,' Graham announced, tossing the cash bag on my desk.

'I guess we need to start giving prospective volunteers math tests.'

'Or start using paid staff again,' he suggested.

'Graham, you are looking at the future of theatre. If the Board of Directors could get away with it, you and I would be replaced with volunteers. Any other problems?'

'Nope. Everyone had the right ticket for the right seat and there were no complaints about the price of drinks, for a change. There was a huge line-up for the washroom, though.'

'Everyone has to check out the scene of the crime, I guess. Were they disappointed that there was no chalk outline of the body or police tape left?'

'No one complained.'

'Good.' I turned back to the computer, saved my file then printed it, taking a sip of coffee before continuing. 'OK, there's the list. I've divided it into sections. First are the people she had serious relationships with; then are the others who I know she was casually involved with.'

He pulled the pages off the printer and read them over. 'That's a lot of names.'

'Well she has worked here for three years. Tomorrow I'll go to human resources to confirm who still works here and get addresses and phone numbers for the ones who don't. I'll update you as soon as I can.'

'OK. Are we doing this as a team?' he asked.

'I think we should split up,' I said. 'We can meet every day and compare notes.'

'Cool. I thought I'd head up to the Box Office Bar tonight and see if anyone from the list is up there.'

The Box Office Bar, or the BOB as we call it, is on the mezzanine level of Restaurant Row, overlooking the court-yard. It is open as late as legally possible and is a popular hangout for most of the Plex staff.

'You keep track of what you spend, Graham. I'll pay you back.'

'Kate, you don't have to do that.'

'No argument allowed. I pay for this or I do it on my own.'

'OK, OK. Do you want me to take this list down to security for you? Detective Lincoln can pick it up the next time he's in.'

'Thanks.' I gave him an envelope out of my desk to put it in. 'So tomorrow is Sunday and I think we both need the day off. Let's meet for a couple of hours early on Tuesday and see if we have any news. Of course, if someone confesses to you tonight, feel free to call me at home.'

'All right,' he agreed.

'And Graham, nobody finds out about this,' I warned him.

'I understand,' he said. 'I am a professional actor, after all. I think I can stay in character for a couple of hours.'

'One paid job does not make you Laurence Olivier, Graham. Just remember – somebody drove a nail into Peter Reynolds' skull. This is for real.'

'Understood,' he said. 'But isn't there one person we're forgetting here?'

'Who?' I asked.

'The grieving widow herself.'

'I didn't forget her,' I said. 'I spoke to her this afternoon and arranged to meet her for a coffee tomorrow.'

'Isn't she going to be suspicious?' he asked.

'Not at all. She called me.'

We made it through the rest of the night without any problems. I missed catching a ride with the techies, who sometimes subbed as my chauffeurs, decided I was too lazy to walk and it was too late to take the C-Train, so I called a cab and was home just before midnight. I hadn't heard from Cam at all and was hoping there would be a message on my machine, but there wasn't.

The apartment seemed kind of chilly and empty, so I put my robe on and curled up on the couch with a blanket and a book. I opened a bag of chocolate-chip cookies and dunked them in my coffee while I read.

It was almost one o'clock when I called Cam's house again. I got his machine and left another message. I was getting really annoyed that I couldn't get in touch with him. Finally, after reading the same paragraph a dozen times, I put the book down and made another pot of coffee. Good thing it doesn't affect my sleep. I took a sip of coffee, dunked another cookie, and tried to decide if I should go to bed or not. I had just started up the stairs when the doorbell rang. I ran to the door and opened it, relieved to see Cam standing there.

'Where have you been?' I asked.

'Did you miss me?'

I pulled him into the apartment and wrapped my arms around him. 'I hate you.'

'You have a strange way of showing it, Katie.'

'I never used to sit around in my bathrobe, missing someone and worrying about where he might be. I was happy being alone and selfish.'

'I love you,' he said.

'Where have you been?' I asked again.

He held up blue-stained fingertips for me to see. 'At the police station.'

'Were you arrested?'

'No, I'm cooperating,' he said, closing and locking the door behind him. 'I promise I'll answer all of your questions, but I really want a bath and a beer first, OK?'

'OK. I'll get you some towels . . . and a beer.'

He kissed me and then went into the bathroom. 'Thank you.'

I heard the water running in the tub as I went to the kitchen. I got a beer out of the fridge and poured it into a glass. I poured myself another cup of coffee and had another cookie before I put the bag away. I grabbed a clean towel from the linen closet, threw it over my arm, and carried everything into the bathroom.

The bathroom was already hot and steamy and the mirrors were fogged over. I handed Cam his beer and laid the towel over the vanity.

'Want your back washed?' I asked, watching him lay back in the steaming water.

'In a minute. I'm too exhausted to move right now.'

I sat on the closed toilet seat. 'Are you OK? You look awful.'

'I'm fine, just tired.'

'I saw Detective Lincoln this afternoon, Cam. He told me pretty much everything.'

'Yeah. Well, he talked to me for quite a while too. Got my fingerprints to check against the prints on the nail gun.'

'Will they be on it?'

'I signed one out and did some drywalling on Thursday. If that's the same one, then I'm sure my prints will be all over it.'

'Did you tell the police that?'

'Yes, Katie.'

'And . . . ?'

'They said they understood but were doing this as a precautionary measure, or something like that.'

I picked up the sponge and soaped it up. 'Lean forward.'

He did and I started washing his back.

'You're really tense,' I said, rubbing the sponge over his shoulders.

'I think you would be too, under the circumstances.'

'Cam, I'm not going to wait for the police to investigate this.'

'What do you mean?' he asked.

'I mean that Graham and I are going to start talking to people and try to find out what happened.'

'Katie, leave it to the police. It's their job.' He turned around to look at me.

'Lean forward, I'm not finished with your back yet. And I'm not going to sit around and wait for them to arrest you. Did you know that this is Detective Lincoln's first murder case?'

'No, I didn't, and they are not going to arrest me.'

'What if they don't find anything else, Cam? They've got all this great circumstantial evidence against you. It's an easy way to close the case.'

'Is there anything I can say to make you change your mind?' he asked, sounding exasperated with me.

'Nothing.' I was firm.

'And you're doing this all for me?'

'Yes.'

'Did you also mean what you said when I came in?' he asked. 'About never worrying about anyone before?'

'You know, I used to come home and love being able to do whatever I wanted, all alone. Tonight when I came home, the place just seemed empty. I had all this stuff that happened today, that I wanted to talk about, and nobody here to talk to.'

'Katie, those are the nicest things you have ever said about me.'

'I love you.' It was so much easier to say than I thought it would be. 'But this really terrifies me.'

'Why?' he asked.

'All I've ever wanted is a nice man and a good relationship with him, maybe a family. I never thought that would mean I would feel so dependent. I've worked really hard to be independent. I know that you really want a family, but you're fresh from a divorce and I don't know if I'm ready for a family yet.'

'Katie, if all I wanted to do was to replace a family, I could have found someone else who was much easier to deal with than you. Haven't you noticed that every time you tell me to go away, I come back?'

'Yes,' I admitted.

He pulled the plug in the bathtub and the water started to drain out. 'So what do I have to do to convince you?' he asked as he stood up and wrapped the towel around him.

I reached out to pull it off him, but he was too quick for me tonight.

'Quit trying to avoid the subject.'

'OK, I guess I have to convince myself, but I did think you might want to stay here for a while. At least until this whole thing simmers down a bit.'

'Why don't you make us both some tea?' he asked.

I went into the kitchen and filled the kettle. 'Does that neat little side-step around my offer mean that you're going to turn me down?'

He came out dressed in his sweatpants. He wrapped his arms around me as I faced the stove and fussed with the tea bags.

'Katie,' he started, 'I would love to move in with you, but not on a two-week trial basis.'

'Oh God, you *are* turning me down,' I groaned, but he didn't let go of me.

'Katie, if we're going to move in together, I need us both to be sure about it. Then we make the commitment to do it, not just try it out for a while.'

52

'But what if things don't work out, Cam?' I asked, pouring hot water into the teapot. The whistle hadn't gone off yet but I needed to keep busy so I didn't have to look at him.

'Then we have to work them through. If I still have my own place, it's too easy – we could call it off over any small thing.'

'I know.' I finally turned around to face him, but he didn't let go of me. 'So if I asked you to live with me, you would give up your place and do it?'

'Yes,' he said.

The kettle started whistling. I had forgotten to turn the burner off. Cam let me go as I turned it off and then poured the tea. I carried the cups over to the couch and he sat down beside me.

'Are you angry with me?' he asked.

'No, you've been perfectly honest with me. Now let me tell you what is really important to me.'

'OK.'

'Finding out who killed Peter Reynolds. Will you help?'

'Yes, Katie, I will.'

I reached over and picked a little box up off the coffee table. 'I can't believe I'm doing this.'

'What?' he asked.

I handed him the box. 'You don't want me to investigate this murder, but you're willing to help because it's important to me. Well, that's helping to convince me that you really do care. Inside that box is the spare set of keys to this place. I'd really like you to be here.'

'Even knowing how I feel about moving in?'

'You can give notice on your place tomorrow,' I said.

'Katie, are you sure?'

'I'll type your notice myself if you like.'

'You have made me a very happy man.' He put his tea down and kissed me. 'We should celebrate.'

'With what?' I thought about my empty fridge.

'Did you have dinner?' he asked. 'I didn't have time, so I'll call Waiters en Route,' he said. 'We'll get some food and some champagne.'

'Let's just get some champagne. I'll walk down to the liquor store.'

'It's late, Katie. I'll go with you.'

'Cam, it's only two blocks. I'll be fine and I'll be back in ten minutes. You can cut up some cheese or something while I'm gone.'

I ran upstairs and got into my jeans and a sweater. I shoved some money in my pocket and ran back downstairs, kissing Cam on my way past.

'I'll be back in a flash,' I promised.

The streets were deserted, but very well lit. I always felt safe in Calgary. I made it to the liquor store and I picked out a nice bottle of champagne. I wasn't much of a drinker, and there were only two types of champagne that I knew. I couldn't afford the Dom so I grabbed a bottle of Mumm's, paid for it, and headed back to the apartment. It was chilly tonight and I could feel winter in the air, so I walked quickly, wishing I had brought my jacket.

At the door to my building I set the bottle down and dug the keys out of my pocket. The front door always sticks, so it takes two hands to open it. The key had just started to turn and I was grumbling, like I always did, wondering whether they were ever going to fix the lock or not, when someone grabbed my arm.

I thought someone was trying to help me with the door, but they had my arm, not the door. I was confused and tried to turn to see who it was, but before I knew what was happening, my arm was twisted up behind my back and I was shoved up against the brick wall. I tried to scream, but he slammed me harder against the wall, knocking the breath out of me.

'Shut up,' a harsh voice whispered in my ear.

My stomach was churning as I felt his hot breath on my ear. I tried to pull away and felt my arm twist further behind my back. My heart was beating a million miles an hour, feeling like it was going to explode. I was being pressed into the wall and struggled to catch my breath. I tried to gasp in some air, hoping to calm myself down and gather my wits about me. I knew that if I panicked I would never get out of this.

'What do you want?' I gasped.

54

'Don't investigate this murder.' The voice, still a harsh whisper, sent a shiver of terror down my spine.

'What do you mean?'

My arm was twisted further and I screamed. He pulled me away from the wall and then pushed me roughly against it. I felt my cheek scrape against the brick.

'Don't ask questions,' the voice ordered.

I thought I recognized the voice and could almost place it when he pulled me away from the wall and shoved me roughly towards the street. I felt myself falling to the curb. I threw my arms out in front of me to stop my fall. I landed on my right side and felt a sharp pain in my wrist. I took a deep breath, trying not to faint, and rolled on to my back, expecting the attacker to jump me. He was gone. I couldn't see anyone around. I picked myself up and stumbled back to the door. I tucked the champagne under my arm and managed to get the door open, one-handed.

I looked at myself in the elevator mirror. My cheek was scraped and bleeding, my lip was bleeding, and my arm was throbbing. By the time I got to the apartment door my hands were shaking so badly that I couldn't get the key in the lock. I finally gave up and rang the bell.

Cam opened the door and his jaw dropped in shock. He had changed into his jeans and was pulling a sweatshirt over his head, stopped with it half on and half off as he pulled me inside and closed the door.

'What in the hell happened to you?' he demanded.

'Cam, it looks worse than it is. I'm OK.'

He took the bottle from me, setting it on the floor, and pulled me into the bathroom.

'What happened?' he asked as he wet the facecloth and started dabbing at my cuts.

'Ouch, that hurts. Be careful.'

'Katie, please tell me what happened.'

'Somebody grabbed me outside the front door.'

'Were you mugged? Did they take your money?'

'No.'

'What then?'

'He said I shouldn't investigate the murder.'

'What?'

'You heard me,' I said.

'Then that's what you are going to do.'

'No, Cam.'

'You're bruised and bleeding. What will happen next if you keep snooping around?' he asked, still dabbing at my cheek.

'Cam, something is wrong with this.'

'You're right about that.'

'No, Cam, think about it. I have barely started asking questions, yet suddenly somebody is beating me up?'

'Someone must have overheard something,' he said.

'Whoever it was had to be close by. Cam, that means the murderer is close by.'

'Can we just change the subject for a few minutes?' he asked.

'Fine.'

He handed me a piece of gauze he had found in the medicine cabinet. 'Hold this to your lip, I'll help you get your sweater off.'

I pressed the cloth to my lip and turned around. He slipped the sweater over my arm.

'Ow! Let's just leave it on for now.' I grimaced as he tried to slip it over the other arm.

'Can you move your fingers?' he asked.

'I can if I want to.'

'So move them,' he ordered.

'I don't want to.'

He pulled my sweater back on over my left arm. 'We're going to the hospital.'

'No, Cam, it's probably just sprained. I fell on it.'

'We'll let the doctor decide, OK? Now, even if I have to pick you up and carry you, you're going to the hospital.'

'OK.' I was too tired and too sore to argue any more. I was also too scared.

'I'm just going to finish dressing,' he said. 'Will you sit here until I come back down?'

'Yes. Will you bring my bag with you?'

We were at the hospital for about three hours and I was now the proud owner of three stitches in my lip and a cast on my fractured right wrist. It was four in the morning when we got home and all I wanted to do was go to sleep. Instead, Cam made me tea, propped me up on the couch with some pillows, and promised I could go to bed as soon as he called the police. He'd only been officially living here for four hours and he was already taking over.

It took the police about a half an hour to get to the apartment, but we were honoured to have Detective Lincoln himself show up. He turned down a cup of tea as he sat on the couch. Cam made himself comfortable on the floor beside me as Lincoln pulled out his notepad.

'I thought you worked for Homicide?' I asked after we were all settled.

'I do,' he replied.

'I'm not dead,' I felt the urge to point out, despite Cam's dirty looks in my direction.

Luckily the detective chuckled. 'No, but you are associated with a recent homicide, so they called me when your report came in.'

'Oh, I bet your wife was pleased.'

'She's getting used to it. You're probably going to have a nice shiner there,' he pointed out.

'Just what I always wanted.'

'Do you want to tell me what happened?' the detective finally asked.

'I was coming back from the liquor store. I had my key in the door, and someone grabbed me from behind. He pulled my arm up, twisted it behind my back and then shoved me against the wall.'

'You sound very calm,' the detective pointed out.

'I think she's in shock,' Cam said. 'She was shaking pretty good when she first came into the apartment, but now she's back to her regular sarcastic self.'

'Could be the Demerol the doctor gave me too,' I added.

'Did the attacker take your money?' the detective continued.

'No. I asked him what he wanted and he told me to quit asking questions. Then he pushed me on to the ground, which is when I did this,' I held up my new cast for all to see, 'and by the time I got up, he was gone. I thought he'd taken my

57

keys and gone into the building, but my keys were still hanging from the lock on the front door.'

'Did you get a look at him?'

'No. He had on jeans, a dark sweater and gloves. He also had a ski mask on.'

'How do you know it was a man?' Lincoln asked.

'By his height and size. He was pretty broad across the shoulders. He was also pressing me into the wall pretty hard and he felt solid, muscular.'

'Could you tell how tall?'

'Somewhere around Cam's size, I think. About five foot eleven.'

'Anything else that you can remember? Something he said or did? Even if it seems like nothing, it might help us find him.'

'I smelled cologne,' I recalled.

'Did you recognize it?'

'I think so. It's the stuff you wear all the time, Cam. I can't think what it's called.'

'Antaeus,' Cam said.

'That's right. I'm pretty sure that's what it was.'

'OK.' Lincoln was scribbling notes in his pad. 'Now what was this he said about you asking questions?'

I hesitated, wondering how much I should tell him, when Cam saved me the trouble.

'Katie has decided that she is going to run her own murder investigation, against all my better advice,' he tattled.

'I thought we went over this when we spoke this afternoon,' Lincoln said sternly.

'Detective, I haven't even started asking any questions. I just talked with a couple of friends about asking some questions. Don't you think it's really strange that someone is coming after me before I've even started?'

'You shouldn't be surprised, Kate. We've determined that the murderer is at the Complex, so it's not surprising that he might have overheard you. This may help us narrow the field a little. I need to know who you talked to and who may have overheard you.'

'I can't remember everyone who worked tonight, but I can

go over the schedule tomorrow. The people I spoke to directly were Graham and Cam. But Graham is just a kid.'

'So that leaves Mr Caminski here?' the detective asked.

I felt myself growing defensive again. 'If you'll recall, Cam was in the apartment when this happened.'

The detective stood up. 'Well, that should do it for now. I would strongly suggest that you let the police do the investigating from now on.'

'I'll be careful,' I promised, avoiding any commitments to stay out of this. 'Tell me, Detective, is it true what you told me this afternoon?'

'What would that be?' he asked.

'That you have never been to a live theatre performance before?'

'Yes, it's true. I'm almost embarrassed to admit it, though.' He grinned.

'Well, let me know when you're free and I'll have some tickets waiting for you at the box office.'

'Really? That would be great. I'll talk to my wife and let you know.'

Cam got up and saw him out. I heard him double lock the door before he came back into the living room. 'You ready for bed?' he asked.

'Bed and aspirin,' I said. I tried standing but I suddenly felt dizzy. Cam was there immediately, grabbing me under the arms and holding me steady.

'I think you still have enough painkillers in you for now,' he said. 'But bed would probably be a good idea. Come on, I'll help you up.'

I happily let him lead me up the stairs and into bed. He brought me a glass of water and then crawled in beside me.

'I put the champagne in the fridge for tomorrow,' he said.

'I'm sorry I messed up the celebration.'

'I don't think it's really your fault,' he said as he reached over and turned the light off.

'I'm sure glad you're here,' I mumbled.

'Me too.'

'Don't forget to set the alarm.' I was fighting to keep my eyes open.

'Why do you want the alarm set?'

'I have to meet Gladys tomorrow.'

'Kate—' he started to protest but I cut him off.

'Cam, she called me. She asked if we could have a coffee and a chat.'

'What time?' he asked, giving in.

'I have to meet her at three, so set it for one, OK?'

'OK, but I'm going with you,' he said.

'You don't have to do that.'

'Katie, after what happened tonight I am not letting you go anywhere alone. Not until they catch the guy who did this.'

'I love you when you're macho,' I said dreamily. 'Now, kiss me before I go to sleep, please.' He leaned over me. 'On the good cheek,' I warned.

That was the last thing I remembered. I was asleep the instant my head hit the pillow.

Sunday

It seemed only minutes had passed when the alarm went off. Cam reached over and hit the snooze button. I was surprised he was still in bed, since it was past noon, but I guess we'd both had a pretty stressful weekend and needed some extra sleep. It was one of those wonderful Sundays where I didn't have to go to work. Actors' Equity, the union, only allows actors to do eight shows a week, and since we had matinees on Tuesday and Wednesday last week, we got Sunday off. And there was nothing that anyone could do about it.

'You awake, Katie?' Cam asked.

'Hmmm.' It was the best I could do before I had some coffee.

'How are you feeling?' He was pushing his luck again, trying for a conversation this early.

'I hurt everywhere,' I groaned.

'Wow, Katie, that was a whole sentence. You better watch it or you'll turn into a morning person.'

I swung my arm over and tried to slap him. 'You're lucky that isn't the arm with the cast on,' I warned him.

'How about a nice bath?' he asked. 'It might loosen up your muscles.'

'I will. Soon. I just need to lie here for a few more minutes.'

He rolled over on to his side, propped his head on his arm and looked at me.

'Do I have a black eye?' I asked, dreading the answer.

'No, but your cheek is a really interesting colour, though, and I think there's a little bit of a goose egg too,' he said as he ran his finger gently over my bruised cheek. 'Your lip is kind of swollen.'

'Does it look awful?'

'It's not so bad,' he said. 'Is it sore?'

'A little.'

'How about your arm?'

'It's not too bad, but this cast is going to take some getting used to. I think I hit myself with it a couple of times during the night.'

'Well I know you hit me a couple of times,' he laughed.

'Sorry.' I tried to apologize, stifling a giggle at the thought of decking him in my sleep.

'Funny girl,' he said. 'You have a very strange sense of humour.'

'So, Cam, what do you think Gladys has to say to me today?'

'We'll never find out if we don't get out of bed,' he said.

'OK, OK, I'm getting up. I think I am going to take a bath. Are you going to make us something wonderful to eat?' I asked hopefully.

'I get the feeling you are going to take great advantage of that cast and the fact that you are not able to do anything,' he said. 'Am I right?'

'Cam, as long as you're here, cast or no cast, I am never going to cook again. I thought it would be a much better idea to let you spoil me.'

'Are you at least planning to do the dishes?' he asked.

'I'll buy you a dishwasher.'

'You have a dishwasher,' he reminded me.

'It leaks.'

'I suppose you want me to look at that, too?'

Breakfast was wonderful. Cam really is a genius at whipping things up out of nothing. It's going to be great having him here, I thought, trying to focus on the positive. I was still having trouble believing that I had asked him to move in. Every time I thought about it, the walls started closing in on me, so I kept eating instead of thinking. Food is such a wonderful substitute for avoiding life's problems.

I arrived at Vaudevilles early, hoping to beat Gladys there and scout the place out a bit. Vaudevilles is the biggest restaurant in the Plex. It is designed like the theatres – a main level and a mezzanine bar, with an open courtyard in the centre. The place is covered with show posters and the tables have lucite tops with theatre programs embedded in them. Upstairs, in the bar, the lucite tabletops open to reveal backgammon, chess, checkers, and Trivial Pursuit games.

There are mannequins all over the restaurant, dressed in costumes borrowed from the wardrobe department, show tunes blasting from the speakers, and all sorts of mismatched furniture bought from the props department's yearly auction. When you sit in Vaudevilles, you know you're in a theatre bar.

I climbed the stairs to the mezzanine bar, passing a mannequin dressed as Mozart, from *Amadeus*, and found myself a seat in the corner at the Trivial Pursuit table. I had a great view of the entrance from where I sat, and kept an eye on everyone's comings and goings while I waited for Gladys. A waitress brought me a cappuccino, without having to ask, and raised her eyebrow at the sight of my face. I shot her questions down with a dirty look, which I regretted almost instantly as she turned and headed back for the bar. I sat, sipping my cappuccino, pleased with the scene I had set and waited for Gladys to arrive. Cam found an empty booth across the balcony from me and pretended to be engrossed in a book.

Gladys came in the front door and I noticed her immediately. She ordered from the bar on the main floor and pointed up to where I was sitting. She then made her way up the stairs and sat down across from me. She hasn't changed since the day I'd met her. As a matter of fact, she probably hasn't changed since about 1965. She has long, kinky red hair that hangs past her waist, with long bangs that almost cover her eyes. She has always reminded me a bit of Janis Joplin on a drug-free day. Gladys wears that Egyptian-style black eyeliner that was really popular in the sixties. I never understood why she hadn't updated her look, but the mixture of that and her intriguing Scottish accent seems to attract men like nothing I have ever seen before. They must think she is exotic and, maybe, that's why she hasn't changed. Her clothing was toned down a little now, maybe because she was in mourning. Normally she wears the brightest flowered pants she can find, Doc Martens, and a turtleneck sweater – never with a bra. I don't think she even owns a bra, but she should – Gladys is a little top-heavy. Sometimes she even wears love beads. She really has got the perfect early hippie look.

'Hello, Katherine, how have you been?' she said without looking at me. She settled herself, lit a thin cigar, and then looked up. 'What the hell has happened to your face?'

Even insults sounded good with an accent. Once, when she was really stoned, she had slipped back into her natural voice and I had been shocked to hear such a middle-class sound come out of Gladys's mouth. That's when she confided that she had spent years teaching herself to speak with the more acceptable upper-class accent – something else that intrigues me about her.

'Good to see you too,' I said with a chill in my voice, but then I realized I shouldn't be too sarcastic if I was planning on pumping her for information. 'Sorry, I'm still a little sensitive about this. I was mugged last night. How are you holding up? You doing OK?'

'Well, frankly, no. I'm feeling pretty shitty. My ex-husband has been murdered, my sons are a mess, and the police are hovering around waiting for me to confess.'

'I am very sorry for your loss,' I said. 'This has been hard on everyone.'

'Yes. Well, I suppose we should get down to business.' The waitress brought her drink and she took a sip.

'Business?' I asked.

'We haven't seen each other for over a year. Do you think I just picked this moment in time to catch up?'

'Gladys, I haven't the slightest idea why you wanted to see me.' I figured it was best to play dumb and let her do the talking.

'I wanted you to know I didn't kill Peter,' she said simply.

'Why would you want to tell me that? Or care what I think?'

'Katherine, I know you're planning on asking some questions about this murder.'

A lot of people seemed to know that, I thought, but said, 'Shouldn't you be talking to the police?'

'I have been – endlessly. However, I want you and your little ushers to leave me alone. I don't want you asking questions about me. I didn't do it, but I really think that someone here, someone I know, did it.'

'Who?' I asked, hoping for an answer but knowing I wasn't going to get one.

'If I knew that, I would be talking to the police and not to you, dear.'

'So who should we talk to?' I asked. 'Who do you think killed him?'

'Katherine, please don't treat me as though I'm stupid. I want you to honestly believe that I didn't do it.'

'OK, then suppose you tell me why I should believe that you didn't kill him.'

'Do you think I murdered Peter?' she asked me.

'I wasn't there,' I replied noncommittally. 'I have no way of knowing what went on.'

'All right, let me rephrase the question. Do you think I'm capable of killing someone?'

'Gladys, I don't think that's a fair question. I'm no expert and I don't think I could judge whether someone is capable of an act like this.'

'You're avoiding the question,' she said.

'All right. What I really believe is that anyone is capable of murder, given the right circumstances.'

'Thank you for being honest. Now, I want you to believe that I did not kill Peter. We are . . . were divorced last year. The fighting between us is all over. We are, I mean *were*, becoming friends again.'

'I heard, but I thought you were staying together for your sons.' I resisted the urge to say they were really staying together for their dogs. 'What happened?'

'He fell in love with someone else. Don't you find that ironic? I was the one desperately searching for someone special and Peter is the one who succeeded in finding someone. The divorce was his idea. He wanted to marry her. But he was very generous to me.'

'Did he marry her?' I asked.

'Two days after our divorce was final.'

'Did that hurt, Gladys?'

'Did I want to kill him, you mean? No, I didn't. I was over

65

Peter long before he ever divorced me. He gave me the house, a substantial cash settlement, and lots of money for the boys' education. I don't have to work for several years, if I don't want to. It turned out quite well for me and I was surprised at how happy I was when he left. The house was mine, my life was mine, and I didn't have to sneak around any more. Peter actually did me a huge favour.'

'And was he happy?' I asked.

'Deliriously,' she smiled. 'He was madly in love with a young and beautiful woman. He loved his work, they were travelling, and the boys adjusted quite well. He even left the dogs with me. We all decided this had turned out for the best.'

'So you had no reason to kill Peter,' I said.

'None,' Gladys agreed. 'Nor did anyone he knew. That's why I believe it is someone from the Plex.'

'Why? What makes you think that?'

'Katherine, you know my reputation. As a matter of fact, I was the one who told you about my affairs. There are a lot of wounded hearts in this building.'

'I'm sorry, Gladys, but it sounds to me like you rate yourself quite highly.'

'No, dear, I don't think all that highly of myself. But the men I slept with did. There were several very ugly break-ups. I had no intention of leaving Peter, at that time, and several men wanted me to. They threatened to tell him about our affairs, to try and force him into leaving me.'

'But that was a long time before Peter left you. Isn't that carrying a grudge a little far?'

'That's what I don't know,' she confessed. 'Except that I can't think of anyone else who would have cause to do this. If it's not someone from the Plex, then we are at a dead end. I don't know who else would kill him.'

'And you want to me question everyone? Find out who doesn't have an alibi, who is still carrying a torch for you?'

'Yes, I do,' she said.

'Why not go to the police, or ask these questions yourself?'

'People are not going to talk to the police, Katherine, and I seriously doubt whether they would talk to me. If Peter was killed to hurt me in some way, the murderer is not going to admit that to *me*.'

'You've got a point.' I finally took another sip of my coffee and found it was cold. 'So who do we go after?'

'You want a list?' she asked.

'Yes I do. Gladys, I know that there are a lot of rumours floating around this building about you and every man who has ever worked here, but I don't think you slept with them all. I'd like the truth.'

'All right, fair enough. I'll start at the beginning. Here are the names of all the men I was involved with and also the men I approached but weren't interested,' Gladys said as she pulled a sheet of paper from her purse and handed it to me. Cam's name was noticeably absent from the list.

'What about Cam?'

'How is Cam?' Gladys asked, a smile coming to her face.

'He's fine. Why do you ask?'

'I heard he spent the better part of yesterday at the police station answering a lot of questions.'

'I'm afraid I seem to be missing your point, Gladys.' My arm was starting to ache and she was starting to annoy me.

'Katherine, I want you to be very motivated to help me out. I don't believe Cam killed Peter, but the police seem to be leaning in that direction. The only connection between Peter and Cam is me. If you help me out, you may be keeping Cam out of jail as well.'

I suddenly remembered what I didn't like about Gladys – the woman can be a real cold-hearted bitch when it suits her purpose.

'Well, you don't have to worry,' I said. 'I am taking this all very seriously.'

'Good.' She stood up and threw some bills on the table. 'This will be my treat. After all, I've become quite a wealthy woman recently.'

She left the table and I watched her go down the stairs towards the door. I noticed the eyes of most of the men in the place following her out. Yep, the look still worked. Maybe I should grow out my hair and get a bad perm.

I looked up and Cam was standing beside the table.

'Well?' he asked, waiting for me to fill him in.

'I have a headache,' I said, rubbing my forehead. 'Let's talk about this later.'

'OK. You want to go home?'

'Yes, I do, but I might as well go up to human resources as long as I'm here. I want to get copies of Thursday's time sheets and the names and addresses for some of the people we want to talk to.'

'Katie, you should go home and go to bed for a while.'

'This will be a quick trip, Cam, I promise. I'm almost on my last legs. Why don't you pull the car into the loading dock and I'll be down in ten minutes?'

'Promise?' he asked.

'Promise.'

I headed up to the admin tower, hoping that I wouldn't have to tell the story of my bruises to anyone. Luckily, being Sunday, it was fairly quiet in the administrative side of the theatre business and almost everyone was off. I was in and out of personnel in ten minutes and in the Fish with Cam in another five. I had been tempted to go to my office for a couple of minutes, but I knew he would give me hell and I didn't have the strength for an argument.

'You look tired,' Cam said as I belted myself into the passenger seat.

'I'm exhausted,' I admitted.

'Well I have a great plan for tonight.'

'What's that?' I asked.

'I think we should pick up something to eat, go home, turn the phone off, cuddle on the couch and put a movie in. We can crack open that bottle of champagne and talk about anything, except what happened to Peter Reynolds last Thursday night.'

'God, that sounds like heaven.' I turned up the stereo, leaned back, closed my eyes, and relaxed as Cam drove us home.

He pulled into my parking space, helped me out of the car, and we walked arm and arm into the building. Cam pretended he was being romantic but I think he was afraid I was going to collapse at any minute. He was closer to the truth than I was willing to admit.

After we had eaten, I changed into a T-shirt and Cam propped me up in bed with some pillows. We decided to watch the movie upstairs so Cam wouldn't have to carry me up later when I fell asleep on the couch. He brought the VCR up and hooked it up to the TV. Then he disappeared back downstairs for a minute, coming back up with four champagne glasses on a tray. Two of them were filled with strawberries soaking in champagne and the other two were for drinking. He set the tray at the foot of the bed.

'What do you want to watch?' he asked when he got everything settled. 'How about *Sleepless in Seattle*?'

'Let's watch an Arnie film,' I suggested.

'I hate Schwarzenegger,' he said. 'Besides, haven't you seen enough senseless violence in real life, or do you actually want to see more?'

'You do not hate Schwarzenegger,' I said. 'You've watched his movies with me before.'

'I hate him now; his movies are too much like real life. Or at least too much like our life.'

'Good point,' I said. 'Something non-violent would be much better right now.'

'How about *Casablanca*?' he suggested.

'OK, you win, but maybe we can put *Total Recall* in later.'

He popped the movie in and sat on the bed beside me. I had a sip of champagne as the opening credits began.

'Pass me a strawberry.'

I felt my eyelids growing heavy as I nibbled on the fruit. I leaned against Cam's shoulder.

'This is nice,' I mumbled.

'Goodnight, Katie.'

'I'm not going to sleep.'

'Whatever you say.'

My eyelids closed and I felt Cam take the champagne glass from my hand. I was going to miss 'As Time Goes By', I thought, and tried to open my eyes. I didn't even have the energy left to manage that.

Monday

The quiet bliss of Sunday night faded quickly when I awoke to the reality of Monday morning. My head hurt, this time from the champagne, and the cast had rubbed my arm raw. I rolled over, trying to find a more comfortable position, and hit my bruised cheek with the cast.

'Shit,' I groaned.

'Good morning,' Cam called from downstairs.

'Morning,' I said.

'Do you want me to bring some coffee up?' he asked.

'No, I'll come down,' I said as I got up and straightened the bed. I headed for the kitchen and curled up in a chair. Cam set a cup of coffee down in front of me and I gratefully took a sip.

'How come you're up so early?' I asked.

'I went for a run,' he said, sitting down across from me.

'So, what's the game plan for today?'

'Well, I thought I'd wait and see if you were still planning on setting up your amateur detective agency or if you'd finally come to your senses,' he said, smiling sweetly at me.

'Do you really need an answer to that question?'

'No, Katie, I know how stubborn you are and you know you make me crazy.'

'Yeah, well, are you still in?' I asked, sipping my coffee.

'I'm in,' he said. 'And I'm going to be your bodyguard. I'm not letting you out of my sight. I intend to make sure that your arm is the only thing that gets broken.'

'Well then, after I figure out how to take a shower, we should get to the office. I need to make some calls and arrange to meet with Graham.'

'Showers are easy,' he said. 'Hold out your arm.'

He got a plastic shopping bag and pulled it over my arm, then taped it closed just above where the cast ended.

'Very clever,' I said.

'When you play rugby in school, you learn how to deal with broken bones,' he said as he kissed me and pushed me towards the bathroom. After I was out of the shower, he cut me loose from the plastic bag and I pulled on some jeans and a sweater.

When I came back downstairs, Cam was in the shower. I poured myself a fresh cup of coffee and sat down at the computer. I couldn't write but I figured I could at least peck with my left hand. I started typing. I started with Thursday, listing any clues, ideas, and people, and then did the same for Friday and Saturday. I was hoping that when I printed the pages it would suddenly be clear that 'the killer is . . .', but of course no such luck. I stared and stared and all I saw was a bunch of unrelated names and events and the knowledge that Peter Reynolds had possibly been killed by one of them, in my theatre, on Thursday night. I typed another page with the list of names that Gladys had given me and compared lists, only to find I still had a bunch of unrelated names. Damn, it never worked like this in the books. By this point the heroine had a pretty good idea of who did it and spent the next several chapters teasing the readers with obtuse clues. Unfortunately I was the one being teased. Or maybe I was just obtuse. I sipped my coffee and turned around to see Cam standing behind me.

'So, who did it?' he asked.

'Very funny.'

'Do you want to leave this to the police now?'

'Cam, have you ever heard of reverse psychology? The more you want me to quit, the more I will want to investigate.'

'This is dangerous,' he reminded me needlessly. 'What do you know about solving crimes?'

'I've read every Agatha Christie and Sherlock Holmes, as well as the latest Sue Grafton. I know all about finding clues.'

'Katie, this isn't a book.'

'No it isn't, Cam, this is real. I could lose you. I feel like if I don't find out what's going on, the police are going to offer you the Criminal of the Month club. I finally allowed you into my life; I'm not letting anyone take you away from me. Got it?'

'OK, but where do we go from here? You've printed the lists and nothing stands out. What are you going to do now?'

'I guess I have to wait until I see Graham. I tried calling him while you were in the shower but he wasn't home. We'll pool all our resources and see if anything new stands out.'

'Does that mean you've done all you can for today?'

'Pretty much,' I said. 'Unless I decide to stare at these print-outs for the next two or three hours and get totally frustrated.'

'I've got a better plan,' he suggested. 'Let's do something fun.'

'Fun? What's that?'

'Like what we used to do,' he said. 'Go to Banff, have dinner, see a movie, take a walk. Any one of the things we used to do before you became Kate Carpenter, girl detective.'

'Oh, you are a funny man. Keep this up and you won't physically qualify to be a Hardy Boy.'

'Katie,' he reached over me and turned the computer off, 'I've got a beautiful white 1971 Hemi Barracuda in your garage with five hundred horse power under the hood, just begging to do some highway driving. It's shift change for the RCMP, so we can drive like demons if we leave right now. I will go in any direction you choose, if only you will say yes and leave with me now.'

'How fast are you going to drive?' I asked.

'How fast do you want me to drive?'

'I want you to drive real fast.' I smiled at him. 'Let's see if the Fish still has it or not.'

'I'll drive real fast,' he promised. 'But you've only got three minutes to make up your mind.'

'Let's go west.'

Soon we were in the car, cruising down Memorial Drive and heading for Highway One towards Banff. Having the Rocky Mountains and all that wild territory only a ninety-minute drive from Calgary – less if Cam was driving – is one of the great pleasures of living here. I like the drive, I love the mountains, and I love Banff, when it isn't overrun with tourists.

We hit the highway and were almost at the city limits. Canada Olympic Park and the two ski jumps were on our left. It was too early in the year for the park to start making snow but, as I craned my neck and peered out the window, I could see several foolish people bungee jumping off the ninety-metre tower.

'They're insane!' I exclaimed.

'I did that last year,' Cam said. 'What a rush.'

'You're insane too, then.' I popped a tape into the deck and cranked up the volume.

I watched another man throw himself off the jump and cringed. Nothing in the world would make me climb up there, let alone throw myself off with only a thin cord saving me from crashing to the ground. I did decide that I would finally come out and watch the ski jumping sometime this winter. I had lost out on the lottery for Olympic tickets and I figured that was long enough to hold a grudge. It was time to go see those crazy Canucks in person.

As we passed the Olympic Park, I sank back into my seat and watched the city fade behind us. We passed through the farms and ranches of the foothills, with the mountains gradually growing closer. I love to come out here in the fall and watch the trees change colour. It never fails to take my breath away – the fall leaves ranging from bright yellow to deepest orange, the mountains rising in the background, already snow-capped at this time of year, and the huge blue sky framing it all. I had actually read a book once that explained why different trees turned different colours, and I bore everyone with this trivia every fall.

'The trees are beautiful,' Cam said, reading my mind.

'Do you know why all the leaves turn different colours?' I asked.

'You told me this last fall, Katie,' he said.

'Pretend I didn't.'

'Why do the leaves turn all those different colours, oh all-knowing one?' he asked sarcastically.

'It has to do with the different amounts of sugar in the sap,' I said. 'The redder they are, the more sugar there is. That's why maple trees are so spectacular.'

'That's every bit as interesting as it was last year.'

73

'If you didn't want to hear it, why did you ask?'

'Turn the tape over,' he said, changing the subject.

I turned it over and then turned my attention back to the scenery. I knew there would be a strong wind any day now, blowing all the leaves off the trees and leaving us with empty sticks until the first snow fell and iced them with frost.

Cam pulled over into a picnic area, beside Lac des Arcs, turning the ignition off.

'Want to go for a quick walk?' he asked.

'Sure.'

We got out and followed a path around the edge of the lake. Even though it was late in the season and the water was freezing, it was covered with small sailboats and windsurfers. In a few more months the lake would be frozen over and it would be covered with ice surfers, probably the same guys who were out there right now. I looked out over the lake and saw a picnic table on a small island.

'I've never noticed that before,' I said, pointing out to the island.

'I guess it's there for the boaters,' he said. 'You sure wouldn't want to swim over there, not through this glacier water.'

The sun was starting to go down and I could feel the chilled air coming off the same glaciers that fed the lake.

'I'm getting chilly,' I said. 'Are you ready to head back to the car?'

'Sure.'

He took my hand and we headed back down the path to the car. He started it up and adjusted the heat for me. I popped another tape in and Cam sped off until we reached the gates of Banff National Park. Cam never speeds in the park. We turned off the highway and headed into Banff township. He found a parking spot and we got out of the car. I stretched and took a deep breath of the clean mountain air. It was almost enough to make me want to quit smoking. I felt totally relaxed as I watched Cam check the locks on his door, and was very happy I had let him talk me into this trip.

I linked my arm through his and we spent what was left of the afternoon wandering up and down the streets, browsing in all the neat little shops set up specifically to rip off the tourists. Worked on me, too.

Banff is full of neat little things to buy that you can't buy anywhere else, or at least if you can, they're not this expensive. There are a lot of stores with hand-made crafts and clothes, souvenirs for the tourists, art stores and galleries, and my favourites, the candy stores. I made sure we got to those before they closed for the day. We found a bench just outside the second candy store and Cam dug into his bag of salt-water taffy while I munched away on my sponge toffee. I had our fudge tucked into my backpack for later. We sat there, stuffed our faces and watched the people go by until it was too cold and too dark to sit there any longer.

'I'm hungry,' I said as we got up and started to walk again.

'You've got to be kidding.'

'We can't come up here and not have dinner,' I said. 'It's like a tradition.'

'Where do you want to go?' he asked.

'Rose and Crown?' The Rose and Crown is a big, loud pub and I figured if I was lucky, I might get Cam to dance with me after dinner.

'Rose and Crown it is,' he agreed.

We wandered down the street and climbed the stairs up to the pub. The waitress got us a booth and we cuddled together on the same side of the table, giggling over a bottle of wine.

'Having a good time?' he asked me.

'The best. How about you?'

'Not bad. I wanted to go to Lake Minnewanka and watch the divers for a while.'

'Cam, you can't watch the divers, they are under the water.'

'You know what I mean.'

'You mean that you wanted to talk to the crazy men who scuba-dive in that freezing water and find out what they had seen and done on their dives. Why don't you just take some scuba lessons and get it over with?'

'I will,' he said. 'When I find the time.'

'I don't know why you would want to dive in that sub-zero water,' I repeated.

'They all seem exhilarated when they come up,' he said.

'That's lack of oxygen to the brain. Seriously, Sam and I told you that if you and Ryan want to do it, we will gladly wait on the shore with the resuscitation team for you.'

'Just think, Katie, if I qualify here, we have a great excuse to go to the Caribbean.'

'That's the first thing you've said that makes sense,' I said. 'Have you decided what you want to eat?'

'I want ribs,' he said. 'Covered in barbecue sauce, with the biggest baked potato they can find.'

'That sounds good,' I agreed. 'I think I'll have that too. Do you see our waitress anywhere?'

It had been at least twenty minutes since she had last shown her face, but what the hell, we weren't in any sort of hurry. She finally found her way back to our table and we ordered dinner and more wine. We watched a darts tournament while we ate. Cam stopped drinking after dinner but I didn't. I made him dance with me several times and, when I realized it was almost midnight, I finally allowed him to load me in the car and head for home.

Tuesday

Monday night in Banff had been a total blast, even after Cam got a speeding ticket on the way home. I guess he didn't know the RCMP schedule as well as he thought. Luckily the police had clocked him when he was slowing down, otherwise they might have cut up his driving license on the spot. We got home very late, stayed up even later drinking beer and playing backgammon and, even though I was exhausted, I felt like I had a new lease on life. I was ready to delve back into the life and death of Peter Reynolds. Cam must have felt better too. When I left him at the security desk in the morning he had a twinkle in his eye and not a single sarcastic comment passed his lips.

Cam had made the mistake of answering the telephone at my place that morning and the Spaz had told him he had to come into work. Imagine, the nerve of the Spaz, calling my house looking for Cam. Lazlo said the department needed help with the inventory, so Cam was now somewhere in the basement, counting screws and nails and being a good team player. I was in my office, making copies of lists for my meeting with Graham later.

I checked my watch to find that I had another hour before everyone showed up. Time to go to the bathroom and then grab a cappuccino at Gus's place. I took a five-dollar bill out of my wallet, shoved it in my pocket and left the office. As the door was closing behind me I automatically felt in my pocket for my keys.

'Shit!' I muttered under my breath, realizing I didn't have them just as the door clicked shut.

Every door in this building locks automatically. That's why I always keep the keys in my pocket, so I won't accidentally lock myself out. Except when I leave them on my desk. That has happened at least once a week since I started working at the Plex. Security always gives me a hard time about locking myself out, and they are becoming much slower at responding to my calls. I'm sure they think that letting me sit outside whatever room I'd locked myself out of for ten or fifteen minutes will teach me not to forget my keys. So far, it hasn't worked.

I headed through the hallway and down the stairs to the main lobby to call the security desk. I knew Nick was on duty; I'd seen him when I signed in. Why was Nick always the security supervisor on duty when I locked myself out of the office? He gives me such a hard time about it.

Nick had graduated with honours from the Mount Royal College criminology program, and all he wants to do is be a cop. He sent in his application and received a reply saying they were very interested in him but, due to funding cutbacks, there was a hiring freeze. The letter had said he would remain on the waiting list and that if there were any openings, he would be contacted. If this had upset Nick, he hid it very well. He continued to upgrade and generally improve his odds, getting a first-aid certificate, learning to swim, and anything else that might possibly help. I have never been sure if anyone would take Nick seriously as a cop, because we don't take him very seriously around the Plex. He is tall and muscular, but has blonde hair and freckles. Body of a man, face of a boy.

I reached the bar, picked up the phone and dialled. Nick answered on the first ring.

'Security desk, Nick here.'

'Hi, Nick, it's Kate.'

'We'll be right there,' and the phone went dead.

I tried dialling again but it rang endlessly and no one picked it up. About thirty seconds later, three guards came running into the lobby from three different directions.

'Are you OK?' Nick demanded, breathing heavily. 'Cam warned us that someone was after you. Which way did he go? Are you OK? Did he hurt you? Did he take anything?'

'Nick, calm down and take it easy,' I said, trying to reassure him.

'Katie!' I turned to see Cam getting out of the elevator.

'What happened? Are you all right?' He grabbed me by the shoulders, surveying me for any new damage.

'Cam, what are you doing here?' I asked, perplexed by this sudden, huge show of force.

'Nick alerted me after you called him. I got here as fast as I could.'

'Do you mind telling us what is going on, Kate?' Nick asked.

'It's OK guys, I just locked myself out. I called to see if you could send somebody down to open my office door.'

The tension level in the room dropped almost instantly. I looked around at everyone, feeling guilty that I had started this stampede.

'Sorry, guys, I had no idea you'd be so worried,' I offered weakly. Somehow, I just knew my great day was starting to go downhill.

I managed to calm everyone down and Nick let me back into my office. I grabbed my keys and went down to Gus's place, where I finally got my cappuccino and muffin. I headed back to the office, avoiding the security desk, and started sorting through the paperwork. Sales reports wait for no man, and I knew that once Graham got here I would want to talk about the investigation without worrying about tonight's work.

Graham and Cam ended up walking in together, five minutes before three. I shoved the theatre work to one side and printed off the Peter Reynolds file. I handed the pages to the guys, waiting anxiously to hear what they had to say.

'I saw Gladys yesterday and this is the information she gave me,' I said, growing impatient for someone to start our meeting. No one replied, so I decided to take charge. 'Let's split up the names and see if we can talk to all of them in the next couple of days. I've separated them into the serious suspects and rumoured lovers. Any questions so far?'

Cam sat on the edge of my desk and read his list.

MAIN SUSPECTS

Burns Enevold – messy break-up, heavy drinker
Douglas Mendlesson – long term, nasty break-up

Jeremy Rawson – unknown, very private
Gene Unrau – lived together, in Germany after break-up

SECONDARY SUSPECTS
Plex ushers – check them all, coordinate rumours
Concert Hall: Mike, Russell, Tom
Heritage Theatre: Howard, Jimmy, Stan
Centenary Theatre – unknown, Kate will talk to them

Cam brought a fresh cappuccino and lit a cigarette for himself and one for me when he had finally finished reading. He was being awfully cooperative and I wasn't sure if I should trust this new behaviour or not. I had a steno pad in front of me, ready to take notes, feeling like Laz the Spaz.

'So how did you do last night, Graham?' I asked.

'Nothing much, boss. There weren't too many people in the bar on a Monday night. What did you get?' Graham was drinking orange juice again. He was totally obnoxious about being healthy. He coughed every time I blew smoke in his direction, and I was surprised he hadn't said anything about my two cappuccinos. Gus always told me he would be broke and out of business within a week if anyone actually listened to Graham's advice on healthy living.

'All right, first on the list is Burns Enevold. Gladys said they dated for two months and, in their last month together, Burns broke up with his wife. A week later Gladys broke up with Burns. That's when he started drinking. According to his personnel records, he's been sent home for drinking on duty at least three times, and it probably should have been several more, but it seems everyone actually feels sorry for him.'

'He'll be easy to find,' Graham said. 'He's pretty much a regular in the BOB after a shift, and he doesn't like drinking alone because then he has no one to complain to. We've all had several free drinks on him.'

'Well take it easy on the drinks – you've still got to be here bright-eyed and bushy-tailed for your shifts. We agreed that this was extra-curricular,' I warned him, thinking I was starting to sound like Cam.

'Yes, Mom,' he piped up. He knew I hated it when he called me that.

'Next, there was Douglas Mendlesson.'

'Douglas?' Cam asked. 'I didn't think Gladys would be his type.'

'You mean his sex? Well, that's quite a story. Apparently, after Gladys broke up with him, he was so devastated that he swore off women. Now, that's only a rumour, but who knows?'

'So who's going to take him?' Graham asked. 'He's management.'

'Not me,' I said. 'He hasn't spoken a civil word to me since I wrote him up for not scheduling any staff on an opening night last season.'

'I'll talk to him,' Cam said. 'I see a lot of him when I'm in the Concert Hall, and I'm sure I can find some excuse to get over there in the next few days.'

'What a trouper,' I said. 'I didn't think I was going to get you to pitch in without a fight.'

'Well, if you can't beat 'em—' he started.

'Save the cute domestic stuff for home,' Graham said. 'Let's get on with this list.'

'OK, OK. Surprisingly there aren't too many more.'

'No?' Cam asked, looking down at his list. 'Then where do all these rumours come from?'

'Well, Gladys said she used to ask a lot but not everyone said yes.'

'Really?' Graham asked. 'I find that hard to believe.'

'I don't,' Cam said dryly.

I shot him a dirty look. 'You'd better not. Anyway, she's over fifty, whether she looks it or not. Most of the people who work here are well under thirty. Not everyone is interested in older women.'

'And some people are actually in monogamous relationships,' Cam said, glancing at me. 'Believe it or not.'

'So, after Douglas, she dated Gene Unrau.' I tried to get back on track.

'Gene Unrau is twenty years old,' Cam pointed out.

'Yeah, well, he was seventeen when they started seeing each other and she thinks he was really hung up on her. They saw each other on and off for two years. She said that every time she tried to break up with him, he refused. He told her that he would have her any way he could, no strings attached. If she wanted to see others, that was fine with him. So she ended up dating him "in between" several other men. When she finally broke off with him, he packed up, dropped out of university, and went to Germany for several months.'

'And he's back at the Plex now,' Cam concluded.

'They all come back to the Plex,' Graham said.

'Well, it makes it easier for us,' I said. 'As they said in *Casablanca*, round up all the usual suspects.'

'Anyone else?' Graham asked.

'Several turn-downs but I don't think any of them would be driven to murder.' I flipped through my notepad. 'She admits to several one-night stands, but I don't think any of them would be involved enough to want to murder anyone either. We can always come back to those if our leads don't pan out.'

'Or, we could turn this over to the police,' Cam suggested.

'Gladys said she did but they didn't seem all that interested. She thinks they've already decided who they want to pin it on and don't want to waste their time checking out anyone else.'

'Besides, Cam, if we left all the investigating to the police, what would we do with our spare time?' Graham laughed.

'Back to the subject here,' I said. 'The only other really serious relationship she had was with Jeremy Rawson.'

'The catering coordinator? I thought he was gay,' Graham said.

'That's what everyone thinks,' I said. 'But he's not, he's bisexual. They dated for a month or so and he wanted her to marry him. When she wouldn't, he took another lover so she would know how he felt.'

'Sounds like a movie: *The Caterer, the Usher, her Husband, and his Mistress*. Was there a futon involved in there any-where?' Cam asked.

'You're watching blue movies, Cam?' I asked. 'Anyway, the lover he took was Douglas Mendlesson. And I bet neither of you know that they are still together.'

'Sorry, Katie,' Cam said, 'but I'm really finding it hard to be serious about this. This place sounds like a soap opera.'

'If you hung around with ushers more often, you'd believe it,' Graham said. 'Most of our gossip makes this stuff seem tame.'

'So maintenance is the safest department to work in?' Cam asked.

'Or the most boring,' Graham replied. 'Front of house has much more fun.'

'OK, let's try not to drag this discussion down to an even lower level.' I lit another one of Cam's cigarettes.

'Either quit smoking or buy your own,' he warned me.

'She smokes much less when she smokes yours, Cam,' Graham said. 'At least when you're here we get a little oxygen.'

'Be nice, Graham. I sign your pay cheque.'

'Right, boss. So what's the plan?'

'I think you should go to the BOB after work again tonight and see who you run into. Cam, maybe you can spend some of your shift in the Concert Hall lobby. I hear Douglas is working tonight.'

'I'll do it, but I don't think I can ever look at Douglas the same way again. I can't believe he and another of Gladys's ex-lovers are shacked up. This is too damn strange for me. You're going to owe me big time for this, babe!'

'I'll let you cook and clean for me,' I said. 'So, can we meet back here tomorrow and see if we've come up with anything?'

'Be here with bells on,' Graham said.

'Cam, are you still with us?' I asked, needing his reassurance.

'I'm not planning on letting you out of my sight, so I guess I'll be here,' he promised. 'But remember, it's under protest.'

'Your undying support is gratifying,' I said.

'Well, I have to get to work.' He stood up, 'Promise me that you won't do anything stupid until I get back.'

'I'll give it my best.'

'Give me a kiss and I'm out of here.'

'That might be misconstrued as doing something stupid,' I protested.

He kissed my cheek and headed for the door. 'That has yet to be determined. Could also be the smartest thing you've done in your entire life.'

I got up from my desk and put the coffee on. Cam hesitated at the doorway.

'I liked you two much better before you got all romantic and soft,' Graham said. 'Now I feel like I need a shot of insulin after I've been around you.'

I shot him my best dirty look. 'Don't you have something better to do than stand here and make fun of me? Or perhaps I can find something for you to do? I don't think we've picked the gum off the theatre seats for several months, you know.'

Graham grabbed his key. 'I'm outta here, but thanks for the thought.'

Cam waited until Graham was out of earshot and then turned to face me. 'All kidding aside, Katie, I want you to know I'm scared for us. This is turning into serious stuff.'

'I know, Cam, I'm starting to feel like there's no one I can trust.'

'What do you mean?' he asked, looking worried.

'Base to ten.' His radio interrupted us. He pulled it out of the holder. 'Ten here, go ahead base.'

'Cam, Douglas wants you in the Concert Hall lobby.'

'What's up, Nick?' Cam asked.

'Plumbing problems.'

'On my way. Ten out.'

'Plumbing problems?' I asked. 'What's that mean, another flooded toilet?'

'Yeah, for this I studied four years to get my building operator's ticket.'

'Well, I'm coming with you,' I said. To hell with the coffee.

'Why? I thought you were going to leave Douglas to me.'

'I just need to go over these time sheets with him.' I picked a file folder off my desk and tucked it under my arm.

'You didn't even look at those,' he said. 'What's really going on?'

'It's Gladys. I don't know if I believe her. She was here Thursday night.'

'Here, at the theatre?' he asked.

'Yep. She started her shift at Bud's Bar upstairs and then Douglas called to see if I could spare a couple of bartenders. Apparently some of his staff didn't show up. So I had Graham send over two people. When I was looking over the records on Friday, I discovered she was one of them. I didn't realize that until later. I just want to confirm when she signed in at the Concert Hall.'

'To see if she has any time unaccounted for?' he asked.

'To see if there's any possibility she could have been around here before we found Peter Reynolds.'

'OK, let's go. My toilet's waiting.' Cam kicked the doorstop out and held it open as I walked through. The door slammed shut behind us.

'Wait!' I shouted. 'My keys . . .'

Cam held out his hand, and there were my keys. 'What is it with you and these keys?'

'I seem to have other things on my mind these days,' I said. 'I don't normally forget them this often.'

'I want you to keep them on you,' he admonished me. 'If someone is after you and you don't have your keys, Katie, you're trapped. Do you understand?'

'Yes, I promise I'll keep my mind on track,' I said.

He opened the fire exit door.

'Where are you going?' I asked, hesitating at the door.

'Short cut,' he said. 'Remember, I have the keys of power and I can go anywhere I want in this building. I always take the short cuts.'

'But Cam, there are two flights of stairs.'

'Yes, Katie, but you're young. I'm sure you can do it.'

'We could take the elevator if we went the other way,' I said, knowing he wasn't going to go for it. Instead of listening to my protests, he grabbed my hand and led me down the fire escape.

A flight of stairs at the Plex isn't like a flight of stairs in a regular building. They are longer. We were three floors underground when we finished our descent. The basement corridors are all unfinished and unpainted concrete. This is an area that the public never sees so, like my office, there is no point in spending any money decorating it. There are security doors at the bottom of each flight of stairs. Getting through them is easy, getting back is impossible. I have always thought the security in this place is what you might expect on a military

85

base, not an arts centre. There are security doors separating the corridors at the end of each theatre, on every level. The architects wanted to ensure that no one gets any further than the theatre they are assigned to. Cam, as well as all the engineers and security staff, has access to every level. He and I just kept cutting through hallways and opening locked doors, taking the most direct route possible.

Cam estimates that he climbs an average of fifty flights of stairs and walks about sixty city blocks for every shift he works, and that's on a quiet night. He always takes the direct route when answering a call in order to save a little wear and tear on those old legs of his. He may like working out on his own time, but at work his attitude is get there, get the job done and get out before they find something else for you to do.

I, however, prefer to take the elevator. My theatre is the second highest in the building and has the most stairs. The Concert Hall is the highest, but is equipped with an elevator and two escalators. I, on the other hand, have 144 stairs from street level to the top of the second balcony. We do have an elevator but it is reserved for patrons only. Besides, rumour has it that my elevator was built on an Indian burial ground, because it acts like it's possessed. I figure I climb from top to bottom an average of five times a night; ten if we have a matinee. Unlike Cam, I think that's more than enough exercise for one lifetime. 'Cam, could you walk just a tiny bit slower?' I asked, trying to catch my breath.

'Katie, you broke your arm, not your leg.'

'Well my legs are about five inches shorter than yours and if I wear them out trying to keep up with you right now, I may not have enough energy for you-know-what later on tonight.'

'Subtlety was never your strong point, was it?' He slowed down slightly. 'So how do you feel about your little meeting with Gladys?'

'Suspicious,' I said, waiting for him to unlock yet another door. 'I mean, I haven't seen the woman socially in about a year, and suddenly she wants me to investigate this mystery for her? I don't think she's doing this because she's worried about you going to jail.'

'What do you think she really wants?' he asked.

'I don't know, but I do know I've never really trusted her. Gladys uses people. I just have to find out what she wants from me.'

'Well, she could be using you as a diversion. If she did it, then asked for your help, she might think she was diverting suspicion from herself.'

'That's possible,' I agreed. 'But I don't know why she would want to kill him. She was free of him, well off, and happy.'

'If she really hated him, divorce wouldn't end that,' Cam said, sounding like he might know this from first-hand experience. 'Remember, it was Gladys that wanted to end the marriage. She might have been quite surprised when Peter actually left her. Some people don't like those kinds of surprises.'

'What was she like when you turned her down?' I asked, not really wanting to know. I prefer to pretend that Cam didn't have a past and he seems content to think that way about me as well.

'Well, she seemed slightly disappointed,' he laughed. 'But that could have been an act for my benefit.'

'I don't think so, Cam. Gladys was never one for sparing other people's feelings.'

'Well then, I guess I'm honoured, in a strange sort of way. Anyway, she didn't seem too upset. I saw her at Vaudevilles later that night with someone else.'

'Bounces back quick, our Gladys,' I said sarcastically.

'She seems to.' Cam opened the last door before we went up the stairs into the lobby of the Concert Hall. 'But do you think she did it?'

'I just don't know.'

The Concert Hall always takes my breath away. No matter how many times I see it, my reaction is the same. It was designed as a concert hall and is indeed a world-class facility. The lobby is marble and brass and, looking up, you can see magnificent crystal chandeliers hanging thirty feet above your head. Each floor opens on to a central courtyard, giving people up in the balcony levels a spectacular view. There is a huge brass and oak bar on the main floor, with a crystal sculpture as its magnificent centrepiece. When lit with multicoloured lights, it is the focal point of the whole lobby. Marble, oak and brass as far as the eye can see, complementing furniture of the finest butter-soft leather. The place reeks of money and taste, which is probably why my theatre has such a low decorating budget.

Cam had started across the lobby to the Rodeo Lounge. The front of house staff don't have their offices on-site, as I do, so they tend to congregate in the Rodeo Lounge. That's the VIP area. If you donate enough money to the Symphony, Ballet or Opera, you are issued with a beautifully engraved gold card that gives you access to the lounge and free drinks all season long. Probably the most expensive free drinks in the city. Douglas sat in one of the tapestry armchairs, watching a football game on the thirty-three-inch TV that sits at one end of the lounge. After all, you can't expect a gentleman to come to the Symphony and not be able to find out the sports scores during intermission.

'Hey, Douglas,' Cam called out.

'Hi Cam.' Douglas turned to me, trying to decide whether he had to greet me or not. 'Katherine.'

'Hello Douglas, how are you?' I really love talking with Douglas or, more correctly, making him talk to me. He would much prefer it if I ignored him so that he could do the same to me.

'Fine, thank you.' He turned quickly back to Cam. 'Sorry to call you on this, but it's the women's washroom in the main lobby. We can't have that out of order with a full house tonight.'

'Not a problem,' Cam said. 'I'll go have a look. If it's really bad I can call in a real plumber and I won't have to do it.'

'See you later,' I called after him as he headed across the lobby.

Douglas sat down and turned his attention back to the Calgary Stampeders game.

'Do you have a minute?' I asked.

'I'm sorry,' he apologized, quite insincerely. 'I didn't realize you wanted to speak with me.'

'I have to check some time sheets. I had two people sent over here on Thursday night and they forgot to sign out. I need to see what time they signed in here.'

88

'You could have just sent a memo to payroll,' Douglas suggested.

'I know.' I smiled sweetly at him. 'But I haven't been over here for a while and I thought the walk would do me good. I also needed a break from my theatre. Things are a little serious over there these days.'

'I'll bet they are.' He stood up. 'I'll just go get my clipboard. That's where the weekend time sheets are. Do you mind waiting here a minute?'

'Not at all. I appreciate your help.'

Douglas left the Rodeo Lounge and walked towards the coat check.

I have never really liked Douglas much. He always seems remote, slightly better than the rest of us. I have tried to give him the benefit of the doubt, thinking he is shy or uncomfortable with new people, but he has never opened up to any of us. Perhaps with the exception of Jeremy Rawson. After he and Gladys parted ways, things had become even icier.

Douglas is very tall, very slender, soft spoken, and balding quickly. If it weren't for the fact that he is always impeccably dressed in a three-piece suit, you might mistake him for a monk with the ring of brown hair that's left on his head. He walked across the room gracefully and erect, like he had either studied ballet for years or had a broomstick shoved up his ass. I sometimes wonder if my latter assumption might not actually be true. That would certainly explain his ill humour.

Soon he returned, breaking up my reverie, flipping through the sheets on his clipboard.

'Who are the employees you are looking for?' he asked.

'Phil Jackson and Gladys Reynolds.'

He looked up at me but said nothing and continued to sort through his papers. 'Phil signed in here at eight forty-five; Gladys signed in at nine fifteen.'

I scribbled on my notepad, not writing anything significant. I was far enough away that he couldn't tell what I was doing.

'OK, thanks, Douglas.'

'Anytime, Katherine.' He spoke as if I were a small child who he was being forced to deal with. He sat down in his armchair but I couldn't leave him in peace yet.

'So, what are the rumours?' I asked.

'Rumours?' he repeated.

'About the murder. I'm in the middle of things over there, so I don't hear what everyone is saying. I'm just kind of curious.'

'I don't listen to rumours,' he said, and clicked the TV back on.

My time was obviously up, so I left. Besides, I couldn't really concentrate on bugging Douglas too much; I had other things to worry about. I had sent Gladys and Phil to the Concert Hall at the same time on Thursday night, only Gladys had signed in a half-hour after Phil. I had to find out where she was and what she had been doing for those thirty minutes.

I walked back to the Centenary, through the public corridors this time, and caught the elevator. I was tempted to go up to my office but was pretty sure the way the day was going that someone would find me there, and I felt like being alone for a while. I pushed open the theatre door. Only the dim rail lights were on, casting a mysterious blue glow across the set. I walked down to the front row and sat right in the middle.

I love the theatre before a show. It is quiet, peaceful, cool and, for some reason, no one ever thinks to look for me there. The set for *Much Ado* was lovely. It was the courtyard of an Italian villa set around Shakespeare's time. There were vines and leaves trailing over marble pillars, red tiled roofs, a working fountain, and the silhouette of a church in the background. The sky could go from blue and cloudless to raging and stormy. It was black now, since the lights were off. When they turned on the projector and lowered the house lights, it would become a lovely summer afternoon in southern Italy. It was too bad I couldn't just climb up onstage and really be there.

I don't know how long I'd been sitting and daydreaming when I heard a door open backstage. Maybe, I thought, if I sat really still, no one would notice me and I could have a few more minutes to myself.

'Oh my God, there's management in the house!' Scott shouted, coming out and sitting on the stage, his legs dangling over the edge. 'What the hell are you doing here so early?'

'Scott, just go away and pretend I'm not here,' I begged, slouching low in my seat.

Scott O'Brien is our stage carpenter. He is tall and good-looking and one of the sweetest guys I have ever met. He has dark hair, olive skin, and sky-blue eyes. He can never keep a girlfriend, and I have never figured out why.

He jumped down off the stage and sat in the seat beside me. 'You having a bad day, you sexy hunk of woman?'

'I'm having a bad week.'

'Turn that way,' he said, pointing away from him. 'What's bothering you? Is it that nasty murder thing that happened?' He started massaging my shoulders.

'You have the most amazing hands,' I said, melting into him. 'And, yes, that nasty murder thing is making my life difficult.'

'So you want to tell me how you got the cast and those stitches?'

'I was mugged,' I said, not wanting to get into it.

'Is that all?' He doubled his efforts on my shoulders, knowing I would be putty in his hands.

'Scott, if you did this to all your girlfriends on the first date, you might start getting some second dates.'

'Save the sarcasm for later,' he said. 'I want to know what happened.'

'I started asking some questions about the murder and I guess someone didn't approve.'

'Kate, what the hell are you doing that for?' he asked. 'You think what you see in the movies is true? You think anybody can investigate a murder?'

'I'm OK, Scott,' I insisted. 'Someone was just trying to scare me.'

'Well, I hope they succeeded.'

'Not really,' I said. 'I have to keep asking questions. The police think Cam did it.'

Scott didn't answer right away. 'OK, I understand, and there will be no further lectures on the subject for now,' he promised. 'So what are you doing to keep yourself safe?'

'Security is keeping an eye on me while I'm in the building.'

'That's a laugh.' He stopped rubbing my shoulders and sat back in the seat. 'Why don't you let us watch out for you?'

'I don't think I really need babysitting,' I protested.

'And how long are you wearing the cast for?' he asked, reminding me that I might need a little help.

'OK, if it will make you happy, you may babysit me,' I said, giving in.

'Just let one of us know when you're in the building and where you are. I could even get you a radio,' he said. 'Of course, we'll put it on a different frequency than security.'

'No, please not a radio. I'll let you know where I am and what I'm doing, but I think I'm relatively safe here. Cam isn't letting me out of his sight when we're out of the building.'

'Well, I may not trust security to look after you, but I do trust Cam,' Scott said. 'Come closer and let me see your face.'

I leaned towards him. 'Careful, it's still sore.'

'Somebody did a real nice job of stitching this up,' he commented.

'When did you become a doctor?' I asked.

'Kate, I've had so many stitches in my lifetime that I'm sure I could qualify for a medical degree,' he laughed. 'These look like they're ready to come out.'

'I was supposed to go today,' I confessed. 'But I chickened out.'

He stood up and pulled me up off my seat. 'Come on, we'll get Trevor to take them out for you.'

'I don't think so.' I tried to pull away from him.

'It's OK, you know he was a paramedic, and he takes all mine out for me.' Scott dropped my arm and jumped up on stage. 'Come on, he's just sitting in the green room having a beer.'

'That certainly reassuring,' I said sarcastically.

Scott leaned over and held out his hands. Against my better judgment, I took them and he pulled me up on stage. Scott is tall and slim but he is incredibly strong. He has a black belt in karate or something and is an avid triathlete, among his many other accomplishments. It always amazes me when I see him shinning up ropes or moving the stage weights around like toys.

Once I was on the stage, Scott took my hand and led me through the stage-right exit and into the green room. He poked his head around the doorway and called to Trevor.

'Hey, doctor, I have a patient for you tonight.'

'What you talking about, butthead?' Trevor asked, before Scott pulled me through the door so Trevor could get a look at me. 'Lordy, girl, what have you gone and done to yourself?'

'She's been putting her nose in where it doesn't belong. Literally,' Scott answered on my behalf.

Trevor E. Lee stood up and put his beer down. He had been named after Robert E. Lee, almost, even though his parents were from California and had never been to the Deep South. He has straight brown hair, John Lennon glasses and a southern accent. Trevor admitted to me once that the accent was fake, but he got so sick of all the Robert E. Lee jokes that he decided if he couldn't beat them, he'd better join them. So he came up with the southern accent, a fake life story, and everyone believed it. As Trevor stood up, he pulled his shirt down over the stomach he was developing from drinking too much beer. It always amazes me that someone who has a job as physically demanding as Technical Director could possibly develop any flab on his body. Scott sat me on the couch and Trevor brought the first aid kit over and set it on the coffee table.

'You're not going to tell me Cam did this, are you?' Trevor asked.

'God no!' I said.

'She's getting involved in this murder investigation,' Scott said, speaking for me again.

'Scott, I *can* talk,' I protested.

'I know you can talk, but I know you won't tell him the truth.' He turned his attention back to Trevor. 'She was supposed to get those stitches out today.'

Trevor probed my bruises gently. 'This could have been a whole lot worse,' he said. 'I hope Scott mentioned that you should let the police handle this.'

'It looks like Cam is becoming the main suspect,' Scott said.

'Scott, stop answering questions for me.'

'Sit still,' Trevor commanded, pulling some tiny scissors out of his kit.

'Trevor, I'll get these out tomorrow.' I pulled away from him. 'I don't have time right now.'

'Have you ever had stitches before?' Scott asked.

'No.'

'Did it hurt when they put them in?' Trevor asked.

'Yes,' I admitted.

'Well, calm down because it doesn't hurt when they come out,' Scott said, but he reached down and took my hand in his as he sat beside me on the arm of the sofa.

'He's right,' Trevor added. 'I promise this won't hurt, OK?'

'OK,' I agreed, moving to the edge of the couch.

Trevor snipped the first stitch and pulled it out gently with tweezers. 'That OK?' he asked.

'Yes,' I said, squeezing Scott's hand.

'OK, only a couple more,' Trevor reassured me.

'I told her we would keep an eye on her,' said Scott. 'She said security had promised to watch her but I thought we could do a better job.'

'I think that's a good idea,' Trevor agreed, dropping another stitch into the ashtray. 'And I suppose you don't think you need watching.'

I didn't answer, waiting for Scott to respond for me. 'My turn to talk?' I asked sarcastically when Scott failed to respond. 'No, Trevor, I agreed. I don't think I'm in any danger here, but I told Scott I would let you guys know when I'm in the building and where I'm going.'

'Good. Do you want us to get you a radio?' he asked, pulling out the last stitch.

'No, I really don't want a radio. I can barely remember to keep my keys on me.' I touched my lip gently, expecting to feel a gaping hole where the stitches had been. 'That really wasn't so bad.'

'I told you,' Trevor said. 'How about a wireless transmitter? We could rig something up for you to wear.'

'I don't think this is that serious. Besides, all I'm doing now is asking some harmless questions about where certain ushers were on Thursday night. I'm making it sound like I'm doing payroll.'

'Scott, Dwayne and I will talk about this tonight. We'll see if we can come up with something that you can live with,' Trevor said. 'But for now, you either stay in your office with your door locked or call us if you're going some-where.'

'I really appreciate your concern,' I said. 'And I promise I will let you watch over me, but only because I know I will get no peace until I agree.'

'Well, that's good enough for me,' Trevor said. 'For now.'

'How does it look?' I asked, still feeling my face.

'It looks really good,' Scott said. 'I'd marry you.'

Trevor laughed. 'Not much of a compliment considering that this butthead would marry anything with a pulse just to get sex on a regular basis. But you look fine.'

'Thanks, guys.' I stood up, looking at my watch. 'But it's time for me to get to work.'

'OK.' Scott stood up so I could pass. 'I'll be up later to see how you're doing.'

'All right.' I kissed him on the cheek. 'You guys really are sweet. Talk to you soon.'

I heard them opening beers as I walked down the hall, past the dressing rooms, and back into my side of the theatre.

Graham was talking to one of the bartenders in the storage area behind the Broadway Bar as I came into the main lobby. We still had a half-hour before we had to get to work so I left him there, trying to get a date. When I got to my office I poured a fresh coffee and sat in the window watching the traffic go by. I heard a rustling sound and turned to see an envelope slide under my office door. For a moment I was afraid and didn't move, but then curiosity overcame my better judgment. I picked up the envelope and ripped it open. Inside, there was a piece of paper covered with letters clipped from the newspaper. I thought this must be some sort of joke until I read it.

THIS IS YOUR SECOND WARNING.
STRIKE THREE AND I WILL TAKE YOU OUT.

I felt a shiver run through me and the hair on the back of my neck stood up. I lunged for the door, making sure it was locked, and then grabbed my phone and dialled the extension for the green room.

'Green room,' Scott answered.

'Scott, it's Kate.'

He must have heard the fear in my voice. 'We're on our way,' was all he said before the phone was slammed down. Suddenly there was a knock at my door.

'Who's there?' I shouted, knowing Scott and Trevor couldn't be here yet.

The pounding continued but no one answered my question.

'Who's there?' I screamed through the door, backing up into the corner of the office.

Then I heard a key in the door and saw the knob begin to turn. Time seemed to slow down and the knob turned forever before the door finally started to open. Suddenly, time returned to normal as Cam pushed his way through the door, followed by Scott and Trevor.

'Katie, are you all right?' he asked, grabbing me by the shoulders.

'Why didn't you answer me?' I shouted at him. 'What are you doing up here?'

'Katie, calm down. Tell me what's going on.' Cam pushed me down on to the window ledge and lit a cigarette for me.

'What are you doing up here?' I asked him again.

'I was finished in the Concert Hall and wanted to check in on you before I headed down to the basement,' he explained. 'Now, will you tell me what the hell is going on?'

I looked down at the floor where I had dropped the letter. 'Someone just shoved that under my door,' I said.

Scott bent down to pick it up and all three of them read it over. Trevor immediately got on his radio and called security, asking them to call the police. Cam sat down on the ledge beside me and put his arm around me.

'I'm sorry, I didn't mean to scare you,' he said. 'I just heard you screaming.'

'Cam, you must have seen someone in the corridor.'

'There was no one out there,' he said.

'You must have seen someone,' I insisted, taking a deep drag on a cigarette. 'It was slid under the door just before you knocked.'

'There was no one out there,' he said again.

'But Cam, there *must* have been. I swear, it came under the door just a couple of seconds before you knocked.' I looked around at all of them. 'One of you must have seen someone out there. I am not imagining this!'

'Cam, why don't you get her out of here. We'll wait for the police. They can come by Kate's place later and talk to her,' Trevor suggested.

Cam looked at me, trying to figure out if I was going to put up a fight or not, but I didn't argue. I suddenly felt very tired. Graham could run the show tonight. I just wanted to go home.

Detective Ken Lincoln was becoming a permanent fixture at my apartment. Once again, we all sat in the living room and, once again, I was the centre of attention as I told my story.

'So after the letter was pushed under the door, you read it, then Cam started knocking on your door?' Ken was rereading his notes, making sure he had everything correct.

'That's right. I panicked and started screaming and then he panicked and thought I was in trouble, so I didn't realize it was him knocking . . .'

'And I didn't realize she was yelling to see who was there,' Cam finished for me.

'You didn't see anyone in the corridor?' the detective asked.

'No one,' Cam said. 'I just came down the hall to her office, knocked, and then she started screaming.'

'That's what I don't understand,' I said. 'There was not enough time between the letter coming under the door and Cam knocking for someone to get out of the corridor.'

'What if they went down the fire escape?' Ken asked.

'No, the fire escape and the main door are right beside each other. There had to be someone in that corridor,' I insisted.

'There wasn't anyone,' Cam said.

'Did anyone check the bathrooms?' Ken asked. 'They are right outside your office.'

I looked at Cam and he shook his head.

'We were all pretty shook up,' he said. 'Nobody thought of it.'

'By the time the officers got there, it was too late.' Ken closed his notebook and took a drink of his mineral water. I had sent Cam to the store for some after we got home. I always feel like such a bad hostess if I have nothing to offer my guests.

'There were ushers, security guards and office staff everywhere,' Ken continued. 'You are becoming the main attraction at the arts centre.'

'Not by choice,' I said. 'I'd be quite happy if everyone would just forget all about this and leave me alone.'

'That's only going to happen if you stop asking questions,' Cam said.

'I'm not in the mood right now—' I started.

Ken cut me off. 'He's right. This episode should convince you that this has turned into a very dangerous game for you. Whoever is responsible for this thinks you know something, and I'd like to find out what it is.'

'I don't know anything,' I said. 'I have racked my brains trying to put this together, but nothing fits. All I know right now is what I've told you.'

'Well, whoever is after you seems to think you're very close. You have *got* to stay out of this for a while. Send word around the grapevine that you are getting nowhere and aren't asking any more questions.'

'All right,' I agreed, thinking it wasn't really a lie. I could tell everyone I wasn't asking any more questions, but that didn't mean it actually had to stop.

'You've got to keep your eyes open. Pay attention to who is around when you're talking and maybe we can find out who's been listening in to your conversations.'

'OK,' I agreed again.

'And you shouldn't be alone.'

'I'm not going to be babysat,' I said.

'Kate, someone has been murdered. This is real life, not some play at your theatre. If this person gets caught they are going to jail for life. Whoever it is would be very willing to murder you to save himself. It's only the first murder that's hard, the second one is much easier.'

'I understand,' I said.

He smiled at me. 'You don't fool me, Kate. You're a headstrong woman and you still think that I suspect your boyfriend of this. You are going to sit here and agree with everything I

98

say, and then you are going to go ahead and do whatever you want to do. Am I right?'

I stared back at him, trying to look innocent. Apparently it wasn't working.

'God, just like my wife. You both make me crazy sometimes.'

Cam laughed. 'I'm glad I'm not alone there.'

Ken turned back to me. 'Kate, I know you're going to do as you please, but I need your promise that you will at least try to be careful. I don't want to be up here again talking to you, unless it's a social occasion. Understand?'

'OK. I'll watch my front. I'm not worried about my back because I have all these overprotective men at the Plex watching out for me.'

'OK,' he said. 'I'm out of here. I'll let you know if we find anything.'

Cam let the detective out and went straight back into the kitchen. He was banging the pots and pans pretty good when I decided to go and see what was wrong.

'Cam?' I began tentatively.

'What?' He was very short with me.

'What's up?'

'You, Katie. You are what's up.'

'What have I done?' I asked.

He threw a pot into the sink and I heard a dish break. 'What have you done? You have put yourself right into the middle of this mess and almost got yourself killed. Twice. What if I hadn't come down the hall just then? He could have come into your office and killed you.'

'Calm down, Cam, nothing happened.' I put my hand on his arm, but he shook it off.

'Yeah, this time. You've already been beat up. I want you to stop this, Katie.'

'I can't,' I said quietly.

'You stop this or I'm out of here.'

'Why? You said you would help.'

'That was before you got hurt, but this is too much. I am not going to stand around and watch you get killed. You say you are doing this for me but I don't care any more. I know

I'm innocent and the police will find out who is responsible,' he said.

'It's not just you, Cam, it's me too. I want to find who's doing this to me.'

'I mean it, Katie. If you don't promise to stop now, I'm out the door.'

'I can't,' I said.

He threw down the dish towel, grabbed his jacket and left. I sat at the table in shock. When I heard the door slam, I felt a tear run down my cheek. In all our time together, all my pushing Cam away from me, he had never once walked out. I had no idea what this meant. I had never seen him angry before and I didn't know if he'd get over it, if I should go running after him or if I was about to live alone again. I reached across the table for the pack of cigarettes and opened it. It was empty. I spent the next hour searching drawers and pockets for a cigarette, but with no luck. I could have walked a block to the corner store, but I was scared to go out alone. I was also scared that Cam might come back and I wouldn't be there.

I made some coffee and paced around the apartment. I tried playing the piano, working at the computer, watching a movie, but I couldn't concentrate on anything. I finally turned the TV on and tried watching the music channel. I called the theatre at about eight o'clock to see how everything was going. Graham told me everything was fine and to get some rest. He sounded busy, so I didn't keep him on the phone long. I tried to concentrate on the TV again but wasn't very successful. I wrapped a blanket around me, laid down on the couch, and cried myself to sleep.

I woke up with a start, feeling a hand on my neck, and I reached out into the darkness, trying to push whoever it was away from me.

'Katie, it's me.'

'Cam?' I asked.

His hand reached out and turned on the lamp beside the couch.

'Cam, I'm so glad you're back.' I wrapped my arms around him and he hugged me back.

'I'm sorry I left like I did,' he said.

'Where have you been?' I asked. 'I've been so worried.'

'I've been walking around and around.' He laughed. 'I couldn't get far. I forgot to take my car keys with me.'

'Why didn't you come back?'

'I had to wait until I wasn't angry any more,' he said. 'I've been known to get very unreasonable when I'm angry. I was afraid I might say something I would regret.'

'I've never seen you like that before,' I said. 'You scared me.'

'I know, but it's just that I'm so frustrated, Katie. Somebody is after you. I thought I could protect you. I'm not doing a very good job of it though, am I?'

'Is that what this is about?' I asked. 'You feel like this is your fault?'

'It *is* my fault, Katie. It's all my fault.'

'No, Cam, we just stumbled into this. It's not your fault.'

'I wish I could believe that, but you're not safe around me.'

'Cam, I'm safer around you than anyone else.'

'No,' he insisted. 'The only way you'll be safe is to stop this. But you're not going to stop and I can't do anything to save you if you keep asking questions.'

I stood up. 'Cam, you're upset and I'm exhausted. I think we should go to bed. We can talk about this in the morning.'

'I'm so sorry, Katie, for everything.'

'It's OK,' I said again, getting up off the couch and turning the light off in the living room. 'Let's just go to bed now.'

He followed me silently up the stairs, neither of us saying a word as we climbed into bed. There didn't seem to be anything else to say.

Wednesday

We did go to bed but I didn't get much rest. My mind wouldn't turn itself off. Cam got up around eight and went for a jog. I pretended I was still asleep and, when he was gone, I turned over and tried to actually get some sleep. I didn't have much luck. I didn't like fighting with Cam like this. Normally we just disagreed and made up. Somehow, we had missed the making up part this time. I finally gave up trying to sleep and went downstairs to put the coffee on.

While I was waiting for the water to boil, I started wiping down the counter tops. The only time I ever clean productively is when I am upset. I took a spray bottle and a paper towel to the table and continued my never-ending battle against fingerprints on the glass top. When I was satisfied, I dropped the paper towel into the garbage. Yesterday's newspaper sat on top of the pail, so I pulled it out. It seemed fairly clean and dry and I hadn't read it yet, so I set the paper on the table, poured myself some coffee and sat down. I sipped coffee and leafed through the paper, not finding anything that really caught my interest. I flipped to the classifieds, looking for the crossword puzzle, and was surprised to see several holes cut out of the newspaper. I continued turning the pages and found more cut-outs. As I flipped, page after page, I couldn't help but think of the awful letter I had received the day before.

'Oh my God,' I heard myself say out loud. Then I heard Cam's key in the door.

I quickly put the paper back together and set it back in the garbage pail, then I sat back down with a fresh cup of coffee.

'Hi, Katie.' Cam came around the corner and smiled at me. 'I didn't expect to see you up already.'

'I couldn't sleep,' I said, holding my quivering hands between my knees.

'I brought the paper in.' He set it on the table and poured himself a coffee. 'Mind if I read the sports section?' Cam settled himself at the table across from me and started to search through the paper.

'Sure.' He found the sports section and shoved the rest of the newspaper across to me. 'I was hoping to read yesterday's paper first. Have you seen it?'

'I thought you'd read it already, so I threw it out,' he said, reading through the score board summary.

'Oh, maybe I can rescue it,' I said as I stood up.

'I doubt it,' he said. 'I'm afraid I cut it up a bit.'

'What?' I sat back down and watched his face carefully, trying to catch him in a lie.

'There were some ads for car parts I wanted, so I cut them out and took them to work with me. Sorry.'

'That's OK,' I said. 'There should be a copy at the theatre I can read. What are you looking for?'

'What?' He looked up from the paper.

'What car parts are you looking for?'

'I thought I'd try and replace the rear window. I'm sick of looking in the rear-view mirror and seeing that gravel chip,' he answered.

'I thought they were expensive.'

'Very,' he agreed as he pushed his coffee cup across the table. 'Can you pour me another cup?'

'Sure.' I stood and brought the coffee pot back to the table. 'So did you find one?'

'No, not yet. Lots of other stuff, though. I thought I might pick up some spare parts, just in case.'

'Find anything interesting?'

'No, nothing you'd understand. Why the sudden interest in cars?' he asked.

'Just curious. I want to make sure you're still spending more of your money on me than you are on the car.'

He laughed and then turned his attention back to the sports section.

I was sure he wasn't lying. I would be able to tell if he was,

103

wouldn't I? As my mind spun, trying to figure all this out, the phone rang, saving me from an irreversible brain cramp. Life had become so complicated. Cam jumped up and answered the phone.

'It's for you,' he called from the living room.

'Who is it?' I asked as I walked into the living room carrying my coffee.

He handed the phone to me. 'The Plex.'

'What now?' I put the phone to my ear and switched to my cheerful house manager demeanour. 'Hi, this is Kate.'

'Hi Kate, it's Grace,' the receptionist bubbled. She must have something juicy to tell me. 'How are you doing?'

'Grace, I'm fine, and you?'

'Oh, busy, busy, busy,' she said. 'But I have news for you from the head honcho himself.'

Oh, God, I thought, what did the artistic director from hell want now? 'Go on,' I instructed Grace.

'You know that the funeral is today?' she asked me.

'Funeral?'

'You know, for Peter Reynolds. Anyways, he asked me to call you. They want you there as the official Foothills Stage representative!' Grace sounded like she was ready to burst with the news.

'Me? Why? I thought that's what the public relations department was for.'

'Well, you know the widow, and you were there at the time of the murder. So you're the lucky winner.'

'Oh, God, will this never end?' I didn't realize I had said this aloud.

'What?' Grace asked, sounding disappointed that I wasn't as excited as she was.

'Nothing. Do you know where it's being held?' I recovered.

'Jackson Funeral Home, on 4th Street, and then he's being buried at Queen's Park Cemetery.'

'All right. What time?'

'The service starts at three. Be there or be square,' she enthused.

'OK, I'll be there. Thanks for the message.'

104

I hung up the phone, cutting her off before she could give me any more news.

'Cam,' I called. He was back in the kitchen, going through the classifieds in his ceaseless quest to perfect the Fish.

'What is it?'

'Did you have any plans for this afternoon?'

The only good thing about the funeral was that I could wear this really great black dress that I had bought a couple of weeks previously, with a simple strand of pearls and a cute little black straw hat to complete the look. It did have a red ribbon, but I didn't think that was too disrespectful. Funerals and weddings, the two legitimate times I can wear hats without people thinking I was a kook. Cam went back to his place and picked up a suit. He also finally brought a few other things over. I had started to wonder if he really did want to live with me. I couldn't blame him, though, not with what had been happening over the past couple of days. I figured we were due lots of fun, carefree times when this was all over.

Cam looked stunning and I thought we made a great couple. I had no idea we would actually make the six o'clock news on both local channels.

We parked several blocks away from the funeral home. I couldn't believe the number of cars and, as we approached our destination, the number of people outside. I recognized some people from the Plex but had no idea who made up the rest of the crowd. Either Peter Reynolds had been a hugely popular man, or the public was very interested in this event. Perhaps this was the consequence of living in a relatively crime-free city. A murder was big news. We elbowed our way through the crowds and the media, and found a seat in the chapel. I couldn't believe that some of the press had actually approached me with questions. What I really couldn't believe was that any of them would even know who I was.

The service was non-denominational and short. The ex-wife, widow, and children sat in the front row, and several people, who I assumed were family friends, rushed to surround them after the service was over. The rest of the crowd just mulled about, waiting for something to happen. After the service was over, Cam and I made our way out quickly, trying to beat the rush to the graveside. I actually said 'No Comment' twice on our way out. I knew Graham would be jealous as hell.

We drove to the cemetery and parked a few blocks away, walking slowly as we waited for the crowd to arrive. There was a huge throng following the family to the graveside at a suitable distance. I was astounded by the number of people who had actually come for the internment. I was also astounded by the number of people who had come from the Plex. It was as though all the suspects had gathered for a fond farewell. Just like a mystery novel. I was also surprised to see Detective Lincoln hovering uncomfortably in the background.

'What do you think he's doing here?' I asked Cam, pointing to the policeman.

'Probably the same thing you are,' he said. 'Checking out the suspects.'

'I am not.' I elbowed him. 'I am here as an official representative of Foothills Stage Network.'

'Lucky they asked you to attend. Otherwise you would have to come up with some other excuse.'

'You're cruel,' I said. 'But should we take advantage of everyone being here and just have a little chat to see what motivated them to come today?'

'I don't mind,' Cam said. 'But keep the conversation light. I don't want anyone thinking you're back to your snoop routine.'

'I promise. We can just wander over and thank them for coming, on behalf of the Plex. You know, the old team-spirit stuff?'

Cam looked like he might put up a fight, but instead held out his hand. 'Just remember, you're not going anywhere without me. Detective Lincoln is watching you too.'

The minister offered a few short words and the casket was lowered into the ground. A flower was thrown in and a symbolic shovelful of earth was dropped into the grave. I guessed there would be a bulldozer, after the family left, to finish the job.

The family formed a reception line. Cam and I wandered slowly towards it, smiling at the few people we recognized.

We found ourselves standing in the line a few people behind Douglas Mendlesson. I hesitated, knowing that Douglas wasn't keen to talk to me under the best of circumstances. But then Cam came through for me, calling out Douglas's name and extending his hand in greeting. I always envied the easiness that men seem to have with each other. All you have to do is extend your hand, give a firm shake, and the conversation seems to flow from there.

'Hey, Cam,' Douglas greeted. 'How are you doing?'

'Good, and you?' Cam asked.

'Not bad. I'm kind of surprised to see you here.'

'Well, I was there when they found him,' Cam explained. 'Katie was coming, so I figured I might as well tag along.'

'Well, I suppose none of us is really here by choice, but it does look good, having the Plex represented like this.'

I was almost ready to jump in with my own questions when Cam surprised me again.

'Did you know him?' Cam asked Douglas.

'No. I've known Gladys for a while, but I never met Peter.' Douglas suddenly looked uncomfortable.

'Cam, I'm just going to go say hi to Susan,' I said, sensing we might get further if I wasn't around. 'I'll be back in a minute.'

'All right, Katie.' He let go of my hand and I wandered off towards a group of ushers I knew.

I saw Cam turn back to Douglas. 'Well, who didn't know Gladys Reynolds?'

I overheard his last comment as I walked away, but then I was out of earshot. I chatted for about five minutes before Cam joined me again. I made my excuses and we moved a discreet distance away.

'Well?' I asked.

'He's a bit of a tight-lipped bastard,' Cam said, shaking his head. 'Not much into opening up.'

'Did he have anything to say?'

'He's still in love with Gladys.'

'Did he tell you that?' I asked.

'No, but I could tell. It's the way he spoke about her, how he kept looking over at her. He did say he had hoped to start

107

seeing her again when she got divorced, but she never returned any of his calls. He came here today to let her know he was there if she needed him.'

'I never really thought Douglas had that much depth,' I said. 'Do you think he could have done it?'

'Katie, I only talked to him for a couple of minutes. We didn't exactly get into accusations.'

'But what do you think?' I asked.

'I don't think he could have done anything to cause Gladys pain, no matter what she did to him. If Douglas was involved in a crime of passion, he would have killed Gladys herself,' Cam said. 'But I don't think it matters.'

'Why not?'

'Because he was on duty at the Concert Hall from six o'clock until midnight on the night the murder took place.'

'I don't think he was there the whole time,' I suggested.

'How would you know? You were on duty at your theatre.'

'Because when he called me and asked me to send over some extra staff, I heard music in the background.'

'Of course you did, the Symphony was performing,' he said.

'No, I heard rock and roll music. Not the Symphony, more like a radio. I bet he called me from his office, not the lobby. He didn't have to be back at the theatre until intermission at about nine thirty.'

'That doesn't prove anything,' Cam said.

'It may not *prove* anything,' I agreed. 'But it doesn't put him in the clear either. Sitting alone in his office won't provide him with much of an alibi.'

'Katie, I thought the whole idea was to eliminate people. All you seem to be doing is proving that it could be anyone. If that's going to be your theory, it could have just as easily been me that did it. I was alone in the basement until I got your call. I have no witnesses or alibi.'

'You're not helping, Cam,' I said.

'Douglas may have been in his office when he called you, Katie, but I don't think he did it. I just don't buy it.'

I stopped arguing with Cam when I noticed Douglas walking towards Gladys. He kissed her gently on the cheek and murmured a few words I couldn't hear.

'I thought you were going to leave the murder investigation to me.'

I turned and saw Ken Lincoln standing beside us. 'Well, Detective, fancy meeting you here,' I said conversationally.

'This is standard procedure for the police,' he said. 'We always check out the funerals, to see who turns up. What's your excuse for being here?'

'The theatre asked me to represent them.' I smiled back at him.

'So you're here for legitimate reasons? Well, the funeral is over, so why don't you let Cam take you home and let us do our job?'

'That sounds like a good idea to me,' Cam agreed.

'I haven't had a chance to speak with Gladys yet,' I said.

'There's a big line-up, Kate,' Ken said. 'You'll be here for hours if you wait to see her, and that probably isn't the healthiest thing you could do for yourself right now. You should probably go home and rest that broken hand or something.'

'Detective, are you ordering me out of here?'

'Would you listen if I ordered you?' Ken asked hopefully.

'I doubt it,' Cam answered on my behalf. I didn't like the way my friends kept turning on me these days.

'Then I won't order you,' Ken said. 'I'll suggest that you have had enough adventure for one week and that lying low and not asking questions might be a good idea at this point. If that doesn't work, I might also mention interfering with an official investigation. That's a bad thing, you know.'

'It's been a pleasure seeing you again, Detective,' I said, turning and heading for the car. Cam shook hands with him and followed me across the cemetery.

We drove home slowly, taking the longest route possible. Cam seemed to be in the mood for driving and for silence. I stared out the window and tried to figure out what was going on with him. He was so on and off with this whole thing. I understood that he was upset and worried about me, but what I couldn't understand was his moods. One minute he was furious, the next minute everything was just fine. Cam had never acted inconsistently before; he usually left that type of behaviour to me. I was feeling really uncomfortable with his being so emotional, and I didn't know how to talk to him about it.

If I'm honest, I wondered if I really wanted to talk to him about it at all. I was starting to feel really crowded. I hadn't had any time to myself since I had been mugged. My over-protective male friends were guarding my every move and I was feeling the need for some space. Under normal circumstances I would have just gone out for a walk in the park, but I didn't dare suggest that. Cam didn't want me out of his sight, and I didn't want to argue the point and have another blow-out with him. Maybe when we got home, I could disappear into the bath for a blissful hour or two alone with a book and a glass of wine.

When we got home, Cam beat me into the bath, so I grabbed a book and curled up on my lounge chair on the balcony. I was hungry, but lazy, so I took an apple out with me. I had read a couple of chapters when Cam joined me on the balcony.

'Feel better?' I asked him.

'A little,' he said, towelling his hair. 'I thought I'd go out for a run, if you don't mind.'

'No, I don't mind. I'm just going to read for a while.'

'Promise me you won't go out?' he asked.

'Cam, please don't treat me like this. I'm not a captive and I'm being careful.' I took a deep breath and decided I didn't want a fight. 'But I'm not planning on going anywhere. Good enough?'

'OK.' He leaned over and kissed me. 'I'll be back in about an hour.'

I heard Cam leave and secure both locks on the door. I tried to turn my attention back to the book but my mind was wandering. I looked over the balcony and watched all the other people enjoying this beautiful fall day. They were jogging, rollerblading, walking, sitting – doing all the things that I used to do before I was placed under house arrest. I really wanted to go and sit on the grass for a couple of minutes and feel the sun's rays from ground level, not my balcony.

What the hell, I thought, throwing my book aside. Cam wouldn't be back for an hour and the park was right across the street. I was going to go, alone, and dip my feet in the fountain. Hopefully I would get back before Cam and not have to explain my absence. But even if I didn't, it would be worth it.

I ran up to the bedroom and changed into some shorts and a T-shirt. I threw on a straw hat for good measure. After all, in Calgary, one enjoys the good weather while it lasted. It could change in minutes.

I hit the street and felt amazingly free. I had honestly planned just to go to MacDougall Park, across the street from the apartment, but when I got outside and felt the sun on me, I had to keep going. I walked down the path along the Bow river, dodging skaters and bikes, and stopped at Eau Claire Market for an iced cappuccino. The market is in downtown Calgary and is supposed to be a great combination of a farmers' market and a shopping centre. What it has turned out to be is a huge warehouse-like structure, painted bright blue, red, and yellow. You can't miss it. I have yet to see a farmer selling his wares there. They do have horse-drawn carriage rides, street musicians, artists, and a lot of overpriced stores, though. There are always huge crowds of people spending huge sums of money every day the market is open. Go figure. But what could I say? I was there spending money with the rest of them.

I made my way through the market, not even stopping to window-shop. I wanted to be outdoors. I got back on to the river pathway and headed across the bridge to Prince's Island. This is my haven, my bastion from the hectic downtown lifestyle. As I crossed the bridge, I felt like I was entering another world. The skyscrapers fell behind me and the trees filled the sky over-head. No vehicles are allowed on the island, which is covered by acres of grass, trees, bushes, ducks and geese. For a city girl like me, it feels like the country. I strolled to the north side of the island and sat on the grass, leaning against my favourite tree. I could watch the canoes and ducks float by on the river on one side, and the people wander by on the other. I stuck my legs out into the sunshine, trying to take advantage of the last of the fall sun. Boy, this felt good, alone at last.

I lost all track of time but didn't care. I was enjoying myself too much to worry. I suppose I should have worn my watch, but that would have just made me feel guilty about not being home yet.

After a half-hour or so, the guilt was winning out and I had decided to get up and head for home when I saw Cam jogging across the bridge. My first instinct was to call out to him, until I remembered that he would probably be furious with me for being out. So I sat still, wrestling with my conscience, and watched him stop and stretch against a tree when he reached the end of the bridge. I decided to get up and go face the music when I saw him straighten up and turn around, then raise his hand and wave to someone. He hadn't said anything to me about going to meet someone and I was suddenly curious. I sat down again, slightly behind the tree, waiting to see who crossed the bridge. When I saw Gladys walk towards him, my stomach lurched. When he put his hands on her shoulders and greeted her with a kiss on the cheek, I started running for the far end of the island. I didn't stop running until I was back at the apartment.

I paced around the living room for a couple of minutes, not knowing what to do. I really didn't want to see Cam when he came back. He had lied to me. What else had he lied about? Just Gladys, or everything since the day we'd met? I felt the walls closing in around me and I knew I had to get out of there.

I scribbled a note to Cam, saying I was going out to dinner with a friend and would see him later. Then I grabbed my bag and keys and left. When I got out of the elevator I realized I really didn't know where I was going. I didn't want to go to the theatre; Graham would just be getting everyone signed in. I'd left him in charge again tonight, not knowing how long the funeral would last. I knew that if I dropped in I would have to take over or sit there and watch him work. My only girlfriend, Sam, was on holiday with her husband and little girl, and everyone else I knew was at the Plex.

I hopped on the C-Train and wound up at the Plex despite my resolve not to go there. My instinct had taken over where my indecision had left off. I took the public corridor in to avoid security and snuck through a fire escape so the front of house staff wouldn't see me.

I let myself into the green room, knowing it was still too

112

early for the actors to be there. Their call for this show was a half-hour, which meant seven thirty. The crew would be in soon, but for now it was deserted.

I grabbed a beer out of the fridge and tossed a couple of dollars into the pot. It isn't my favourite drink but I didn't feel like making coffee. I sat on the couch and sipped the beer but I was too hyper to sit still. I turned on the monitor and watched the empty stage for a while. Then I saw Graham climb up on the stage, look around to see if anyone was watching and, when he felt sure that he was alone, he started tap-dancing. The kid was amazing. I always suspected he snuck in early and did stuff like this. I was used to hearing him sing while he was in the auditorium and in the lobbies, but had never caught him on the stage before. Graham wanted to be an actor more than anything else in the world, and he still had all the unbridled enthusiasm that went with being eighteen. It was delightful to see. I didn't know if he would ever be a successful actor, but it had been a long time since I had seen anyone that wasn't cynical about the theatre.

'You've got to talk to that kid,' I heard a voice say from behind me. 'We're getting sick of chasing him off the stage.'

I turned my head and saw Scott standing in the doorway.

'He's not hurting anything. Let him enjoy himself while he can.'

Scott grabbed a beer and sat down beside me. He draped his arm on the back of the sofa and I curled up beside him, laying my head on his shoulder. Scott is like a brother to me and it was nice having him so close with my real brother so far away.

'You look like you're having a bad day.'

'Scott, I'm having a bad week, remember? It's like a nightmare.'

'So why aren't you at home relaxing instead of sitting here whining? You certainly wouldn't catch me spending my days off here.'

'I was at home but I needed to get away for a while,' I said.

'You and Cam have a fight?' he asked.

'Not yet.'

'Oh, now that sounds promising. Just the kind of secure

113

home life I've always hoped for.' He shook his head at me. 'I really think you have to decide what you want, Kate. Do you want Cam around? Do you want a relationship or not?'

'Me, taking advice on relationships from you? This sounds like the blind leading the blind.'

'I'm serious, Kate. I like him and I think he's a good guy for you. Quit pushing him away, or one of these days he might not come back.'

'Scott, I think he may be involved in this murder.'

'What do you mean?' he asked, sitting a little straighter.

'I caught him on Prince's Island with Gladys,' I said, bitterness creeping into my voice.

'And what did he have to say about it?'

'I didn't ask him. I panicked and ran away. He didn't even know I was there. I was supposed to be back at the apartment.'

'Well, talk to him. There's probably a very simple explanation.'

'He told me he didn't know Gladys. He said she had approached him once and he had turned her down, and that was that.'

'Kate, I don't think there is any point in beating this to death until you talk to Cam. He'll tell you what happened and you can either believe him or not, so why get all worked up until you know what's going on?'

'You're probably right,' I said. 'But I don't want to go home. I don't want to face him. What if I don't believe him?'

'Then I will drive you straight down to the police station and you can tell Detective Lincoln all about it. Then I will personally throw Cam out of your apartment and stay with you until you feel safe.'

'Really?'

'Of course.'

'You'd do that for me?'

'Anything, babe. I'll even drive you home now if you like.'

'How about in a little while?' I asked, wanting to avoid a confrontation as long as I could.

'Tell you what,' he suggested. 'Why don't you watch the play with me in the tech office and I'll drive you home later.'

'That would be nice,' I said.

'Does Cam know where you are?'

'I left a note for him saying I went out to dinner with a friend. He shouldn't be too worried.'

'I gotta go sweep the stage. Why don't you grab a couple of beers and come sit in the office before anyone else arrives?'

I stood up and got the beer while Scott turned the monitor off. We took the stage-right door and snuck around behind the blacks – the huge black curtains that hang downstage of the scenery. This provides a crossover area where cast and crew can move from stage-right to stage-left and keep the audience in the dark, literally. I could hear Graham dancing on the stage as we crossed. Scott tucked me into the corner of the tech office and turned the monitor on.

'Watch this,' he told me.

I turned and watched Graham dancing. Scott took the mike and switched it on. He cleared his throat and then held the mike close to his mouth. 'I warned you about being on my stage!' he bellowed.

In the monitor, I saw Graham almost fall off the stage in shock. 'Shit!' I heard him yell from the theatre. 'You said you weren't going to do that any more.'

'So stay off my stage, you junior butthead,' Scott yelled back, taking a broom out on to the stage. I stifled a giggle and took another sip of my beer.

Scott and I had a great time watching the play and giggling. Luckily the tech office is far enough from the stage that you can get away with a lot before having to worry about the audience hearing you. *Much Ado* is a low-tech show, so Scott and Trevor didn't have much to do except make fun of the actors. Dwayne sat in the technical booth, at the back of the auditorium, running the lights. After the show, Scott drove me home. He wanted to come up and make sure everything was OK, but by that time I had calmed down and was ready to talk with Cam.

I let myself in and found the apartment dark, except for a small light shining from the loft. I locked up, took off my coat, dropped it by the door, and climbed up quietly, not knowing if Cam was awake or asleep. He was awake, sitting up in bed with the latest copy of *Car and Driver*.

'Hi, Katie, did you have a good time tonight?' He smiled at me.

'Yes, I did actually.' I took off my clothes, feeling strangely self-conscious with him watching me. I pulled on my T-shirt quickly and sat on the side of the bed.

'How's the arm feeling?' he asked.

'Not bad.'

'Your bruises are fading nicely,' he said, touching my cheek gently.

'I feel much better,' I said. 'How was your run this afternoon?'

'Great. It was such a beautiful day out. I ran down to Prince's Island. Boy was it crowded.'

'I bet.'

'And you'll never guess who I ran into.'

I felt a chill of anticipation run down my spine. 'Who?' I asked innocently.

'Gladys Reynolds.'

'Really?' I didn't have to fake the shock in my voice.

'Yeah, I was just stretching by the bridge, and there she was.'

'What a surprise.' I hoped my voice didn't actually sound as icy as it felt in my throat.

'No kidding. I figured she should be home with the boys, welcoming the neighbours, or whatever it is you do after a funeral. But there she was, in shorts and sandals, eating an ice-cream cone, certainly not looking like she'd just buried a husband.'

'Did you talk to her?'

'I just got a quick hello,' he said, putting his magazine away. 'She said she was meeting someone so she didn't have much time.'

Cam had told me almost everything, without my having to ask. I should have felt relieved but, somehow, I didn't. I climbed over him and crawled under the covers.

'I missed you tonight,' he said, turning off the light and rolling over on to his side, watching me as I settled myself under the covers.

'Me too.'

He leaned over and kissed me.

'Cam, I'm really tired.'

'OK,' he said, moving closer and wrapping his arms around me. 'Sleep well and we'll see how you feel in the morning.'

'Good night,' I whispered, trying to sound sleepy.

'Love you,' he said.

'Me too.'

I fell into an uneasy sleep long after Cam's breathing had become regular.

Thursday

I woke up when I felt Cam stirring beside me. He got up, went downstairs and I heard him puttering about in the kitchen for a while. I could smell coffee, then I heard the front door open and close as he went out for a run. I snuggled back under the covers, the sun shining through the window and warming me. I fell asleep and didn't wake up until I heard the front door slam and the shower start. I rolled out of bed and headed slowly down the stairs even though I still felt exhausted. I think all the nervous tension I had been feeling for the past week was beginning to get to me. I knew I had to find some energy to get into the theatre. I hadn't been there for two days and could imagine the mounds of paperwork I would have to work my way through before I could even think of the night's show. I had better start drinking coffee now; I was going to need the caffeine in my system.

Cam had left his cigarettes on the table and I decided a smoke would taste good with my coffee. I lit one and sat down with the newspaper. Cam came out of the bathroom with a towel wrapped around his waist. I thought briefly about ripping the towel away, but couldn't work up the energy. I was in worse shape than I thought.

'Oh, now there's a healthy picture,' he said. 'Coffee and a cigarette before eight in the morning.' Oh, God was it only eight? 'And I bet you haven't had anything to eat, either,' he continued. 'I'll just throw some clothes on and make breakfast.'

He ran up the stairs and kept talking while he dressed.

'What would you like? I think there's some eggs left. Do you remember when you bought them? They're probably a

118

couple of months old, like everything else in your kitchen, aren't they? If they're OK, I could make eggs florentine. I think I saw some spinach in the freezer. That is if I can chip the box out of the ice. By the way, would you be insulted if I defrosted and disinfected your fridge?'

He was back downstairs and poured himself a coffee, refilling mine as well, before he put the pot back on the stove.

'Feel free to do anything you want to the fridge,' I said icily. He missed my vocal pun.

'We really need some groceries, but I'd like to do the fridge first, and maybe the oven too.'

'Whatever, Cam. You know I really don't understand things like defrosting fridges and cleaning ovens.'

'I think you understand just fine,' he laughed. 'You just avoid doing them until someone else comes along and offers to clean up for you. Or you move out when it gets too bad.'

'Well, if a system works, why change it?' I asked.

'So, do you know how old these eggs are?' He pulled the carton out of the fridge and looked for an expiry date.

'They're less than a year and more than a month old,' I said. 'I really can't remember when I bought them.'

'Well, should we risk it?' he asked.

'Sure, eggs would be nice,' I said.

'So, are you going in to the theatre tonight?' he asked.

'Yeah, I've already missed two nights in a row. I think that's a record for me. What time do you have to be in?'

'I told the Spaz I'd be there about nine thirty. He really wants to finish the inventory today.'

'That's too early for me,' I said. 'I need to do a load of laundry this morning. Maybe I'll get really motivated and dust or something.'

'Can I throw some stuff in the wash?' he asked.

'It'd be pretty rude of me to say no after you cooked breakfast for me.'

'Katie, are you OK?' he asked.

'I'm fine,' I said, not looking up from the newspaper. 'Just tired.'

'Are you sure? I want you to tell me if there's anything bothering you.'

119

'Why do you think something's wrong?' I asked, finally looking up at him.

'You seem different – quiet. Have I done something? Are you mad at me?'

I stood up and took my coffee cup over to the counter. 'I'm not mad, Cam, I promise. I'm just really stressed out.'

'I want you to promise me that if there's anything wrong, anything at all, that you'll talk to me about it,' he said.

'I will,' I promised, filling my coffee and watching him crack eggs and toast English muffins.

'I mean it.' He put his fork down and turned to me. 'If you're feeling crowded with me here, I don't want you to be afraid to say so. We need to be able to talk if this relationship is going to work.'

I hugged him, afraid the expression on my face might betray me. 'Cam, I swear that if something's bothering me, I'll talk to you about it.'

But I couldn't talk to him about this; about the fact that no matter what he had said last night, I was beginning to feel I couldn't trust him. Cam had been the one person who made me feel safe this past week – until now. As I hugged him, I felt very much alone.

We ate breakfast in relative silence. I was pretending to be my usual grumpy self, watching Cam wolf down his meal so he could get to work on time. He rinsed the dishes, gave me a quick kiss, and headed out the door.

When he was gone, I seriously thought about doing laundry but decided I would rather soak in the tub. I could drop some stuff off at the dry-cleaners instead.

Amazingly, by ten o'clock, after a long bath, I felt quite energetic. So rather than waste my energy on housework, I decided to go into the theatre early. I threw some clothes into a plastic bag, dropped them off at the cleaners on the main floor of my building and then walked to the C-Train. I figured I could get a couple of hours worth of work done and then find someone to have lunch with me. I really needed to get started on the schedule for the next show. I found it amazing how normal, everyday life kept happening, no matter what ugly events tried to interrupt. I could barely think ahead to closing-night the following weekend, let alone the fact there was already another play in rehearsal, about to hit the stage in three weeks.

Nick was sitting at the security desk, drinking coffee and looking much more bored than he should be at this early stage of a shift.

'Hey, Nick, what's up?' I asked as I signed my name into the log.

'Absolutely nothing and boy am I enjoying it,' he smiled. 'How about you?'

'Where's the Spaz today? He hasn't left you alone for the last week.'

'For the next four hours he's locked upstairs, in the main conference room, stuck in a board meeting he has no way of getting out of. I intend to sit here with my feet up for each of those four hours.'

'Well, unlike you, I work for a living, so I'm about to go and bury myself in a pile of paper for the next four hours.'

'Well, I'll be thinking of you, Kate, while I'm sitting here doing nothing.' He smiled.

'I really appreciate that. Have you seen Cam around?'

'No, but I don't think he's due in until noon today. Management has been on the Spaz's case about the amount of overtime the maintenance department has been pulling this week.'

'Oh?' I felt that icy feeling in my stomach again. 'Well, tell him I'll buy him a coffee when he gets in, OK?'

'Sure thing, and try to keep your keys in your pocket today, OK?' he instructed.

'Yes, yes, yes.' I started down Tin Pan Alley, towards the backstage area of my theatre.

'And keep your office door locked,' he yelled after me as he buzzed me through the security door.

I pretended I couldn't hear him as the door closed behind me. Besides, I was much too busy worrying about Cam lying to me again to care about Nick's warnings.

I got out my keys and let myself into the dark hallway at the back of the theatre, cutting through the stage – something I was not encouraged to do without a technician at my side – out the other side and into the public corridor. I took the fire-escape stairs up one flight to my office. I propped open the door and started the coffee. It is always my automatic reaction to dive into work while my brain tries to deal with what was happening to me.

I tried to balance the deposit sheets that were sitting on my desk and failed miserably. I tried working on the inventory sheets, and then on the schedule, but they were both beyond my powers of concentration. Finally, I dumped the deposits on my desk and started to roll coins. That I could manage.

I watched the clock nervously, waiting for twelve o'clock to arrive. I didn't know what I was going to say to Cam, but I decided I had to confront him. I couldn't keep pretending that everything was all right, and I couldn't bear the thought of going home to him that night if I was still feeling that way. I had to know. I had to ask him and look straight into his eyes while he answered me. I had to find out whether he loved me or was lying to me. I knew I would be able to tell. Then I looked up to check the clock again and he was there.

'Oh God!' I jumped a foot out of my chair and tried to grab my coffee before it tipped over. 'You scared me.'

'Sorry, Katie. I thought you would hear me coming. I didn't mean to sneak up on you.'

'You didn't come in at nine this morning.' I had decided to be subtle and break into the conversation slowly. Obviously I was not doing a great job.

'What do you mean?' he asked.

'Don't lie to me, Cam. You've been lying a lot recently and I need to know why.'

'I was here, Katie, at the Plex. I came straight here after I left the apartment.'

'Cam, when I signed in, Nick hadn't seen you yet. I saw your keys hanging on the board right under your name tag and I bet your radio was there too.'

'OK, it's true.' He sat down in the chair across from me. 'I was here. I just wasn't working, I was at Vaudevilles.'

'You were with Gladys again, weren't you?'

'No, I was with Detective Lincoln. We met at the restaurant and had a coffee,' he admitted.

'Why are you doing this to me?' I was hurt by his admission

and covering my feelings with anger. 'How can I trust you any more?'

'Katie, I only lied to protect you.'

'Well, Cam, that's not very reassuring. I seem to have someone chasing me and I'm starting to think it's you.'

'Katie—' he tried to interrupt me, but I was on a roll.

'And why shouldn't I, when you've lied to me twice in the past two days?'

'What do you mean, twice?' he asked.

'You lied about meeting Gladys on Prince's Island yesterday,' I said shortly.

'How would you know that?' he asked. 'You promised you would stay in the apartment.'

'Well, I broke that promise. I saw you on the island, I saw you waiting at the bridge for someone, and then I saw you give Gladys a very friendly greeting.'

'All right, it was me she was meeting there. I needed to talk to her.'

'About what? Your involvement in the murder of her husband? Or perhaps the affair you had with her that you insist on denying.'

'Katie, it's not what you're thinking.'

'Well, what is it then?' I demanded. 'It had better be the truth and it had better be good. I'm finding it hard to believe anything you say.'

'OK. Let's start with Gladys. She is a close friend of my wife – I mean ex-wife. I've known Gladys for years. I asked her to meet me at the island because I wanted to convince her to talk to you and ask you to get out of the investigating business. You may not believe it, but she was as upset as I was about your attack, and she is as concerned about you as I am.'

'Oh, right. That would be why she asked me to help out in the first place.'

'It's true, Katie. I asked her to call you and tell you anything she could think of to get you to back off.'

'If she was friends with your ex-wife, why didn't I know about it? I hung around with Gladys for almost a year on a regular basis.'

'Gladys is a strange woman. Haven't you ever noticed that she keeps all aspects of her life very private? I bet you could tell me everything about what happened to her here at the Plex, but do you know one single thing about the rest of her life?' he asked. His eyes looked as angry as I felt.

'Not really,' I admitted.

'Well that's the way it was. I bet you didn't even know she had other friends. Did you ever hear her mention any friends, or anything she did outside of this building?'

'No, I didn't,' I said quietly.

'Well, that's the way she liked it. She was always worried that I might say something. She talked to me about it before she started working here. I had to swear up and down that I would never admit I knew her, and when she came over to my house, I never heard anything about her work here. You would never have known that she even had this job. Patsy would try and ask how certain shows had been, or if she'd made any new friends, but Gladys always changed the subject. It used to make Patsy crazy. I think she thought she could get some inside gossip on what I did during the day.'

'OK. I'll buy most of this so far.'

'When I met her at the island, Gladys told me that she wasn't going to waste her breath trying to talk to you. She knows how stubborn you are and told me the more we tried to talk you out of something, the more you would want to do the opposite.'

'What about today? If you were meeting Ken, why couldn't you tell me?' I asked. 'What's the big secret?'

'He wanted to talk to me about the funeral and the people we talked to.'

'Well, why didn't he call me too?' I asked.

'I told him I wouldn't talk to him if you came along. I didn't want you to get all excited again about finding the killer. You've hardly said anything about it in the last day, and I was hoping you were losing interest.'

'Oh, I get it.' I felt my anger flare again. 'You couldn't change my mind, so instead you decided it would be better to lie to me.'

'God, Katie, only with the best of intentions. I don't want

you to get hurt. I have been worried sick about you.' He shook his head, not knowing what to else to say.

'Did you think I wouldn't find out?' I asked.

'I hoped you wouldn't, but I knew you might. I knew you'd be pissed when you did find out, but I decided I would rather have you safe and alive and hating me than dead.'

I got up and poured myself a coffee. Then I turned my back on Cam and stared out the window, not knowing what to say. I was still torn. Trust was never one of my strong points. Could I forgive him?

'Do you want me to leave?' he finally asked.

I turned around and walked over to where he sat, then punched his shoulder, as hard as I could. 'Damn you! Don't you ever lie to me again! About anything!'

'I am so sorry, Katie.'

'I mean it. You know about my past relationships.' I hit him again. 'You know how hard it is for me to trust anyone. How dare you lie to me, for whatever noble reason you may come up with?'

I hit him once more for good measure. I was really starting to feel better.

'Katie, I will do anything in the world to make you believe me,' Cam promised.

'And don't fucking call me Katie!' I like this getting rid of my hostility stuff. I was suddenly beginning to see why primal scream therapy had caught on. I would have to do this more often.

He stood up, rubbing his shoulder where I had hit him. 'I'll leave.'

It was now or never, I thought, to forgive and forget or to end our relationship. Suddenly, I realized that no matter what he had done, I couldn't bear the thought of losing him right now.

'Wait,' I said.

He turned and looked at me.

'I don't want to lose you, Cam, but I need you to tell me that you will never lie to me again.'

'I swear it.' He smiled. 'But I'm still going to call you Katie.'

I smiled back. 'I can't believe I thought you were the killer.'

'Why?'

125

'You're too sensitive, you could never murder anyone.'

'How do you know this isn't all an act?' he asked, still smiling at me.

I moved closer and hugged him, wishing he hadn't made that last remark. There were some things I just didn't find funny any more. 'Maybe you should just shut up while you're ahead of the game,' I told him.

Cam kissed me, but then his radio summoned him to some emergency, so he left me and headed off to work. I sat back down at my desk and found I was able to concentrate much better now. I actually saw those stacks of reports getting smaller.

'Yo, boss, am I happy to see you!'

I jumped out of my chair again. This time I didn't save my coffee before it tipped over. I grabbed some paper towels and started swabbing up the mess. 'What is it with everyone today? Are you all trying to give me a heart attack?'

'Sorry,' Graham said, flopping down in a chair. 'I'm just glad to see you.'

'Did you have problems with the shows?' I asked. 'Or are you just stressed from making all the big decisions by your-self for the last two days?'

'No, the work stuff was fine.' He pulled an orange juice out of his backpack and shook it up. 'But I have lots to tell you about my investigation.'

I felt my interest growing. 'Really?'

'Yes, really. I spent the last two nights sitting in the BOB until all hours while several drunks poured their hearts out to me.'

'Well, fucking A,' I said. 'Maybe we are finally going to get somewhere with this.'

'Haven't you been successful?' he asked, almost gloating.

'No, all I've accomplished over the last few days is several very loud fights with Cam.'

'Well, I know a lot more about some of our leading sus-pects now than I did a couple of days ago.'

I cleared everything off my desk and pulled a legal pad out of the drawer, ready to take notes, before turning my atten-tion back to Graham.

'OK, what have you got?'

He smiled and took another swig of his juice, enjoying making me wait.

'Anytime soon,' I suggested.

'OK, OK. Keep your britches on.' He finished his juice and tossed the bottle into the recycling bin. 'Two points!' he cheered when he hit the can.

'One of these days you're going to miss and you're going to have a hell of a mess to clean up.'

'I don't miss, Kate. Anyway, the first person I ran into was Burns. I guess that wasn't much of a surprise. He was pretty well corked by the time I got to the bar and I spent most of Tuesday night with him. He has some real trust problems, you know? It took me hours to get him to open up and I had to bitch about you a lot.'

'So, what did he have to say?' I asked, ignoring his last comment.

'Well, he's very bitter, as predicted. Doesn't see his wife or kids any more, just sends alimony cheques to the lawyer's office. That's why he's still working here. Needs all the extra money he can get to keep up those payments. Apparently his wife cleaned him out really good. He also really hates Gladys, again as predicted. But strangely enough, he isn't fond of you either.'

'Me? Why?' I asked. 'Guilt by association?'

'No, it turns out he applied for your job, the same time you did, but he didn't even get an interview. He thinks you told Foothills Stage Network some stories about his behaviour and that cost him the chance to work here. He thinks the job would have been his if it wasn't for you.'

'Well, that's interesting, but it doesn't really help us much,' I said, flipping to a clean page.

'Don't be so quick to brush him off, Kate. He's a very bitter man who might stoop to anything to get even. He as much as told me he would do anything to get back at Gladys. Even asked me if I had any ideas.'

'So, do you think he was desperate enough to murder Gladys's husband then try and frame her for it?' I asked.

'Well, there is only one drawback to that idea,' Graham observed.

'Yeah?'

'He's pretty much drunk all the time, or so the bartender told me. I don't know if he could stay sober long enough to plan something like this.'

'Maybe he could if he finally thought he was going to get his revenge,' I suggested.

'Maybe.' Graham didn't look convinced. 'What about an alibi for Thursday night?'

'He said he was in the bar most of the night. The bartender thought he remembered him being there, but couldn't be sure. I guess Burns is like a fixture in the bar. Nobody really notices him any more.'

'Well that doesn't help a lot – or answer any of our questions.'

'It's something we can look into later, and a warning for you too, Kate. He wouldn't mind getting even with you, either. You should probably keep your eye on him.'

'Idle talk from a drunk,' I said. 'I'm not too concerned about him, and I don't think he'll be around the Plex much longer anyway. He's on his last warning for being late, being drunk, being rude, or any combination of the above.'

'Well, just remember what I said,' Graham warned.

'OK, I'm warned. Who's next?' I asked.

'I ran into Gene at Gus's place.'

'You went to Grounds Zero?' I asked.

'Yes and Gus almost dropped to the floor when he saw me come in. But I saw Gene go there on Wednesday afternoon and figured I might not have a better opportunity to talk to him.'

'So, how is Gene?'

'Well, Gene is now practicing some sort of strange Eastern religion. He found peace, harmony, and free love with a group of people he met at an airport in Germany. He was apparently quite heartbroken when Gladys dumped him, so I guess these religious people found him at the most opportune moment and took advantage. It must have worked, because boy, is he mellow.'

'Really?'

'Yeah, swears he's celibate and only came back to town to finish up some business here so he could head back and become a missionary, or whatever it is these people do. He also wanted to make peace with Gladys. He told me it was bad karma to have things end the way they did, and he needed to know that she loved his spirit and forgave him his human frailties or he could never be at peace with the universe.'

'He's hooked,' I commented.

'You should have seen him. From the look in his eyes, I would have sworn he was stoned.'

'Could it be an act?'

'While we were in Grounds Zero, he stopped Gus from killing a fly. He spent twenty minutes chasing the stupid thing through the restaurant before he finally caught it and let it outside. After seeing that, I'm pretty sure he couldn't kill anyone.'

'Graham, you're not helping us. All we're doing is eliminating everyone from the list.'

'Have you or Cam talked to Douglas yet?'

'We spoke to him at the funeral,' I said. 'He may be a stuck-up arrogant jerk, but I guess we've ruled him out as the murderer. He was away from the Concert Hall on Thursday night, at about the right time, but no one here saw him hanging around.'

'So that leaves us with Jeremy Rawson, our friendly caterer,' Graham said.

'Have you spoken to him yet?' I asked.

'Nope. I haven't seen him anywhere. I'm starting to think he's avoiding us. You're going to have to take him on yourself. Pretend you want to talk about a special event or something.'

'That's easy enough to do,' I said. 'We've got an opening-night party coming up in a couple of weeks. It won't seem too strange if I want to see him about that.'

'You know what I think?' Graham asked.

'What?'

'I think we've missed someone. Everyone on our list seems to have ironclad alibis except Gladys – but then she seems to have absolutely no motive and no access to the murder weapon. Maybe we're looking at this the wrong way.'

'What do you mean?'

129

'I don't know for sure, but maybe there's another angle to this, other than Gladys's involvement.'

'Like someone trying to frame Cam . . .' I said, thinking out loud.

'Could be,' he nodded. 'Maybe we should find out who doesn't like Cam.'

'What if Peter Reynolds was just in the wrong place at the wrong time? What if someone stole that hammer, knowing Cam was the last person to sign it out, and then they just waited for someone to come into the bathroom? Maybe it doesn't really matter who was killed.' I was speaking rapidly, afraid I might lose this train of thought if I didn't get it out quickly.

'That sounds like a plot out of a bad novel,' he said.

'Think about it, Graham. What if the fact that it was Peter Reynolds, who was the ex-husband of one of the Plex staff, was only a horrible coincidence?'

'Does someone hate Cam that much?' he asked.

'I don't know, but maybe I should find out.'

'Maybe.'

'I'll talk to Cam tonight. We should talk to Detective Lincoln too.' Then I glanced at the clock and noticed it was getting late. 'But for now, let's get back into theatre mode. I haven't been here for two days and you are going to help me with this mound of paperwork. When we finish that you can explain to me why you go on to an empty stage that you're not supposed to be on, in an empty theatre, and sing and dance your heart out.'

'You saw me?' he asked. 'Shit, I can't get away with anything around here, can I?'

'Not as long as I'm in charge.' I handed him the bag of coins I had been rolling. 'But you can try to make it up to me by starting with these.'

'Not fair,' he said.

'Very fair, when you consider that I have to try to balance your deposits for the last two nights. How can you be over by two hundred dollars?' I asked. 'We don't sell anything for more than fifteen dollars. How difficult is this?'

'OK, I'll roll coins. You knew I couldn't balance anything when you hired me.'

'When you're finished with the coins you can go down and start a complete inventory.'

'Aw, Kate . . .' he began.

'You haven't done an inventory for two days, Graham, it won't kill you,' I insisted.

'OK, but I'll have to sing onstage later, to let my artist's spirit free after hours of endless brain-dead counting,' he said, getting to his feet.

'Like I said, you'll live.'

'I may live, but I won't like it,' he said as he left.

Graham counted and I spent several hours trying to balance his messed-up deposits. It took me until almost four o'clock. When I finished he was still down in the main lobby, counting T-shirts and redesigning the displays for that night's show. I always let him set the displays up and later, when he was out of the immediate vicinity, I would rework them. Graham had problems restraining his artistic expression in every way, including setting up T-shirt displays. I piled all the reports into my in tray. I didn't feel like diving into the schedule right then, but I did feel the urge to walk over to the catering offices before they closed. I pulled out my file for *Rock and Roll*, our next show, then grabbed a copy of the script I had been reading and threw it in for good measure. I made sure my keys were in my pocket and headed for the main lobby.

I heard something from *The Phantom of the Opera* coming from the lobby and followed the music to where Graham stood, obliviously belting out the tune as he folded T-shirts.

'You need to sing something with a faster tempo,' I admonished him. 'Then maybe you would work faster.'

'I know you grew up with that horrible disco mistake of the seventies, but I don't do the Hustle.'

'So I've noticed.' I figured he had at least another hour's worth of work left. 'I'm heading over to catering and then I'm going to grab some takeout. Do you want me to bring anything back for you?'

'Yeah, a vegetarian on wholewheat, please.'

'I can't believe you really expose your body to so much healthy stuff, Graham. When was the last time you had a hamburger and fries?'

131

He ignored me. I ducked in behind the Hollywood Bar and out through the service corridor. It opens straight on to the Meeting Place, which is where the catering offices are located.

The Meeting Place is a small annexed corner on the second level. There are stairs that lead straight down to Restaurant Row, and straight up to the Improv Arena. There are four meeting rooms, the catering office, and a set of washrooms. The washrooms are a blessing, because none of the designers had thought to put in appropriate plumbing for dish-washing or coffee preparation in the meeting rooms. So, if you arrive early for a meeting and went to the washroom, chances are you'll find an usher at the sink, making the coffee for your meeting. I have never thought that was such a good idea, but the Plex seem to think it's much better than putting in new plumbing and a food prep room.

The designer had tried for an Italian look in this area, but heaven only knows why. All of the meeting rooms and offices have big windows with shutters for privacy and red, white, and green striped awnings. Wicker furniture sits outside the rooms, and lots of trailing ivy and grapevines hang on the walls. It is slightly pretentious, but comfortable.

Catering had the shutters open, which meant there were no high-level meetings going on and anyone could barge right in, so I did. Luckily the secretary wasn't there, so I walked through the common area and straight into Jeremy Rawson's office.

Jeremy is a bit of a mystery to me. He's a small man, both in height and girth, with straight blonde hair, nondescript brown eyes, and glasses. He isn't very outgoing and usually only engages in conversation when he has to. He would be described as mousy if he were a woman, yet he was never alone. Women seem to gravitate to him – beautiful women. I have never really seen the attraction, but maybe that's because I'm dating someone. Perhaps Jeremy has something he turned on and off when eligible women are around him.

Jeremy sat at his desk, typing furiously at his computer, his back to me. I knocked lightly on his door, not wanting to startle him by barging right in. Once in a while I could be subtle.

'Come in,' Jeremy called and then looked over his shoulder to see who was there. 'Oh, hi Kate.'

'Hi Jeremy, I came by to talk about opening night,' I said casually.

'Have a seat,' he said, turning back to his computer and clearing the screen.

I am envious of these offices. They are located in the public areas, so are painted every year; they have furniture that doesn't need reupholstering, and oak desks and filing cabinets. A far cry from the office where I spend most of my days.

Jeremy finished playing with his computer and pulled a file out of the drawer labelled FOOTHILLS STAGE NETWORK.

'OK, *Rock and Roll*. Opening night in two weeks, right?' He looked up from his paperwork to confirm with me.

'Yes.'

'Kate, I must say, it's a little early to be doing this. You know I don't meet with the chef until a week before opening.'

'I just wanted to make sure that you had everything you needed,' I lied.

'I do, thanks.' He closed the file and looked ready to end our conversation.

'Actually, there was something else I wanted to talk to you about,' I began.

'I don't think so,' he said, turning his back on me as he put the file away.

'Excuse me?' I was startled by his response.

'I know what you want to talk about, and I don't wish to discuss the matter.'

'I'm not sure I know what you're talking about,' I tried.

'That's not going to work with me,' he said, sitting back at his desk. 'You want to talk to me about the murder of Peter Reynolds and my relationship with his widow. Am I correct?'

'Well, I had hoped to get into it much more subtly than this,' I said. 'But, yes, you're right.'

'I'm sorry, but I have no intention of discussing that with you. So, is there anything else?' he asked abruptly.

'Jeremy, why don't you want to talk about this?' I asked.

'All right, that I'll answer. First of all, my private life is none of your business or that of anyone else who works in this building. I have had enough rumours spread about me to last a lifetime. I have decided that will not happen any longer, so my private life is strictly off-limits. Secondly, you are not an official investigator on this case. I have spoken to the police already; I do not have to speak to you. I find this whole affair appalling. I also feel that if people, like you, insist on sticking their noses into this and asking questions, they will damage the Plex's reputation. Therefore, I do not wish to participate in any conversations with you about the murder. Do I make myself clear?' he said in a calm, clear voice.

'Yes, you do,' I said. 'But I want you to know that Detective Lincoln and I are in close contact. I intend to mention your reluctance to discuss this with him. Perhaps he will want to come back and talk to you again.' My not so subtle stab at a veiled threat.

'You do that, Kate, at which point, I'm sure he'll tell you that I offered an ironclad alibi for that night, and that the thirty or so witnesses I provided have already confirmed with the police that I was nowhere near this building last Thursday. Now, is there anything else?' he asked, standing up.

I felt stupid and decided a graceful exit would be quite appropriate. 'Just let me know when you have the menu ready for opening night,' I said, edging toward the door.

'I always do.'

I left the office quickly, taking the stairs down to Restaurant Row two at a time, hoping to outrun the humiliation I felt. I picked up a couple of sandwiches from the deli and took the elevator back up to the theatre. Graham was sitting in my office filling out time sheets when I got back. I set his sandwich in front of him and sat in the window.

'Well, have a nice talk with Jeremy?' he asked, tearing into the plastic wrap covering his dinner.

'Let's just say I had a talk with him. We can take him off our list, too.'

'What did he have to say?' Graham asked.

'I really don't want to talk about it.'

I bit into my sandwich. I figured that if I had a full mouth I couldn't answer any more questions. Graham raised an eyebrow. Curiosity was burning in his eyes but he said nothing. I guess he had worked with me long enough to know when I meant what I said. After several bites of my sandwich, my pride once again intact, I felt ready to start talking again.

'So we really have no suspects left,' I said.

'Unless you count Gladys,' Graham pointed out.

'The jury is still out on that one,' I said. 'I just don't think she did it. But I can't really rule her out until we find out where she was between the time she left here and the time she signed in at the Concert Hall on Thursday night.'

'OK, so other than Gladys, no, we don't have any suspects left,' Graham agreed. 'We must be really good at this to prove everyone innocent so quickly. What do you think?'

'Well, we're not the world's greatest detectives but I don't think we're totally stupid,' I said, not really believing it myself at this point. 'I think we're on the right track though, Graham. I don't think any of these people did it. We just have to find a new angle.'

'That Cam has an enemy somewhere?' Graham asked.

'It seems like the next best assumption. He has been made to look like the prime suspect and we know he didn't do it. Someone is trying awfully hard to make it seem like he's the killer.'

'OK,' Graham said between bites. 'What about his ex-wife?'

'Patsy,' I said, feeling uneasy.

'Is that her name?' Graham asked.

'Yes, but that's about all I know about her.'

'Why did they split up?'

'I have absolutely no idea,' I said. 'Cam and I don't really talk about our past relationships. He never wants to talk about his marriage.'

'Have you ever met her?'

'Never,' I admitted.

'That's strange.'

'Why?'

'You're living with the man, Kate. You tell me you know nothing about his ex-wife?'

'Like I said, we prefer not to talk about the past,' I said with a touch of irritation in my voice.

'So he never bitches about her? They don't have fights about alimony or anything?'

'Not that I've ever heard of. I just assumed it was a fairly civilized divorce.'

'Maybe you need to talk to Cam about her tonight,' Graham suggested.

'Do you think that we should seriously consider his ex-wife – who I don't think has ever even entered this building – as a suspect?'

'To begin with,' Graham said, wadding his plastic wrap up and throwing it into the garbage can. 'That's always the way it happens in the movies.'

'I keep telling you to remember that this is real life, not the movies.'

'OK, OK. What about people here at the Plex?' he asked.

'Cam is probably the most loved person here. Everybody likes him,' I assured him.

'You're right. I've never heard anything bad about him from anyone. But maybe he had a fight with someone. Or maybe he got a raise when someone else didn't. Who knows? Frankly, I'm stumped.'

'Me too.' I wadded my plastic up and tossed it towards the garbage can. When I missed, as usual, Graham leaned over and picked it up for me.

'Want to try two out of three?' he asked.

'Don't be a smart-ass,' I said. 'Do you think we're in over our heads, Graham?'

'Of course we are,' he said. 'But that's not the point. The point is we are trying to help Cam. Do you trust the police to exonerate him?'

'No, I don't. I just keep thinking that if they hit a dead end, Cam might be an easy out for them. There's lots of circumstantial evidence here. Maybe enough to indict him.'

'Well, do you want to keep this up?' he asked.

'I want to find out who did this.' I held up my cast. 'And I wouldn't mind getting a shot at him before the police do.'

'Well?'

'I guess we just keep blundering onwards,' I said. 'Follow our instincts and best guesses and watch all the repeats of

Murder, She Wrote. Jessica Fletcher always seems to figure out who did it. Maybe we can learn something from her.'

'Actually, I've been rereading my *Compendium of Mystery Theatre*,' Graham said.

'Has it helped?'

'Not in the least. Remember this is real life, Kate, not the movies.'

'You're right, and in real life we only have one hour to get ready for the show. I'll start the coffee,' I offered.

'Only because you're going to drink it,' Graham said. 'Why don't I ever get the easy jobs?'

'Because you're not the boss. You know, the under-qualified overpaid pain in the butt that always makes you do the jobs she doesn't like doing?'

'Oh, yeah, now I remember. So what horrible lowlife job don't you want to do right now?' he asked.

'I really don't want to stock the bars,' I said. 'I would much rather you did it, for the experience. Then I can get started on the scheduling for *Rock and Roll*, which I seem to have been putting off all day.'

'OK, I'll do the bars,' he gave in. 'I've already done the sign-in sheets for tonight.'

'Good. We've got the floats ready and you've done your lovely displays so we can rook the public out of their hard-earned dollars. As soon as we change, we should be ready for another night in paradise.'

'With another sold-out show,' Graham said.

'How long do you think this sold-out run will last?' I asked. 'Are they never going to forget that a murder took place here?'

'I hope not,' Graham said. 'If these big houses keep up, I might stand a chance of getting a raise.'

'Don't hold your breath on that one. You know that every single extra dollar we make will be put on stage with the most lavish scenery since *Phantom of the Opera*. You know what they say about Krueger, our hallowed leader? He directs the best scenery in the business. It's actors he has a problem with.'

'Krueger?' he asked.

'Shit, I shouldn't have said that. But it's more polite than

137

Pizza Face,' I said. 'You'd better swear this goes no further. It's what they call Russell, our artistic director. Freddy Krueger. You know, the burn victim with the claws from *Nightmare on Elm Street*? I personally think it's a great comparison.'

'I promise it will go no further,' Graham assured me. 'There's no way I would risk having Mr Dyck hear me call him that. He could hurt me.'

'Yes, he could,' I agreed. 'And worse, he can make sure that you never act in this city.'

'A fate worse than death.'

'OK, get out of here. I want to change and get back to work.'

He grabbed a liquor inventory sheet from the filing cabinet and headed for the stairs.

'Is this punishment for not balancing the deposits for the last two nights?' he asked as he started down the hall.

'Think of it as character building,' I yelled back.

'I think I have about enough character for one lifetime, Kate.'

That was the last time I heard from him as the door at the far end of the hall closed. I noticed his key sitting on my desk so I took a doorstop down and propped the fire door open. That way he could get back in. If security found it they would scream bloody murder but they weren't due on their rounds for another half-hour or so. Once a month I went down to security, got a lecture on fire safety and keys, then reclaimed all my doorstops.

When I came back to my office, I heard a song from *Les Mis* coming over the office speaker as Graham cut through the theatre to the bar in the upper lobby. You just can't shut that boy up.

I decided to get dressed before I got down to work so that I wouldn't have to stop and change later. I picked a nice drop-waist summer print off the rack and a pair of pumps to go with it. A quick glance in my mirror and I decided I didn't need to freshen my make-up. I took the dress off the hanger, grabbed a pair of pantyhose and went around the corner into the ladies' room. I left my keys on the desk, knowing this was the one place I could go in this building where there were no locked doors to get through.

I stripped off my jeans and sweater and pulled on my pantyhose. God I hate those things. I'm sure they were designed by a man. No woman would ever come up with an idea like pantyhose. I slipped the dress over my head and smiled. It was the prettiest dress I owned, garnered me lots of compliments every time I wore it, and felt like an old nightgown, broken in and comfortable. As I bent down to put on my shoes I heard a noise in the hall.

'I'm in the bathroom, Graham, I'll be right out,' I yelled.

I finished dressing and decided I looked good. I was having one of the best days I'd had in a week. I felt good about Cam again, was totally caught up at work, and had had a great afternoon with Graham. He always lightens my mood.

I folded my jeans and sweater and took one last look in the mirror before I headed for the door. I pushed the door, but it didn't open. I pushed again, not quite understanding what was wrong. It still wouldn't open. I took a deep breath, feeling panic beginning in the pit of my stomach. I didn't want to panic because I knew that if I stayed calm I could figure this out. I set my clothes on the counter and walked back to the door. I pushed with both hands but it didn't budge, so I threw all my weight against it, with the same results. This door didn't have any sort of latch on it and I couldn't understand why it wouldn't open.

I decided to try a new approach. I pounded my fist on the door and panicked.

'Graham!' I yelled. 'Graham, are you there?'

There was no reply, so I pounded harder and yelled some more. I totally gave up on trying to control my panic and started screaming and pounding on the door, almost completely out of control. Ten minutes later I gave that up too. My throat felt raw from screaming and my fist hurt. I sat on the counter and wished I had a cigarette. I tried to concentrate on my nicotine craving and not on who had locked me in. I had to believe that as long as I was locked in, I was safe. Someone was just trying to scare me.

In another ten minutes, I heard singing in the hall. I jumped off the counter and ran back to the door.

'Graham!' I yelled, pounding on the door again. 'Graham, let me out.'

'Kate? Where are you?'

'In the bathroom,' I yelled back. 'I can't get the door open.'

I heard some scraping sounds and then Graham pulled the door open. I wrapped my arms around him, relieved.

'Thank you,' I said as I kissed his cheek.

He blushed slightly and pulled back from me. 'What's going on? This was wedged under the door.'

He held up a doorstop. I let go of him and straightened my dress. 'I think someone was trying to send me another warning,' I said carefully.

'How long have you been in here?'

'About twenty minutes,' I said. 'Way too long.'

'We better call security,' Graham said, heading toward my desk.

'Why?' I asked. 'So they can search for someone who has had over twenty minutes to get away? I don't think so.'

'Kate, Cam will kill me if I don't make you report this,' Graham warned.

I grabbed my clothes from the counter. 'I don't want to talk about it right now. I'd also rather not discuss it in the bathroom. I think I've been in here long enough for one day.' I shuddered involuntarily.

I pushed past him and into my office, set my clothes on the window ledge, poured a coffee, and sat down at my desk.

'What's this?' I asked, holding up a Foothills Stage envelope with my name on it.

'I don't know,' Graham said. 'I haven't been into the office yet. I went straight to the bathroom when I heard you screaming.'

I ripped open the envelope. 'Shit,' I whispered, suddenly scared again. 'Call Cam, call security, and call the police. Ask for Detective Lincoln.'

'What's it say?' he asked.

'Please call security, now,' I begged him.

He picked up the phone and dialled the security desk. 'Hi Nick, it's Graham at Centenary. There's been another problem up here. Can you page Cam for Kate, and get up here. Call the police, too.' There was a moment of silence and then Graham continued. 'No, she's OK. But she looks like she's seen a ghost. I think you better get Cam up here fast, OK?'

He hung up as I reread the note.

Dear Kate,

Just wanted to remind you that I was watching you. Don't get overconfident now. I told you to stop asking questions and I meant it. I'm getting quite tired of having to remind you. So I've taken the liberty of borrowing the keys to your apartment for a while. Also, you shouldn't be wearing black panties with a white dress. Very tacky. See how vulnerable you really are.

Your friend.

Someone grabbed the letter from my hand. I looked up and saw Cam standing beside me.

'We should be careful with this, just in case he left some fingerprints on the paper. Or the doorstop,' I added, turning to look at Graham.

'Are you all right?' Cam asked, ignoring my warning as he finished reading the note and switched it to his other hand.

'Cam, please put that down on the desk. I don't want anyone to touch it until Detective Lincoln gets here. Graham, put the doorstop down too.'

Cam dropped the letter and Graham set the doorstop beside it.

'Are you all right?' Cam asked again.

'I'm fine,' I said. 'He just wanted to scare me.'

'Well he scared me,' Cam said. 'When I heard the call on the radio I figured he'd finally made good on his promise to shut you up.'

'He didn't, Cam. I'm OK. But he's got the keys to the loft.'

'Don't worry about that. We'll get the police to take us home tonight and I'll call George and have him meet us there.' George is the Plex's handyman and locksmith. 'I'll pick up a

141

new lock from the supply room and George can change it tonight,' he continued.

'Will he do that for you?' I asked. 'We won't be home until after midnight.'

'I've covered some shifts for him,' Cam said. 'He owes me one anyway, and when I tell him why we need the locks changed, he'll definitely be there.'

'OK, then I'm not going to worry about the apartment. There's nothing there that can't be replaced.' I held out my coffee cup to Graham and noticed my hand was shaking. 'Can I get a refill?'

'Sure, Boss,' he said, taking my cup.

'Can I have a cigarette, Cam?' I smiled weakly at him. He reached into his pocket and handed me a smoke, without a lecture this time. 'There's just one thing I want you guys to know,' I said.

'What's that?' Cam asked, lighting my cigarette for me.

'I am fucking sick and tired of being scared.' I felt all the unused adrenalin flooding my veins. 'I've been scared for the last week, wondering if someone was following me, waiting for me to be alone for one minute so they could come after me. I didn't ask for any of this to happen, and I am goddamned sick and fucking tired of feeling like this.'

'Katie, calm down—'

'No! I am going to find out who this asshole is, and I am going to fucking see him in jail, if it's the last thing I do. He may think he's going to scare me into crawling off into a corner somewhere, but all he has succeeded in doing is really pissing me off.' I felt like a ranting maniac.

'Katie—'

'No way, Cam, I am not going to calm down. I am going to find out who is doing this to me,' I exploded. 'I want my life back.'

Graham reached over timidly and set my coffee in front of me. I heard the security guards coming down the hall and I also heard a police siren in the distance, approaching the Plex.

'Feel better now that you've got that out?' Cam asked.

'A little,' I admitted. 'But I meant what I said.'

'OK,' Cam said. 'Then we are going to find this guy. We're going to stop pussyfooting around and find out who did it.'

'But what if he comes after Kate again?' Graham asked. 'I mean, look what he's done already and we've been fairly subtle so far. What's he going to do when we're more aggressive?'

'Graham, he's come after Kate three times so far. I don't think he's going to stop even if we back off right now. I think somehow we're really close to finding out what this is all about. We don't realize who or what it is we've stumbled across, but *he* does and I think he's scared that we're going to finally put it all together. So, the way I see it, even if we stop now, *he* won't.'

Way to go, Cam, I thought, he must be getting angry about this too, just like me.

'So now we get aggressive,' Graham said. 'And what about Kate?'

'What about me?' I asked.

'You're obviously in danger,' Graham said.

'That's the easy part. This guy has never had the balls to go after her when she's with someone else, so we make sure she's not alone. Ever.'

'That's true,' I said. 'He's done everything when I'm alone. He's either scared of crowds, or men. We're all asking questions, but I'm the only one he's bothered with.'

'So we're dealing with a coward,' Graham said. 'Someone who thinks he can scare a woman by spying on her and pushing her around a bit.'

'He's obviously never lived with Katie,' Cam commented, 'or he'd know it's not such a good idea to push her around.'

'He's obviously never worked for her either,' Graham added.

'I'm going to take that as a compliment,' I said. 'Now where are the police? I want to get on with this.'

'They're on their way up,' Nick said from the doorway. 'We've done a complete search of the theatre and it's empty.'

'Thanks for checking so quickly,' Cam said, and then he turned back to me, disappointed. 'I was hoping we could catch this guy.'

'I figured the creep would be long gone,' I said. 'I spent over twenty minutes locked in the bathroom.'

'The bastard has got keys,' Nick said. 'This place was locked up tight as a drum when we got here.'

'Have you found any keys missing?' I asked.

'Not one.' Nick gave the answer I didn't want to hear. I was still hoping we could find this guy the easy way. 'Every single key that has been cut since the building opened is accounted for.'

'That's not a big help,' I said. 'He may be a coward, but he's smart. Somehow he's got a key without anyone knowing about it. And he's got a key that will open almost anything.'

I heard someone else coming down the hallway and turned to see Detective Lincoln.

'Well, Kate, I figured I'd be hearing from you soon. After all, it's been a couple of days since you got yourself into any trouble.'

'Detective, despite your sarcastic comments, you are a sight for sore eyes. May I have my trusty assistant fetch you some juice and I can tell you all about my day?'

He sat down in the chair across from me. 'Why don't you call me Ken?' he asked. 'I think we know each other well enough to be on a first-name basis.'

'Can I get you a juice?' Graham offered.

'Yeah, OJ would be great,' he said.

'Be right back.'

Graham disappeared downstairs and Ken turned his attention back to me. 'OK, let's hear all about your latest adventure.'

'Well, someone locked me in the bathroom with that doorstop.' I pointed to the edge of the desk. 'And left this note sitting on my desk.'

Ken leaned over the desk and turned the letter around so he could read it. 'Did you see anyone?' he asked.

'Nope.'

'Hear anything?'

'Not a thing,' I confirmed.

'This guy must have a key,' Nick jumped in. 'When we got here this place was locked up. There is no way he could get in and back out again without one.'

'I suppose you better go back over the key count again,' Ken said. 'Either there is one missing or someone has managed to copy one.'

'We've counted twice,' Nick complained at the thought of going through the inventory again.

'Do you make copies on the property or do you send them out?' the detective asked. He had his pad out and was taking notes.

'We send them out. There's only one place in town that can make these keys and it requires a form filled out in triplicate, signed by two of the three people who can authorize key duplicates.'

'You guys really go overboard on security around here. Does someone think this is Fort Knox or something?'

'Well, Lazlo gets a little carried away sometimes,' Cam offered.

'I can relate to that. I worked with him for a year.'

My ears perked up at that comment. 'Do you happen to know why he left the police force?' I asked quickly.

'Sorry, privileged information,' Ken said as he turned quickly back to his notepad. 'I would like one last key count to make certain that nothing has been missed. I suggest we go over all the records of keys copied in the last year as well. I'll get a fingerprint man down here to dust the door handles. Maybe we'll get lucky this time. How many people have touched this letter?' he asked as he slipped it into a plastic evidence bag.

'Just Cam and me,' I said. 'We tried to be careful.'

'OK, and the doorstop?' he asked, placing it into a separate bag.

'There are hundreds of those in the building,' Cam said.

'He could have picked it out of the box I have in the bottom of the file cabinet. Everyone knows that's where I keep them.'

'Not much help there. This guy is going to make us work to catch him.'

'What about my apartment?' I asked.

'I'll send some uniformed officers over and have the landlord let them in. We'll make sure that the apartment is safe and someone will stay there until you get home. I can recommend a locksmith to replace the lock.'

'It's OK,' Cam said. 'I'm making arrangements for the Plex locksmith to meet us at home tonight. I'll pick up a lock from maintenance and replace it tomorrow.'

'Good, as long as you're safe.'

Graham came back with an orange juice.

'Thanks.' Ken opened the lid and took a sip. 'I'll be off for now then.' He turned to Nick. 'Will you make sure that everyone stays away from that washroom until the lab guys get here?'

'Not a problem,' Nick said.

'I'll leave the letter and doorstop here for them as well,' Ken said. 'Make sure no one else touches them.' He stood up to go.

'What, no lectures for me today?' I asked.

'They don't seem to be doing much good, Kate. You seem determined to do what you want no matter what I say.'

'Try working for her,' Graham said and I shot him a dirty look.

'So, my best advice to you is don't go anywhere alone.'

'We've already taken care of that,' Cam assured him. 'She's not going to be alone again until the killer is behind bars.'

'Good. Then that's the best I can do.' He started down the hall but then stopped and turned back towards us. 'Were you serious about getting me some tickets to this play?'

'Sure.'

'Well, I checked with my wife and she says that next Friday or Saturday would be great, if that's possible.'

'Just pick the night, Ken, I'll have tickets waiting for you at the box office.'

'Well, let's say Friday.'

'I'll order the tickets for you tonight,' I said.

His face broke out into that boyish grin again. 'Thanks, that's really great of you.'

'No problem,' I assured him.

'See you later then.' And he continued on his way.

I love giving out theatre tickets. People who have no idea about how the theatre works always think I must break every rule in the book to get them complimentary tickets. In truth, there are some nights when half the audience has been 'comped' in. If a show is selling poorly, we totally paper the house. I remember one night when we had only sold ten tickets. It would have killed the actors to play to a house with only ten people in it, so the admin staff had spent two days trying to give out over seven hundred free tickets. We never told the actors about that one. I have ten tickets per play that I can use for promotional purposes as giveaways. I also have four house seats for each night to use as 'trouble' seats for audience members who are not happy with their own seats, or if there are seats that have been double sold. Luckily situations like this rarely happen so I'm pretty liberal at giving my friends the house tickets. It has only ever backfired on me once. So free tickets really aren't a big deal. But everyone is always so grateful and impressed; I'm not about to tell them the truth. I certainly never get tired of a little adulation from my friends.

I checked my watch and was surprised to see how late it was. 'Graham, you better go and unlock the doors. The staff should be getting here soon. Let's keep everyone in the Diamond Lounge until the police are finished up here.'

'OK. On my way.'

I tossed his key to him. 'You'll probably be needing this.'

'Thanks, Boss.'

'Graham,' Cam called after him. 'I want you to promise you'll stay beside Katie all night tonight.'

'I promise.'

'I'll stay here until you get back upstairs. When you're finished for the night, I want you to walk her to the security desk and I'll pick her up there.'

'OK,' Graham promised. 'Anything else?'

'Just have security radio me if she gives you any trouble.'

'Yes, sir.' Graham took off down the stairs.

'Excuse me, but "she" is still in the room,' I pointed out.

'Sorry, Katie. I'm just worried.'

'Cam, I swear I will not cause any problems. I have decided that I really don't want to be alone any more. You guys just better be prepared to move fast to keep up with me. I wasn't kidding about finding this guy and putting a stop to this.'

'Neither was I,' he said.

'You're really with me on this?' I asked. 'You're not going to lecture me later about how dangerous it is?'

'No, I really mean it. Someone means to scare the hell out of you or really hurt you. The only way we can stop all this is to find him.'

147

'Good.' I stood up and wrapped my arms around him. 'I'm so glad you're back on my side.'

'I never left your side,' he whispered in my ear.

I should have known it would be a bad night at the theatre, the way my afternoon had gone, but I had hoped my luck would change. I was wrong. It was a hell of a night.

We had to hold the show for ten minutes because one of the actors was involved in a minor car accident and was late getting to the theatre. We had two sets of double sold tickets and spent fifteen minutes trying to placate angry audience members. Intermission brought a round of complaints about drinks prices, which wasn't all that unusual, but wasn't something I felt like dealing with right then. At the end of the show, we spent fifteen minutes on our hands and knees helping a patron look for a lost diamond earring, which she later found in her purse, and another twenty minutes waiting for a lone patron to pick up a coat that had been left in the coat check. I had just decided to lock up and put the coat in lost and found, when a man came running in explaining and apologizing on behalf of his wife who had forgotten she'd worn a coat that evening. And people think theatre is glamorous.

I changed into my jeans with Graham standing guard outside the bathroom door. I made him talk to me the entire time I was in there. I hung my dress up and dropped the deposits into the safe. We locked the office, did a quick check of the theatre, and headed through the stage-right corridor to the security desk.

There was laughter coming out of the green room so I poked my head around the corner to say goodnight.

'Hey, Kate, let me buy you a beer,' Trevor said. 'And then you can tell us about what this butthead did to you this afternoon.'

'I'm supposed to meet Cam at security,' I said.

'Give him a call and ask him to pick you up here,' Scott suggested.

'I'm not supposed to leave her,' Graham protested. 'Cam threatened me with my life.'

'We'll take full responsibility for her. Now go call security and I'll open you a beer,' Trevor commanded.

'OK with you, Kate?' Graham asked.

'OK with me. I'll see you tomorrow,' I told him.

Graham headed off down Tin Pan Alley to sign out. I went over to the phone and dialled security.

'Security desk, Nick here,' the guard answered on the second ring.

'Hi, Nick, don't you ever go home?'

'Well Kate, if you would quit getting yourself into trouble, maybe I wouldn't have to pull all these double shifts to fill out incident reports. What can I do for you?'

'Is Cam there yet?'

'Haven't seen him.'

'When he gets up there, will you tell him I'm in the green room with the guys?'

'Sure thing,' Nick answered. 'Is everything all right?'

'Everything is fine. I'm just having a beer with the boys.'

'OK, I'll let Cam know.'

I hung up the phone and sat down beside Scott, hoping I could talk him into another shoulder massage. Trevor leaned across the coffee table and handed me a beer. I really don't like beer much, but I do like drinking with the boys. Even on a bad night they are very entertaining.

'So how true is this story we heard today?' Trevor began.

'What did you hear?'

'We heard that you got another threatening letter and spent a little while locked in a bathroom.'

'Well, it's pretty much true,' I said.

'What was in the letter?' Trevor asked.

'It said he is watching me, knows what I was doing and that I had better stop it. He also said he took my apartment keys and that I was very vulnerable, as he can get to me any time he wants.'

'Now, if that were true, why didn't he get you right then?' Trevor asked. 'Sounds like this guy is just trying to scare you.'

'Well he's doing a pretty good job,' I said. 'He was there, watching me change, and I never realized it. I thought I was being really careful, but I guess I'm not being careful enough.'

149

'I guess it's hard to be on guard every second,' Scott said. 'And it's hard for people like us to realize the lengths these sickos will go to.'

'What about your apartment?' Trevor asked. 'Have the police checked it out?'

'They're waiting for us right now, and Cam has arranged for George to meet us there to change the lock tonight.'

'Good,' Scott said. 'I told you Cam would take care of you.'

'You were right, Scott,' I said. 'All I had to do was talk to him.'

'Did I hear my name mentioned?' Cam asked, coming around the corner.

'Yes, dear,' I said. 'Your timing is perfect.'

'Are you ready to go?' he asked.

I took a last sip of beer and stood up. 'I'm more than ready. Thanks for the beer, guys. See you tomorrow.'

Cam and I headed for his car. We were home fifteen minutes later and found two uniformed police officers sitting in the living room. George arrived a few minutes after that and changed the lock in almost no time at all, while Cam went upstairs and changed. The police made sure the new lock was secure and headed out with promises that patrols around the apartment building would be doubled for the next couple of nights. Cam offered George a beer but he turned him down, anxious to get back to his own bed. Cam locked up after George left and I headed straight upstairs, hearing the bed calling my name. I undressed quickly, dropping my clothes on the floor and pulled on a T-shirt.

'Do you want a cup of tea?' Cam called up from the kitchen.

'No thanks, I'm exhausted.'

'OK, I'm going to make myself one. Be up in a minute.'

'All right,' I said. I caught sight of my reflection in the mirror and saw my black panties under my T-shirt. I changed those quickly, feeling violated. He had seen them, whoever he was, and I didn't think I'd ever wear them again. I turned off the overhead light and switched on the bedside lamp. Then I threw back the comforter and screamed. Cam must have taken the stairs three at a time because he was at my side before I could even catch my breath to scream again.

'What?' he asked.

I pointed to the bed where I had thrown back the comforter. There was a red rose lying on the sheets with a Foothills Stage Network envelope attached to it. My name was written on it in the same handwriting that had been on the envelope in my office a few hours ago. Cam took my arm and pulled me away from the bed.

'Come on, let's go downstairs. I'll call the police.' I couldn't stop staring at the bed. 'Come on, Katie.' He pulled me towards the stairs. 'He's not here now. The police searched everywhere. You're safe. Let's call the police and have them check this out, OK?'

'OK,' I agreed and followed him down the stairs. 'But this does it. He crossed the line tonight, Cam. He came into my house, my private life. He violated the one safe place I had. I am going to fucking kill him.'

We called the police and a dishevelled Ken Lincoln showed up looking like he had just got out of bed. They packed the rose and note into evidence bags, asked a few questions, did another search of the apartment, then left us alone.

I made Cam come upstairs to help me change the bed, because I couldn't stand the thought of sleeping on sheets that that man had touched. I changed the comforter too, deciding I would take the whole lot to the cleaners and have them sanitized. It was after three o'clock when we finally got into bed. I was exhausted but my mind wouldn't switch off. I felt myself start to shake, probably from the adrenalin rush I had experienced earlier. Cam must have noticed too, because he rolled over and pulled me into his arms. The shaking finally passed and I fell into a troubled sleep.

Friday

I woke with the sun streaming through the bedroom window and feeling surprisingly refreshed. I looked at the clock and saw it was almost noon. Cam was still in bed beside me, which was also a pleasant surprise. He's only slept in a few times since I've known him, preferring to be up early jogging or doing something else disgustingly healthy. He must have been just as exhausted as I was. In a sadistic way, it made me gloat to know he was feeling the effects of the last few days too. He seemed to be holding together so well during the past week that I was beginning to wonder if all the jogging and other healthy crap really does make a difference. I guess it doesn't after all. Good.

I decided I could sleep for another hour or so since Cam showed no signs of stirring, so I closed my eyes and drifted off almost immediately. When I opened my eyes again Cam was awake and watching me.

'Morning,' he said.

'Good morning. Have you been awake long?'

'No, just a few minutes.'

'It's really nice waking up with you here,' I said, hoping a little positive reinforcement would convince him to do this more often.

'I've enjoyed it,' he said. 'We don't do this often enough.'

'So why aren't you out jogging or something?'

'I didn't really feel like it,' he said, smiling at me. 'I actually had another form of workout in mind for this morning.'

'Oh?'

'I was thinking that team sports would be a good idea.'

'Well I think it's about time I got some exercise,' I said. 'Why don't you show me what you had in mind?'

* * *

It was two o'clock in the afternoon by the time I hit the shower, feeling even better than I had when I first woke up. Cam had wrapped my arm for me and I was gloriously wasting natural resources, standing under the steaming water singing a Supremes song at the top of my voice. I heard Cam yell that lunch was ready but I ignored him and turned the hot water a notch higher. I didn't actually have to be at work until four. I could shower for an hour if I wanted. That's when I was hit by a stream of ice cold water. I screamed and jumped out of the tub, landing on Cam, who had turned the hot water off.

'You're getting me wet,' he said, trying to pull away.

'Serves you right,' I said as I reached for a towel. 'That's a dirty trick to play on someone.'

'I didn't realize you were planning to spend the whole afternoon in there.'

'I would have come out eventually,' I said. 'I was just enjoying the peace. I haven't had much of that recently.'

'Well, lunch is ready and then we've got to go. You may not have to be at work until four, but I'm already running late,' he said.

'I don't want to go yet.'

'You don't have a choice,' he said. 'You're not to be left alone, remember?'

'How could I forget? Do I have time to run upstairs and dress or should I go like this?' I asked, dropping my towel.

'I think putting some clothes on would be a good idea,' he said.

'OK, I'll be quick.'

I ran upstairs, found some clean jeans and grabbed the first sweater in the closet. I was back downstairs, sitting at the table in no time. Cam served up some sort of bean soup and fresh biscuits. He is amazing in the kitchen and I had no idea how he does it. I really can't cook to save my life. To be honest, I can't even unthaw. That he could come up with a meal like this from what was in my pantry and make it taste good too absolutely amazed me.

I loaded the dishwasher while Cam went upstairs and changed. I had just put the soup pot in the fridge when Cam came downstairs, ready to go. He checked the fridge and pulled the soup pot back out.

'You have to cover things you put in the fridge, Katie,' he said.

'But we're just going to eat it tonight.'

'It dries out,' he explained. 'We've discussed this before.'

'Always worked for me in the past,' I said.

'Chinese takeout doesn't count. Now grab your bag and let's go.'

'OK, I'm ready. Calm down. You're not about to get fired for being an hour late. They could never find anybody else who would work as many hours as you do for as little money as you get.'

'Very reassuring,' he smiled. 'Now can we go?'

We were at the Plex in under five minutes. Luckily there were no speed traps on the way. Cam helped me out of the car and locked it up.

'I want to go get a cappuccino,' I said when we reached the stage door.

'I don't have time, Katie, I'm late.'

'Just walk me down there. You can leave a message for whomever my first babysitter is to pick me up there.'

'Promise you won't leave Gus's until someone comes to get you?' he asked.

'I swear,' I said. 'I swear on my caffeine addiction.'

'OK.' He started walking me towards the corner. He opened the door for me and gave me a quick kiss on the cheek.

'Can you leave me a couple of cigarettes?' I asked.

He pulled out his pack and put it in my hand. 'Stay put.'

'I will. See you later.'

I walked over to the counter and pulled up a stool. Gus finished up with a customer at the cash register and then came over to where I was sitting.

'Kate, I heard you got yourself into some trouble.' He studied my face closely, inspecting the fading bruises.

'You should see the other guy,' I joked.

'That's not what I heard,' he said. 'I heard the other guy is doing pretty well and that you are the one getting most of the battle scars.'

'Maybe so. You don't seem to miss much, do you?'

'Why haven't I seen you in the last few days?' he asked.

'I've been busy. There's also this group of men at the Plex who seem to be producing too much testosterone. They've been doing all this macho "let's protect the little woman" crap.'

'That doesn't seem to be such a bad idea, considering that technicolor face of yours. What can I get you today?'

'I'll have a mochachino now and a cappuccino to go please.'

'You know, I'm putting my second kid through university right now, thanks to you.'

I ignored him. 'So, what's the buzz these days, Gus?'

'I've heard a lot about you. Not much else.'

'Come on, you know everything that goes on in this building. Why don't you just tell me who did it and I can end all of this right now.'

'Well, if I did that it would take all the fun out of it.'

'Seriously. Do you have any ideas?'

'The only thing I know for sure is that you need to ignore the obvious.'

'What do you mean?'

'From what I hear, this murder isn't about what it appears to be about. But I think you've probably figured that out on your own.'

'I'm beginning to,' I said. 'That only makes it harder, not easier. I have no idea where to look.'

'I think you're looking in the right places, Kate, otherwise whoever it is that's after you wouldn't be so nervous. I think what you have to do now is figure out why. When you know why, you'll know which one of these people is responsible.'

'Easier said than done,' I said, starting to feel a little depressed.

'Well, kiddo, I'm keeping my ears open here. If I hear anything, you'll be the first to know,' he promised.

'Hey, Kate.'

I turned around and saw Scott standing at the restaurant door. 'Oh, there's my knight in shining armour now,' I said. 'Guess I gotta go.'

'Hey, Gus, how's it hanging?' Scott called from the doorway.

'It would be going better if you drank as much coffee as you did beer,' Gus joked.

'You ready to go, Kate? I promised Cam I'd take you to the theatre and keep an eye on you until Graham gets in.'

I put some money on the counter and grabbed my takeout cup.

'Thanks, Gus. I'll see you later.'

'You watch your back, Kate,' he warned.

I followed Scott out into the street and up the stairs through the stage door. We signed in and Scott picked up his radio. We headed down Tin Pan Alley and past the scenery shops. The huge, airplane hangar doors that led into the workshops were open and I slowed down to look inside.

'Is this for us?' I asked Scott, looking at the piles of half-finished scenery scattered all over the shop. There was a bright red 1957 Cadillac convertible in one corner.

'Yeah, for *Rock and Roll*. It's starting to look pretty good.'

'I can hardly wait to see this on the stage. What's the car for?' I asked, hoping Scott would take me inside for a closer look.

'What do you think a car like that was used for in 1961?'

'Are we going to have sex onstage?' I asked, raising my eyebrows.

'Only a little smooching, nothing serious. And there's a ghost that lives in the trunk.'

'Cool.' I lingered by the open door until Scott grabbed my arm and pulled me back out into the alley.

We continued down the corridor and Scott opened the door into the backstage-right corridor. I unlocked the green room for him and he put a pot of coffee on for me.

'I don't suppose you would let me go up to my office?' I asked.

'Only if I come with you.'

'Can we just go up and I'll bring some work down here?'

'Sure, let's go.'

We ran up and I grabbed some time sheets and the scheduling I had been putting off, and headed back to the green room. I dumped my bag and jacket on the couch and my papers on the coffee table.

'You can't work in here,' Scott said.

'Why not?'

'Cause I've got to work onstage and I can't see you from there.' He picked up my papers. 'Follow me.' Scott led me out on to the stage and dumped my stuff on the chaise lounge set up in the courtyard area. 'You can work here,' he said.

'I am not going to sit on stage and do my paperwork,' I protested. 'I'll sit down in the auditorium.'

'No, I can't see you if you sit there, but if you stay right here, I can watch you on the monitor if I have to go into the tech office and I can see you from the tech booth as well.'

'All right, but I feel really stupid.'

'Just pretend you're acting,' he said. 'Seems to work for everyone else.'

'Are you going to put some tunes on?' I asked.

'Sure, what do you want?'

'Anything upbeat and loud.'

Scott jumped off the stage and disappeared into the tech booth at the back of the theatre. A minute later Supertramp came blasting out of the speakers. Nothing like having a seventy-five-thousand dollar sound system for your own personal enjoyment. It kind of ruins you for a home stereo system, though. Scott came bounding back down the aisle and leapt up on to the stage.

'I'll either be back in the tech office or up there.' He pointed up to the fly towers overhead. 'I want to hear you scream loud and long if anyone comes into this theatre. Do you understand?'

'I think my simple brain can process that, Scott. However, you'll never hear me over the music.'

'I'll hear. Now work hard and don't move.' He disappeared backstage.

I looked up to the infrared video camera and waved at it.

'I said work hard,' he yelled from backstage. 'I didn't say make faces into the camera.'

'Just making sure you're watching,' I yelled back.

I worked through the schedule really quickly; I was able to copy most of the list from *Much Ado*. I put everything beside me on the floor and lay back on the chaise lounge. I stared up into the flies and saw Scott hanging over the top tower,

157

trying to pull up a stage weight. I felt a shiver going through me and closed my eyes.

The guys have taken me up there several times, telling me the only way to get over my fear of heights is to face it head on. Both Scott and Trevor have worked as rock-climbing instructors and are full of little insights like that. I don't know anybody who wouldn't be scared up there. There are two cat-walks, one at thirty feet and one at forty. Neither has solid flooring, just metal grillworks. When you look down at your feet you can see straight to the stage floor. There are metal railings running all around for a handhold. So, when I was up there I only had a thin metal grillwork supporting my weight and a thin metal bar to grab on to, and the guys were surprised that I didn't like it! Seeing Scott leaning over the edge just made my stomach lurch. I felt like I was falling.

The guys told me once that their ultimate goal was to fly me. That meant they would put me in a harness, attach a thin wire, and drop me over the edge with only God and their good-will to keep me from plunging forty feet to the ground. They would have the harness set up in December for *A Christmas Carol* and said that was my deadline. Once a week they drag me up there to get used to it.

The sick part, which really worries me, is that I sort of want to do it. I'll never admit it to anyone, of course, but it's a secret thrill. That's why I haven't been protesting too much.

'Is this what they pay you to do?'

I opened my eyes and looked up to see Scott leaning as far over the edge as he could. I didn't know if he was trying to impress me or scare me to death. 'Just concentrate on what you're doing up there, Scott. You're making me nervous.'

'Do you want to come up here today?' he yelled down.

'Not today, thanks.'

'OK. Well, I'm on my way down. I'll be there in a minute.'

'Don't rush,' I cautioned him. 'Take the stairs, it's safer.'

I heard the door at the top of the towers open and shut, and I waited for Scott to appear. A second later all the lights flickered out.

'Scott!' I screamed, feeling panic rising inside me. 'Scott, where are you?'

I heard a door open.

'Don't move!' Scott yelled back. 'I'm coming.'

The lights suddenly came back on and I saw Scott rushing across the stage towards me.

'Are you OK?' he asked.

'What happened?' I demanded, ignoring his question.

'Sorry,' a voice yelled from the back of the house. I turned to see where it was coming from and saw a cleaner cowering in the back of the auditorium.

'I'm new here,' he stammered. 'I was just trying to get the cleaning lights on so I could vacuum the aisles.'

'What's your name?' Scott yelled angrily at the cleaner.

I put a hand on his arm to restrain him. 'No, Scott, it was an honest mistake,' I said. 'Let's not make a big deal out of this.'

Scott looked back up at the man. 'Go call your supervisor and get him down here to show you how to work the lights.'

'Right away,' the man said, making a hasty exit.

I took my hand off his arm and smiled. 'I have used up more adrenalin this week than I have the rest of my life.'

'I got a little rush there myself,' Scott laughed. 'I guess we're a little on edge these days.'

'I guess we are.'

Graham showed up about a half-hour later and he and I went back up to my office. We rushed through our prep work, had everything ready to go, and I got changed with Graham standing outside the bathroom door again. Then we decided to go for a walk around the building to see who we could run into. I grabbed a couple of dollars from my wallet so I could buy some takeout on the way back up.

I headed off down the hall with Graham trailing behind me. As soon as I heard my office door close I realized my keys were sitting on my desk. 'Oh shit,' I said, turning around.

'Is this what you're missing?' Graham asked, holding up my key chain.

'Now this is why I hired you,' I smiled, reaching out to grab the keys.

Graham put his hand behind his back, hiding them from

me. 'No. First I want to know where we're going and what kind of trouble we're going to get into.'

'Just follow me,' I instructed.

'Kate, I really want to know who we're going to piss off before we go and do it.'

'Well, I don't really have a plan, Graham – not a fully formulated one anyway. I thought we'd try and find everyone on our original list. We've decided that one of them has to be the murderer, right? No matter what the reason for this killing?'

'Maybe.'

'OK, so we should make them all think we have proof that each one of them did it. Then I thought we could tell them that if they don't back off, I'm going to the cops.'

'But we don't have any proof,' he said.

'I don't think that really matters,' I said, holding out my hand for the keys. 'It always works for Agatha Christie.'

He dropped them into my hand. 'What works? Barging into somebody's office, accusing them of murder, and then waiting for them to kill you?'

'First of all, they're not going to kill me as long as you guys don't leave me alone.'

'Great, so they'll kill both of us?' he asked.

'Graham, if you would just try to follow along here for a minute?' I started down the hall and he had no choice but to follow me. 'What it does is get them freaked out. Whoever the murderer is will think that we have found some proof. Then he will get scared. And if he's scared he may just do something stupid and give himself away.'

'You're insane,' he said. 'Does Cam know about this plan?'

'Yes,' I said. 'Sort of.'

'Kate, why don't we wait and talk to him about it?' Graham suggested.

I cut behind the main bar and let myself into the service corridor. 'No way. I told you guys I was mad and I wasn't going to put up with this any more.'

'That's fine and good, but how about having a sensible plan before we go jumping in head first?'

'This is going to work,' I insisted. 'We just have to really pressure them. Make them really believe that we know something. It's my turn to scare him.'

'I still say we wait for Cam,' Graham insisted.

'You don't get a vote, Graham.' I stopped when we got to the Meeting Place. 'You're either with me or you're not.'

'Fine, I'm with you. As if I had a choice.'

'Then I want the performance of a lifetime out of you,' I told him.

'What am I supposed to do?' he asked.

'Improvise and follow my lead.' I took a deep breath. 'OK, the catering door is open. I do believe Jeremy Rawson is in and open for business. Let's go.'

We walked into the catering office and found the secretary sitting at her desk this time. We were going to have to get by her first.

'Kate,' she greeted me. 'What can I do for you today?'

'I'm here to see Jeremy,' I said, barely stopping at her desk. When in doubt, barge in, I thought.

'I'll just buzz him for you,' she offered.

'I don't think so.' I pushed past her desk and threw open the door to Jeremy's office.

'Kate, did we have an appointment?' he asked, obviously annoyed at my presence.

'No, Jeremy, we didn't.' I could play the bitch as well as anyone.

'Then I'm afraid we'll have to make one for later, I'm rather busy right now.' He had already turned back to his computer, thinking I was dismissed.

I slammed the door to the office.

'I think you'll see me now, Jeremy. I have something very important to discuss. Peter Reynolds, as a matter of fact.'

'I think I have made my position on that subject perfectly clear,' he said, but he finally looked up at me.

'Yes, you certainly did. But now it's my turn to make my position clear.'

'Kate, I'd like you to leave this office right now or I'll call security.' He picked up the phone.

Graham reached over and slammed the phone back into the cradle. 'I think you should hear the lady out,' he snarled.

Jeremy had a shocked look on his face, but for once said nothing.

'Now hear this,' I began. 'I know who killed Peter Reynolds. I know why, and I have proof. Now if this mysterious murderer doesn't leave me alone, for good, I am going straight to the police with the information I have. Do you understand what I am saying?'

'I don't see how this has anything to do with me,' he said.

'Well then, you just think about it for a while and maybe it will start to make sense. Either way, I want you to believe that I meant what I said.'

Graham picked the phone back up and handed it to Jeremy. 'Feel free to call security now, if you'd like,' he said with a smile. 'And thanks for your time.'

We left the office as quickly as we'd come in and walked straight back into the theatre without looking back. When the door to the service corridor closed behind us, I finally stopped and turned to look at Graham. We both broke out into a serious case of the giggles.

'That felt good,' I laughed.

'You were great,' Graham said. 'I think you should consider a career on the stage.'

'God, my knees were knocking the whole time. I was scared he'd hear them.' I wiped the tears from my eyes. 'That was a nice touch, slamming the phone down.'

'Well, I did get an A in improvisation last year. I saw someone do that in an old movie.'

'So, shall we go find our next victim?' I asked.

'Sure, where to?' He was full of enthusiasm now.

'There's some sort of community concert on in the Concert Hall. I bet Douglas Mendlesson is in the lobby right now, just waiting for us.' We headed for the elevator and I pushed the button for the ground level.

'Do you think Jeremy did it?' Graham asked as the elevator took us down. 'I thought he pretty much had an ironclad alibi.'

'No, I don't think he did it, but I did think he would be the easiest one to start with. I wanted some practice. I've never done this sort of thing before.'

'You couldn't tell,' Graham said.

The elevator doors opened and we headed down the hall. The Concert Hall and the Centenary Theatre are at opposite ends of the Plex. It's almost two blocks of corridors to get from one to the other. The route takes people past all the restaurants and retail areas, which makes everyone at the Plex happy. People spending money is what everyone likes to see. I stopped to admire some earrings in one of the windows until Graham grabbed my arm and pulled me after him.

'So, are we going to do the same thing?' he asked.

'It seemed to work,' I said. 'We'll just wing it and see how Douglas reacts.'

'Can I use you as a reference at my next audition?'

'You kidding?' I asked. 'Do you think anyone would ever believe that two non-institutionalized people would actually try to piss off a murderer?'

'I suppose you're right. Did you get the new locks on your apartment door last night?' he asked.

'I did. Were you worried?' I asked, making him blush.

'A little. I have a confession to make,' he said.

'Go ahead.'

'I put a deadbolt and chain lock on my door last night.'

'Graham, have you been getting threats?' I asked.

'No, but this is all getting a little close to home, you know?'

'I know. Do you want to get out of this little investigation?'

'No, I'm cool. I just thought better safe than sorry,' he said. 'I guess it was a good idea considering what we're doing today. Life is becoming quite an adventure around you these days.'

'I liked it better quiet,' I admitted.

'Too late.' He stopped in front of the Concert Hall doors. 'Do you want to get out of this?'

'Too late,' I said. 'Someone was in my apartment last night, my bedroom. I'm not letting that happen again. I am flushing this guy out.'

'OK, let's go find Douglas.'

We walked in, smiled at the ticket takers, and strolled right past them. I figure if you dress well and look like you know where you are going, you can get into any theatre in the world without a ticket. They never stop me, even the new ones who don't have a clue who I am. Then I realized that my ticket takers probably do the same thing. I decided I'd have to bring that up at the next staff meeting.

I stopped at the main bar. 'Is Douglas around?'

'He's in the Rodeo Room,' the cashier said. 'Do you want me to go get him for you?'

'Don't bother. We can find him.'

Graham and I walked purposefully into the Rodeo Room and found Douglas sitting in front of the TV. There was another game on. Graham walked straight up to the TV and turned it off. I liked his style.

'Katherine, Graham.' Douglas looked at both of us. 'Is there something I can do for you?'

'No, Douglas, but there is something I can do for you,' I was back into my bitch-mode again.

'And what is that exactly?' he asked.

'I can keep you out of jail,' I told him.

'Excuse me?'

'Let me keep this brief,' I began. 'I know who the murderer is and I have proof. I intend to keep it to myself just as long as he leaves me alone. However, if he threatens me once more, I will be at the police department so fast it will make your head spin. Have you got that?'

'Kate, you have to go to the police. If you know anything, you have to tell them,' Douglas pleaded.

Shit, that wasn't the way it was supposed to go. 'This is the deal I'm willing to make,' I continued. 'My silence if he leaves me alone. I just wanted you to know that.'

'There's one thing I have to know,' he said.

'What?' I didn't know where this was leading.

'Is Gladys in any danger?'

'Douglas, I believe that's one question that only you can answer,' I said. I turned to leave and Graham began to follow me.

'I beg you, if Gladys is in danger, please go to the police. Please, Katherine.'

That was the last thing we heard from Douglas as we left through the main doors. I headed straight through the next set of doors and right outside on to the street.

'I need a coffee,' I said.

164

'Let's go to Grounds Zero,' Graham suggested.

'You're willing to go to Grounds Zero twice in one week?' I asked.

'He's got a juicer now,' Graham said. 'Fresh squeezed anytime I want.'

'All right, follow me.'

We turned the block, went around the corner and walked into Gus's place. My favourite stool at the end of the counter was empty and waiting for me. Graham climbed up on the stool beside mine.

'Hey, Kate, you out causing trouble?' Gus asked.

'How do you hear about these things so quickly?' I asked him.

'I didn't. That was a lucky guess and you just confirmed it.' He laughed. 'What can I get you?'

'I'll have a cappuccino,' I said.

'Do you have any mangos?' Graham asked.

'They got a boy that's not old enough to drink coffee looking after you?' he asked.

'Oh, give him a juice,' I said. 'I'm working on corrupting him but it's taking longer than I expected.'

Gus turned to the back counter and started making our drinks. I pulled a cigarette out of my pocket, leaned over the counter and grabbed a book of matches from Gus's stash.

'Buy a lighter,' Gus said.

'Don't need one,' I said. 'I'm quitting.'

Graham waved his hand in front of his face, fanning the smoke away from him. 'Aren't there rules about smoking in restaurants?' he asked.

'This is a coffee house,' Gus said. 'Different rules.'

'Besides, Graham, you know that ninety per cent of the people in this building smoke. Gus would be cutting his own throat if he banned smoking. No one would come.'

'I still think it's disgusting.' Graham let out a fake little stage cough.

'Let's talk about you,' I said. Gus shoved my coffee across the counter to me. 'Where is all your anger coming from?'

'What do you mean?' Graham asked.

'Slamming Jeremy's phone down, shutting off Douglas's TV.

165

I have never seen that sort of aggressive behaviour from you before.'

'It's called acting, Kate.'

'Are you sure there's not this evil, macho, testosterone-filled beast inside you just begging to get out?'

Graham blushed. 'More like frustration from years of working for you.'

'Now that I can understand,' Gus said, handing Graham his juice.

'Why is it that whenever there are two men and me in a room, the two men take immense pleasure in ganging up on me?' I asked.

'You're just too easy a target, Kate,' Gus told me.

I heard the door open and both Graham and I turned to see Burns Enevold walk in.

'This is too good to be true,' I whispered to Graham.

'Don't you think we've done enough for one day?' he asked.

'We can't pass this up. This is like a gift from the gods,' I insisted.

Burns walked up to the counter, ignoring Graham and me. 'I'll have a cappuccino to go,' he said, throwing some money on the counter.

'Coming up,' Gus said.

'Burns, how have you been?' I asked, starting in gently for a change.

He didn't even look at me, just stared straight ahead, watching Gus make his drink.

'I don't think ignoring me will make me go away.' Still no response. He was going to be a tough one. 'As a matter of fact, it might piss me off,' I said. 'And if I get pissed off, I might go to the police.'

Finally he turned to me. 'I'm sorry, did you say something?' He swayed slightly while he stood there. He must have been drinking already, or maybe he needed a drink.

'Just a friendly warning,' I smiled. 'Back off, asshole. I know you did it. I know you've been hassling me, and I want you to stop.'

I punctuated my threat by pointing my finger in his face.

166

He grabbed my finger and pulled it away. 'Your mother didn't teach you any manners, did she?'

Graham moved so fast, I almost missed it. He had Burns's wrist in his hand and was obviously squeezing tightly by the look on Burns's face.

'And I don't think your mother taught you how to treat a lady, did she?' Graham asked. 'So you pay attention. You take your coffee, go wherever you're going, and think about this. You have been warned. You back off or you'll find your ass in jail. Do you understand?'

Burns pulled his arm free, grabbed his coffee and left without his change.

'Graham, I swear, you keep this up and you're going to start turning me on.'

Graham blushed again but Gus interrupted before he could respond. 'That's a dangerous game you're playing, Kate,' he warned.

'It always has been dangerous, Gus, but now I'm fighting back.'

'I hope you know what you're doing,' he said, refilling my coffee.

'So do I.'

I got a takeout cup and then a subdued Graham and I headed back to the theatre. Burns had scared me a little. I hadn't expected anyone to fight back, but I had forgotten to factor Burns's drinking into the equation. It made him unpredictable. But I felt much safer knowing that Graham had stood up to him. Burns might act tough, but it was the booze, not his character. I didn't think he would be bothering us again. I just hoped Cam didn't hear how this had gone. If he did he would lock me in my room and never let me out again. He already thought I was crazy; now he'd think I was totally insane. I made Graham swear that Cam would only hear an edited version of the story from us – and I intended to edit a lot.

We spent the next hour trying to get ready for the show. I was sick of filling in time sheets and counting floats. I can always tell when it's near the end of a run. Soon, I thought, I would have ten days off and then come back refreshed and

167

ready to do it all again. For now though, I asked Graham to count the floats and I did the less distasteful meaningless tasks.

We were just about done when Cam called and offered to buy me supper. I promised Graham I'd bring him something back if he let me go. He did. Cam and I sat in a corner booth and had a wonderful chat. I didn't tell him about my afternoon, though; I figured I'd save that for when we got home. I returned to the theatre feeling refreshed, ready for the show, and slightly guilty about not confessing my deeds to Cam. That feeling passed quickly.

When I got back to the theatre Graham had everyone signed in, in uniform, and in position. The audience had started to arrive, the theatre was in order, and I was pleased. Graham is a good kid and I am lucky to have him working for me. I would never admit that to anyone, but I vowed to try to get him a raise. I checked my watch and walked over to the tech booth. Just inside are the microphone and controls that feed the lobby PA system. I pulled the microphone down to my level and flicked the switch to the on position.

'Good evening, ladies and gentlemen, and welcome to Foothills Stage Network's presentation of *Much Ado About Nothing*. This evening's performance will begin in fifteen minutes.'

I ended up having a lovely, quiet, peaceful night with a theatre full of happy people who didn't complain about anything. I actually got the deposits balanced and everything locked up by eleven. Cam was already waiting for me at the security desk and was in a great mood. He'd had an uneventful night as well. We were out of the building by eleven fifteen and home by eleven thirty.

As soon as we got home, Cam ran upstairs to change as I went from room to room, turning on every light. Cam heard me banging around and leaned over the railing to watch me.

'What are you doing?' he asked.

'Checking.'

'Checking for what?'

'For mice,' I said sarcastically. 'What do you think?'

'Katie, the place is safe. That's an incredibly expensive

lock on the door, and you and I have the only keys that will open it. There is no way that anyone can get into this apartment.'

'Cam, just let me check everything out and then I'll feel much safer, OK?'

'OK.'

'Do you want a beer?' I asked, opening the cupboards.

'I'd love one,' he said. 'But do you seriously think that someone could be hiding in the cupboards?'

'No, I don't. I told you, I'm checking for mice,' I said.

I pulled a beer out of the fridge for him and set it on the stairs. Then I checked the bathroom and the front closet. I tried the front door, to make sure it was locked, and began to turn some of the lights off.

'Feel better?' he asked.

'A little.'

I poured myself some iced tea from the pitcher in the fridge and set it on the piano. I went back to the bathroom and took my clothes off, dropping them in the laundry basket. I put on my robe and went back to the piano.

I love my piano with all my heart and don't play it nearly enough. It's a Roland digital piano, eighty-eight grand size, with fully weighted keys, over one hundred orchestral voices and ten-track recording. It can be a completely electronic keyboard or a fully functional piano with a touch of a button. Perfect for whatever mood I'm in. I turned it on and brushed some dust from the keys.

'You coming up?' Cam asked. 'Or do you want me to come down?'

'I'm going to stay here for a while,' I said, playing a chord with my good hand and adjusting the volume control. Most of my neighbours would be in bed at this time of the night and I didn't want to risk any complaints.

Cam came down the stairs and grabbed his beer. He flung himself on the couch, set the beer on the coffee table, and grabbed the book that he was reading from under the couch.

I started playing. My fingers felt really stiff and it was awkward with only four free fingers on my right hand, and those restricted by the stupid cast. It was a long time since I

169

had last played. I really should start working on some scales again. Maybe.

'Have a good show?' Cam asked.

'Not bad,' I said. 'You have a good night?' I continued attempting to play while we talked.

'Nice and quiet for a change, and not a single plugged toilet. Which brings up a question I have always wanted to ask.'

'What?'

'Why do women try to flush sanitary napkins down public toilets? They wouldn't do it at home. They know it won't work and their toilet will just flood. So why do they do it in public washrooms?'

'It's high heels, Cam. When we wear them it throws off our centre of gravity and our brains tilt. That makes the part of our brain that deals with reason and logic receive less blood supply than normal. Which means we do things like try to flush sanitary napkins, or date men.'

'Funny.'

I turned off the piano and twisted around on the bench so I faced him. 'Would you like to know what I did today?'

'Maybe,' he said cautiously. 'Do I really want to know?'

'Probably not,' I admitted. 'But in keeping with our open and honest policy, I thought I should tell you.'

He folded the corner of his page down and put the book back under the couch. 'Go ahead, I'm ready.'

'Graham and I had several interesting talks with some of our suspects today,' I said.

'Yeah . . .'

'Basically I told them that I knew who the murderer was and that I had proof.'

'I knew you would do something like this,' he said, looking like he felt a headache coming on.

'I also told them that if they didn't leave me alone, I would going to the police and turn them in.'

'Katie, just tell me you had some sane, logical reason for doing this.'

'I did. I'm trying to flush him out. If he thinks I'm about to turn him into the police, he's going to get scared or desperate. And if he's desperate, he might do something stupid.'

'What, like kill you?' Cam asked.

'No, like give himself away.'

'You have been reading too many mystery novels,' he said. 'This is real life, Katie.'

'Cam, I told you, I'm not going to put up with these scare tactics any more. I told you I was going on the offensive.'

He took a deep breath. 'I guess there's nothing I can do, since it's already done. Tell me how everyone reacted.'

'Jeremy Rawson was in shock. Personally, I don't think anyone has ever spoken to him like that before. Douglas was worried about whether Gladys was in danger or not. I think you were right about him; he's still in love with her. And Burns Enevold almost broke my finger.'

'What?' Cam sat up quickly.

'Oh, he was probably drunk. It wasn't anything serious. Graham jumped right in and did the chivalrous male rescuer thing and Burns backed right off. I don't think I have to worry about him.'

'Katie, you're insane.' Cam shook his head. 'If one of those guys really is the murderer, you have just given him an open invitation to come after you. For real this time.'

I walked over to the couch and sat beside him, putting my arm around him. 'But you guys aren't going to let that happen to me, are you?'

'I hope you know it is taking every last ounce of my self-restraint to not lock you in the bathroom and never let you out again,' he said.

'And I appreciate it.' I kissed his ear, an act usually guaranteed to get his mind off any subject.

'Katie, stop that. I think we need to discuss this.'

'OK,' I said, moving my attention to his mouth. 'But we have all night to talk about it.'

'Katie, I really wish you wouldn't do that right now,' he said.

'Do you really?'

'No.'

Saturday

I knew everything was back to normal when I woke up around nine, alone. I didn't hear any noise in the apartment, so I knew Cam was out jogging. I got up, checked the door to make sure he had locked it after going out, and decided to have a quick shower. He still wasn't back by the time I got out.

I wrapped a towel around me and went upstairs. I opened the closet and pulled out a pair of jeans and a sweater and threw them on the chair. I grabbed some socks and underwear and added them to the pile of clothes. I leaned over the bed to straighten the comforter, which is the closest I ever come to actually making the bed. I heard the floor creak behind me and turned to see where the sound had come from. All I saw was the blurred outline of a man as he leapt across the room and landed on top of me, pushing me on to the bed.

I landed hard and had the breath knocked out of me. I waited to catch my breath, thinking Cam had come home and was playing some sort of sick game. I tried to roll over so I could see him and give him hell. A hand shot out, pushing my head into the mattress.

'Don't move,' a gruff voice said. It wasn't Cam.

I felt a knot of fear in my stomach and began to struggle, trying to kick the man, but I was lying on my stomach – not a good defensive position. I opened my mouth to scream but before I could get a sound out, he had pushed my face into the mattress again. I struggled like a crazy woman, trying to get my arms out behind me and grab whoever was holding me down.

The hand lashed out again, slapping me on the back of my

head. I stopped struggling as I saw stars dancing in front of my eyes. I didn't want to pass out. I struggled to breathe, turning my head slightly to try and get more air into my lungs and slowly the stars began to fade.

'What do you want?' I asked.

'Don't move,' was all I was told.

Not knowing what else to do, I lay still, waiting to see what he wanted.

His hands moved, one to the centre of my back, pushing me firmly into the bed. I felt the other on the outside of my thigh.

'Your skin is so smooth,' he whispered.

I felt sick to my stomach. I gasped, trying to breathe deeply and evenly, to remain in control of the situation. His hand moved higher up my thigh and slid under the towel.

'No!' I screamed.

'It'll be easier if you don't fight,' he said.

'Let me go!' I felt a fresh surge of adrenalin enter my bloodstream and tried to lash out. I felt him undo the towel and his grip slipped for just a second. I flipped over and kicked him in the stomach. All I saw was a flash of brown hair before a pillow came down over my face.

I was panicked, terrified, trying to scream. He was so strong I couldn't loosen his grip. My lungs were empty, straining for fresh air but I couldn't get any. I was suffocating. I saw spots dancing before my eyes and I knew I was going to die.

Suddenly, I became very calm. I'd be goddamned if I was going to let him kill me and get away with it. With the last of my strength I reached up for his face and tried to get my fingernails into his eyes. I missed but felt my nails make contact with his cheek. I was unbearably dizzy and my arms dropped to the bed, growing heavy and weak.

'I warned you,' I heard him growl. 'I told you I could get you.'

I caught a faint scent of cologne and I knew this was the same man who had attacked me before. What a shame, I thought. Here I was in the same room as the killer and I couldn't even see who he was. I waited for my life to flash before my eyes, but nothing happened.

'I warned you,' he said again.

That was the last thing I heard.

I knew I was alive when I realized I could still smell his cologne. It seemed to be everywhere. Then my brain, functioning very slowly, informed me that if I could still smell the cologne, he must be close. I should do something. As my senses slowly returned I decided that all I had the strength to do was scream. I let out a really good one and opened my eyes.

'Katie, calm down,' Cam said. 'You're all right. I've called an ambulance.'

'Cam?' I couldn't understand why Cam was sitting beside me. Where was the killer?

'You're OK, Katie.' Cam was feeling my forehead, not knowing what else to do.

'He's here!' I screamed and sat up quickly. 'He's here!'

'No, Katie, I checked. The door was locked when I got back. There's no one in the apartment except you.'

I reached over and touched his cheek. 'What happened? You're bleeding.'

'I fell while I was jogging.'

I brushed some dirt away from the scrape on his cheek. 'You should wash that.'

'I will.' He smiled. 'Tell me what happened.'

'He was in here. He attacked me, put a pillow over my face. He must have thought I was dead when I passed out.' I suddenly felt nauseous.

'Did you see him?'

'No. Just his hair. Brown hair.' I was breathing deeply, trying to settle my stomach.

'Nothing else?'

'No, but how did he get in here?' I was feeling a little better now, physically, but I was starting to get angry. 'How did he get a key? You promised me that I was safe! You said that no one could get in here but us!'

'I don't know how he got in, Katie. I swear I thought you were safe. I would have never left you alone otherwise.'

I hit his shoulder again; it had felt so good when I did it

the other day. Then I started crying. Cam took me in his arms and rocked me slowly back and forth.

'I told you this was dangerous. You're too close to the murderer. He's not going to let you get away with this.'

I pulled away from him, feeling really angry now. 'Don't you dare lecture me,' I said. 'Don't you fucking dare lecture me. I am making my own decisions here. I told you I am not going to live in fear of someone stalking me.'

'No, you're going to let him kill you instead.' Cam's words scared me, but I wasn't going to let him know that.

'He didn't kill me,' I snapped.

'How much closer could he get without actually doing it?' Cam asked. 'I'm not letting this happen again. I'm taking you out of here.'

'What?' I was starting to feel nauseous again.

'I said, I'm taking you out of here. We can go visit my sister in Saskatoon. Stay for as long as we need to.'

'No way. I told you I'm staying here and I'm going to find this guy.' I breathed deeply, trying to hide my discomfort.

'Katie, he almost killed you.'

'Yes, Cam, he almost killed me. It's me he's decided to go after. Me! I am not going to take it. I told you I was going to flush him out and, damn it, it's working.'

'Yeah, working really well,' Cam said dryly

'We just have to be more careful,' I said. 'I'm going to go back to the Plex and see every one of those guys again.'

'What, someone trying to smother you isn't enough? What is it going to take to stop you, Katie?'

'He's going to have to kill me to stop me. It's him or me, Cam, and if I have anything to say about it, it'll be him. In jail. All you have to do is promise me that you'll never leave me alone. Ever. I'm not safe anywhere.'

'You'll be safe in Saskatoon,' he insisted.

'If you're not willing, I'll talk to Graham, or Scott or Trevor. Or I'll hire a bodyguard if I have to. But I am not giving him another chance at me.'

'Katie—' But he was cut off by a pounding on the door.

'I'm serious, Cam. I'm scared out of my wits, but I'm not letting him get away with this.'

'I don't want to lose you,' he said.

'You're not going to lose me. The guy was stupid this time. I almost saw him. It's a start. He's getting desperate.'

The pounding on the door got louder.

'OK, OK. I'll agree,' Cam gave in. 'But only if you tell Detective Lincoln about your plan. If he's willing to help protect you, then I'll go for it. If not, we go to Saskatoon.'

'OK,' I agreed. I could always change my mind later. Besides, I really wanted to go and throw up.

The pounding started again. 'Open up! Police!' a voice yelled.

'Go and let them in,' I told him. 'I'm going to the bathroom.'

When I came out of the bathroom I did feel better, and I convinced the paramedics that I didn't need to go to the hospital. After arguing with the police, they realized they were not going to get me into the ambulance, and left. Ken Lincoln had two uniformed officers outside the apartment door, while the three of us sat in the living room. I had talked Ken into trying some herbal tea, promising it was caffeine-free. Cam had a beer in his hand and I was chain-smoking while working on my second coffee.

Ken took copious notes as I told him what had transpired in the loft, and then there was a moment of silence while he reread what he had written.

Cam broke the silence. 'You need to know what Katie has been doing.'

'What have you been up to?' Ken asked.

'I've been talking to the suspects,' I admitted.

'Threatening them,' Cam clarified.

'And you thought that would be a good thing to do?'

'Yes, I did.'

'Could you tell me why?' There was a look of disbelief on his face.

'Are you anywhere near solving this crime?' I asked.

'We are following several leads,' he began.

'I want the truth. Don't give me that official department bullshit. I want to know where you really are with this investigation.'

'All right,' Ken said. 'I suppose you deserve the truth at this point. We have several leads and all of them seem to be going nowhere. I think that if we actually solve this murder, it's going to happen a long way down the road.'

'That's what I thought. So I decided we should try and flush this guy out. Scare him and hope he makes a mistake.'

'I'd say it worked,' Ken admitted. 'But I wouldn't say it was smart.'

'Maybe not, but this guy is after me. He's been in my office, in my house, broke my arm, and almost suffocated me. I won't just sit here and wait for him to come after me again. I don't want to be a victim any longer.'

'Look, Kate, I can understand the frustration, the fear—'

'You're not going to change my mind,' I insisted. 'Cam is ready to take me out of the province, for God's sake. Do you think that's the solution?'

'No, I don't. But, Kate, you aren't a cop. You have absolutely no experience with a situation like this and you don't know what you're doing, how to handle yourself.'

'So you've got to help,' I said.

'And how do you propose I do that?' he asked.

'I don't know. You're the cop; you come up with the ideas. Put a wire on me, send someone in undercover, or something.'

'I don't think I can justify any of those things with the department. We don't even have a suspect.'

'Ken, when I turn up alive at work tonight, don't you think that somebody is going to be really shocked?'

'Probably.'

'Wouldn't you like to be there to see who it is?'

'What time are you going to work?' he asked.

'About five.'

'OK, I have to go back and talk to my boss. I don't know about any of this. I want you to promise not to leave this apartment before you hear from me, and I promise I'll call you before five.'

'I promise,' I agreed quickly, before he changed his mind.

'I'm not making any promises,' he warned. 'I'm leaving this decision up to my boss.'

'Just talk to him, tell him what's happened, how I feel,' I pleaded.

'You won't go anywhere?'

'I swear.' I crossed my heart.

He stood up. 'OK. I'll call you as soon as I can.'

'Great.' I finally allowed myself a smile.

'But you know, Kate,' Ken smiled as he started toward the door, 'they say Saskatchewan is beautiful at this time of year.'

The afternoon passed very slowly. I, of course, was not in the best of moods and Cam finally decided that keeping his distance would be his best defense. I decided house cleaning would be mine. I did the bathroom, dusted and oiled everything that didn't move, and then I had all the dishes out of the cupboards to wash them. The clock moved slowly, getting closer and closer to five o'clock, with no word from Detective Lincoln. I was getting edgier, wondering what I was going to do when Ken said no. I really didn't think I would be able to talk Cam into helping me further. I suspected that Graham, Scott and Trevor would all be urging me to go to Saskatoon as well. I didn't know how I was going to live, always wondering who had been after me, if he was never caught. Always looking over my shoulder, hearing footsteps behind me in the dark. I scrubbed harder, trying to block those thoughts out of my mind, when there was a knock on the door. I heard Cam come in from the balcony, but I ran from the kitchen, beating him to it.

I opened the door and saw Ken Lincoln standing in the hallway. He didn't look happy. My heart sank. I knew he didn't like the idea, and now he was going to tell me he wasn't going to help. I wondered what the weather was like in Saskatoon in September.

'I want you to know that I have always hated using decoys, especially when they are civilians,' he began before I invited him in.

'I understand.' I tried not to let any emotion show on my face as I waited for his decision.

'The department was grateful for your offer of assistance.'

'It's OK, Ken,' I said. 'I understand.'

I felt Cam's hand on my shoulder and turned to offer him a weak smile. He had won.

'So, as much as I protested,' Ken continued, 'my boss thought it might work.'

'What?' I asked, shocked.

'You heard me. He wouldn't have agreed to it except for the fact that you're already in danger. Doing this isn't going to make the situation any worse than it is already. So maybe we can catch the guy, if we all work together.'

'Are you serious?' I asked. Cam's hand fell off my shoulder.

Ken stepped into the apartment and was followed by a young man I hadn't noticed.

'This is Constable Young,' Ken said.

The man looked too young to be a policeman. But then, as I grow older everyone looks young to me. He wore a white shirt and black trousers. He looked like he had just finished a shift at a restaurant, or a theatre.

'Young here is going to be your new usher, starting tonight. He is not actually going to usher; his job is to watch you. I don't care how you explain it to everyone, but he is going to follow you every second you are at work. I have another officer who is going to be on duty outside this apartment door every second you are at home. I may not like it, but at least I can try to keep you from getting killed.'

'Ken, this is wonderful!' I exclaimed.

'There is one rule. You do not talk to anyone or do anything stupid without clearing it with me first. Is that perfectly understood?' he asked.

'Yes,' I assured him.

'If you blow it, if you so much as think about crossing that line, I will personally put you on a plane to Saskatoon,' he said. 'I hope I am making myself clear?'

'Perfectly,' I promised.

'Then I will see you two later. Young is going to drive to the theatre with you. I'm going home to pick up my wife. We have tickets for the show tonight.'

I was feeling much better, and insisted we get ready to go to the theatre. Cam was very quiet on the ride over, gave me a kiss on the cheek at the security desk and headed down to the basement. Clint Young and I took the back way to the theatre and up to my office. I found the spare keys in the bottom of my bag and gave them to him. We did a tour of the theatre, starting at the fly towers and ending in the basement. Clint caught on to the key system quickly, but seemed a little overwhelmed by all the various levels, corridors, twists and turns. We got back to my office and I showed him how the coffee pot worked, got him a uniform, and showed him some of the basic paperwork. I figured we could always use an extra hand and, since he was supposed to act like a real usher, I put him to work. He was quite serious about protecting me, but I could sense his underlying excitement at being in the theatre. It happened to everyone at first. After all, the theatre is a magic place.

Graham wandered in about a half-hour later. I had explained to the officer that Graham was working with us and Clint thought it would be all right for me to tell Graham who he really was.

Graham was surprised to see a new face in the office. I usually consult with him when I hire new staff. 'Graham, meet Constable Clint Young. Clint is going to be working with us, undercover.'

'Cool,' Graham said, shaking Clint's hand. 'Glad to have you here.'

'No one but you, Cam and myself knows about him, all right? Everyone else is going to think he's just an usher.'

'So does this mean our investigation is officially sanctioned by the police now?' Graham asked.

'I guess so,' Clint said.

'Actually, our plan worked better than we could have hoped,' I joked. 'Someone broke into my apartment this morning.'

'No way!'

'Yes, but it wasn't serious,' I said.

'There was an attempt on Kate's life this morning,' Clint jumped in. 'You need to know how serious this is.'

'Kate, is he telling the truth?' Graham turned to me, disbelieving.

'Yes, but I'm OK. I told you this guy was desperate.'

'Did you get a look at him?' Graham asked.

'I only saw a bit of his hair. It was brown. I did manage to scratch his face.'

'Brown hair. Well that rules out Douglas; he doesn't have enough hair for you to notice. I have some news,' Graham said.

'What?'

'I managed to get Gene assigned to the main bar tonight. He was the only one we didn't talk to yesterday.'

'Good,' I said. 'So we just watch and find out who is really surprised to see me.'

'And who has a scratch on his face,' Clint added.

'All right, back to work for now. Graham, can you unlock the side doors and let the staff in? The time sheets are ready and the coffee is on. I don't feel like counting money tonight, so we'll use the cash boxes from last night and I'll figure the whole mess out later.'

'OK. I'll be right back.'

'And Graham, you're going to have to do cash tonight. I'm going to tell everyone that I'm training Clint. He's supposed to stay with me all the time.'

'Oh, Kate, don't make me do cash. I'll do anything else,' he pleaded.

'Graham, I want you nearby. So shut up and go where I tell you to.'

'I'll make a mess of it. You know I can't balance anything.'

'It will be good practice for you.' I smiled. 'Now go. I expect you back here in five minutes.'

The ushers straggled in over the next ten minutes and everyone introduced themselves to Clint. They were going to be really pissed off when they found out that Clint was an undercover cop and I had kept it a secret. I was anxious to get on with the show. I wanted to find out who was surprised to see me. I managed to send the ushers and volunteers to their positions. I took Clint into the theatre with me while I gave everyone a pep talk and reviewed evacuation procedures. After the talk, the staff and volunteers went out into the lobbies to await the paying public, while I showed Clint how the seats in the theatre are arranged. It didn't matter if he was a real usher or not; people were going to ask him for assistance and he would need to know where to direct them.

181

When I was sure that Clint knew his way around and everything was ready for the audience, I decided it was time for a coffee. I wandered across the lobby to the main bar, trying to arrive there when Gene was standing alone. He was the one I wanted to talk to. I guess Clint didn't understand my ulterior motive, because he was following close behind me.

'Hi,' I greeted the second bartender, disappointed that Gene had ducked back into the supply room. 'I'll have a coffee, please.'

'And for you?' she asked Clint.

'Club soda, please.' He smiled at the girl.

She poured his drink first and then finally gave me my coffee. I stood, playing with the stir stick, waiting for Gene to return. I heard his voice in the back and then he appeared, carrying a case of wine.

'Kate!' he yelled, setting the wine down and running towards me.

I saw Clint tense for a moment, ready to spring into action, and then relax when Gene wrapped his arms around me in a huge bear hug of an embrace.

'Gene, nice to see you,' I said, trying to free myself.

'God is blessing me,' he said. 'I feared I wouldn't see you before I left on my mission.'

'I heard you've made a new life for yourself.'

Gene finally pulled away and I examined his face. Not a mark on it. Gene smiled at me and I thought Graham was right, he did look stoned. I suddenly lost all interest in him.

'We'll have to talk after the show,' I said.

'Please, let's do that. I have so much to share with you.'

'Great.' I was definitely going to have to sneak out the back way tonight. I did not want to get into a 'God is Good' talk with him. 'We'll arrange something after intermission.'

'God is great,' he told me, still smiling.

I turned away quickly and walked back towards the tech booth. I took Clint inside and showed him the three cubicles where the stage manager, sound and lighting technicians sit during the show. He was very impressed by the technology. He insisted on climbing the ladder to the projection booth to make sure it was empty. I think he just wanted to see what

182

kind of equipment we have up there. I shooed Clint out of the booth and made my first announcement. We opened the doors to the theatre and a few patrons wandered in and found their seats. Most of the ticket holders preferred to remain in the lobby until the last minute.

I did my rounds, talking to the coat check staff and ticket takers, and stopping at both bars. I also made sure Ken's tickets were waiting for him at the box office. Then we did another circuit of the theatre, stopping to make sure all the ushers and volunteers were in position. Volunteers have been known to get carried away with the festive atmosphere and decide it's more fun to mingle than seat people. Graham and I always check on everyone several times a night and gently herd the few strays back to their positions.

I delivered a bouquet of flowers backstage to one of the actors and introduced Clint to Scott, Trevor and Dwayne while we were back there. After chatting for a few minutes, we went back to stand by the tech booth and watched the people watching us.

I made announcements at ten minutes, five minutes, and three minutes. At one minute before show time, I got back on the PA to convince the few people remaining in the lobby that the play really was about to begin and that they should find their seats. Then I instructed the ushers to close the doors.

The technicians successfully took the house to black and the actors were quiet when getting onstage, but somehow the ushers still didn't manage to get all the doors to whisper shut at the same time. It's difficult with almost all volunteers working the doors. They only work one shift a month and never quite get it together. But I was ever hopeful that one magical night we would actually do it. Until that perfect moment was achieved, when I ordered the doors closed, Graham took off up the house-right stairs and I went up the house-left ones, managing to close all the errant doors within about twenty seconds. I should run the hundred-yard dash in the Olympics.

I came back down the stairs, much more slowly than I had ascended them, with a winded Clint following me, and met Graham in the main lobby. I found my shoes, which I had kicked off as I ran, and put them back on. I can manage the run in flats, but I never dare with heels on. Clint got himself another club soda and we sat on the couch, waiting for late-comers.

We never run a show where we got the doors to close simul-taneously and we never run a show without latecomers. True to form, two couples appeared. We vacated the sofa and I turned on the monitor so they could watch the play until late-comers'call. At the prearranged cue, Graham turned his flash-light on and led them into the darkened theatre. When we had the lobby back to ourselves again, I kicked off my shoes and flopped down on the couch.

'Wow!' Clint exclaimed. 'I never realized there was so much running around involved in this. Whenever I've been to the theatre, it's always seemed so calm. I thought being an usher was an easy job.'

'Think again,' Graham said. 'And if you want a real chal-lenge, try to balance my pre-show sales.'

'I don't think we need Clint doing that on his first shift,' I said. 'We want to encourage him. If he tries to balance your sales, he'll be suicidal.'

'Funny.' Graham shot me a dirty look.

'Did you see Gene?' I asked.

'Was he the one who found God?' Clint asked.

'That's him,' I said.

'And not a mark on his face,' Graham confirmed.

'Are you sure you scratched the man who attacked you?' Clint asked me.

'Yes, I had blood under my nails.' I felt a shudder run down my spine as I remembered the struggle.

'Did Ken take samples for the lab?' he asked.

'No,' I said. 'I washed before he could. I guess I wasn't thinking very clearly.'

'That would have been our first piece of real evidence,' Graham said.

'I know,' I snapped at him. 'I've been through this with the police already. I'd rather not do it again, please.'

'OK. Do you need me right now?' Graham asked.

'Why?'

'I want to go for a walk.'

184

I realized I wasn't the only one this was hard on. Graham must have been just as disappointed as I was. I truly believed that something would happen tonight and this would be all over.

'Go ahead,' I said. 'Be back by intermission.'

'Thanks.' He grabbed his key off the sales table and headed down the stairs.

'So, is there anything we should be doing?' Clint asked.

'Regaining our strength for intermission.'

The rest of the evening was busy, but nothing out of the ordinary. I had to admit I was feeling pretty down by the time everyone had signed out. Graham, Clint and I locked everything up and waited in my office for Cam to pick me up. He had called to say he was going to be a few minutes late.

Graham had been very quiet all night. I figured he was feeling depressed, like I was. We had expended a lot of energy and stretched our nerves to the limit, with nothing to show for it.

Clint stood up, breaking the silence. 'I need to use the bathroom,' he said. 'Graham, do you mind watching Kate for a minute?'

'Go ahead,' Graham answered.

'Not that I don't trust you,' Clint told us both, 'but I'm going to close and lock the office door.'

'That's OK,' I said.

When the door closed and Clint was gone, Graham leaned across the desk and took my hand in his.

'Kate, I need to talk to you. Quickly, before he comes back.'

'What is it?' I was concerned.

'You're not going to like what I have to say.'

'Then just say it, Graham.'

'I went for a walk so I could check everyone out. I saw Jeremy, Burns, and even Douglas. No one had a scratched cheek. I checked every usher, cleaner and security guard in this building. Not one of them had a scratch, a bruise, anything.'

'What's your point?' I asked, knowing there was more.

'I ran into Cam at the security desk,' he said quietly.

'No.'

'Yes, Kate, you need to think about this.'

185

'No,' I insisted, knowing what he was going to say.

'Kate, he was the only one I could find with brown hair and a scratch on his cheek.'

'He fell while he was running,' I explained.

'Kate, please think about this.'

'Graham, this is stupid. Why would Cam kill someone and then try to frame himself?'

'Maybe he thought if it looked like he was being framed he would take some suspicion off himself.'

'And then move in with me to protect me?'

'Or watch you. Make sure you didn't get too close to finding out the truth.'

'We are not having this conversation.' I pulled my hand from Graham's.

'Kate, just think about it. Promise me you'll think about it.'

Clint knocked on the door. I stared angrily at Graham until he got up and let the policeman back in the office.

'You can go, Graham. I won't need you until five tomorrow.' I felt ice in my voice.

'I'll see you, Kate.' Graham picked up his backpack and left quickly.

'Something wrong, Kate?' Clint asked.

'No, nothing. Let's get out of here. We can meet Cam at the security desk.'

We picked Cam up and drove home in silence. Clint made sure we were locked into the apartment and that there was someone stationed outside our door. I made a pot of coffee and offered him a Thermos-full. He accepted with a smile and sat down in the chair we brought out for him. He poured himself a cup of coffee and opened a worn paperback novel.

Cam made sure the door was locked tightly, put the chain on and turned off the hall light.

'You're really quiet tonight,' he said.

'I know.'

'Something I said?'

'No. I'm going to bed.' I started up the stairs, changed into a T-shirt and climbed into bed. Cam turned the lights off downstairs and came up. He sat in the chair by the window.

186

'Do you know we haven't seen a movie for five days?' he asked.

'I never thought about it.'

'I think that's a record for me.'

'We can go tomorrow if you like.' I knew I didn't sound very enthusiastic.

'It doesn't matter,' he said as he stood up and undressed.

'I wish none of this had ever happened,' I said. 'You and I were finally working things out, the play was going well, now everything's such a mess.'

'Katie, you and I have never had a normal relationship. This is just another chapter in that strange book of ours.'

'I want this to end.'

'It will,' he promised.

'I want to go to the movies, drive to Banff, get speeding tickets.' I punctuated my thoughts with the best sigh I could manage.

'You sound depressed. Remember, this whole investigation was your idea.'

'I believed it would work,' I said, defending my actions. 'I thought we could catch the guy and end it.'

'Tell me what you're really depressed about,' he asked.

'Graham and I had a disagreement tonight.'

'About what?' he asked.

'Nothing.' I hated it when I said that. A typical woman response that really meant 'I want you to drag it out of me'.

He sat on the bed. 'If it was nothing, why are you so upset?'

'I can't tell you, Cam.'

'Will you tell me later? When you're ready to talk about it?' he asked.

'I'll try.'

'OK.' He turned the light off and crawled under the covers.

'Graham told me that you were the only one he could find in the Plex with a scratch on his face.' I guess I felt like talking now. I don't know how these things kept coming out of my mouth. There was no response from Cam. I waited in silence for several minutes. 'I told him you fell.' I needed to break the silence. 'I was panicked, oxygen-starved; I probably didn't really scratch the guy. Or maybe I got his arm or something.'

'I'm sure Graham just said that because he's concerned about you,' Cam whispered.

'I don't doubt you, Cam,' I said. 'I need you to believe that.'

'I do, Katie.'

'Cam, will you please hold me?'

There was another minute of silence, and I actually thought he wouldn't do it. Then he turned to me and took me in his arms.

Sunday

I woke up, alone in bed, and rolled over to look at the clock. It was nine – time to get up and face the day. I dragged myself out of bed, went downstairs and turned the coffee on. Then I checked the apartment door and found it securely locked. I couldn't resist opening it and checking around the corner. It was a relief to see the policeman still in place, guarding me. He stood up when he noticed me peering out the crack in the open door.

'Morning, ma'am.' He smiled.

'Good morning, officer.'

'Your friend said to tell you he went out for a jog. He left about ten minutes ago and said he'd be back in an hour.'

'Thank you. Can I get you a coffee or anything?'

'No, thanks, I've got everything I need.' He held up his Thermos to show me. 'I came prepared.'

I closed the door, made sure the locks were secured, poured myself a coffee and went back up to the bedroom. Cam's jeans were still lying on the chair where he had left them. I looked at them for a minute, feeling an urge to do something I shouldn't, stopped myself, then made the bed. I turned back and picked up the jeans. I should hang them up, I thought, or put them in the laundry. I rummaged through the pockets, finding his wallet and some loose change. Then I found an address book. I set the wallet and change on the bedside table and took the jeans and address book downstairs. I tossed the jeans in the laundry basket, making it look like laundry had been my real intention, and wandered back into the living room, flipping through the address book. I found the number I was after and walked over to the phone. I couldn't believe I was even thinking of doing this, but my finger had a mind of its own.

189

'Hello.'

I only hesitated for a second. 'Hello, Patsy?'

'Yes, who's this?' asked the voice on the other end.

'You don't know me,' I said. 'I work at the Plex with Cam. My name is Kate Carpenter.'

'I don't have anything to say to you.'

'Please,' I implored. 'Don't hang up. I really need to talk to you.'

'About what?' The woman was hesitant. I was afraid she was going to hang up despite my pleas.

'About Cam,' I said, deciding it was better to jump right in.

'I told you, I don't have anything to say to you,' she said.

'Patsy, please, I'll only take a minute of your time.'

'Are you seeing Cam?' she asked.

'Yes, I am.' I expected her to hang up then.

'Well, I'm very happy for you. What do you want?' Her voice was short, but at least she was still on the phone.

'I need to know about Cam,' I told her, feeling guilty.

'I don't want to talk about him.'

'Please, Patsy, I need to know what happened between the two of you.'

'I think you should talk to Cam. I have to go now.'

'I can't talk to him,' I said. 'I'm scared of him.'

'Look, Kate, I'm very happy you're with Cam. He's left me alone and now I suggest you do the same.'

'What do you mean, he's left you alone?'

'Just what I said. I have a restraining order. I don't want to use it but I will if you call me again.'

She hung up. I set the receiver quietly back into the cradle and closed Cam's address book. I carried it upstairs and put it on the table beside his wallet. I came back downstairs and poured myself another cup of coffee. I sipped the coffee and stared out of the kitchen window for a moment, trying to decide whether I was a totally despicable person for what I had just done. I decided I could live with myself for now, went back to the phone, and dialled Graham's number. I figured I should make up with him before that night's show. The phone rang four times before his answering machine picked up.

190

'Hi, this is Graham. Sorry I can't take your call right now, but if you leave your name, number and time you called, I'll get back to you as soon as I can. If this is about an acting job, say so now and I'll pick up the phone. It's only my friends that I don't want to talk to.'

I heard the beep. 'Graham, it's Kate. I'm sorry I was so hard on you last night. Please call me and let's make up. I'll see you at the theatre tonight if I don't hear from you sooner.'

I hung up and poured my third cup of coffee. I was drinking a lot, even by my standards, but I just felt at odds with everything. I didn't know what to do, where to go, or who to believe. I didn't want to start believing that Cam was guilty again; I had gone through that with him already. I believed he was innocent, but then who *did* do it? I needed to know – and soon. I was beginning to feel like a yo-yo, and getting very tired of it.

I took my coffee and a chocolate croissant out to the balcony, fulfilling the first two food groups: chocolate and caffeine. I sat on the lounge chair and didn't even try to read. I didn't have the energy to concentrate on a book. I stared over the rail at the city, drank my coffee and nibbled on the croissant.

Cam came in about a half an hour later and I felt a sudden stab of guilt. I took a deep breath and tried to get over it before I had to face him. I had done what I had done, there was no going back. I fervently hoped that Cam would never find out unless I told him, and I wasn't planning on doing that any time soon. He came out on to the balcony with a cup of coffee and sat down beside me.

'Good morning,' I said, noticing he looked a little tired.

'Good morning. You feeling better?'

'A bit. I've made a resolution not to be too much of a bitch today.' I tried for the light touch.

'OK,' he said. 'I can live with that.'

'Wrong answer,' I said.

'What, you think I'm dumb enough to argue with you any more? I haven't won a fight with you in over a week now.' Cam was smiling, but it looked forced to me.

'I'm getting good.'

191

'You've had lots of practice.'

'So, what are we going to do today?' I asked.

'Saskatoon is still an option.'

'Don't give up that dream, Cam. It's actually starting to sound better to me.'

'Good.'

'I have made a decision.'

'What's that?' he asked as he kicked off his shoes and put his feet up on my lap.

'I've decided that if this isn't over by closing night, we're going to Saskatoon between shows.'

'Really?'

'Yes. We close next Saturday. If this isn't all wrapped up by then, I'll need a break. If the police can't find this guy, then I don't know what made me think I could.'

'You're an optimist,' he said.

'And look where it's got me so far.'

'Katie, don't change. Believe it or not, all these little quirks are what make me love you.'

'Is that a compliment?' I asked.

'Mostly.'

'Good. So, did you manage to run today without kissing the pavement?'

'I knew you were going to bring that up.'

'You are the most athletically gifted and graceful person I have ever met. I don't think I have ever seen you fall.'

'Well, I was distracted.'

'By what?' I was suddenly interested.

'There was a girl in a thong bikini,' he said. 'I couldn't help myself.'

'That'll teach you. You're supposed to only have eyes for me.'

'I guess I'm lucky I don't have black eyes.'

'Is there any coffee left?' I asked him, handing him my cup.

'Let me just run and check that out for you.' He jumped up and was back in a minute with a steaming cup in his hand. 'Want me to cook, too?'

'No, this is nice. I'd rather not get back to reality just yet.'

'OK.' He settled back down and put his feet up again.

'Tell me about Patsy,' I said, hoping he wouldn't notice my sudden interest in his ex-wife.

'I thought we had agreed that we weren't going to talk about our past relationships.'

'Well, maybe it's time we did,' I said. 'I'll tell you anything you want to know about mine.'

'Katie, I really loved Patsy, but I'm not proud of my last six months with her. It's something I'd rather just put behind me.'

'I'm not proud of all my relationships either, Cam. But, good and bad, they have made me who I am.'

'Well, I don't want to be who I was when Patsy and I were together. I'm hoping I've evolved a little since then.'

'What do you mean?'

'Katie, please,' he protested.

'I just think that if we're going to move into a more serious stage of our relationship, we need to be able to talk about anything.'

'I will talk to you about anything, Katie. Including my marriage, but only when I'm ready. Which I'm not.'

'You've never told me why you broke up with her,' I persisted.

'You've never asked.'

'I thought you would talk about it when you were ready,' I said.

'And I will.' Cam was beginning to sound tired of this conversation.

I turned away from him and pretended to stare at the clouds. I felt tears in the corner of my eyes and I blinked, willing them away. 'I feel like I don't know you,' I said. 'I feel as though you're hiding something from me.'

'I'm not hiding anything, Katie. There are just some things I'm not ready to admit to myself.'

I wanted him to tell me everything, something, anything. His avoidance was only making me wonder what he was hiding. I tried to push those feelings aside, wanting to trust him. I felt him reach over and take my hand. He squeezed it and I looked over at him and smiled. I think he was about to kiss me, which would have made me feel a whole lot better, when the phone rang.

'Shit.'

'I'll get it,' he said.

'It's OK. You got the coffee, I'll get the phone.' I picked it up on the fourth ring, just before the answering machine cut in. 'Hello?'

'Kate?'

'Yes.' I was trying to place the voice.

'This is Ken Lincoln calling.'

'Hi, Ken, have you got any good news today? I could use some right about now.'

'Kate, I've sent a police car over to your apartment. It should be there in a few minutes.'

'What's wrong?'

'I need you to come to the Foothills emergency department. I'll meet you there.'

'Ken, tell me what's happened.' I looked up and saw Cam standing beside me. He raised his eyebrows in a silent question, wondering what this was all about.

'It's your assistant, Graham,' Ken said calmly.

'What about him?' I heard panic in my voice.

'He was brought in about a half an hour ago. He was rollerblading on Prince's Island and someone beat him up.'

'Is he OK?'

'I don't know yet. I'm calling from my car. A squad car will pick you up downstairs and they'll get you here quickly. I promise I'll let you know everything as soon as you get here.'

'OK, we'll be there.' I slammed the receiver down and ran up the stairs with Cam following close behind me.

'What?' Cam asked.

'It's Graham. He's been beaten up.' I threw off my robe and pulled a sweater out of the closet. 'They've taken him to the Foothills.'

'What happened?'

'Ken said he was sending a police cruiser for us.'

'You finish dressing, I'll lock up.'

I dressed faster than I ever had before. I didn't care what I was putting on. I grabbed my bag and brought Cam his wallet and keys. Cam locked the door and the policeman, who was already outside, escorted us downstairs. The driver sped to the hospital, sirens blasting, and dropped us at the emergency entrance, where Ken Lincoln was waiting.

'Is he OK?' I asked, hardly out of the car.

'The doctors are still with him,' Ken said. 'I don't know how he's doing. He looked pretty bad.'

'Where is he?'

'We can't see him yet,' Ken said, taking my arm and leading me inside. 'They've given us a room to wait in.'

'I want to see him,' I protested.

'Calm down, Katie.' Cam put his arm around my shoulder and started leading me down the hall, following Ken. 'The doctors will talk to us as soon as they know anything.'

We waited for about an hour in the private room. None of us had much to say. When the doctor finally came in, we all looked up expectantly, waiting for him to speak.

'It's not as bad as it first seemed,' he said. I breathed a sigh of relief. 'We think he's got a concussion. He's badly bruised, but there doesn't seem to be any internal damage. His knee is hurt but I've called in an orthopaedic consultant and we'll let him make the prognosis on that.'

'Thank God.' I think we all said that at once.

'Have the boy's parents been notified?' the doctor asked Ken.

'They're in Vancouver. I've got someone working on that now,' Ken said. 'It will be nice to be able to give them some good news with the bad.'

'Can we see him?' I asked.

'He's sleeping. He was sedated before we did the CAT scan. He's going to be pretty much out of it for the rest of the day.'

'Please, I'd like to see him anyway,' I said. 'Just for a minute.'

'All right,' the doctor agreed. 'I'll have a nurse take you to his room.'

I held my hand out for Cam. He took it and we both looked at Ken.

'Go ahead,' the detective told us. 'I'll meet you back here.'

We followed a nurse down the corridor into one of the treatment rooms. Graham lay on the bed, looking as pale as the sheet that covered him. His face was splattered with dried blood and there were stitches in his cheek. He had a bandage wrapped around his head, his right leg was in a brace, and his neck was in a cervical collar. There were bruises showing around his neck and shoulders. I walked over, stood beside the bed, and took Graham's hand.

'I'm so sorry,' I whispered.

Cam put his hand on my shoulder. 'Katie, it's not your fault.'

'Look at him,' I said.

'They said he'll be OK.'

'I should have never involved him in any of this.'

'Katie, you don't even know what happened yet. It could have been a robbery or something.'

'No, Cam, it's the same guy. I know it. He couldn't get me yesterday, so he's going after my friends.'

'Katie, don't do this to yourself.'

'I've got to find him,' I said. 'This has got to end.'

'I know, Katie, I know.' He wrapped his arms around me and we watched Graham sleep until a nurse chased us out of the room.

Ken drove us back to the apartment, made sure we were locked in, and made me promise not to leave for the theatre until Clint Young arrived to pick us up. Cam and I both puttered around the house without much enthusiasm for anything. At three, Cam decided to hit the shower and get dressed for work. I was fine with what I had on and figured I could change at the theatre.

I phoned Graham's parents while Cam was in the shower and learned that his mom was flying out, even though his injuries weren't as serious as we had first thought. I had already decided that Graham could move in with me, and if he needed help getting around at first I'd be happy to look after him. His mom thanked me, but said she'd feel much better being here and tending to Graham herself. It was probably for the best, since I hadn't even run my plan past Cam yet. This living together thing had so many rules to adapt to. We agreed to meet at the hospital the next day and have a coffee. Cam came out of the bathroom just after I'd hung up and headed upstairs to dress.

'Have you seen my jeans?' he called down.

'Yes, I put them in the laundry basket,' I shouted back, feeling another of those annoying stabs of guilt.

'Katie, those were clean.'

'Sorry, I'll bring them right up.'

'Thank you.'

I pulled his jeans out of the laundry basket and took them upstairs. I sat on the edge of the bed and watched him dress.

'You are so sad today,' he said. 'You need to brighten up a little.'

'Under the circumstances, I think it's justified.'

'This morning,' Cam said, 'when you asked all those questions about my marriage, you had tears in your eyes. This mood isn't just about Graham, is it?'

'Maybe,' I said.

'What's going on, Katie?'

'Nothing. I just need to think some things through,' I lied, sort of.

'The fact that Graham is in the hospital isn't your fault,' Cam said. 'Hell, Katie, it might have just been a robbery. This might not have anything to do with our little murder.'

'I think that's pushing the coincidence barriers a little far.'

'Why don't we let the police decide,' he said. 'Now that you're actually willing to let them do their job, take the final step and let them decide if this is connected with your investigation or if poor Graham was just in the wrong place at the wrong time.'

'Or said the wrong thing,' I suggested.

'What do you mean?' Cam asked.

I looked at the scratch on his cheek and flashed back to the attack on me the day before, my fingernail scraping down a man's cheek. Graham had pointed out that Cam had been the only one in the Plex with a mark on his face. I had told Cam what Graham had said to me, and then Graham got beaten up while Cam was out running . . .

'Katie, tell me what you mean,' Cam interrupted my thoughts.

'Maybe he just really pissed someone off when we were talking to our suspects the other day,' I said, trying to recover quickly. 'He was a little aggressive. Maybe the murderer decided that he would go after him, instead of me. You know the squeaky wheel gets the oil.' I finally shut myself up, thinking I was starting to rant. Hopefully Cam wouldn't sense that I was trying to cover up my real thoughts.

'What is wrong with you?' he asked.

So much for my Academy Award this year. 'I'm just upset, overtired, and very emotional right now,' I said. 'Just ignore whatever I say.'

'OK, I'll ignore you for now, but remember you can talk to me if you need to.'

The look of love in his eyes made my stomach turn and the horrible guilt returned. I smiled back at him, trying to believe everything was fine. Why was I sitting here, once again ready to believe that Cam was the murderer? The smart part of my brain was screaming at me to talk to him. To tell him how I felt and level with him. The other ninety per cent of my brain was screaming at me to get out of there. Always being one to follow my instincts, I sat there and kept smiling. I just didn't have a clue of what else do. Luckily, there was a knock at the door and I was spared having to make a decision for a little while longer. I ran downstairs.

'You guys ready for work?' Clint Young asked.

'Just about. Come on in for a minute,' I said, stepping aside to let him in. 'There's coffee on if you want it.'

'Sorry, Kate, I know I am a cop and I have a reputation to maintain, but even a career officer can't drink as much coffee as you do.'

'Funny man. Keep working in the theatre, Clint, and we'll even have you smoking soon.'

Cam came down the stairs. 'You ready to go?' he asked us both.

'Might as well,' I said. 'I'd rather get tonight over with as quickly as I can.'

We all piled into Cam's car and headed for the Plex. He dropped us off at the stage door and made us promise to wait by the security desk while he parked across the street. We walked through Tin Pan Alley towards the theatre. The shop doors were open but none of us cared about what was going on in there. I guess we all had other things on our minds.

Clint went ahead of Cam and me, and checked the wash-rooms and my office before we were allowed in. Clint started the coffee for me and I opened the safe and pulled out the deposits. I knew I would regret it later, but I dumped the two previous nights' deposits into a cash bag and put it back into the safe. I would try and balance it all another day when I had more energy. If I couldn't balance, no loss. It wouldn't be the first time we hadn't balanced, and probably wouldn't be the last time either.

I counted fifty-dollar floats into the cash boxes and locked them in my bottom desk drawer. I pulled out Graham's key before I realized he wouldn't be in, then dropped it back into the drawer. Cam watched me and smiled across the desk.

'It'll be OK,' he promised.

'I don't want to talk about it right now,' I said. 'Do you mind?'

'No, I don't mind. Can I do anything for you?'

'Not really. Are you sure you just want to sit here and watch me all night?' I asked. 'Clint is here to babysit me. I'll be OK.'

'Don't you want me here, Katie?' he asked. His eyes looked so sad.

No, my mind screamed, I don't. 'Of course I do, Cam. It's just that you'll probably be bored.'

'Maybe I'll go in and watch the play,' he suggested.

'I forgot to ask Ken how he enjoyed it last night.'

'He loved it,' Clint said. 'He couldn't stop talking about it this morning.'

'Really?'

'Really. He couldn't believe how involved he got. Said he thought theatre would seem fake.'

'You'll have to give him some tickets for the next play. He can come and enjoy it and not worry about dead bodies,' Cam said.

'I wanted to meet his wife too,' I said. 'Apologize to her for getting him up in the middle of the night so many times.'

'Oh, don't worry about Becca,' Clint said. 'Her dad was a cop. She's used to it.'

'Shit, look at the time. I'd better open up, I'm sure I've got staff downstairs wondering where I am.'

199

'I'll go,' Cam said, pulling out his keys.

'No, we'll go,' Clint said. 'I'd rather keep everyone together.'

'I'll be fine,' Cam said. 'I don't think this asshole will bother me. I can fight back.'

'Let him go,' I said firmly.

'All right,' Clint said. 'Do you want some coffee, Kate?'

'Sure, black please,' I said, then turned to Cam. 'Please don't say anything to the ushers; I want to tell them.'

'Don't worry, I'll keep quiet.' He took off down the stairs.

When I heard the door close at the far end of the corridor I turned to Clint. 'I'm afraid,' I admitted.

'I know, Kate, that's why I'm here.'

'I'm afraid of Cam.'

'Excuse me?' Clint looked surprised.

'I think there are things about Cam I don't know, things that maybe I should know.' I stopped and caught my breath. 'I can't believe I'm saying this to you.'

'Tell me what you know, Kate.'

'I called his ex-wife this morning. She had to get a restraining order against him.'

'Does he know you called her?' Clint asked.

'No. But I had to; he wouldn't talk to me about it. I don't even know why they divorced. What if he was violent?'

'I'll call Ken tonight and have him check it out,' Clint promised.

'Thank you.'

'What else?' he asked.

'I don't know what you mean.'

'What else is scaring you? You didn't bring this up just because of this restraining order. Is there something else about Cam that I should know?'

'No,' I said quickly.

'Kate, you have to level with me.'

'I can't,' I said. 'I can't turn on him. All I have are some suspicions, things he's said that don't really add up, but nothing I can really put my finger on.'

'OK. I'll call Ken tonight and talk to him about this. Maybe he can take you out for coffee tomorrow and let you know what he thinks.'

'No, I shouldn't have even brought it up,' I said.

'Kate, if there is any chance at all that Cam is responsible for any of this, you need to know. If he decides to go after you while you're alone with him, there is nothing we can do to protect you.'

I heard the door at the end of the corridor open and quickly turned back to Clint. 'Please don't say anything to Cam about this,' I begged.

'Promise,' he answered.

'I told them you were late because we were having wild sex on the desk,' Cam joked, followed by ten curious ushers.

'There are some things about your boss that you just shouldn't know,' Leonard piped up.

'I hope you've washed the desk,' Charlotte said.

'Thanks for preserving what little dignity I had left,' I told Cam. 'But there is something I have to tell you before we get started tonight.'

'What's up?' Leonard asked as they all found seats.

'Graham won't be in for a while,' I began. 'He was attacked this afternoon on Prince's Island.'

'In broad daylight?' someone asked.

'Is he OK?' someone else said.

'He's going to be OK,' I assured them. 'He looks awful, but the doctors have promised it's not as bad as it looks. He only has a minor concussion, a few stitches, and lots of bruises. He will need some physiotherapy on his knee and maybe a minor operation, but he should be fine.'

'Which hospital is he in?' Charlotte asked.

'He's at the Foothills. I don't have the room number yet, but I'll get that before we leave tonight and let you all know.'

'Are we going to send something?' Charlotte asked.

'We should,' I agreed. 'Does anyone have any ideas?'

'A stripper.'

'Thank you, Leonard,' I said. 'Perhaps we should think about this for a while and make a decision after the show.'

'Can he have visitors?' Martha asked.

'I think so. He'll probably be glad to have some company.'

'What happened?' Leonard asked.

'The police aren't really sure. It might have been a robbery attempt. I guess we'll know more when they have had a chance to talk with him.' I looked around the room and saw a subdued bunch, just as I expected. 'Let's try and stay positive tonight, guys,' I said. 'We still have a show to get through. Since I was late and Graham isn't here, would you guys split up and do a walk through for me. I'll change and meet you downstairs.'

They shuffled out, dropping coats and bags, and headed off into the theatre. I picked something off my rack, not even noticing which outfit it was, and went into the bathroom to change. When I came out, some volunteers had started to wander in. I assigned everyone to their positions, left Charlotte in charge, and went down to the lobby to check the bars.

I saw Douglas standing by the Hollywood Bar and tried to change direction before he saw me. Too late; he was coming across the lobby. I had no choice but to talk to him and I probably deserved whatever shit he was about to heap on me.

'Katherine, we heard about Graham,' he began. 'Nick in security told me when I signed in. The Plex staff all want to take up a collection and get something for him. We wondered if you had any ideas?'

'Douglas, that's very thoughtful,' I said, relieved. 'We were going to discuss it at the end of the show. Why don't you come up to the office later and we'll shoot some ideas around.'

'Thanks, I'll do that,' he said. 'And I don't want you to worry about the bars tonight. I'm going to stay on the floor all night and supervise. I'm sure you have enough on your mind right now.'

I looked at him and saw a sweet, sensitive man. What an about-face. 'That's really very nice. I appreciate it.'

'Just let me know if there's anything you need,' he said, turning back to the bar.

I almost felt guilty about what we'd done to him the day before. I turned around, not sure where I was going. I didn't really have anything to do. I would have preferred being busy. I decided I'd just take a wander backstage and see what was up. At least that would kill a couple of minutes.

I headed down towards the backstage-right hall, followed closely by Clint. I smiled and said hello to several actors and poked my head in the green room. No one there. I headed for the door to the stage and wandered through, hoping to run into someone who could offer some diversion. The house lights were on full, as were the stage lights, but no one was around.

'Look out below,' I heard. I tilted my head upwards and saw Scott and Trevor on the tower.

'What are you guys up to?'

'Come on up and we'll show you,' Trevor said.

'I've got my heels on,' I said. 'I'll come up tomorrow.'

'We're getting the harness ready,' Scott explained.

'I thought you didn't have to fly anyone until the Ghost of Christmas Future?'

'So did we,' Trevor yelled down. 'But Krueger decided that Elvis's ghost should be able to fly in the next show.'

'So we're rigging it to test on Trevor,' Scott said. 'He's a little heavier than Elvis, but it'll be a good test.'

'Shut up butthead,' Trevor said. 'We're rigging it for me because I'm always the first one to test it. That's why I'm the technical director.'

'Whatever,' I heard Scott mutter.

'Where's Dwayne?' I asked.

'Changing gels,' Trevor said, pointing to the massive rack of lights hung in the back of the theatre. Dwayne was leaning out at an impossible angle, putting new filters on the lights.

'These guys are crazy,' Clint said.

'You haven't seen the half of it,' I said. I turned back up to the towers. 'I'll catch you guys later when you're back on the ground.'

'Take it easy,' Scott said.

I led Clint down the stairs at the edge of the stage and into the auditorium. We cut back through the house and into the lobby.

'I couldn't do that kind of work,' Clint said, shaking his head.

'They have no fear.'

'I think I'll stick to ground level and chasing bad guys. It's much safer.'

I laughed as we headed back to the office. I didn't really know where else to go.

Cam was still sitting in the office. He had a cup of coffee and a cigarette going. He didn't smile when I came back in, and I could understand his sentiment. I sat down at my desk and Clint moved towards one of the benches.

'Would you mind?' Cam asked. 'Can we have a couple of minutes alone?'

'Sure,' Clint said. 'I'll just be in the hall.' He closed the door behind him.

I let out a sigh and leaned back in my chair, closing my eyes. 'Are we going to fight now?' I asked.

'Why would you think that?'

'Because that seems to be almost all we do these days.'

'You know, high-stress situations like this can either make or break a relationship.'

'Cam, I don't want to do this here,' I said.

'Do what here?'

'I don't want to do my personal life at work.'

'Well, with the police following you around everywhere, we don't really have a private place to talk any more.'

'I tried to talk this morning but you didn't seem all that interested.'

'I want to know where that came from?' he demanded.

'Where what came from?' I hoped playing innocent would get me out of this.

'This sudden interest in my marriage,' he said. 'You seem to have lasted quite a while without needing to know about it. What made you bring it up all of a sudden?'

'I don't know,' I lied.

'I'm sure you do,' he said. 'I'm sure it's not just idle curiosity.'

'Doesn't matter, anyway. You don't want to talk about it.'

'I'm not the murderer,' he said.

I opened my eyes and looked at him. 'Where did that come from?'

'It's what you're thinking, isn't it?'

'Don't be ridiculous,' I said.

'I don't think I *am* being ridiculous. I think that's what you're thinking. Again.'

'Cam, I really don't want to do this right now.'

'When do you want to discuss it?' he asked. 'After I'm in jail?'

'I'm in this mess because I'm trying to keep you out of jail.'

'That's how it began,' he said. 'But is that still the way you feel?'

I stood up. 'I'm going down to the lobby. I don't want to deal with this right now.'

'If you won't talk to me, I'm going home.'

'Fine,' I said, starting down the corridor.

'Katie, don't do this to us.'

'We'll talk when I get home,' I said, starting down the stairs towards the lobby.

Clint followed me downstairs. I got a coffee at the bar and watched Cam head down the stairs and out into the street. I turned and looked out through the window, watching him walk down the street and into the parking lot. I checked my watch and decided I'd better get my mind back to the theatre. I headed for the tech booth. Time for my first announcement.

Clint got me home by twelve thirty and turned me over to the police officer sitting in the hall. He stood and introduced himself, and then I let myself into the apartment.

The place was pitch-black and I thought Cam must have gone out. I turned the kitchen light on and dropped my bag on the table. It was stuffy in the apartment and I decided to sit on the balcony for a while. I was startled to see Cam lying on the couch watching me.

'Why are you lying here in the dark?' I asked.

'I was sleeping.'

'Sorry, I didn't mean to wake you. Why didn't you go to bed?'

'I didn't know if you'd want me there tonight.'

'Do we have to do this, Cam?' I asked. 'I just want a good night's sleep and we can talk or fight or whatever you want tomorrow.'

'Fine,' he said flatly.

'Thank you.'

I turned around and climbed the stairs. Forget sitting on the balcony, I was going to bed. I pulled off my clothes and put on a T-shirt. I leaned over and pulled the comforter down. I heard the floor squeak behind me and turned in a panic to see Cam coming up behind me. He pushed me on to the bed and pinned me under him.

'Let me go!'

'Not until you believe me,' he said.

'Fine, I believe you, now let me up.'

'Not yet. Tell me what hand you used to scratch him with.'

'What are you talking about?' I was trying to get him off me but I could barely move.

'What hand did you use to scratch him with? Think, Katie, when he had you pinned down on the bed, what hand did you use?'

'Is there a point here?' I asked, starting to get really pissed off.

Cam flipped me over and I began to feel very scared. He was so strong, I didn't have a hope of fighting back.

'OK,' he said. 'You're lying here, he's got a pillow over your face. Show me how you scratched him.'

'You should know,' I said.

'Well, humour me,' he insisted.

'I don't remember. I was scared.'

'Try to remember.'

'Cam, this isn't the least bit funny. You are scaring me.'

'Try to remember.' He picked up one of the pillows and brought it toward my face. I screamed, but he pushed the pillow on to my face, muffling the sound. Now I really began to struggle. This wasn't going to happen twice. I reached up for his face and felt him grab my wrist. He lifted the pillow off my face and I gulped in the fresh air.

'See, you used your left arm. The one without the cast,' he said, holding my wrist tightly.

'Let me go. You're hurting my wrist.'

'You used your left hand, Katie. That means you would have scratched him on the right side of his face. Look at my face.'

And I did. The right side of his face was covered with healthy, tanned, unbroken skin. It was his left cheek that had been scratched.

'I'm not the murderer,' he said, getting off me and going downstairs. He never came back. I knew I should have gone down and made up with him, but I didn't have the strength.

Monday

I woke up in a panic, to the sound of someone screaming. I didn't realize it was me until Cam came upstairs and put his arms around me.

'It's OK,' he said, rocking me gently. 'You're safe, you were dreaming. It's only a dream.'

I closed my mouth and the screaming stopped, but then there was a frantic knocking on the apartment door.

'Are you OK in there?' a policeman yelled through the door.

'We're OK.' Cam stood up and yelled over the edge of the loft. 'Just a bad dream.'

'I'm sorry,' I said, trying to gather my wits. I looked around the room, wanting to make sure I was truly awake. I was in my apartment, it was daylight, and no one was trying to kill me. I took a deep breath and tried to calm myself.

'It's OK,' Cam said, back on the bed beside me, his arms around me again. 'Do you want to talk about it?'

'I don't remember,' I lied. 'I think someone was chasing me.'

'You're safe now.' He held me tighter. 'Why don't you lie down and try to go back to sleep for a little while?'

'Not alone,' I begged, grabbing his arm when he tried to stand up.

'I'll stay with you,' he said, lying beside me as I settled back under the covers.

'Thanks,' I said, finally relaxing into his arms.

'Why did you call Patsy?' His arms tightened around me as he asked the question. I could feel his body grow tense. Shit, I was not going to be allowed to forget that phone call. I was not together enough to try and lie to him. I had the sinking feeling we might be headed for a fight and I really didn't want to be alone right then.

'Please don't be angry,' I said, trying to see if avoidance might work.

'Why shouldn't I be angry?'

'I don't know. I'm confused, Cam,' I admitted as I looked into his eyes.

'About what? Don't you know that I love you?'

'Yes, I do know that. It's just that I feel I don't know anything else about you.'

'I wish you had asked me, instead of calling her,' he said, letting go of me and running his hand through his hair. He always did that when he was nervous.

'How'd you find out that I called her?' I asked.

'Is that really important?'

'No, I guess that's not the point, is it?'

Cam got up from the bed and began pacing the room. He finally sat in the chair by the window.

'I called Patsy yesterday,' he began. 'When I came home from the theatre. She and I still have a few things to work out and I decided it was time to start mending some fences. I just hadn't planned on doing it this soon. I'm really not proud of the way my marriage ended, Katie.'

I pulled the covers up around me, feeling chilled, and propped my head on some pillows. I was quiet, for once, waiting for him to continue. He didn't say anything else.

'Cam, she told me she had to get a restraining order to keep you away,' I said, breaking the silence.

'That's true.'

'I have a right to know what happened,' I said in a determined voice.

'Why?' he asked, anger flaring in his eyes. 'My marriage with Patsy has nothing to do with you and me.'

'It does have something to do with us. If you were abusive, I want to know right now, in case it's going to affect our relationship,' I explained, trying to remain calm.

'It won't affect us!'

'How do I know that?' I was on the defensive again.

'The same way that I knew you wouldn't go through my stuff or call my ex-wife,' he said pointedly. I didn't have an answer for that one.

209

'Patsy and I started to make our peace last night. I want you to know that. I also want you to know that I will tell you all about her, but not until I'm ready to. I think that you and I have to do a little bit of rebuilding here first. Regain some trust.'

'Cam, I need to know what happened.' I felt hurt, but I couldn't let this go.

'That's where the trust comes in,' he said. 'You have to learn to truly trust me.' He stood up and started down the stairs.

'Where are you going?' I called after him.

'I'm going to take a shower,' he said. 'Don't worry, I'm not leaving. I have no intention of walking away from this relationship without a fight.'

I laughed at his choice of words. 'I think we've already covered that.'

He didn't smile at my joke, just turned and walked down the stairs.

Cam and I were dressed and ready to go within the hour. Ken Lincoln had arranged a ride for us so that we could visit Graham. Cam locked the apartment door and we headed for the lobby with our police escort. We got into the cruiser and started for the hospital, a little slower than yesterday, and without the benefit of lights or sirens.

Graham was in a private room. The curtains were open, the sun streaming in, and there was a great view of the mountains. He was awake and talking quietly with his mom.

'Hi,' I greeted them, entering the room with my cheeriest face. 'How are you doing?'

Graham turned and offered me a weak smile. I saw his two front teeth were broken and fought the urge to giggle at this new look.

'Hi Kate,' he lisped. 'What are you doing up this early?'

'I had hoped this adventure might improve your sense of humour,' I said. 'I see it's had no effect at all.'

'Nice shiner,' Cam said, moving closer to the bed.

'Thanks for coming,' Graham greeted him.

'How are you feeling?' I asked.

'Very sore and everything hurts. The doctors keep telling me that's a good thing.'

'That's because they're not lying here in pain,' I joked.

Graham's mom reached across the bed and gave my hand a squeeze. 'It's nice to see you here, Kate. Graham's told me what's been happening at the theatre.'

'Good to see you too, Rose. I'm glad you could get here so quickly.'

'How are you doing?' Graham asked me.

'Fine. Nothing new. I guess our murderer is getting bored with trying to scare me,' I said, sitting gently on the edge of the bed.

'Don't believe it,' Graham warned. 'He's still out there; I'm proof of that.'

'So what happened?' Cam finally asked what we had both been thinking about.

'I don't remember,' Graham said. 'I don't remember anything about it.'

'Nothing?' I asked.

'No. The doctor told me that's normal. I may remember something, I may never remember. Some sort of traumatic amnesia.'

'Well, it's probably better that way,' Cam commented.

'When are they going to spring you?' I asked.

'Today, if I don't start seeing double or talking in tongues,' Graham joked. 'And I can hardly wait to get out of here.'

'So soon?' I asked, shocked.

'I guess I'm taking up valuable bed space. I'm seeing a dentist this morning to get something done to these teeth and then I guess they figure there's nothing else they can do for me.'

'Are you going to be OK at home?' I asked.

'I'm staying until he's better,' Rose assured me. 'He'll be just fine.'

'It's not fair, Kate,' Graham said. 'I just got my own place a couple of months ago and now my mom's moving in with me.'

'It'll be good for you,' I said. 'Maybe she can teach you some manners.'

'Manners?' he asked.

'Yeah, that's what separates us from the animals, remember?'

211

'The guy that attacked me, he said something about manners,' Graham said.

'What do you mean?' Rose asked.

'I don't really remember. It's just that manners is ringing a bell somewhere. I'm sure he said something like that,' Graham said with a puzzled look on his face.

I took Graham's hand and squeezed it. 'Don't worry about it, kiddo. It'll come back to you. Don't get all stressed out now.'

'I need to remember who did this,' he said.

'You'll remember,' I promised him.

'Kate, I'm sure the guy who did this is the same guy who's been after you. If I can't remember, you won't be safe.'

'Don't worry,' Cam said. 'They've got so many police officers around, no one can get to her. Not even me.'

'Hello, hello,' I heard from the doorway. We all turned and saw a group from the theatre coming into the room.

'Look, he's got one of those hospital nighties on,' Charlotte said. 'Is it true they don't have backs in them?'

'Stand up and turn around for us, Graham,' Martha said.

'Mom, can you pull up my covers, please?' He was blushing.

Everyone piled into the room, bringing balloons, stuffed animals, and more flowers. I leaned over and kissed him on the cheek.

'We'll come back when it's less crowded. You take it easy.'

Cam and I fought our way out of the room and when we were in the hall I took his hand. 'You are a nice man,' I said to him.

'I try.'

'I want to go out for breakfast,' I said.

'With two policemen? Why don't we go home and I'll make something?' he asked.

'Aren't you tired of doing all the cooking?'

'No. You play piano to relieve your stress, I cook.'

'OK, take me back to the prison,' I said.

That's what it was beginning to feel like. I moved out to the balcony, settling myself on one of the lounge chairs. I felt better on the balcony, less trapped. I heard Cam rattling pots and pans in the kitchen but I tuned it out as I lay back in my lounge chair, trying to sleep. I did doze off for a little while but came right back to life when I smelled food. I opened my eyes and saw Cam standing over me holding a plate. I sat up and took the plate from him.

'This smells great,' I said.

'Thanks.'

'What is it?'

'Blackberry crepes.'

'Where do you keep finding all this stuff?' I asked. 'I know I didn't have blackberries in the fridge.'

'I stopped at the grocery store on the way home last night.'

'I was beginning to think there was a magic fairy that just kept refilling the fridge at night.'

'There is, Katie. His name is Cam.'

'Someday you're going to have to teach me how you do all this,' I said as I dug into my breakfast.

'I don't know if I'm really up to that,' he laughed.

'I've got to go into the theatre today.'

'It's Monday,' Cam said. 'No show, remember?'

'I've got three days' worth of sales receipts to balance.'

'If you have to.'

'Are you going to come in with me?' I asked.

'Do you want me to?'

'Clint will be there,' I said. 'I should be safe. I really don't expect you to sit there all day and be bored to tears.'

'OK, I'll think about it,' he said. 'I can always find something to do in the workshop. I've got a few projects waiting for me. I would feel safer being close to you.'

'It's up to you,' I said non-committally. 'I do like having you close by, no matter what I said before.'

'Thanks,' he smiled at me. 'Do you want another crepe?'

'I'd like several more crepes.'

After we finished eating, Cam did the dishes and decided he would come to the theatre with me. I called Clint to let him know what our plans were. We were escorted to Cam's car and Clint was waiting for us at the stage door.

'Sorry to spoil your day off,' I apologized to Clint.

'No problem. I'm making great overtime.'

We went through the same procedure as the night before,

213

with Clint preceding us, checking everything before finally letting me into my office. I opened the safe and buried myself in sales reports. Clint opened up a paperback he had brought along and Cam made coffee. By the time the first pot was finished and he was making a fresh one, I could tell that he was getting bored. He finally gave up trying to entertain himself.

'I'm going down to the workshop,' he said. 'If you don't mind.'

'I'll probably get more done if I'm not watching you pace,' I agreed. 'We'll be OK without you.'

He leaned over the desk and kissed me. 'Call me if you need me.'

'OK,' I promised, returning to my paperwork.

I managed to work through all the reports in a couple of hours. My deposits weren't exactly balanced but the accounting department could figure it out. That's what they get paid for after all.

I checked my watch. It was four o'clock and I still had another hour or two's worth of work before I called it a day. We were still playing to sold-out houses and it would be nice to come in the next day knowing everything was done. I decided to take a break before I got back to it. Sales reports aren't the most exciting aspect of my job. I called the green room to see if anyone was around.

'Green room,' Scott answered.

'Hey, Scott, it's Kate.' I was glad to hear his voice. 'You got a beer you can crack for me?'

'Sorry Kate, no beer. We're working in the towers today. Why don't you come on up and watch us rig this thing?'

I tried to come up with a good excuse, but couldn't think of one on such short notice. I decided I hated sales reports more than I hated the fly towers.

'I'll meet you in the green room in a couple of minutes,' I agreed. 'But you're not putting me in the harness today.'

'Don't worry,' he promised. 'Trevor hasn't tested it yet. Nobody flies until Trevor flies.'

'See you in a minute.' I hung up the phone and turned to Clint. 'Come on, we're going to go conquer my fear of heights.'

214

'What about my fear of heights?' he asked.

Scott and Trevor were waiting for me outside the green room. 'Who's your friend?' Trevor asked. 'Did you replace Graham already?'

'No, he's a cop,' I confessed, despite the look I got from Clint. 'He's here to make sure you don't throw me off the tower.'

'Who's going to protect *him*?' Scott asked.

'Cut the wisecracks and let's get this over with,' I said as I opened the door to the stairwell, ushering them onwards. We climbed the stairs, forty feet up, and everyone but Scott was breathing hard by the time we got to the top.

Scott held the door open and I stepped over the ledge. The catwalk over the stage was to my right; the catwalk over the auditorium to my left. I took a few steps forward, never trusting the floor in this room. I knew that I was standing on the ceiling of the theatre and if I took a few steps in any direction there was grilled floor where I could look down on the theatre. I didn't usually do that, preferring to pretend that I wasn't up so high, about to risk my life. Not that it's that dangerous, but I always become totally melodramatic when I'm terrified.

Scott and Trevor veered to the right, out over the stage.

'Aren't you forgetting something?' I asked, following Scott to the edge of the fly tower.

'What?' he asked.

'Me.' I held out my hand.

Scott took it and led me slowly out on to the catwalk. 'Quit looking down.'

'It's a self-preservation thing,' I said. 'I want to fall on the softest part of the stage.'

'What about the cop?' Trevor asked, noticing that Clint wasn't following us.

I glanced over my shoulder and saw Clint sitting on the steps, pulling out his paperback. 'Come on in, the water's fine,' I called to him.

'I'm happy right here,' he insisted. 'You guys have fun.'

'It's perfectly safe,' I said. 'You'll be fine.'

'I'd find that easier to believe if you didn't look so terrified.'

Clint laughed. 'I can see you just fine from here. Go ahead without me.'

Scott walked me out to a point just beyond where they were working. He put my hand on the rail and took a step back from me. 'You OK?' he asked. They are very patient with me and never fool around when I'm up here with them. Most important, they never make fun of my fear.

'I'm fine,' I said, pretending to relax. 'Just don't make any sudden moves.'

Scott kicked some stage weights out of his way and I felt a shiver run up my spine as the catwalk shook ever so slightly.

'We've got the harness hooked up already,' Trevor said, holding up a wire so thin that I didn't believe it would hold anyone up. 'This hooks on to the harness that the actor wears. We just set up the counterweights to match the actor's body weight, and the rest is all a matter of physics.'

'What if they lie about their weight?' I asked.

'I weigh them myself on my office scales,' Trevor said. 'We don't fool around when we're flying someone.'

'The insurance rates are a killer ever since we dropped that one actor,' Scott joked.

'You're scaring the lady, butthead,' Trevor said. 'We've never dropped anyone. Scout's honour. That's why I'm the one who flies first. Nobody else goes out until I'm satisfied.'

'Who weighs you?' Scott asked.

'I do.' Trevor scowled.

'And he never tells anyone what he weighs,' Scott told me. 'What if the counterweights are wrong?'

'That's why I always check up on you,' Trevor said.

Scott was tying off some ropes while Trevor double-checked the entire system. He turned around so Scott could hook the wire to his harness. Trevor climbed over the railing and I felt that shiver up my spine again as I watched him hang over the edge. 'I don't think I can watch,' I said.

'It's OK,' Trevor said calmly. 'Normally we'd have a small platform here, like a diving board, for the actor to stand on. We'll set that up closer to production. For now, if Scott's ready . . .'

'Ready,' Scott confirmed, checking the rigging.

'Then I just step off.' Trevor pushed off from the rail and Scott slowly let him down a couple of feet.

I closed my eyes tightly, expecting to hear Trevor scream as he plunged to the floor. When I didn't hear anything, I opened my eyes and saw Trevor hanging in mid-air.

'Swing me out centre-stage,' he ordered.

Scott did as he was asked. They tried several other positions, then raised and lowered him a few times. I actually started to feel much more confident, especially since it wasn't me hanging out there.

'I think that's good for today,' Trevor called over to us. 'Let me down to the stage.'

'Now I threaten to leave him here,' Scott told me.

'And then I threaten to fire him,' Trevor yelled back.

'At which point I immediately lower him to the stage.' Scott watched Trevor sink to stage level and then secured the ropes. 'Now, we go down.'

He reached out for my hand and I gave it to him gladly. We joined Clint and trekked back down the stairs. Scott led us backstage to where Trevor was dangling about a foot above the stage.

'Very funny, butthead,' Trevor said. 'Now let me down.'

'Sorry, I must have misjudged that last foot,' Scott laughed, moving into the wings and lowering Trevor to the floor.

'You better watch yourself, butthead,' Trevor yelled after him. 'Tomorrow, I'm flying you.'

'I think it's time for us to leave,' I said to Clint. 'Thanks for the lesson, guys.'

'Come by for a beer after the show, Kate,' Scott called after us. Clint and I cut through the house and back up to my office.

'That's the most amazing thing I have ever seen,' he said when we were settled back in.

'What's really amazing is that they want me to do that.'

'If you do, you're as crazy as they are,' he said, opening his book.

'The fact that I'm sitting here on my day off doing the books seems a good indication of my mental condition,' I said as I looked out the window and realized what a beautiful day I was missing.

'We all do strange things on our days off,' Clint said. 'Take me, for example.'

'I think I should finish up as quickly as possible and then we'll all go out for dinner.'

'You're the boss.'

'Sorry. I'm assuming you have no life, like me,' I apologized. 'I'll just finish up here and then you can head on home.'

'It's OK, Kate.' He smiled. 'I don't have a life, not right now at least. Dinner would be fun.'

'I'll treat,' I offered.

'I'll accept.'

Motivation made my pen fly and I managed to finish the paperwork within an hour. Cam wandered back into the office and I mentioned the dinner idea to him. I figured that asking was better than telling. I was determined to work on this relationship thing. It was hard though, after thirty-three years of doing things my own way. Cam agreed dinner was a great idea and I locked everything up in the safe. I wanted to get out of the theatre before anyone changed their mind. I craved Italian food, Cam wanted a steak, Clint said he liked Mexican, so we settled on Chinese. We decided on a buffet, so we wouldn't argue over which dishes to order, and picked a place close to home.

We managed to totally stuff ourselves and get to know Clint a little better. All for under twenty-four dollars plus drinks. I couldn't believe it when I glanced at my watch and saw it was almost nine o'clock. Considering I had spent my day off more or less under house arrest, it had turned out to be a pretty good day.

Clint saw us back to the apartment, checked in with the constable on duty, and said his goodbyes. I promised him I wouldn't need to be at the theatre until around three o'clock the next day, so he could sleep in. When Cam and I were finally alone and locked up tight in the apartment, it suddenly became very quiet.

'Want to watch a movie?' I finally asked.

'Sure,' he agreed. 'What would you like?'

'You pick. Do you want me to make popcorn?'

'No, I'm stuffed. I'll take a beer though,' he said.

'I don't know if there's any left.' I wandered into the kitchen and opened the fridge.

'I picked some up last night when I got the groceries,' Cam called from the living room.

'What else did you get?' I asked, staring into the fridge. I looked over the fridge door and saw Cam staring at the videos.

'Oh, some coffee beans, fresh vegetables, and a bottle of wine, just in case you felt the urge to switch from caffeine.'

'Let's get drunk,' I suggested as I pulled some beer out of the fridge.

'You want a comedy or drama?'

'Comedy,' I said, grabbing the bottle of wine before I closed the door. 'You'll have to open the wine.'

'I'll be right there.' He pulled a movie from the shelf and put it in the VCR, then came into the kitchen and got out the corkscrew.

'You bought wine with a cork? I'm honoured.'

'Sometimes you just have no class, Katie.'

'It's all my mother's fault.'

'How do you figure that?'

'She wanted me to be a lady. This is my unique form of rebellion.'

He popped the cork and pulled a huge glass down from the cupboard for me. 'Speaking of no class, even I know that's not a wine glass.'

'If you want to get drunk, there is no point being delicate about it.' He filled the glass and handed it to me, then grabbed the beer off the counter for himself. 'Shall we?'

'After you.' I turned off the lights in the kitchen.

Cam plopped himself on the couch and grabbed the remote control.

'Will you brush my hair? I haven't been able to do it properly since I got this cast on.'

'Get your brush.'

I ran to the bathroom and grabbed my brush before he could change his mind. I sat on the floor at Cam's feet and handed him the brush.

I've been trying to grow my hair and it's halfway to my waist now. Most days I like it but there are times I feel ready

219

to drive to the nearest hairdresser and have it all cut off. I had been having a lot of those days since I got the stupid cast, but I am thirty-three and if I'm ever going to have long hair, I have to do it now. Another few years and I will be too old. In truth, I'm probably too old now, but I'll never openly admit that. I love having my hair brushed and, as an added bonus, Cam seems to enjoy doing it.

I settled into a comfortable position and he put his feet into my lap and started the movie. This was our trade off. He brushed my hair; I massaged his feet. I sipped some wine and felt a little buzz. I'm not much of a drinker. Cam reached over and shut off the table lamp. Sitting in the dark, watching a thirty-three-inch TV with surround-sound speakers made me feel like I was in a movie theatre.

My mind was wandering. I wasn't really into the movie, but I was even less into sitting in silence with Cam all night. At least the movie gave us an excuse not to talk to each other. I was enjoying the closeness and the pretence that everything was normal. I finished my first glass of wine and Cam stopped brushing long enough to refill it for me.

'I've missed this,' I said.

'Missed what?'

'Doing this kind of thing together, like we used to. Do you know it's only been two weeks since the murder? It feels like forever.'

'Katie, everything will be back to normal soon. There's only one more week to go before the play closes. I'm sure the police will catch him by then.'

'Promise?' I asked tiredly.

'Promise.'

'What do you think Graham meant at the hospital – something about manners?'

'Hmm?' Cam was trying to watch the movie.

'You know. He thought the guy that attacked him said something about manners.'

'Katie, Graham was probably high on medication. He was rambling.'

'It could be a clue. If I could only figure out what it means, maybe it could lead us to the murderer.'

He leaned over and refilled my glass. 'Drink up, you're starting to sound like a cop again.'

'You're right,' I said, sipping some wine. 'No more murder talk.'

'That's better. I'm going to get another beer. You want anything?'

'I want you,' I leered at him, definitely feeling the effects of the wine.

'I'll be back in a minute.' He returned with two beers. As he resettled himself on the couch I put the brush into his hand.

'Enough already,' he protested.

'Not enough. More wine too,' I said, holding out my empty glass.

'Are you driving anywhere tonight?' he asked as he poured.

'No, officer. I'm staying at home watching sick movies that my boyfriend insists are comedy classics.'

'Then drink up. And if you'd actually watch the movie instead of talking, you might realize that it *is* a classic.'

'You want a comedy classic, then let's try this.' I tried to stand and found that something had happened to my legs. They didn't work properly. Cam steadied me and I weaved my way to the movie shelf. I found the tape I wanted, ejected his and started mine.

'*Barefoot in the Park*?' he asked. 'Funny movie, hardly a classic.'

I made my way back to the couch and sat beside him. 'I think I'm a little bit drunk.'

'You just realized that?'

'Yes. When I stood up. Funny how that happens.' I giggled. 'What should I do now?'

'I think I should get you to bed before you pass out.'

'I'm not going to pass out,' I said defensively.

'You always pass out. You hardly ever drink and you have no resistance. I guarantee that within twenty minutes you will be dead to the world.'

'I don't want to go to bed,' I protested. 'I want to stay up all night and watch movies.'

'Why don't we watch this upstairs?' he suggested. 'Then if you do pass out I won't have to carry you up.'

'OK.' I tried to stand again and fell back down on to the couch, landing on top of Cam. 'It's a good thing I don't drink often. I hate not being able to walk.'

'But you're a cheap date.'

'Sure, like I want that on my gravestone. "Here lies a cheap date",' I said, trying to stifle another fit of giggles. I was really enjoying feeling so light-hearted.

'It'll be our little secret.'

'I am going to be so sick tomorrow,' I said, trying hard to remain serious.

'I have to work in the morning. I'm so sorry I'll miss all your suffering.'

He managed to lead me up the stairs and into the bedroom. I stood in the middle of the room and took my clothes off, dropping them on the floor, then climbed into bed. Cam picked everything up, folded it and set it on the chair. He undressed, turned off the light, and crawled in beside me.

'You said we could watch the movie up here,' I said, trying to fluff up the pillows.

'I lied.'

'Cam, did you beat Patsy?' I asked. Where did that come from? I wondered. Did I actually say that? Damn, we'd been having such a good time. Well, maybe he hadn't heard me.

'Katie, I don't want to have this conversation when you're drunk.'

Shit, he had heard me. No use turning back now. 'I just can't stop thinking about it. I need to know. Did you beat her?'

'No, I never beat her,' he said quietly. Then there was silence and I thought Cam must have fallen asleep. Then, very softly, he whispered, 'I only hit her once, Katie.'

I didn't know how to answer him, so I pretended I was asleep.

Tuesday

There was sunlight shining in my eyes and it hurt. I had a headache, my teeth felt like they were all wearing little woolen sweaters, and my stomach had shut down in protest. I rolled over, pulling the covers over my head and wanting to go back to sleep, but moving just made me realize how badly my head was pounding.

'Do you want some aspirin?'

The voice of an angel. I must have died during the night. 'Yes,' I croaked.

I felt Cam get out of bed and heard him trot down the stairs. He returned with three aspirin and a glass of water, which he put into my outstretched hand.

'Thanks,' I said, taking them greedily. 'I'm sorry I passed out last night.'

'That's OK,' he said. 'I was pretty tired, too.'

'What time is it?' I asked, trying to avoid opening my eyes wide enough to see the clock.

'It's only seven thirty,' he said. 'You can sleep for hours.'

I pulled the covers back up around me. 'Thanks for the aspirin. Are you going into work?'

'In a few minutes. Do you want me to set the alarm for you?'

'No, I'm sure I'll wake up on time.'

'I'll set it anyway,' he said, kissing me on the cheek and getting out of bed.

I lay still for several minutes, listening to him puttering in the kitchen. I finally heard him go out the door, then the apartment was silent. I got out of bed and headed for the shower. My headache was already starting to fade and I was hoping

223

that a shower and brushing my teeth would take care of the rest. By the time I was dressed and had a coffee in my hand, I almost felt human.

I took the phone into the kitchen and sat down at the table with a coffee and a bagel. I dialled Graham's place first. His mom picked up on the second ring.

'Hi, Rose, it's Kate,' I greeted her, sounding much more cheerful than I thought possible.

'Kate, good to hear from you again,' she said.

'Did you get Graham home?'

'No, the doctors decided they wanted to keep him in for another day or two. I was just on my way up to the hospital. Do you want to come with me? I can stop by and pick you up. I'm sure he'd love to see you.'

'I'd love to,' I said. 'But I'm not allowed to go anywhere without at least half the police department following me.'

'Oh, that's right. I forgot about that.'

'I'll see you up there in an hour or so,' I promised. 'Is there anything he needs?'

'Just cheering up.'

'I'll do my best, Rose. See you soon.' I hung up, then picked the phone up again and dialled another number.

'Ken Lincoln.'

'Ken, it's Kate Carpenter.'

'Hi, Kate.' He sounded so cheerful I could almost feel his grin. I hate morning people. 'Thanks for the tickets. The play was great.'

'I'm glad you enjoyed it,' I said. 'Ken, I called because I need a ride to the hospital. I want to look in on Graham.'

'You can ask the officer sitting outside your door,' Ken said. 'There shouldn't be any problem.'

'Actually, I was hoping you could give me a lift. I want to talk to you,' I confided.

'All right, I think I can get away from here for a bit. I'll meet you out front in half an hour.'

'Thanks, Ken.' I hung up, hesitated and finally dialled one last number.

'Security desk, Nick speaking.'

'Hi Nick, it's Kate.'

224

'Hi, Kate. What's up?'

'I just wanted to leave a message for Cam.'

'He's downstairs, Kate, I'll transfer you,' Nick said.

'No! I mean, I don't want to bother him. Just tell him I'm going to the hospital this morning and I'll see him at about three, when I get into work.'

'OK, will do.'

'Thanks, Nick. See you later.' Having covered all the bases, I hung up.

I loaded the dishwasher, grabbed my coat and bag and was escorted to the lobby by the officer on duty. Ken was waiting for me as promised. I jumped into the car and he put it into drive.

'Don't forget your seatbelt,' he warned me.

I fastened it and opened my window. 'You don't seem quite as cheerful as you were on the phone.'

'I've got some news for you,' he said. 'And I don't think you're going to like it. I know I didn't.'

'What?' I asked, dreading the answer.

'The department has decided it is not cost-effective to continue with these security arrangements any longer.'

'What?' I asked incredulously.

'It's been three days, Kate, and there have been no further attempts on your life. The threat appears to be over. The officers are needed elsewhere.'

'Oh my God.' I let the news sink in. 'What about Clint?'

'He'll be with you tonight,' Ken said. 'If nothing happens, he'll be reassigned tomorrow. Kate, I'm very sorry.'

'It's OK,' I said, not believing it. 'You're probably right. I haven't heard or seen anything in days. I'm sure the murderer thinks he's gotten away with it.'

'Can I guess what it was you wanted to talk to me about?' Ken changed the subject.

'Go for it.'

'You wanted to talk about Cam,' he said, looking over at me to confirm his guess.

'Did Clint talk to you?' I asked.

'Yes, he did. I looked into the complaint against Cam and the restraining order. His ex-wife went to court after he beat

225

her up. She refused to press charges but she did get a restraining order. He's not allowed within fifty feet of her.'

'He said he only hit her once,' I said.

'It must have been a good one,' Ken replied. 'He broke her jaw.'

I felt sick to my stomach.

'Other than that, Cam is clean,' Ken continued. 'He has had a few speeding tickets, but nothing else.'

'Does this make him a suspect again?' I asked.

'Truthfully, yes. But, Kate, we still have a lot of suspects and not a lot of evidence. We have no evidence against Cam except that he was the last person to use the murder weapon, which is only circumstantial at best. I don't think he did it. It's not logical; there's nothing to tie him to the crime.'

'I don't know what to do,' I said, slumping back into my seat and closing my eyes. My headache was returning quickly.

'Do you know anything else?' the detective asked. 'Any evidence that he might have done it, any suspicions?'

Everything I had was circumstantial, too. 'No.' I decided that I loved Cam, I was living with him, and I had to make myself believe in him.

Ken pulled up in front of the hospital entrance. 'You have to do what is right for you.'

'But I don't know what that is,' I admitted.

'I don't think Cam is a threat to you, Kate, but I have a feeling this case is going to be open for a long time. Can you live with that kind of doubt?'

'No, I don't think I can.' I sighed.

'Then listen to me. I've been on the police force for over ten years. I have good instincts and I don't believe he did it.'

'You fool,' I laughed. 'This is your first murder investigation.'

'How did you know?'

'I eavesdropped the first day I met you. So what do those instincts of yours tell you now?'

'OK, they're my wife's instincts. I've told her a lot about this and she insists there is no way that Cam could be responsible for any of this.'

'Thanks, Ken,' I smiled. 'Are you coming up to see Graham?'

'Not now. I thought I'd talk to him again after lunch.'

'OK, I'll see you later. Thanks for all your help.'

Ken waved as he pulled out of the driveway.

Graham's room was filled with flowers, balloons and stuffed animals. Graham himself was looking much more cheerful and alert today. He was sitting up, holding court with a cute student nurse. She saw me and smiled.

'I better get going.' She turned her smile to Graham. 'I'll be back this afternoon to give you a sponge bath.'

I watched her walk out of the room and turned to see that Graham was doing the same. 'I see you're feeling better,' I said, teasing him.

'Kate, this place is great! I don't think I've ever felt so good.'

'I thought they were springing you yesterday?'

'When I met Mandi yesterday afternoon, I decided I should stay for another day and get to know her better. I told them I was having dizzy spells.'

'Does your mother know about this?' I asked.

'No, and don't you dare tell her,' he ordered. 'I'll be home living under her rules soon enough. Let me have a little fun now.'

'They did your teeth,' I said, noticing he had his old smile back.

'Yeah, the dentist came up today and put temporary caps on. Said I can have the permanent ones done whenever I feel up to it.'

'They look good. How's the rest of you feeling?'

'A little sore when I move,' he said. 'Not so bad when I'm lying here. The doctor said I'd be my old self again in a couple of weeks.'

'Glad to hear it. So does this mean you want tonight off, or do you think you can make it in?'

'I think I'll stay right here. Mandi and I have plans for a sponge bath and then dinner.'

'You are so obvious,' I said. 'I bet she sees right through you.'

'I hope so.' He laughed. 'Now tell me about you.'

227

'Nothing to tell.'

'Kate, I've been worried sick.'

'Graham, there's nothing to tell. Absolutely nothing has happened in the last three days. The police think it's over. Whoever was trying to scare me thinks he got away with it. He's faded back into the scenery.'

'Really?'

I was just guessing, but I was pretty sure Graham didn't believe me. 'Really,' I assured him. 'So quit worrying about me and concentrate on getting back to work. I don't have anyone to give the dirty work to and I'm very tired of doing the inventory myself.'

'It's character building, Kate, remember?'

I checked my watch and found it was getting close to noon. 'I better get going.'

'So soon?' he whined.

'Don't want to interrupt your sponge bath. Besides, I have something I have to do at the Plex,' I said. 'I promise I'll see you tomorrow, and your mom will be here soon.'

'That's supposed to be comforting? Oh well, say hi to everyone at the theatre for me and thank them for all the stuff.'

I leaned over and kissed his cheek. 'I will. Take care and call me if you need anything.'

'Or remember anything,' he said, losing some of his good cheer.

'Yeah, that too.'

I caught a cab, feeling strangely vulnerable. This was the first time in days I was without an escort. I had the taxi drop me off at the corner and stopped in at Gus's for a coffee. I sat on my favourite stool and waited for Gus to come over.

'Kate, long time no see,' Gus said. 'Where's those police guys you've been hanging around with? Don't they drink coffee?'

'I think they're too busy,' I said. 'I'll have a large African blend please.'

He poured me a cup of the strongest coffee he had brewing and put it in front of me. 'So where are the police today?' he asked.

'Meeting me later. They seem to think the threat is over.'

'They're wrong,' Gus said. 'He's just waiting for the right moment.'

'If you know so much, why don't you know who did it?' I asked, sounding angrier than I had meant to.

'Because he's smarter than we're giving him credit for. He hasn't left a single clue yet. At least not one that we've figured out. Kate, you have to be smarter.'

'I'll try,' I said, picking up my coffee and turning for the door.

'I know you're a smart girl, Kate, but be a careful one too, OK?' he said as I walked out the door.

The sun was shining and I thought it looked like we might have an Indigenous Aboriginal North American Summer – I always strive to be politically correct.

I walked the half block to the stage door slowly, not really wanting to go inside, but feeling very vulnerable out on the street. Ken had almost made me believe this might be over but Gus's warning was still ringing in my ears and I was on edge again. I climbed the steps and entered the building. Nick was sitting at the security desk talking on the phone. He looked up and smiled at me as I approached. I signed the logbook and then waited for him to get off the phone so I could collect my messages. My eyes wandered to the security camera monitors hanging on the wall behind him.

'I'll just be a second, Kate,' Nick told me, putting his hand over the receiver.

'Take your time,' I said. I noticed Cam on one of the monitors, walking down the corridor on the third floor, approaching the Concert Hall. I made a mental note to call him as soon as I got to my office, and let him know I was here early. Then I saw Gladys on the monitor. She had just entered camera range from the other end of the corridor. I saw Cam smile at her and Gladys smiled back. She hugged him and kissed him on the cheek. They stood talking for a minute or so and then she hugged him again. They started walking down the hallway, arm in arm, and then were out of camera range. I couldn't tear my eyes away from the screen.

'Here's your messages, Kate,' Nick said, handing several pieces of notepaper through the window to me.

I stared at him, not comprehending what he was saying. I looked down at the papers held out to me and forced my hand out to accept them. 'Thanks,' I said, and turned down the hall. Nick buzzed me through the security door and I started down the alley towards the theatre.

Cam had lied to me. I refused to believe that he and Gladys were just old family friends – not after seeing that little display of affection. Why was he still lying to me? I had to talk to Detective Lincoln. I wanted to let him know that Cam and Gladys were having some sort of a relationship. I closed myself in my office and wedged a doorstop under the door, locking myself in. I dialled the number for the police department.

'Detective Lincoln's desk,' a voice answered.

'Is he there?'

'I'm sorry, he's away from his desk right now. Can I take a message?'

'Just tell him Kate Carpenter called.'

'Does he have your number?' the voice asked.

'Yes. Thank you.'

I hung up. That hadn't resolved a thing. What was I going to say to Cam tonight? I couldn't tell him I had seen him with Gladys this afternoon, he would just come up with another story and sucker me in. I would end up believing everything he said and feel guilty about doubting him. Everything would be fine until the next time I caught him in a lie. I'd been here before. I was trapped in a vicious circle and I didn't know how to get out of it.

The problem was that despite all this, I knew I loved Cam. I liked having him with me all the time. I depended on him and I didn't want it to end. But maybe it was inevitable. If Cam was having a relationship with Gladys then it was already over between us. I guessed the only thing I could do was go home tonight and see what happened.

Clint showed up about five o'clock. He came by to check on me, and offer his apologies for the way things had worked out. He offered to stay for the night's shift but I assured him I could manage on my own. Clint gave me his business card and told me to call him any time I needed him.

I did a sleepwalking act through the show, working on autopilot. The ushers sensed my mood and were incredibly helpful and very quiet. We finished by eleven.

I hadn't heard from Cam all day. When I phoned Nick, he told me that Cam had signed out at seven. I stopped in at the green room and Scott offered to take me home. We signed out and climbed down the stairs to the street, where I saw Cam parked in the loading dock, waiting for me.

'You want to go with him?' Scott asked, nodding his head in Cam's direction.

'I better,' I said. 'Thanks for your help.'

'See you tomorrow.'

Cam got out as I approached, walked around to the passenger side, and opened the door for me.

'I thought you'd forgotten about me,' I said as I fastened my seatbelt.

'I'm sorry. I should have called you tonight. I had a lousy day.'

'Well, so did I.'

'Katie, when I got home there was no cop at the door.'

'If you'd called me today I would have told you about that. I saw Ken Lincoln this morning and he told me the department decided they couldn't afford to keep protecting me if no one was going to have the decency to try to kill me.'

'I said I was sorry,' he repeated, pulling the car out into the street.

'Me too,' I said. 'I didn't mean to be bitchy. Tell me why your day was so lousy.'

'Same old shit,' he said. 'I do everything in this building but what I'm licensed to do. And then a good friend of mine let me down today.'

'Who?' I asked, thinking I knew the answer.

'It's nothing, Katie,' he said. 'Want to stop for something to eat?'

'I just want to go to bed,' I said. 'Do you mind?'

'No, I'm exhausted.'

Cam parked, turned the engine off and we walked in silence. Cam opened the apartment door and turned on the hall light.

'You go first,' I said.

'You want me to have a look around?' he asked.

'Yes please.' I stayed by the door while Cam turned on every light and checked all the closets.

'Just as we left it,' he said, turning off some lights.

'Thanks,' I said, securing the locks. I dropped my bag and slipped off my shoes.

'Katie, I think we need some help,' Cam started. 'You don't feel safe in your own home and I'm angry all the time, feeling like I can't protect you.'

'What are you suggesting?'

'Some sort of counselling. Crime victims get help all the time. I think there are doctors that specialize in things like this.'

'I'll be fine,' I said.

'But I don't know if I will be.'

'Cam, I've got to go to bed. I'm so tired that I can't even think straight.'

'Katie,' he called after me as I started up the stairs.

'What?' I turned to face him.

'I need you.'

'Come up to bed,' I said. 'You need some sleep, you look awful.'

He turned off the lights and checked the locks again before he came up. The bedroom was dark. He undressed without turning the light on and crawled in beside me. I reached over and brushed a stray lock of hair from his forehead.

'What's wrong?' I asked.

He didn't answer, just moved close to me, wrapped me in his arms and held me tightly.

'Whatever it is, you can tell me.'

'Not now,' he said. 'Tomorrow.'

'OK.' I wrapped my arms around him, hugging him back.

Wednesday

I lay in bed, awake but in no hurry to open my eyes and start the day. I knew it was late by the angle the sun was shining in through the window. I did my best imitation of a cat stretch and slowly turned to look at the clock. It was almost noon. Cam's side of the bed felt cool. He must have left for work hours ago and I hadn't heard a sound. I sat up, feeling well rested, and decided it was time to get moving. I found myself looking forward to the prospect of having the apartment to myself.

In the kitchen I found Cam had left some cigarettes on the table and the coffee on the stove. I poured myself a cup and lit a cigarette. The newspaper was on the table and I opened it to the crossword puzzle, sat down, and began working my way through it.

About an hour later I pushed the completed puzzle aside and put on a fresh pot of coffee. I called the hospital and found out that Graham had been discharged. I decided to give his mom a chance to settle him at home and would call them later. I wandered back into the kitchen and opened the fridge. There were some bagels and a piece of cheddar cheese in the vegetable drawer. I scraped the mold off the cheese, sliced it on to the bagel, spread on a little mayo, and went out on to the balcony to eat. I always feel the urge to be outside at this time of year. Soon we would be snowed in for the winter, the one season in which I didn't enjoy the great outdoors. I know I'm the only person in Calgary who doesn't ski or skate. Winters are very long for me.

I finished my sandwich and had settled into my lounge chair with a book when the doorbell rang. Cam had hooked the doorbell up for me in the spring, after spending an hour in the hallway one night knocking on the door. I had been sitting on the balcony and hadn't heard a thing. Next day, I had a doorbell. Nothing like a little personal discomfort to spur a man into action.

I got up, angry at being disrupted during the first few hours of peace I had enjoyed in weeks. I realized I was still wearing the T-shirt I had slept in, so I grabbed my housecoat, fastened the belt and looked through the peephole.

'Gladys?' I was shocked to see her standing there and threw open the door.

'Hello, Katherine.' She pushed in past me, not waiting for an invitation. 'I won't keep you long. I just feel there are a few things we must discuss.'

'Do come in,' I said sarcastically, closing the door and following her into the living room.

'Your apartment looks lovely,' she said, sitting on the couch. 'I don't see any of Cam's belongings here yet.'

'I don't believe that's any of your business,' I said, still standing, hoping she wasn't planning on staying long.

'Well, actually Katherine, Cam has spoken to me about you. I really feel like this is my fault.'

'You have a lot of balls to discuss me and then show up here to tell me about it.' I was indignant. I went into the kitchen and grabbed a cigarette.

'Well, I'm about to discuss him with you. Perhaps that will even things out and make you feel better.'

I came back into the living room with my cigarettes and ashtray. 'You sanctimonious bitch,' I snarled. 'How dare you?'

'Do stop and sit down,' Gladys said. 'You have no idea what you are talking about. Now if you would like to listen to me for a moment, I can clear this up.'

I sat, not knowing what else to do. 'Just tell me how long you and Cam have been having this relationship?' I asked. 'Has it been going on the entire time I've been seeing him?'

'Katherine, I am not seeing Cam. I've already explained this to you. He and I have known each other, socially, for a long time.'

'Well you seem to be quite close lately.'

'You're wasting my time, Katherine. I told Cam that I

wouldn't be any help. He has been after me for a week to come and speak with you. He seems to think I can make you listen. The problem is that you are too stubborn to reason with. I'm not sure exactly what Cam sees in you.'

If I had been closer, I would have slapped her face. Since I wasn't, I stood up and pointed dramatically towards the door. 'Get out!'

'No, I've come this far and you're going to listen to what I have to say. Then I can wash my hands of this. So, unless you were planning on physically throwing me out, I suggest you sit down.'

I obeyed her again, feeling defeated.

'I'm not here to tell you why Cam and Patsy broke up. That's something he will tell you when he's ready. As your brilliant investigative skills have already uncovered, he did hit her once, and broke her jaw. I think she's lucky he was so restrained. Had it been me in that situation, I would have killed her. Cam was never violent before that, or since. He has spent the last year trying to get over the guilt of what he did. So, dear, you have nothing to worry about; he is not a wife beater and I seriously doubt he will ever hit anyone again, despite the provocation.'

'Thank you for telling me that.' I stood again, ready to see her to the door.

'I'm not finished,' she informed me coldly. I felt like a yo-yo as I sat down again. I lit another cigarette, trying to hide my discomfort. 'Now, as to Cam being the murderer? Get over it, Katherine, he isn't a murderer. I don't know how you could ever believe he could do it, but be assured the very idea is outside the realm of possibility.'

'Why should I believe you?'

'I've known him for years. You will just have to trust me. If I had any idea that asking you to look into this would cause all these problems, I would never have brought it up.'

'Oh, Saint Gladys.' I rolled my eyes. 'You have always done whatever suits your needs at the time. You wanted someone to find out who murdered your ex-husband and nothing would have stopped you from asking me to help.'

'You're right.' She smiled. 'I am used to getting what I want.

235

But I am genuinely sorry that this has caused you so many problems.'

'And not even caught the murderer?' I asked, finishing her thought.

'Yes, we should have at least caught the murderer. Now, I want you to forgive Cam and forget me. Your play closes in a few more days. Go away with him.'

'There is so much more happening between us than you know,' I said. 'He has lied to me so many times.'

'Katherine, he was not ready to deal with any of this yet. He would have told you when the time was right, but you forced it out of him. Forgive him for being human.'

I stood again, determined to end the visit this time. 'I think the rest of this is too personal for me to discuss with you,' I told her, walking towards the door.

'You're right, and I'm really not interested in your personal life – as I've been telling Cam for the last week.' She grabbed her purse and followed me to the door. 'I've done my duty and can sleep with a clear conscience now. What you do with this information is up to you.'

I closed the door behind her and locked it.

I showered, dressed and decided to walk to the Plex. I needed some time to enjoy the sunshine and clear my mind. I walked down the river pathway, enjoying the cool breeze and sunshine and the fact that there were hardly any rollerbladers out. I walked past the market, veering to peek into the shop windows as I went. I wasn't in a buying mood, but I'm always in a looking mood. I was starting to feel better. I might not be able to catch a murderer but I was going to straighten out the rest of my life. I was going to talk to Cam as soon as I could and I wasn't going to be scared any longer. I had secure locks on my doors, my friends were watching out for me, and nothing had happened for almost four days now. I probably had as much chance of getting hit by a bus as I did of being murdered. I certainly didn't cower every time a bus went by. I stopped at Gus's on the way to my office.

'Hey, Gus.' I smiled. 'What's new?'

'Kate, you seem a little more cheerful today. What can I get you?' he asked.

'Cappuccino to go please.' I put some money down on the counter.

He turned to make my coffee, but kept talking. 'That Burns fellow has been in looking for you.'

'Graham warned me about him,' I replied. 'Seems he wanted my job and is holding a bit of a grudge. Frankly, right now, he can have my job.'

'I think you've got to watch out for him, Kate.'

'Why? He's mostly just a harmless drunk.'

'He drinks too much coffee to be a drunk,' Gus said. 'That's usually what they do after they join AA.'

'But he's still up in the BOB every night,' I said. 'If he is going to AA then he's not doing a very good job of it.'

'Well, you watch out for him,' Gus said. 'I don't trust him.'

'I think he's all talk.' Who would try to kill someone over a job like mine?'

He handed the coffee across the counter to me. 'You just keep those big strong boys close to you,' he said. 'Keep me from worrying about you so much.'

'I will. I'll see you tomorrow.'

I walked the half block and climbed the stairs at the stage door. Otis was sitting behind the security desk.

'Good afternoon, Kate,' he greeted me cheerfully.

'Hi, Otis,' I said, signing my name into the logbook. 'Where's Nick?'

'In the bathroom. There aren't any messages for you today.'

'Thanks.' I started down the hall then turned back. 'Will you radio Cam and let him know I'm in my office?'

'Sure thing,' he said as he buzzed me through the security door.

I opened the door into the theatre. The lights were on and I heard some noise coming from the stage as I passed the dressing rooms and headed into the lobby. I wanted to get everything ready for the evening and keep my mood up. I owed my staff a fun night after yesterday.

The light was on in my office, but that didn't worry me. The cleaners often forget to turn the lights off after themselves. I saw an envelope sitting on my otherwise empty desk. I picked it up and tore it open. There was just one line on the page.

I KNOW THE POLICE AREN'T
WATCHING YOU ANYMORE

I crumpled the paper up into a ball and threw it into the garbage can. Then I unlocked my office door and wedged a doorstop under it, defiantly keeping it open.

'You don't scare me, you asshole!' I shouted down the empty hall.

My phone rang and I realized I must look very foolish standing here, screaming into an empty corridor. I sat down and picked up the phone.

'Front of house,' I said.

'Hi, Katie.'

'Hi, Cam. I missed you this morning.'

'I tried to be quiet,' he said. 'You looked like you needed some sleep.'

'Gladys came over this morning.'

'She did?' he asked, surprised.

'Yes. Was she the friend who let you down yesterday?' I asked, and when I got no response from Cam, said, 'I thought so. Have you spoken to her since?'

'Briefly,' he admitted.

'I think you and I need to talk.'

'I can't now,' he said. 'I'm up to my ears in water. We're trying to flush out the heating system.'

'I don't want to talk here anyway,' I said. 'Tonight, at home?'

'Sure.'

'Cam, I want you to be honest tonight,' I said. 'This isn't about the murder any more. This is about you and me now. I know you hit Patsy and I need to know why. I understand that you don't feel comfortable talking about it, but knowing why you hit her is very important to me.'

'I understand.'

'I don't feel there is ever a justifiable reason for a man to hit a woman,' I told him. 'I'm just warning you, I'm going to need to know what made you do it.'

238

'I understand, Katie,' he said quietly.

'If you don't think you can talk about it yet, don't come home.'

'I'll be there,' he said. 'Do you want me to pick you up after work?'

'I'll get Scott to drive me home. I love you.'

'I love you too.'

I put the phone down and decided to call Graham before getting emotional. He picked up the phone on the first ring.

'Whoever this is, please help me. I'm being held hostage by my mother. Please come and rescue me.'

'You idiot,' I said. 'You should be kissing that woman's feet for what she's done for you.'

'Kate, she dusted.'

'Oh my God!'

'She killed my two pet dust bunnies that I kept under the bed.'

'I can see now why you've never invited me over to your place.'

'I'm going crazy,' he said. 'You've got to help me.'

'I'll wait until after she cleans the bathroom,' I said. 'Then I'll come over and see what I can do. Now, tell me seriously, how are you doing?'

'I'm fine,' he said. 'Can I come into work tonight?'

'I wish you could, but I think you'd be more trouble than you're worth. I'd like to see you climb up and down all these stairs with those crutches. Are you lonely?'

'No, I'm surrounded by well-wishers. And Mandi has come over to check on me.'

'That little nurse from the hospital?'

'That's the one.'

'Well, I'll be damned,' I said. 'She must be even dumber than she looked.'

'My type of woman.'

'Should I come over tomorrow and check you out?' I asked.

'I'd like that.'

'I'll call before I come. Talk to you then?'

'Sure. If you have any dust at your place, bring it over OK? Mom's running out of things to do.'

I hung up, feeling my mood rise again. Everything was going to be all right.

The show went well, we laughed and giggled our way through the entire evening, and Scott dropped me off in front of my place just before midnight. I made my way upstairs, wondering if Cam would be there. As I put my key into the lock he opened the door and pulled me to him, hugging me.

'I missed you,' he said.

'Me too.'

'Are you hungry?' he asked, pulling me inside and locking the door behind me.

'No, I grabbed a salad before the show,' I said, dropping my boots and bag at the door. I followed him into the living room. He had some jazz playing, candles lit, and a bottle of wine open.

'Are we celebrating?' I asked.

'Hopefully.'

I sat on the couch, and noticed he had a plate of cheese, crackers, and antipasti sitting on the table. Cam sat down on the couch and poured two glasses of wine. I sat cross-legged and turned so I was facing him. He handed me a glass and I took a sip. He had bought the good stuff again.

'Here's to the truth,' he said, holding his glass up.

I reached over and clinked glasses with him.

'I haven't told anyone this, Katie. I've felt so guilty that I was ashamed to tell anyone. I've finally worked up my courage, so I'm just going to plow through the story.'

He sipped his wine and I let him talk.

'Patsy and I got married when we were just twenty. We both wanted a family while we were young and spent years trying, but she never got pregnant. She went to school, got a job and I was making good money. We had a great place, nice cars, lots of things, but no baby. I had tests done and so did she but there was nothing wrong with either of us. I wanted to adopt, but she wanted to keep trying for our own. Well, fourteen years later she got pregnant. God, I was so happy . . .' He stopped to take another drink. I didn't know what to say, so I just let him continue.

'I thought we had everything then. Patsy thought we had

240

everything before. She liked her job and somewhere along the line had decided she didn't want to be a mother. She told me she didn't want to have the baby. I told her I would raise it, I would leave if she didn't want us around, but I wanted our baby. I guess she didn't care. I came home from work one day and she wasn't pregnant any more. She went for an abortion that morning.'

I reached over and took his hand. I squeezed it, letting him know I was there for him.

'I lost it, Katie. I don't really remember what else happened, I just kind of blacked out. Next thing I knew, she was lying on the ground, screaming in pain. I guess I had hit her. I have never been so angry in my life. But I never thought I could hit a woman.'

'Cam, I don't know what to say.'

'There's nothing *to* say. It happened. I did something I never thought I was capable of. That's why I left when we had that big fight. I felt myself getting angry and I was afraid I might hurt you.'

'You were pushed beyond reason,' I said.

'So that's my story. My ugly past. I don't think there is a justifiable reason to hit a woman either – even that. Can you stand to be around me, knowing everything?'

'I think I can.' I put my wine down and moved closer to him. He put his arm around my shoulder and pulled me even closer.

'Why didn't you ever tell me?' I asked.

'Right. I can picture that. Oh, by the way, the reason my wife divorced me was because I beat her up. Would you have ever had anything to do with me?'

'Probably not.'

'So, where do we stand now?' he asked. 'Have I lost you?'

'No, Cam. You haven't lost me. I haven't exactly told you everything about my past, either.'

'Oh?'

'We'll save that for another time,' I said. 'I think there's been enough true confessions for one night.'

Thursday

I was in the middle of this great dream, just Tom Cruise and me, when the alarm went off, interrupting one of the best times I'd had in months – real or imagined. Cam finally reached over, shut it off and climbed out of bed. Try as I might to stay with him, Tom grew fainter and fainter. I gave up and opened my eyes.

'Where are you going?' I mumbled sleepily.

'To work,' he said. 'Go back to sleep, it's early.'

'Don't go,' I said, grabbing his arm. My dream with Tom Cruise had left me feeling very amorous.

'Katie, I have to go to work,' he informed me coolly, trying to pull his arm free.

'Call in sick,' I suggested.

'I can't. Let me go, I've got to take a shower.'

'I hate it when we work different shifts.' I pouted, finally letting him free.

'I promise I'll drop by your office this afternoon,' he said, leaning over to kiss me.

I wrapped my arms around his neck and pulled him back into bed.

'Katie, I'm going to be late,' he protested.

'You've been late before and didn't seem to mind.'

'I've got a very important meeting at eight o'clock and I can't be late.'

I reluctantly released him and he climbed out of bed for the second time.

'Can we have lunch today?' I asked as he started down the stairs.

'Sure, meet me at the stage door at noon. I'll buy.'

Feeling defeated, I curled up into a ball, pulled the covers around me, and went back to sleep.

I woke up again at eleven o'clock and decided I had better get up if I was going to meet Cam by noon. I was out the door by eleven forty-five and at the Plex by twelve on the nose. Cam was waiting for me at the stage door. We walked around the outside of the building towards Vaudevilles and found an empty table on the patio. We talked, yet again, about going away for a couple of days when the play closed. I protested, yet again, and finally convinced Cam that Saskatoon was not the ideal destination. I wanted to go somewhere we didn't know anyone, or didn't even have to *see* anyone if we chose not to. We were stumped and beginning to become argumentative, so I suggested we could make a decision later. I didn't want lunch to end with an argument. Cam had to get back to work, and I walked with him as far as my office. He kissed me goodbye and disappeared down the fire escape into the basement.

I opened the safe, pulled out the deposit bag and sat down at my desk. I wanted to get my work done right away and then I would go see what Scott and Trevor were up to. I made some coffee and started sorting through the deposits. The floats were counted and locked safely in the desk. I took the liquor sheets down and did a very quick inventory. My least favorite jobs were done for the day. Now I could have some fun. I poured a coffee and lit a cigarette.

Sitting alone, I realized how tired I was. The stress was catching up with me. I needed three or four days' sleep before I would feel like my old self again. My wrist hurt where the cast was rubbing, but the doctor told me to expect some discomfort. Knowing that didn't make me feel any better, just more cranky. I took a final drag off my cigarette and put it out. Time to take a couple of aspirin and go find something constructive to do.

I opened my desk drawer and shook a couple of aspirin from the bottle into my hand. I downed the first one with a sip of cold coffee. I refilled my cup and settled on the window sill, when I heard a noise in the hall. The door was closed and

I couldn't see into the corridor. I sat quietly, every nerve fibre in my body standing at attention, when I heard it again. It sounded like someone was at the end of the corridor, coming in through the fire escape. I picked up my phone and dialled the security desk.

'Nick here.'

'Nick, it's Kate. Do you have any guards in the theatre?' I whispered.

'Nope. We're on shift change, Kate, everyone is standing right in front of me.'

'There's someone here, Nick!'

'Where are you?'

'In my office and I'm locked in. It sounds like there's someone in the hall.'

'Stay there, we're on our way,' he ordered and slammed the receiver down. I set my phone down very quietly and then moved closer to the door. I hadn't heard any other noises and was beginning to believe that my imagination was working overtime. I opened the door a crack, ready to slam it shut in an instant if I saw anyone in the corridor. I didn't; the hallway was empty. The main lights were off, but the sun was streaming in through the windows and there weren't any shadows to hide in. I grabbed my keys, put them in my pocket, and ventured out, letting my office door close quietly behind me. I was not about to let this guy scare me again.

'Hello?' I called quietly, feeling a little foolish. 'Is anyone there?'

When there was no response, I walked further down the corridor, feeling much more confident. There was no one there. I was being foolish and letting my imagination get the better of me.

'Hello?' I called again. 'Is anyone here?'

I opened the door to the washroom and peeked in. It was empty. I moved on further and tried the door to the ushers' locker room. It was locked. At the end of the corridor I tried the door that led into the lobby, but it didn't open either. If there had been someone in this corridor they wouldn't have been able to get back out again. The only other door led into the fire exit. I opened it up and peered in but couldn't see anyone. I felt my pocket to make sure I had my keys, then entered the fire escape, letting the door close behind me.

'Hello?' I called again, braver by the minute. 'Is anyone here?'

'Kate.'

I just about jumped out of my skin and felt an adrenalin rush. I hadn't actually expected to find anyone. 'Hello, who's there?' I yelled, sounding much braver than I now felt.

'Kate, I'm up here,' the voice beckoned.

I ran up the first flight of stairs. 'Where are you?' I called when I reached the landing. But there was only silence.

These stairs go down as far as the third level of the basement and all the way up to the second balcony. It's not the place to try to corner someone. I paused a moment to catch my breath, then started down the stairs. I was going to wait for security, like I should have in the first place, and let them chase the bad guy. When I reached the landing I heard another noise behind me and quickly turned to look. I thought I saw a shadow on the wall. I hurried across the landing, racing for the door, still watching behind me. I took the keys out of my pocket and fumbled to get the right one in the door. I took a deep breath to try and control my panic as well as my shaking hands, and turned my full attention to making the key fit into the lock. Finally, it went in. I glanced over my shoulder one last time when the door flew open. I jumped back, shocked and not sure how to escape. I tried to turn around and run up to the next level but a hand grabbed my arm. I tried to pull away, shocked by who I saw.

'Cam?'

'I'm sorry, Katie.' He grabbed my hand and pulled me away from the ascending stairs.

'Let me go!' I screamed. I struggled, trying to get away, and lost my balance. For an endless moment, I teetered at the top of the stairs, trying to grab a railing to save myself, and then time suddenly returned to normal and I fell.

There was pain as my shoulder hit the concrete stairs, and I felt my nails ripping as I tried to reach for the banister and missed, scraping them across the concrete wall instead. I knew I was going to hit the landing, thinking it was lucky that my head would hit first, since everyone always told me it was the hardest part of my body.

I thought I heard someone calling my name but they sounded very far away. I felt so tired and didn't have the strength to answer. If they would only let me sleep for another few minutes . . . But the voice wouldn't stop. Something cold touched my cheek and I finally opened my eyes.

'Go away,' I slurred, finding it hard to make my voice work.

'Can you hear me?'

'Yes. Just let me sleep.' That was hard work, stringing together a whole sentence.

'Katie, do you know where you are?'

'I'm . . .' Shit, where was I? 'I'm at work. Someone pushed me down the stairs.'

'It's OK. I'm here.' It was Cam talking to me. 'Now I don't want you to move. We've called an ambulance and it'll be here in a few minutes, OK?'

I struggled to open my eyes. 'Cam?'

'Yes, I'm here.'

I saw him kneeling over me, felt him holding my hand. Nick knelt beside him, talking into his radio.

'Am I hurt?' I asked, trying to sit up. The blinding pain that shot through my head convinced me to lie still for a while.

'I don't think so.'

'Any bones poking out, any blood?' I asked.

'No, Katie. Everything looks OK. But I don't want you to move.'

'I'll just sleep for a while.' I decided that would be the least painful option.

'No, I want you to stay awake until the ambulance gets here, OK?'

'OK.'

'Do you remember what happened?' he asked, a worried look crossing his face.

'No. I fell. That's all I remember – starting to fall after he pushed me.'

'He pushed you?' Nick asked.

'Who?' Cam asked. 'Do you remember who?'

246

'No,' I closed my eyes again. 'I can't think right now, I have a headache.'

'OK, we'll worry about it later.' He turned to Nick. 'Can you have someone call Detective Lincoln?'

'Already have,' Nick told him.

'Where's the ambulance?' Cam barked at the security guard.

'Just pulled up,' Nick replied calmly. 'Otis is bringing the paramedics up now.'

Cam turned back to me. 'They're on their way. You still doing OK?'

'I'm fine, I just need to sleep.' And I did.

Friday

When I opened my eyes, the sun was still shining, and I guessed I hadn't been unconscious too long. I had a horrible headache and felt slightly nauseous, but other than that nothing seemed badly damaged. I turned my head and saw Cam sleeping in a chair beside the bed. I sat up a little and did a quick survey of myself. No new casts on any of my limbs, no obvious bandages or stitches. I couldn't see any bruises, but I could certainly feel them.

I pushed the blanket away and swung my legs over the edge of the bed. Slowly, I pushed myself off the bed and tried to stand. I felt my legs grow weak, my head started to spin and I began to crumple, when two hands suddenly reached out to grab me.

'No, let me go!' I screamed, trying to break free.

'Katie, it's me.' Cam resisted my attempts to push him away and sat me back on the bed.

'Cam, I'm sorry.' I breathed deeply, trying to get my head to stop spinning. 'I saw you reaching out for me and I flashed back to just before I fell. All I could think of was those hands reaching out and pushing me down the stairs.'

He wrapped his arms around me. 'You're safe now.'

'Did they find him? Was he in the basement?'

'No, they couldn't find anyone.'

'Then I'm not safe. Detective Lincoln was wrong, Cam, this guy has not gone away. I could have died.'

'But you're OK. I'm not letting you out of my sight again, and you're not going back to work.'

Work? Who was running the show? 'What time is it?' I asked. 'I've got a show to run. I've got to get to the theatre.'

'It's two o'clock. On Friday.'

'Friday?'

'You've been here for a day, Katie,' he explained.

'My God, what about the theatre?'

'Doug Mendlesson is running the show for you. I talked with him before I came to the hospital yesterday and he said not to worry, he could handle everything. He'll manage tonight, too.'

'I can't hide any more. I can't stay in the apartment for the rest of my life. I have to find out who is doing this.'

'No, Katie, let the police handle it. We're finished with it.'

'Cam, I know something or I've seen something and I just haven't figured out what it is yet. Until I do, I'm not going to be safe. Anywhere. No matter what Ken says.'

'Well, you'll be safe here for a week or so,' he said.

'I can't stay here.'

'Katie, the doctors want to keep you here for observation.'

'Why? I feel OK.' I tried to smile to prove I was fine but it only made my headache worse.

'You were very lucky. Lots of bruises, but that's about all. Luckily, you seem to have landed on your head, so there was no serious damage.' He grinned at me, trying to ease the tension.

'Then I can go,' I insisted.

'You have a concussion, Katie. You have to stay here so they can keep an eye on you.'

'Cam, please help me get dressed and take me home. I don't want to stay here.'

'I think it would be better if you did.'

'If you're planning a battle of wills, you know I'm going to win.'

'God, Katie, you make me crazy. Why can't you just do the sensible thing for once?'

I got off the bed again, very slowly, and stood unsteadily, but I did manage to stay standing this time. I walked over to the closet and opened it to find the jeans and blouse I had worn to work. Cam relented and helped me dress.

'I'm doing this under extreme protest,' he said.

'Fine, as long as you're doing it.'

'It'll serve you right if you lapse into a coma.'

'I've got a miserable headache and someone is trying to kill me, so I'm not in a great mood right now,' I warned him. 'I want to go home and have a bath. I don't want to listen to a lecture now or for the next several days. Do you feel you are able to comply with these requests?'

'Fuck, Katie, you are not the only one who is scared here. Do you have any idea how I felt, seeing you unconscious at the bottom of the stairs? Perhaps you could stop for one minute and realize there are two of us involved in this.'

I looked at him, opened my mouth to lash out, and burst into tears instead. 'I'm sorry,' I cried.

'No, I'm the one who should be sorry,' he said, wrapping me in his arms.

'Please, Cam, just take me home.'

He picked up my bag and threw it over his shoulder, took my arm, and walked me out to the nurses' desk. The doctor protested, made me sign all sorts of forms promising not to sue him if something horrible happened, but finally Cam got me home.

I dropped my bag at the door and headed straight for the bath. I filled it with water as hot as I could stand and climbed in. My right shoulder and hip were really sore and I imagined the bruises would be ugly when they finally emerged. I submerged myself into the water and felt better almost immediately. Cam brought me in a cup of tea and then left me alone. I heard him turn the TV on and smelled something wonderful cooking.

Eventually the water began to cool and I reluctantly got out of the bath, put on Cam's robe and walked into the living room. He was lying on the couch watching a movie.

'Feeling better?' he asked.

'Much.' I smiled, trying to prove I meant it. 'I'm really tired but things aren't hurting quite as badly as they were.'

'Good.'

'Is there room there for me?' I asked.

Cam moved over a little and I lay down beside him. He tucked a pillow under my head.

'Comfortable?' he asked.

'Very. Will dinner keep if I sleep for an hour or so?'

'It'll be fine, Katie. Sleep for as long as you like.'

I kissed him. 'Thank you,' I said. 'I'm so sorry I got angry at the hospital.'

'It's OK, don't worry about it. I think we're both just about at the end of our ropes. We could both use some sleep.'

I cuddled close to him and was asleep in an instant.

The hallway was dark. I was running down it, almost blindly. I knew someone was behind me and I had to get away. The corridor seemed to stretch for miles as I ran, trying to get to safety. I finally made it to a door and pushed my way through. I was suddenly standing on the edge of a bottomless cliff, trying to regain my balance.

'I'm sorry,' a voice said from somewhere behind me, and I turned around to see where it was coming from. I saw an arm emerge from the darkness and push me.

'Please don't,' I begged, trying to grab at the arm to keep myself from falling.

It seemed an eternity as I reached out, groping through the darkness for a handhold, as I leaned further and further over the edge of the cliff at an impossible angle. Then I fell.

'Help me!' I screamed. 'Cam!'

'Katie, Katie, wake up.'

I opened my eyes and looked around, not sure where I was.

'Katie, you were dreaming.' Cam shook my shoulders gently. 'Do you hear me? You were having a dream.'

'Cam?' I tried to reorient myself. A part of me felt as though I was still falling off the cliff.

'Are you OK?' he asked.

'I think so.'

'Was it a nightmare?'

'Yes.' The memory came flooding back. 'Oh God, somebody pushed me, I was falling.'

'Katie, did you see who it was?'

'No. Everything was dark. All I could see was his arm. Cam, I'm so scared.' I grabbed him, hanging on for dear life.

'You're OK,' he repeated. 'I'm right here.'

'What are we going to do?'

'Run away?' he suggested.

'How far do we have to go to get away from this?' I asked.

'OK, let's not run away. Let's have dinner and go to bed. Tomorrow's got to look brighter. Detective Lincoln is coming over in the morning; maybe he'll have some good news.'

'I'm so glad you're here, Cam. I couldn't get through this without you.'

'I love you,' he said tenderly.

Cam took me into the kitchen, fed me some homemade soup and biscuits, and helped me up to bed. He made sure I was comfortable, then went down and checked the locks before coming back up and climbing in beside me.

The hallway was dark. I couldn't see to the end of it, but I knew the door was there, miles away. And that was my only way out. I heard footsteps behind me and I started to run. The corridor expanded as I ran, stretching further and further into the distance as I tried to escape. All I could hear was my heart pounding and the footsteps behind me. I reached a door and pushed my way through it. I felt a hand grab my arm. I turned around, trying to see my attacker. He took a step forward and came into the light.

'I'm sorry, Katie,' he said.

Oh my God, my mind screamed, not believing what was happening to me. Cam stood there, staring at me with an evil look. His hand reached up for my shoulder and I took a step backwards. He moved closer and closer until I was at the edge of the cliff with nowhere else to go. And then he pushed me over the edge.

I sat up in bed, trying to catch my breath. Cam lay beside me, still sleeping soundly. I guess I hadn't screamed out loud. I lay down slowly, trying not to disturb the stranger next to me. The man I thought I knew; thought I loved. Cam moved slightly and I held my breath, hoping he wouldn't wake up. I remembered everything now. I remembered standing in the fire exit, the door opening, trying to run away, someone grabbing me, turning around and seeing that it was Cam.

A hand reached out from the darkness of the bedroom and touched my shoulder. It took every ounce of will power I had not to scream and run right then.

'Did you have another nightmare?' he whispered, his lips close to my ear.

'I'm OK,' I answered, sounding amazingly calm. God, he was awake! What was I going to do?

'Was it the same dream?' he asked, his hand rubbing my back now.

'Yeah.'

I felt tears running down my cheeks. I rolled over, away from him, pretending I was trying to find a comfortable position.

'Are you crying?' he asked, sitting up and trying to look at me through the darkness.

'I'm OK,' I said weakly. 'I just need some sleep.'

He reached up and squeezed my shoulder and then tried to wrap me in a hug.

'It was only a dream, Katie. You're OK now.'

'I know,' I said, lying stiffly in his embrace.

'Did you see who it was?'

'No. I didn't see anything. Just the arm reaching out for me.'

He started massaging my shoulder, lying so close I could feel his heart beating. It took all my strength not to pull away from him. I couldn't believe it. After everything we had been through in the last week, Cam really was the murderer. It had all been a lie. He didn't love me. He had moved in to watch me because he was afraid that I would find out.

I couldn't stay in bed with him a minute longer. I pushed him away, climbing over him to get out of bed and ran for the stairs.

'Where are you going, Katie?' He sat up, reaching for the light.

'I'm just going to have a bath,' I said.

'Do you want some company?'

'No. You go back to sleep. I need to soak for a while.'

'Call if you need me.' He turned the light off and lay back down.

I went into the bathroom and locked the door behind me. I ran a facecloth under cold water then held it to my face. I felt like I was going to faint. I dropped the cloth and turned the water on in the tub. I sat on the edge, my hand in the water testing the temperature, and wondered how I was going to get out of the apartment. I had to get to Detective Lincoln, but I couldn't call him from here. What was I going to do? I was trapped.

I had to think. I couldn't use the phone, and I couldn't figure out how to get upstairs, get dressed, and then leave without Cam hearing me. I didn't want him to suspect that I knew until I could get to the police, where I would be safe.

I opened up the cabinet and took a couple of aspirin. In the mirror I saw a reflection of my clothes hanging on the hook on the back of the door, right where I'd left them. Maybe, if I could change and sneak out quietly, I could get to the police.

I dressed quickly. The bathtub was about half full when I pulled the plug and left the water running, hoping Cam would think I was still in the bath. The noise should cover any sounds I might make.

I opened the bathroom door a crack and peered out. There were no lights on and it was quiet. I was sure Cam was asleep upstairs and hadn't heard anything. I snuck out of the bathroom and closed the door softly. My keys were on the peg beside the door. I took them off the hook and opened the door quietly. When I was in the hallway I let the door close gently behind me and left without locking it.

I ran to the elevators as fast as my feet would take me and frantically pushed the button. The elevator seemed to take forever. It finally opened just as the door to my apartment opened.

'Katie?' Cam called down the hall. I turned and saw his head poke out of the door and I dashed into the elevator. I knew he had seen me. 'Shit,' I muttered under my breath. I pushed the button for the ground floor and then pounded the close button over and over again. 'Come on!' I screamed at the elevator. The door closed just as Cam came into view.

'Where are you going?' I heard him yell.

My heart was pounding as the elevator began its descent. I prayed I would get downstairs before he did. The doors opened on the main floor and I stuck my head out to look around. The lobby was empty and I ran for the exit.

I reached the C-Train station just as a train pulled up. I hopped on and headed for the Plex.

I got off the train before it had stopped moving and ran the half block to the stage door. Nick was sitting at the security desk and looked quite surprised when I came in.

'I thought you were supposed to be in a hospital bed.'

'Nick, you know me. Can't keep me in bed for a week. I'd be bored silly,' I gasped, still breathing heavily from my run but trying to sound normal.

'How are you feeling?' He looked concerned.

'Little bit of a headache, but not bad. I just thought I'd come in and catch up on some paperwork. After all, I've been away for two days.'

'Kate, it's after midnight. Are you sure you want to be alone in your office?' Nick asked, looking puzzled.

'Yes, Nick. I don't think anyone would risk coming back there, do you?'

I signed in the logbook, trying to stop any arguments. Luckily his phone rang and he had to turn his attention away from me to answer it.

'Hi, Cam, what's up?' Nick said into the phone.

My heart skipped a beat as I moved quietly down the corridor and pulled out my key.

'Yes, she's here at the desk right now, just a sec and I'll let you talk to her.'

I saw him turn back to where I had been standing just as I let myself quietly through the security door and rounded the corner.

'Kate!' I heard him call after me. 'Kate, phone call for you.'

I ran towards my office. I didn't even bother to turn on the lights while I tried to dial Detective Lincoln's number. My hands were shaking so badly it took me three attempts before I finally got it right. It rang several times and then I heard a click as it forwarded to another line.

'Police department,' a strange voice answered.

'Detective Lincoln please.'

'I'm sorry, ma'am, he's not in. Would you care to leave a message?'

'How about Clint Young?' I tried.

'Sorry, neither of them are here. Can I take a message?'

'Yes. This is Kate Carpenter. Tell him I'm at the Plex and that I know who pushed me. I know who killed Peter Reynolds.'

'Your number please.'

'No, he can't call. You have to get this message to him as quickly as possible. Please, tell him he has to come here right now,' I practically screamed into the receiver.

'I'll have him paged,' the tired voice promised.

'Thank you.'

I looked up and saw Cam's car drive by as I hung up the phone. I moved to the window and saw him round the block again before he pulled into the loading dock beside the stage door. I double-checked the lock on my office door and then realized that wasn't going to do me much good. He had the same keys as me.

I hesitated for a second, not sure where I could hide until the police arrived. Then, impulsively, I grabbed my keys and headed into the corridor and straight for the fire exit. There was no place to hide in the lobbies or the auditorium, but if I went down the fire escape I could work my way through the basement corridors and back to the security desk. My feet barely touched the concrete as I ran down the two flights of stairs.

I heard the door I had just come through open again as I stood quietly in the basement, trying to get my key into the security door. I let myself through and pulled the door closed behind me as softly as I could. The sound of footsteps starting down the stairs echoed behind me as I ran down the corridor until I reached the next locked door. It was so dark, I had to try three keys before I got the right one. I took a deep breath and tried to calm myself. This was not the time to panic and lose control. I let myself through, took a deep breath, and let the door close behind me, before I realized I had taken a wrong turn. I was under the stage, not in the corridor that led up to the security desk. The only way I was going to get back on track was to return to the corridor I had just left. I opened the door a crack, but I could already hear footsteps running in my direction. I changed my mind and headed for the orchestra pit. I could climb up and get back into the theatre that way. The footsteps came closer. I ran through the storage area, crashing into a klieg light, and finally made it into the orchestra pit. I crashed into a cymbal, making a horrible noise, and climbed up on to the piano. I reached over the wall that divides the orchestra pit from the theatre and tried to pull myself over. I felt someone grab my hand and yank me up over the edge.

'Jesus, Katie, what the hell do you think you're doing?' Cam was furious. He looked worse than the night he had walked out of my apartment, and it scared me.

'I've called the police, they'll be here any minute,' I warned him.

'If you live that long.' He jumped up on to the stage without letting go of my arm and pulled me up after him.

'Let go. You're hurting me.'

'Better that than the alternative,' he said, getting an even tighter grip on my arm. 'Now shut up and come with me.'

He pulled me across the stage and into the stairwell on stage left. I started struggling, trying to run for the stage-right exit. I knew I would be all right if I could just get away from him and back to the security desk.

'Katie, stop it!' he snarled at me. Cam pulled me close to him, pinching my arm in an iron grip, and slapped me across the face. I saw stars dance in front of my eyes. 'If you want any chance of living longer than tonight, you will quit fighting and come with me. Do you understand?' he hissed through clenched teeth. His anger was palpable.

'Cam, let me go. We can end this right now. Just let me go and I promise I won't say anything.'

'Stop talking nonsense.' He pulled me roughly after him and shoved me into the stairwell. 'Now shut the fuck up and start climbing.'

'Where are we going?' I asked, trying to stall him.

'Up to the tower.' He pushed me, trying to get me to start up the stairs. 'Now, are you going to go, or am I going to have to drag you up?'

I started climbing slowly but Cam was right behind me, pushing me upwards. My mind raced. I had to escape. This stairwell only went in one direction and that was up. The fly tower was forty foot high, and once we were up there, there weren't too many ways to get back down. If I made a run for the door on the opposite side, I might have a chance. If I could just slam the door on Cam, I might be able to get away.

I was out of breath by the time we got to the top. I promised God that if he would get me out of this, I would exercise faithfully every day. I put my key in the door and opened it, with Cam urging me on impatiently. As soon as I was through the door I turned and tried to push it closed. Cam was too close and too strong. He gave it a good shove and knocked me over. He reached down and grabbed me, pulling me back on to my feet, and dragged me out on to the catwalk.

'Let me go!' I screamed, feeling more terrified with every step we took. The theatre had good acoustics and I was praying someone would hear me.

'Shut up, Katie,' he ordered, pulling me further out.

I made the mistake of looking down and felt my stomach do a somersault. I struggled harder, trying to free my arm and get away from him.

'Let me go!' I screamed desperately.

He pulled me to him and clamped his hand tightly over my mouth. I could barely breath. 'I said, shut up,' he said quietly.

He started to pull me further on to the catwalk. I saw the stage forty feet below. Suddenly, a horrible vision of my future flashed through my mind, of what would happen to me if Cam pulled me out any further on to the fly tower. It wasn't a pretty picture. I bit his hand and stomped on his foot as hard as I could. Cam let go and I ran back towards the door to the stairwell. I pulled open the door and felt a hand grab my wrist as I tried to go through, yanking me back. The door slammed shut, blocking my escape.

'Cam!' I screamed as he twisted me around. 'Let me go right now. Please!'

He pulled me away from the door and to the other side of the tower. I twisted around, trying to scratch at his face, his eyes – anything to get away from him. And then I saw who had a hold of me.

'Oh my God.'

'Wrong.' He pulled me to the stage-right side of the tower, away from Cam.

'But Cam pushed me down the stairs,' I said, not comprehending what was happening.

'Wrong again.' He laughed. 'I'm very disappointed. You were getting so close to the right answer. You see, I strung a tripwire on those stairs, hoping you would fall and break your neck. Save me some trouble. Cam was actually trying to catch you. Really bad timing. He almost saw me.'

'I don't understand.'

'You will if you think about it for a while. You see, you've got everything going for you here. Good job, friends, a man you love. Think about that. And then maybe you will realize that not everyone has that, Kate. Not everyone has the job that they want, the people they love. I gave up my life for Gladys, and then you told her I wasn't worth it. I applied for your job, thinking I could start all over again. But I didn't get that either, did I? Thirty years old, divorced, and I'm an usher at a lousy arts centre. Think about that, Kate. That's if I let you live that long.'

He had pulled me out into the middle of the catwalk and had me pinned against the rail. I was looking down at the stage, too scared to struggle.

'Now, where is that boyfriend of yours?' he asked. 'Is he trying to sneak up on us? Call him, please.'

'No,' I said. 'No, you don't want to do this. You'll regret it later, when you've sobered up.'

'Another of your astute observations?' he snarled. 'I haven't had a drink for over a year. I've been too busy planning your demise, so to speak. And not one of you even noticed, did you?' Gus did, I realized too late. 'Now, call Cam for me, please,' he ordered.

'No.'

'Call him!' he screamed at me.

'No, this is between you and me,' I said defiantly.

He pushed me over the rail. I screamed. I was bent at the waist, hanging over the tower, my feet barely touching the floor. He grabbed my belt and lifted me a few inches off

259

the floor. The only thing keeping me from going over was his tenuous grip on my belt.

'OK! Let me up,' I begged.

'Call him!'

'Cam!' I screamed. 'Cam, where are you?'

'Answer her, Cam, or she goes flying without ropes,' he yelled out into the theatre.

'I'm here,' Cam said, walking slowly out on to the catwalk. 'Let her back up now.'

Burns pulled me up. I was gasping and my head was spinning. I breathed deeply, trying to catch my breath. I grabbed for Burns's arm and held on tightly to him.

'Good of you to join us. I wouldn't want you to miss this.'

'Let her go, Burns,' Cam said, continuing slowly towards us. 'The police are on their way. It's too late; you'll never get away.'

'It's never too late. Besides, if I have to go out, I'm going with a splash.'

'Why? What is all this about?' Cam asked. A few more feet and he'd be right beside me.

'It's about Gladys. You know that. I loved her, but she would never leave him for me. Even after I called her husband and told him about us. I quit my job for her, left my wife, lost my children. Your little girlfriend here told her I wasn't good enough for her. I thought I meant something to her, but in the end I was nothing. She valued Kate's opinion more than mine. I was just the first in a long line of flings. And she didn't even have the decency to tell me.'

'But why kill her husband? She left him.' I saw Cam inching closer while Burns turned to answer me.

'Cam was supposed to go to jail for it. It was just pure irony that Peter Reynolds was the one who walked into that bathroom. I was going to kill the next person who walked through that door. I wanted to ruin your life, just like you ruined mine. But you and your little snoops just wouldn't stay out of it.'

'I couldn't let Cam go to jail, Burns.'

'Oh, bullshit. You women are all alike. Five minutes ago you would have pushed Cam over the edge if you could have.' He pushed me harder into the rails to make his point and I

260

felt my hip starting to bruise. I tightened my grip on his sleeve. 'You're all just out to take us for whatever you can get. You should be thanking me, Cam. I'm doing you a favour here, getting rid of this little bitch.' He turned to Cam. 'And if you take one step closer, she's going over the edge right now.'

'You're going to push her anyway,' Cam said.

'But that's the fun of all of this,' Burns laughed. 'What do you do? Wait and hope for a miracle, or come at me now and risk everything?'

He pushed me back over the edge of the railing. I lost my grip on his sleeve and was staring down at the stage again. I felt like throwing up.

'What's it going to be?' Burns asked.

'Cam, stay back. Please,' I begged.

'Well, we have Kate's vote. She wants to wait, grab a few more minutes of life. Maybe she thinks I'll have a stab of conscience and let her go. What about you, Cam? Want to see your girlfriend fly?'

'Please, Burns, don't do this.'

'You'll get your turn next, Cam, but Kate really is the one that deserves to be punished. She's going first.' He lifted me off the ground and pushed me over the edge. I felt his hand on my belt, the only thing between me and the stage floor. I grabbed for a handhold, trying to save myself. I could feel him pushing me further over the edge. I screamed and kicked out at him but it only made me lose my grip on the rail. My mind was racing, trying to find a way out.

'You'll get your turn right after you watch her go.' Burns smiled at Cam and then turned back to me. 'But enough of this. I think the time has come.'

'No!' I screamed. 'Please don't.' I felt myself being pushed further over the edge, his grip loosening on my belt. I couldn't see anything to grab as I searched frantically for a handhold.

'Say goodbye,' I heard Burns say from above me as he began to loosen his grip on me. Then I saw a hand reach out of the darkness.

'Take my hand,' a voice commanded.

I didn't stop to wonder who it was, I just reached out. I was about six inches away when I heard Cam lunge at Burns, who released his grip on me to defend himself, and I went over the rail.

'Help me!' I screamed as I started falling. I kept screaming until I felt my shoulder wrench and I stopped falling.

'Kate, I've got you,' a voice said. 'Grab my other hand.'

'Help me!' I screamed.

'Take my other hand,' he ordered.

'I can't! Oh God, help me!'

'Take my other hand!'

I threw my free arm up and Scott grabbed my hand. He pulled me close to him and I wrapped my arms so tightly around him I was afraid I might break his ribs. We started dropping gently to the stage. When I felt the stage floor under my feet I wrapped my arms around his shoulders and started crying. Scott tried to loosen himself from my grip but I wouldn't let him go.

'It's OK, Kate. You're safe,' he said, and then turned his head to stage right, where Trevor stood. 'She's OK. I got her.'

'Is Cam OK?' I asked between sobs.

'He's OK.' The theatre lights began to come on. 'Dwayne and a couple of security guards are up there.' He pointed up through the grill and I saw several people holding Burns down.

'How did you know?' I asked, trying to get control of myself but failing miserably.

'Cam came to the green room. Luckily we were working late tonight. We've been searching high and low for you. Dwayne was following you down the stairs but lost you in the basement. Then Trevor heard you yelling at Cam from the tower, so we came up on the other side.' Scott released himself from the harness but still had me attached to him. 'Let's get you out of here.'

I hugged him tighter. 'I can't believe you caught me.'

'Neither can I, Kate. Good thing this was rigged for Trevor. Our weight combined still isn't as much as his.'

'I heard that, butthead,' Trevor yelled from the wings.

Scott took me into the green room and cracked a beer for each of us. He took a Kleenex and wiped my eyes for me.

'You got that ugly raccoon thing happening here,' he said.

262

'I never could cry pretty,' I explained, trying to wipe away the mascara.

'You look just fine to me,' he said, sitting beside me.

I moved close to him and hugged him. 'Thank you so much.'

'It's going to be OK, Kate.'

We sat on the couch in silence. A security guard came rushing by with the police and a few minutes later they came down with Burns in handcuffs. Detective Lincoln poked his head into the green room.

'Kate, do you have some sort of problem with me getting a good night's sleep?' he joked.

'I told you I'd catch him,' I said.

'Well, I could think of easier ways to do it,' Ken said. 'I'm going down to the station now. I expect to see you down there tomorrow.'

'I'll be there,' I promised.

Scott got up and came back with a blanket. He wrapped it around me, trying to control my shivering, and sat back down beside me. I leaned against him and sipped my beer.

'This is going to be a great story to tell your grandchildren,' I said.

'Yeah, well Kate, this is one story I could have done without. I almost had a heart attack when you went over the side.'

'You should have seen it from my point of view.'

'You know, we really prefer people not to swan dive off the towers. I think I'll have to teach you how to climb the ropes, so you'll have a different way down next time.'

'Don't worry, Scott. I am never going up the tower again. Ever.'

'We'll see,' he said.

'No way. All three of you couldn't get me up there.'

Cam poked his head around the door. 'Katie?'

'Are you all right, Cam?' I set down my beer.

'I'm fine.'

'Can you ever forgive me?' I asked, feeling tears welling up in my eyes again.

Scott stood up. 'My cue to exit, stage left.'

Cam took Scott's place beside me on the couch. 'Katie, there's nothing to forgive.'

'I thought you were the killer.'

'I know, but it doesn't matter any more. It's all over now.'

'I'm sorry,' I said again.

He wrapped me in his arms and pulled me close to him. 'God, Katie, don't be sorry. I'm the one who took you up there and that was just about the stupidest thing I've ever done. I knew the guys were in the theatre, and I thought they could hear us from up there. I couldn't think of anywhere else to go. But I almost got you killed.'

'If you hadn't come, I would have been killed. He almost did it twice; he would have succeeded this time.'

'The police said they would drive you home,' Cam said.

'I want you to drive me home.'

'Are you sure?'

'All I want to do right now is go home, Cam. With you.'

He stood up and held out his hand. 'Come on, I'll take you back to your place and tuck you into bed.'

I reached out and took his hand. 'Back to *our* place.'

Saturday

We were up bright and early on Saturday morning. We visited Graham and filled him in on everything that had happened, then went on to the police station to answer Ken Lincoln's endless questions. He told us Burns had confessed. He had been planning this for a year, and would be in jail for a while.

We drove home and loaded the car. As soon as I cleared out the theatre after the show, we were hitting the highway and heading for the ocean. I had ten days off and refused to come back until my body was tanned and waterlogged from swimming. We had reservations at the Dolphin Motel in Tofino on Vancouver Island, and I had a spot picked out on the beach where I intended to spend most of my time. I could hardly wait.

I stood at the top of the stairs, watching the ticket takers move the crowd up into the theatre, when suddenly I saw a familiar face.

'Sam, you're home!' I ran over and hugged my best friend. 'I thought you would never get back.'

'It was tempting.' She smiled at me, and then I saw a concerned look cross her face as she noticed the cast on my arm. 'What on earth have you done to yourself?'

'It's more than I can explain in five minutes,' I said. Cam came up beside us and shook Ryan's hand.

'Well, we'll just have to go out for coffee after the show and you can tell me all about it,' Sam insisted.

I looked at Cam and he smiled and nodded in agreement. It would be worth getting away an hour or two late, just to see the look on Sam and Ryan's faces when we told them what had happened to us in the last two weeks. And they thought they had been on an adventure!

Epilogue

We had arrived home after spending ten idyllic days on Long Beach. We brought our luggage up to the apartment, dumped it on the floor and decided to deal with it later. Cam made some coffee for me and grabbed himself a beer. He decided to take a quick shower before we went out for something to eat. I sat on the balcony, waiting for him. I stood at the railing, coffee in hand, watching the clouds go by above me and the traffic below.

In a strange way, I felt sad this was over. It had been the most exciting time I'd ever had in my life. My greatest adventure. And I knew that nothing like this would ever happen to me again. I mean, really, how many times do any of us have a murder take place in our own back yard, so to speak? Then Cam came out on to the balcony, stood very close to me and draped his arm over my shoulder. He smelled musty and was still damp from the shower. Suddenly, I didn't feel like going out. I was getting to like having a man around. Just as I leaned over to kiss Cam, the phone rang.

I looked at Cam, he looked at me, and we kissed.

'You're not answering that,' he whispered as he pinned me against the wall and kissed me again.

The answering machine picked up on the fourth ring.

'Hi, you've reached Kate and Cam. We are still away on a deserted island somewhere, so leave a message, and if we decide to come back, I promise we'll return your call.'

'Hi Kate, it's Graham. You need to come into the theatre right away. You're never going to believe what's just happened!'